Love's Pilgrimage

Upton Sinclair

Contents

LOVE'S PILGRIMAGE

BY

Upton Sinclair

PART I
Loves Entanglement

BOOK I
THE VICTIM

It was in a little woodland glen, with a streamlet tumbling through it. She sat with her back to a snowy birch-tree, gazing into the eddies of a pool below; and he lay beside her, upon the soft, mossy ground, reading out of a book of poems. Images of joy were passing before them; and there came four lines with a picture--

  "Hard by, a cottage-chimney smokes,
   From betwixt two aged oaks,
   Where Corydon and Thyrsis, met,
   Are at their savory dinner set."

"Ah!" said she. "I always loved that. Let us be Corydon and Thyrsis!"
He smiled. "They were both of them men," he said.
"Let us change it," she responded--"just between ourselves!"
"Very well--Corydon!" said he.
Then, after a moment's thought, she added, "But we didn't have the cottage."
"No," said he--"nor even the dinner!"
Section 1. It was the Highway of Lost Men. They shivered, and drew their shoulders together as they walked, for it was night, and a cold, sleety rain was fall-

ing. The lights from saloons and pawn-shops fell upon their faces--faces haggard and gaunt with misery, or bloated with disease and sin. Some stared before them fixedly; some gazed about with furtive and hungry eyes as they shuffled on. Here and there a policeman stood in the shelter, swinging his club and watching them as they passed. Music called to them from dives and dance-halls, and lighted signs and flaring- colored pictures tempted them in the entrances of cheap museums and theatres; they lingered before these, glad of even a moment's shelter. Overhead the elevated trains pounded by; and from the windows one could see men crowded about the stoves in the rooms of lodging-houses, where the steam from their garments made a blur in the air.

Down this highway walked a lad, about fifteen years of age, pale of face, and with delicate and sensitive features. His overcoat was buttoned tightly about his neck, and his hands thrust into his pockets; he gazed around him swiftly as he walked. He came to this place every now and then, but he never grew used to what he saw.

He eyed the men who passed him; and when he came to a saloon he would push open the door and gaze about. Sometimes he would enter, and hurry through, to peer into the compartments in the back; and then go out again, giving a wide berth to the drinkers, and shrinking from their glances. Once a girl appeared in a doorway, and smiled and nodded to him; he started and hurried out, shuddering. Her wanton black eyes haunted him, hinting unimaginable things.

Then, on a corner, he stopped and spoke to a policeman. "Hello!" said the man, and shook his head--"No, not this time." So the boy went on; there were several miles of this Highway, and each block of it the same.

At last, in a dingy bar-room, with saw-dust strewn upon the floor, and the odor of stale beer and tobacco-smoke in the air--here suddenly the boy sprang forward, with a cry: "Father!" And a man who sat with bowed head in a corner gave a start, and lifted a white face and stared at him. He rose unsteadily to his feet, and staggered to the other, and fell upon his shoulder, sobbing, "My son! My son!"

How many times had Thyrsis heard those words--in how many hours of anguish! They sank into the deeps of him, waking echoes like the clang of a bell: they voiced all the terror and grief of defeated life--"My son! My son!"

The man clung to him, weeping, and pouring out the flood of his shame. "I have fallen again--I am lost--I am lost!"

The occupants of the place were watching the scene with dull curiosity; and the boy was trembling like a wild deer trapped.

"Yes, father, yes! Let us go home."

"Home--home, my son? Will you take me home? Oh, I couldn't bear to go!"

"But you must come home."

"Do you mean that you still love me, son?"

"Yes, father, I still love you. I want to try to help you. Come with me."

Then the boy would gaze about and ask, "Where is your hat?"

"Hat, my son? I don't know. I have lost it." The boy would see his torn and mud-stained clothing, and the poor old pitiful face, with the eyes blood-shot and swollen, and the skin, that had been rosy, and was now a ghastly, ashen gray. He would choke back his feelings, and grip his hands to keep himself together.

"Come, father, take my hat, and let us go."

"No, my son. I don't need any hat. Nothing can hurt me--I am lost! Lost!"

So they would go out, arm in arm; and while they made their progress up the Highway, the man would pour out his remorse, and tell the story of his weeks of horror.

Then, after a mile or so, he would halt.

"My son!"

"What is it, father?"

"I must stop here, son."

"Why, father?"

"I must have something to drink."

" *No*, father!"

"But, my boy, I can't go on! I can't walk! You don't know what I'm suffering!"

"No, father!"

"I've got the money left--I'm not asking you. I'll come right with you--on my word of honor I will!"

And so they would fight it out--all the way back to the lodging-house where they lived, and where the mother sat and wept. And here they would put him to bed, and lock up his clothing to keep him in; and here, with drugs and mineral-waters, and perhaps a doctor to help, they would struggle with him, and tend him until he was on his feet again. Then, with clothing newly-brushed and face newly-shaven he would go back to the world of men; and the boy would go back to his dreams.

Section 2. Such was the life of Thyrsis, from earliest childhood to maturity. His father's was a heritage of gentle breeding and high traditions--his forefathers were cavaliers, and had served the State. And now it had come to this--to hall bedrooms in lodging-houses, and a life-and-death grapple with destruction! And when Thyrsis came to study the problem, he found that it was a struggle without hope; his father was a man in a trap.

He was what people called a "drummer". He was dependent for his living upon the favor of certain merchants--men for the most part of low ideals, who came to the city in search of their low pleasures. One met them by waiting about in the lobbies of hotels, and in the bar-rooms which they frequented; and always the first sign of fellowship with them was to have a drink. And this was the field on which the battle had to be fought!

He would hold out for months--half a year, perhaps--drinking lemonade and putting up with their raillery. And then he would begin with ginger-ale; and then it would come to beer; and then to whiskey. He was always devising new plans to control himself; always persuading himself that he had solved the problem. He would not drink in the morning; he would not drink until after dinner; he would not drink alone--and so on without end. His whole life was drink, and all his thoughts were of drink--the odor of it always in his nostrils, the image of it always before his eyes.

And the grimness of his fate lay here--that it was by his best qualities that he was betrayed. If he had been hard and mercenary, like some of those who preyed upon him, there might have been hope. But he was generous and free-hearted, a slave to his impulses of friendship. And this was what made the struggle such a cruel one to Thyrsis; it was like the sight of some noble animal basely snared.

From his earliest days the boy had watched these forces working themselves out. The gentleman and the "drummer" fought for supremacy, and step by step the soul of the man was fashioned to the work he did. To succeed with his customers he must share their ideas and their tastes; and so he was bitter against reformers, who interfered with the gaieties of the city, with no consideration for the tastes of "buyers." But then, on the other hand, would come a time of renunciation, when he would be all enthusiasm for temperance.

He was full of old-fashioned ideas, which would take the quaintest turns of reactionism; his politics were summed up in the phrase that he "would rather vote for a nigger than a Republican"; but then, in the same breath, he would announce some fine and noble sentiment, out of the traditions of a forgotten past. He was the soul of courtesy to women, and of loyalty to friends. He worshipped General Lee and the old time "Virginia gentleman"; and those with whom he lived, and for whose unclean profits he sold himself, never guessed the depths of his contempt for all they stood for. They had the dollars, they were on top; but some day the nemesis of Good-breeding would smite them--the army of the ghosts of Gentility would rise, and with "Marse Robert" and "Jeb" Stuart at their head, would sweep away the hordes of commercialdom.

Thyrsis saw a great deal of this forgotten chivalry. His nursery had been haunt-ed by such musty phantoms; and when he first came to the Northern city, he stayed at a hotel which was frequented by people who lived in this past--old ladies who were proud and prim, and old gentlemen who were quixotic and humorous, young ladies who were "belles," and young gentlemen who aspired to be "blades". It was a world that would have made happy the soul of any writer of romances; but to Thyr-sis in earliest childhood the fates had given the gift of seeing beneath the shams of things, and to him this dead Aristocracy cried out loudly for burial. There was an incredible amount of drunkenness, and of debauchery scarcely hidden; there was pretense strutting like a peacock, and avarice skulking like a hound; there were jealousy, and base snobbery, and raging spite, and a breath of suspicion and scandal hanging like a poisonous cloud over everything. These people came and went, an endless procession of them; they laughed and danced and gossiped and drank their way through the boy's life, and unconsciously he judged them, and hated them and feared them. It was not by such that his destiny was to be shaped.

Most of them were poor; not an honest poverty, but a sham and artificial pov-erty--the inability to dress as others did, and to lose money at "bridge" and "poker", and to pay the costs of their self-indulgences. As for Thyrsis and his parents, they always paid what they owed; but they were not always able to pay it when they owed it, and they suffered all the agonies and humiliations of those who did not pay at all. There was scarcely ever a week when this canker of want did not gnaw at them; their life was one endless and sordid struggle to make last year's clothing look like new, and to find some boarding-house that was cheaper and yet respectable. There was endless wrangling and strife and worry over money; and every year the task was harder, the standards lower, the case more hopeless.

There were rich relatives, a world of real luxury up above--the thing that called itself "Society". And Thyrsis was a student and a bright lad, and he was welcome there; he might have spread his wings and flown away from this sordidness. But duty held him, and love and memory held him still tighter. For his father worshipped him, and craved his help; to the last hour of his dreadful battle, he fought to keep his son's regard--he prayed for it, with tears in his eyes and anguish in his voice. And so the boy had to stand by. And that meant that he grew up in a torture-house, he drank a cup of poison to its bitter dregs. To others his father was merely a gross little man, with sordid ideas and low tastes; but to Thyrsis he was a man with the terror of the hunted creatures in his soul, and the furies of madness cracking their whips about his ears.

There was only one ending possible--it worked itself out with the remorseless precision of a machine. The soul that fought was smothered and stifled, its voice grew fainter and feebler; the agony and the shame grew hotter, the suffering more cruel, the despair more black. Until at last they found him in a delirium, and took him to a private hospital; and thither went Thyrsis, now grown to be a man, and sat in a dingy reception-room, and a dingy doctor came to him and said, "Do you wish to see the body?" And Thyrsis answered, in a low voice, "No."

Section 3. So it was that the soul of this lad had grown sombre, and taken to brooding upon the mysteries of fate. Life was no jest and no holiday, it was no place for shams and self-deceptions. It was a place where cruel enemies set traps for the unwary; a field where blind and merciless forces ranged, unhindered by man or God.

Thyrsis could not have told how soon in life this sense had come to him. In his earliest childhood he had known that his father was preyed upon, just as certainly as any wild thing in the forest. At first the enemies had been saloon-keepers, and wicked men who tempted him to drink with them. The names of these men were household words to him, portents of terror; they peopled his imagination as epic figures, such as Black Douglas must have been to the children of the Northern Border.

But then, with widening intelligence, it became certain social forces, at first dimly apprehended. It was the god of "business"--before which all things fair and noble went down. It was "business" that kept vice triumphant in the city; it was because of "business" that the saloons could not be closed even on Sunday, so that the father might be at home one day in seven. And was it not in search of "business" that he was driven forth to loaf in hotel-lobbies and bar-rooms?

Who was to blame for this, Thyrsis did not know; but certain men made profit of it--and these, too, were ignoble men. He knew this; for now and then his father's employers would honor the little family with some kind of an invitation, and they would have to swallow their pride and go. So Thyrsis grew up, with the sense of a great evil loose in the world; a wrong, of which the world did not know. And within him grew a passionate longing to cry aloud to others, to open their eyes to this truth!

Outwardly he was like other boys, eager and cheerful, even boisterous; but within was this hidden thing, which brooded and questioned. Life had made him into an ascetic. He must be stern, even merciless, with himself--because of the fear that was in him, and in his mother as well. The fear that self-indulgence might lay its grisly paws upon him! The fear that he, too, might fall into the trap!

It was not merely that he never touched stimulants; he had an instinct against all things that were softening and enervating, all things that tempted and enslaved. For him was the morning-air, and the shock of cold water, and the hardness of the wild things of the open. Other people did not feel this way; other people pampered themselves and defiled themselves--and so Thyrsis went apart. He lived quite alone with his thoughts, he had never a chum, scarcely even any friends. Where in the long procession of lodging and boarding-houses and summer-resorts should he meet people who knew what he knew about life? Where in all the world should he meet them, save in the books of great men in times past?

There was not much of what is called "culture" in his family; no music at all, and no poetry. But there were novels, and there were libraries where one could get more of these, so Thyrsis became a devourer of stories; he would disappear, and they would find him at meal-times, hidden in a clump of bushes, or in a corner behind a sofa--anywhere out of the world. He read whole libraries of adventure: Mayne-

Reid and Henty, and then Cooper and Stevenson and Scott. And then came more serious novels--"Don Quixote" and "Les Miserables," George Eliot, whom he loved, and Dickens, whose social protest thrilled him; and chiefest of all Thackeray, who moulded his thought. Thackeray knew the world that he knew, Thackeray saw to the heart of it; and no high-souled lad who had read him and worshipped him was ever after to be lured by the glamor of the "great" world--a world whose greatness was based upon selfishness and greed.

Thyrsis knew no foreign language, and fate or instinct kept him from those writers who jested with uncleanness; so he was virginal, and pure in all his imaginings. Other lads exchanged confidences in forbidden things, they broke down the barriers and tore away the veils; but Thyrsis had never breathed a word about matters of sex to any living creature. He pondered and guessed, but no one knew his thoughts; and this was a crucial thing, the secret of much of his aloofness.

Section 4. In one of the early boarding-houses there had been a little girl, and the families had become intimate. But the two children disliked each other, and kept apart all they could. Thyrsis was domineering and imperious, and things must always be his way. He was given to rebellion, whereas Corydon was gentle and meek, and submitted to confinements and prohibitions in a quite disgraceful manner. She was a pretty little girl, with great black eyes; and because she was silent and shy, he set her down as "stupid", and went his way.

They spent a summer in the country together, where Thyrsis possessed himself of a sling-shot, and took to collecting the skins of squirrels and chipmunks. Corydon was horrified at this; and by way of helping her to overcome her squeamishness he would make her carry home the bleeding corpses. He took to raising, young birds, also, and soon had quite an aviary--two robins, and a crow, and a survivor from a brood of "cherry-birds." The feeding of these nestlings was no small task, but Thyrsis went fishing when the spirit moved him, secure in the certainty that the calls of the hungry creatures would keep Corydon at home.

This was the way of it, until Corydon began to blossom into a young lady, beautiful and tenderly-fashioned. Thyrsis still saw her now and then, and he made attempts to share his higher joys with her. He had become a lover of poetry; once they walked by the seashore, and he read her "Alexander's Feast", thrilling with delight in its resounding phrases:

"Break his bands of sleep asunder,
And rouse him like a rattling peal of thunder!"

But Corydon had never heard of Timotheus, and she had not been taught to exploit her emotions. She could only say that she did not understand it very well.

And then, on another occasion, Thyrsis endeavored to tell her about Berkeley, whom he had been reading. But Corydon did not take to the sensational philosophy either; she would come back again and again to the evasion of old Dr. Johnson--"When I kick a stone, I know the stone is there!"

This girl was like a beautiful flower, Thyrsis told himself--like all the flowers that had gone before her, and all those that would come after, from generation to generation. She fitted so perfectly into her environment, she grew so calmly and serenely; she wore pretty dresses, and helped to serve tea, and was graceful and sweet--and with never an idea that there was anything in life beyond these things. So Thyrsis pondered as he went his way, complacent over his own perspicacity; and got not even a whiff of smoke from the volcano of rebellion and misery that was seething deep down in her soul!

The choosers of the unborn souls had played a strange fantasy here; they had stolen one of the daughters of ancient Greece, and set her down in this metropolis of commercialdom. For Corydon might have been Nausikaa herself; she might have marched in the Panathenaic procession, with one of the sacred vessels in her hands; she might have run in the Attic games, bare-limbed and fearless. Hers was a soul that leaped to the call of joy, that thrilled at the faintest touch of beauty. Above all else, she was born for music--she could have sung so that the world would have remembered it. And she was pent in a dingy boarding-house, with no point of con-tact with anything about her--with no human soul to whom she could whisper her despair!

They sent her to a public-school, where the sad-eyed drudges of the traders came to be drilled for their tasks. They harrowed her with arithmetic and grammar, which she abhorred; they taught her patriotic songs, about a country to which she did not belong. And also, they sent her to Sunday-school, which was worse yet. She had the strangest, instinctive hatred of their religion, with all that it stood for. The sight of a clergyman with his vestments and his benedictions would make her fairly bristle with hostility. They talked to her about her sins, and she did not know what they meant; they pried into the state of her soul, and she shrunk from them as if they had been hairy spiders. Here, too, they taught her to sing--droning hymns that were a mockery of all the joys of life.

So Corydon devoured her own heart in secret; and in time a dreadful thing came to happen--the stagnant soul beginning to fester. One day the girl, whose heart was the quintessence of all innocence, happened to see a low word scribbled upon a fence. And now--they had urged her to discover sins, and she discovered them. Suppose that word were to stay in her mind and haunt her--suppose that she were not able to forget it, try as she would! And of course she tried; and the more she tried, the less she succeeded; and so came the discovery that she was a lost soul and a creature of depravity! The thought occurred to her, that she might go on to think of other words, and to think of images and actions as well; she might be unable to forget any of them--her mind might become a storehouse of such horrors! And so the maiden out of ancient Greece would lie awake all night and wrestle with fiends, until she was bathed in a perspiration.

Section 5. About this time Thyrsis was making his ***debut*** as an author. He had discovered a curious knack in himself, a turn for making verses of a sort which were pleasing to children. They came from some little corner of his consciousness, he scarcely knew how; but there was a paper that was willing to buy them, and to pay him the princely sum of five dollars a week! This would pay for his food and his hall bedroom, or for board at some farm in the summer; and so for several years Thyrsis was free.

He told a falsehood about his age, and entered college, and buried himself up to the eyes in work. This was a college in a city, and a poor college, where the students all lived at home, and had nothing to do but study; and so Thyrsis missed all that beneficent illumination known as "student-life." He never hurrahed at football contests, nor did he dress himself in honorific garments, nor stupify himself at "smokers." Being democratic, and without thought of setting himself up over others, he was unaware of his greatest opportunities, and when they invited him into a fraternity, he declined. Once or twice he found himself roaming the streets at night with a crowd of students, emitting barbaric screechings; but this made him feel silly, and so he lagged behind and went home.

The college served its purpose, in introducing him to the world of knowledge; but that did not take long, and afterwards it was all in his way. The mathematics were a discipline, and in them he rejoiced as a strong man to run a race; and this was true also of the sciences, and of history--the only trouble was that he would finish the text-books in the first few weeks, and after that there was nothing to do save to compose verses in class, and to make sketches of the professors. But as for the "languages" and the "literatures" they taught him--in the end Thyrsis came to forgive them, because he saw that they did not know what languages and literatures were. On this account he took to begging leave of absence on grounds of his poverty; and then he would go home and spend his days and nights in learning.

One could get so much for so little, in this wonderful world of mind! For eight cents he picked up a paper volume of Emerson's "Essays"; and in this shrewd and practical nobility was so much that he was seeking in life! And then he stumbled upon a fifteen-cent edition of "Sartor Resartus", and took that home and read it. It was like the clash of trumpets and cymbals to him; it made his whole being leap. Hour after hour he read, breathless, like a man bewitched, the whole night through. He would cry aloud with delight, or drop the book and pound his knee and laugh over the demoniac power of it. The next day he began the "French Revolution"; and after that, alas, he found there was no more--for Carlyle had turned his back upon democracy, and so Thyrsis turned his back upon Carlyle.

For this was one of the forces which had had to do with the shaping of his thought. Beginning in the public-schools he had learned about his country--the country which was his, if not Corydon's. He had read in its history--Irving's "Life of Washington," and ten great volumes about Lincoln; so he had come to understand that salvation is of the people, and that those things which the people do not do--those things have not yet been done. So no one could deceive him, or lead him astray; he might laugh with the Tories, and even love them for their foibles--quaint old Samuel Johnson, for instance, because he was poor and sturdy, and had stood by his trade of bookman; but at bottom Thyrsis knew that all these men were gilding a corpse. Wordsworth and Tennyson, Browning and Swinburne --he followed each one as far as their revolutionary impulse lasted; and after that there was no more in them for him. Even Ruskin, who taught him the possibilities of English prose, and opened his eyes to the form and color of the world of nature--even Ruskin he gave up, because he was a philanthropist and not a democrat.

Thyrsis had been brought up as a devout Episcopalian. They had dressed him in scarlet and white to carry the train of the bishop at confirmation, and had sent him to an afternoon service every day throughout Lent. Early in life he had stumbled on a paper copy of Paine's "Age of Reason," and he read it with horror, and then conducted a private ***auto da fe***. But the questions of the book stayed with him, and as years passed they clamored more loudly. What would have happened, astronomically, if the sun had stood still? And how many different species would have had to go into the ark? And what was the size of a whale's gullet, and the probable digestive powers of a whale's stomach?

And then came more fundamental difficulties. Could there, after all, be such a duty as faith in any intellectual matter? Could there be any revelation superior to reason--must not reason have once decided that it was a revelation, or was not? And what of all the other "revelations", which all the other peoples of the world accepted? And then again, if Jesus had been God, could he really have been tempted? To be God and man at the same time--did that not mean both to know and not to know? And was there any way conceivable for anything to be God, in which everything else was not God?

These perplexities and many others the boy took to his clerical adviser, a man who loved him dearly, and who gave him some volumes of the "Bampton lectures" to read. Here was the defense of Christianity, conducted by authorities, and with scholarship and dignity; and Thyrsis found to his dismay that the only convincing parts of their books were where they gave a ***resume*** of the arguments of their opponents. He learned in this way many difficulties that had not yet occurred to him; and when he had got through with the reading his mind was made up. If any man were to be damned for not believing such things, then it was his duty as a thinker to be damned; and so he bade farewell to the Church--something which was sad, in a way, for his mother had been planning him for a bishop!

Section 6. But Thyrsis was throwing away many chances these days. He went into the higher regions to spend his Christmas holidays; and instead of being tactful and agreeable, he buried himself in a corner of the library all day long. For Thyrsis had made the greatest discovery yet--he had found out Shakespeare! At school they had taught him "English" by means of "to be or not to be", and they had sought to trap him at examinations by means of "man's first disobedience and the fruit"; and so for years they had held him back from the two great glories of our literature. But now, by accident, he stumbled into "The Tempest"; and after that he read every line of the plays in two weeks.

He lost his soul in that wonderland; he walked and thought no more like the men of earth--he dwelt with those lords and princes of the soul, and learned to speak their language. He would dodge among cable-cars and trucks with their heavenly melodies in his ears; and while he sung them his eyes flashed and his heart beat fast:

> "Good night, sweet prince,
>   And flights of angels sing thee to thy rest!"

There were a few days left in those wondrous holidays; and these went to Milton. There was a set of his works, enormously expensive, which had been made and purchased with no idea that any human being would ever read them. But Thyrsis read them, and so all the beauty of the binding was justified. For hours, and hours upon hours, he drank in that thunderous music, crying it aloud with his hands clenched tightly, and stopping to laugh like a child with excitement:

> "Th'imperial ensign, which full high advanced,
>   Shone like a meteor streaming to the wind,
>   With gems and golden lustre rich emblazed,
>   Seraphic arms and trophies; all the while
>   Sonorous metal blowing martial sounds!"

And afterwards, when he came to the palace that "rose like an exhalation", all of Thyrsis' soul rose with it. One summer's day he stood on a high mountain with a railroad in the valley, and saw a great freight-engine stop still and pour out its masses of dense black smoke. It rose in the breathless air, straight as a column, high and majestic; and Thyrsis thought of that line. It carried him out into the heavens, and he knew that a flash of poetry such as that is the meeting of man's groping hand with God's.

It was about here that a strange adventure came to him. It was midwinter, and he went out, long after midnight, to walk in a beautiful garden. A dry powdery snow crunched beneath his feet, and overhead the stars gleamed and quivered, so bright that he felt like stretching out his hands to them. The world lay still, and awful in its beauty; and here suddenly, unsuspected--unheralded, and quite unsought--there came to Thyrsis a strange and portentous experience, the first of his ecstasies.

He could not have told whether he walked or sat down, whether he spoke or was silent; he lost all sense of his own existence--his consciousness was given up to the people of his dreams, the companions and lovers of his fancy. The cold and snow were gone, and there was a moonlit glade in a forest; and thither they came, one by one, friendly and human, yet in the full panoply of their splendor and grace. There were Shelley and Milton, and the gentle and troubled Hamlet, and the sorrowful knight of la Mancha, with the irrepressible Falstaff to hearten them all; a strangely-assorted company, yet royal spirits all of them, and no strangers to each other in their own world. And here they gathered and conversed, each in his own vein and from his own impulse, with gracious fancy and lofty vision and heart-easing mirth. And ah, how many miles would one have travelled to be with them!

That was the burden which this gift laid upon Thyrsis. He soon discovered that these visions of wonder came but once, and that when they were gone, they were gone forever. And he must learn to grapple with them as they fled, to labor with them and to hold them fast, at the cost of whatever heartbreaking strain. Thus alone could men have even the feeblest reflexion of their beauty--upon which to feed their souls forever after.

Section 7. These things came at the same time as another development in Thyrsis' life, likewise portentous and unexpected. Boyhood was gone, and manhood had come. There was a bodily change taking place in him--he became aware of it with a start, and with the strangest and most uncomfortable thrills. He did not know what to make of it, or what to do about it; nor did he know where to turn for advice.

He tried to put it aside, as a thing of no importance. But it would not be put aside--it was of vast importance. He discovered new desires in himself, impulses that dominated him in a most disturbing way. He found that he took a new interest in women and young girls; he wanted to linger near them, and their glances caused him strange emotions. He resented this, as an invasion of his privacy; it was inconsistent with his hermit-instinct. Thyrsis wished no women in his life save the muses with their star-sewn garments. He had been fond of a line from a sonnet to Milton:

"Thy soul was like a Star, and dwelt apart."

But instead of this, what awful humiliations! In a summer-resort where he found himself, there was a girl of not very gentle breeding, somewhat pudgy and with a languishing air. She liked to have boys snuggle down by her; and so Thyrsis spent the whole of one evening, sitting in a summer-house with an arm about her waist, dissolved in a sort of moon-calf sentimentalism. And then he passed the rest of the night wandering about in the forest cursing himself, with tears of shame and vexation in his eyes.

He was so ignorant about these matters that he did not even know if the changes that had taken place in him were normal, or whether they were doing him harm. He made up his mind that he must have advice; as it was unthinkable that he should speak about such shameful things with any grown person, he bethought himself of a classmate in college who was an earnest and sober man. This friend, much older than Thyrsis, was the son of an evangelical clergyman, and was headed for the ministry himself. His name was Warner, and Thyrsis had helped him in arranging for some religious meetings at the college. Warner had been shocked by his theological irregularities; but they were still friends, and now Thyrsis sought a chance to exchange confidences with him.

The opportunity came while they were strolling down an avenue near the college, and a woman passed them, a woman with bold and hard features, and obviously-painted cheeks. She smiled at a group of students just ahead, and one of them turned and walked off arm in arm with her.

"Good heavens!" exclaimed Warner. "Did you see that?"

"Yes," said Thyrsis. "Who is she?"

"She comes from a house just around the corner."

"But who is she?"

"Why--she's a street-walker."

"A street-walker!"

This brought to Thyrsis' mind a problem that had been haunting him for a year or two. Always when he walked about the streets at night there were women who smiled at him and whispered. And he knew that these were bad women, and shrunk from them. But just what did they mean?

"What does she do?" he asked again.

"Why, don't you know what a street-walker is?"

"Not very well," said Thyrsis.

It took some time for him to get the desired information, because the other could not realize the depths of his ignorance. "They sell themselves to men," he said.

"But what for?" asked Thyrsis. "You don't mean that they--they let them---"

"They have intercourse together. Of course."

Thyrsis was almost dumb with dismay. "But I should think they would have children!" he exclaimed.

"Good Lord, man!" laughed the other. "Where do you keep yourself, any-way?"

But Thyrsis was too much shaken to think of being ashamed. This was a most appalling revelation to him--it opened quite a new vista of life's possibilities.

"But why should they do such things?" he cried.

"They earn their living that way," said the other.

"But why *that* way?"

"I don't know. They are that kind of women, I suppose."

And so Warner went on to expound to him the facts of prostitution, and all the abysses of human depravity that lie thereabouts. And incidentally the boy got a chance to ask his questions, and to get a common-sense view of his perplexities. Also he got some understanding of human nature, and of the world in which he lived.

Here was Warner, a man of twenty-four, and of a devout, if somewhat dull and plodding conscientiousness; and the last eight or nine years of his' life had been one torment because of the cravings of lust. He had never committed an act of unchastity--or at least he told Thyrsis that he had not. But he was never free from the impulse, and he had no conception of the possibility of being free. His desire was a purely brute one--untouched by any intellectual or spiritual, or even any sentimental color. He desired woman, as woman--it mattered not what woman. How low his impulses took him Thyrsis realized with a shudder from one remark that he made--that his poverty did not help him to live virtuously, for about the docks and in the workingmen's quarters there were women who would sell themselves for fifty cents a night.

This man's whole life was determined by that craving; in fact it seemed to Thyrsis that his God had made the universe with relation to it--a heaven to reward him if he abstained, and a hell to punish him if he yielded. It was because of this that he clung to the church, and shrunk from any dallying with "rationalism". He disapproved of the theatre, because it appealed to these cravings; he disapproved of all pictures and statues of the nude human form, because the sight of them overmastered him. For the same reason he shrunk from all impassioned poetry, and from dancing, and even from non-religious music. He was rigid in his conformance to all the social conventions, because they served the purpose of saving him and his young women-friends from temptation; and he looked forward to the completion of a divinity-course as his goal, because then he would be able to settle down and marry, and so at last to gratify his desires. He stated this quite baldly, quoting the authority of St. Paul, that it was "better to marry than to burn."

This conversation brought Thyrsis to a realization that there was a great deal in the world that was not found in the poetry of Tennyson and Longfellow; and so he began to pry into the souls of others of his fellow-students.

Section 8. Warner had given him the religious attitude; and now he went after the scientific. There was a tall, eager-faced young man, who proclaimed himself a disciple of Haeckel and Herbert Spencer, and even went so far as to quote Schopenhauer in class. Walking home together one day, these two fell to arguing the freedom of the will, and the nature of motives and desires, and what power one has over them; and so Thyrsis made the startling discovery that this young man, having accepted the doctrine of "determinism," had drawn therefrom the corollary that he had to do what he wanted to do, and so was powerless to resist his sex-impulses. For the past year this youth, a fine, intellectual and honest student, had gone at regular intervals to visit a prostitute; and with entirely scientific and cold-blooded precision he outlined to Thyrsis the means he took to avoid contracting disease. Thyrsis listened, feeling as he might have felt in a slaughter-house; and when, returning to the deterministic hypothesis, he asked how it was that he had managed to escape this "necessity", he was told that it must be because he was of a weaker and less manly constitution.

And there was yet another type: a man with whom there was no difficulty in bringing up the subject, for the reason that he was always bringing it up himself. Thyrsis sat next to him in a class in Latin, and noticed that whenever the text contained any hint at matters of sex--which was not infrequent in Juvenal and Horace-- this man would look at him with a grin and a sly wink. And sometimes Thyrsis would make a casual remark in conversation, and the man would twist it out of its meaning, or make a pun out of it--to find some excuse for his satyr's leer. So at last Thyrsis was moved to say to him--"Don't you ever realize what a state you've got your mind into?"

"How do you mean?" asked the man.

"Why, everything in the world seems to suggest obscenity to you. You're always looking for it and always finding it--you don't seem to care about anything else."

The other was interested in that view of it, and he acknowledged with mild amusement that it was true; apparently it was a novelty to him to discuss such matters seriously. He told Thyrsis that he could not remember having ever restrained a sexual impulse in his life. He thought of lust in connection with every woman he met, and his mind was a storehouse of smut. And yet he was not a bad fellow, in other ways; he handsome, and a good deal of an athlete, and was planning to be a physician. "You'll find most all the fellows are the same," he said.

Not long after this, Thyrsis was selected to represent his college on a debating-team, and he went away to another city and was invited to a fraternity-house; and here, suddenly, he discovered how much of "college-life" he had been missing. This was a fashionable university, and he met the sons of wealthy parents. About a score of them lived in this fraternity-house, without any sort of supervision or restraint. They ate in a beautiful oak-panelled dining-room adorned with drinking-steins; and throughout the meal they treated their visitor to such an orgy of obscenity as he had never dreamed of in his life before. Thyrsis was trapped and could not get away; and it seemed to him when he rose from the table that there was nothing left clean in all God's universe. These boys appeared to vie with each other in blasphemous abandonment; and it was not simply wantonness--it was sprawling and disgusting filthiness.

One of this group took Thyrsis driving, and was led to talk. Here was a youth whose father was the president of a great manufacturing-enterprise, and supplied him with unlimited funds; which money the boy used to divert himself in the pursuit of young women. Sometimes he had stooped so low as manicure-girls and shop-clerks and stenographers; but for the most part he sought actresses and chorus-girls--they had more intelligence and spirit, he explained, they were harder to win. He had his way with them, partly because he was handsome and clever, but mainly because he was the keeper of the keys of opportunity. It was his to dispense auto-rides and champagne-suppers, and flowers and jewels, and all things else that were desirable in life.

Thyrsis was appalled at the hardness and the utter ruthlessness of this man--he saw him as a young savage turned loose to prey in a civilized community. He had the most supreme contempt for his victims--that was what they were made for, and he paid them their price. Nor was this just because they were women, it was a matter of class; the young man had a mother and sisters, to whom he applied quite other standards. But Thyrsis found himself wondering how long, with this contagion raging among the fathers and the sons, it would be possible to keep the mothers and the daughters sterilized.

Section 9. These discoveries came one by one; but Thyrsis saw enough at the outset to make it clear that the time had come for him to gird up his loins. The choice of Hercules was before him; and he did not intend that the course of his life was to be decided by these cravings of the animal within him.

From the grosser sorts of temptation he was always saved by the fastidiousness of his temperament; the thought of a woman who sold herself for money could never bring him anything but shuddering. But all about his lodging-house lived the daughters of the poor, and these were a snare for his feet. It seemed to him as if this craving came to a man in regular pulses; he could go for weeks, serene and happy in his work--and then suddenly would come the restlessness, and he would go out into the night and wander about the streets for hours, impelled by a futile yearning for he knew not what--the hope of something clean in the midst of uncleanliness, of some adventure that would be not quite shameful to a poet's fancy. And then, after midnight, he would steal home, baffled and sick at heart, and wet his pillow with hot and bitter tears!

So unbearable to him was the thought of such perils that he was impelled to seek his old friend the clergyman, who had lost him over the ancient Hebrew mythologies, and now won him back by his living moral force. With much embarrassment and stammering Thyrsis managed to give a hint of what troubled him; and the man, whose life was made wholly of love for others, opened his great heart and took Thyrsis in.

He told him of his own youthful struggle--a struggle which had resulted in victory, for he had never known a woman. And he put all the facts before the boy, made clear to him the all-determining importance of the issue:

"Choose well, your choice is   Brief and yet endless!"

On the one hand was slavery and degradation and disease; and on the other were all the heights of the human spirit. For if one saved and stored this mighty sex-energy, it became transmuted to the gold of intellectual and emotional power. Such was the universal testimony of the masters of the higher life--

"My strength is as the strength of ten   Because my heart is pure."

And this was no blind asceticism; it was simply a choosing of the best. It was not a denial of love, but on the contrary a consecration of love. Some day Thyrsis would meet the woman he was to cleave to, and he would expect her to come to him a virgin; and he must honor her as much--he must save the fire and fervor of his young desire for his life's great consummation.

Such was the ideal; and these two men made a compact between them, that once every month Thyrsis would write and tell of his success or failure. And this amateur confessional was a mighty motive to the lad--he knew that he could never tell a lie, and the thought of telling the truth was like a sword hanging over him. There were hours of trial, when he stood so close to the edge of the precipice that this alone was what kept him clear.

Section 10. The summer had come, and Thyrsis had gone away to live in a country village, and was reading Keats and Shelley, and the narrative poems of Scott. There came a soft warm evening, when all the world seemed a-dream; and he had been working hard, and there came to him a yearning for the stars. He went out, and was strolling through the streets of the village, when he saw a girl come out of one of the houses. She was younger than he, graceful of form, and pretty. The lamp-light flashed on her bright cheeks, and she smiled at him as she passed. And Thyrsis' heart gave a great leap, and the blood surged to his face; he turned and looked, and saw that she was gazing over her shoulder at him.

He stopped, and turned to follow, his meditations all gone, and gone his resolutions. A trembling seized him, and every nerve of him tingled. He could feel his heart as if it were underneath his throat.

In a moment more he was beside the girl. "May I join you?" he asked, and she replied with a nod.

Thyrsis moved beside her and took her arm in his. A moment later they came to a place where the road was dark, and he put his arm about her waist; she made no resistance.

"I--I've seen you often before," she said.

"Yes," he replied, "I have seen you." And he suddenly remembered a remark that he had heard about her. There was a large summer-hotel in this neighborhood, which as usual had brought all the corruptions of the city in its train; and a youth whom Thyrsis had met there had pointed out the girl with the remark, "She's a little beast."

And this idea, as it came to him, swept him away in a fierce tide of madness; he bent suddenly down and whispered into her ear. They were words that never in Thyrsis' life had passed his lips before.

The girl pushed him away; but she laughed.

"You don't mind, do you?" exclaimed Thyrsis, his heart thumping like a hammer.

"Listen," he whispered, bending towards her. "Let us go and take a walk. Let us go where no one will see us."

"Where?" she asked.

"Out into the country," he said.

"Not now," she replied. "Some other time."

"No, now!" exclaimed Thyrsis, desperately. "Now!"

They had been moving slowly; they came to a place where a great tree hung over the road, shadowing it; and there they stopped, as by one impulse.

"Listen to me," he whispered, swiftly. "Listen. You don't know how anxious I have been to meet you. It's true--indeed it's true!"

He paused. "Yes," said the girl, "and I have been wanting to meet you. Didn't you ever see me nod to you?"

And suddenly Thyrsis put his arms about her, and pressed her to him. The touch of her bosom sent the blood driving through his veins in torrents of fire; he no longer knew or cared what he said, or what he did.

"Listen to me," he raced on. "Listen to me! Nobody will know! And you are so beautiful, so beautiful! I love you!" The words burned his lips, but he forced himself to say them, again and again--"I love you!"

The girl was gazing around her nervously. "Not now," she exclaimed. "Not to-night. To-morrow I will meet you, to-morrow night, and go with you."

"No," cried Thyrsis, "not to-morrow night, but now!" And he clasped her yet more tightly, with all his strength. "Listen," he panted, his breath on her cheek. "I love you! I cannot wait till to-morrow-- I could not bear it. I am all on fire! I should not know what to do!"

The girl gazed about her again in uncertainty, and Thyrsis swept on in his swift, half-incoherent exclamations. He would take no refusal; for half his madness was terror of himself, and he knew it. And then suddenly, as he cried out to her, the girl whispered, faintly, "All right!" And his heart gave a throb that hurt him.

"I'll tell you," she went on, hastily, "I was going to the store for something, and they expect me home. But wait here till I get back, and then I'll go with you."

"You mean it?" whispered Thyrsis. "You mean it?"

"Yes, yes," she answered.

"And it will be soon?"

"Yes, soon."

"All right," said he. "But first give me a kiss." As she held up her face, Thyrsis pressed her to him, and kissed her again and again, until her cheeks were aflame. At last he released her, and she turned swiftly and darted up the street.

Section 11. And after she was gone the boy stood there motionless, not stirring even a hand. A full minute passed, and the color went out of his cheeks, and the fire out of his veins, and he could hardly stand erect. His head sunk lower and lower, until suddenly he whispered hoarsely, under his breath, "Oh, my God! Oh, my God!"

He looked up at the sky, his face ghastly white; and there came from his throat a low moan, like that of a wounded animal. Suddenly he turned, and fled away down the street.

He went on and on, block after block; but then, all at once, he stopped again and faced about. He gripped his hands until the nails cut him, and shut his teeth together like a steel-trap. "No, no!" he muttered. "No--you coward!"

He turned and began to march, grimly, as a soldier might; he went back, and stopped on the spot from which he had come; and there he stood, like a statue. So one minute passed, then another; and at last a shadow moved in the distance, and a step came near. It was the girl.

"Here I am," she whispered, laughing.

"Yes," said Thyrsis. "I have something I must say to you, please."

She noticed the change in a flash, and she stopped. "What's the matter?"

"I don't know just how to tell you," said Thyrsis, in a low, quivering voice. "I've been a hound, and now I don't want to be a cad. But I'm sorry for what we were talking about."

"You mean what *you* were talking about, don't you?" demanded the girl, her eyes flashing.

Thyrsis dropped his glance. "Yes," he said. "I am a cur. I beg your pardon. I am so ashamed of myself that I don't know what to do. But, oh, I was crazy. I couldn't help it! and I--I'm so sorry!" There were tears in his voice.

"Humph," said the girl, "it's all right."

"No," said Thyrsis, "it's all wrong. It's dreadful--it's horrible. I don't know what I should have done---"

"Well, you better not do it any more, that's all," said she. "I'm sure you needn't worry about me--I'll take care of myself."

Thyrsis looked at her again; she was no longer beautiful. Her face was coarse, and her anger did not make it any better. His humility made no impression.

"It is so wrong---" he began; but she interrupted him.

"Preaching won't help it any," she said. "I don't want to hear it. Good-bye."

So she turned and walked away; and Thyrsis stood there, white, and shuddering, until at last he started and strode off. Clear through the town he went, and out into the black country beyond, seeing nothing, caring about nothing. He flung himself down by the roadside, and lay there moaning for hours: "My God, my God, what shall I do?"

Section 12. It was nearly morning when he came back and crept upstairs to his room; and here he sat by the bedside, gazing at the haggard face in the glass. At such times as this he discovered a something in his features that filled him with shuddering; he discovered it in his words, and in the very tone of his voice--the sins of the fathers were being visited upon the children! What an old, old story it was to him--this anguish and remorse! These ecstasies of resolution that vanished like a cloud-wrack--these protestations and noble sentiments that counted for naught in conduct! And his was to be the whole heritage of impotence and futility; he, too, was to struggle and agonize--and to finish with his foot in the trap!

This idea was like a white-hot goad to him. After such an experience there would be several months of toil and penance, and of savage self-immolation. It was hard to punish a man who had so little; but Thyrsis managed to find ways. For several months at a time he would go without those kinds of food that he liked; and instead of going to bed at one o'clock he would read the New Testament in Greek for an hour. He would leap out of bed in the morning and plunge into cold water; and at night, when he felt a longing upon him, he would go out and run for hours.

He took to keeping diaries and writing exhortations to himself. Because he could no longer use the theological prayers he had been taught, he fashioned new invocations for himself: prayers to the unknown sources of his vision, to the new powers of his own soul--"the undiscovered gods," as he called them. Above all he prayed to his vision of the maiden who waited the issue of this battle, and held the crown of victory in her keeping--

> "Somewhere beneath the sun,
>   Those quivering heart-strings prove it,
> Somewhere there must be one
>   Made for this soul to love it--
> Some one whom I could court
>   With no great change of manner,
> Still holding reason's fort,
>   While waving fancy's banner!"

All of which things made a subtle change in his attitude to Corydon, whom he still met occasionally. Corydon was now a young lady, beautiful, even stately, with an indescribable atmosphere of gentleness and purity about her. All things unclean shrunk from her presence; and so in times of distress he liked to be with her. He would drop vague hints as to sufferings and temptations, and told her that she seemed like a "goddess" to him.

Corydon received this with some awe, but with more perplexity. She could not understand why anyone should struggle so much, or why a youth should take such a sombre view of things. But she was perfectly willing to seem like a "goddess" to anyone, and she was glad if that helped him. She was touched when he read her a poem of his own, a poem which he held very precious. He called it

> "A song of the young-eyed Cherubim
> In the days of the making of man."

And in it he had set forth the view of life that had come to him--

> "The quest of the spirit's gain--
>   Lured by the graces of pleasure,
> And lashed by the furies of pain.
>   Thy weakness shall sigh for an Eden,
> But the sword shall flame at the gate;
>   For far is the home of thy vision
> And strong is the hand of thy fate!"

Section 13. Though Thyrsis had no time to realize it, it was in this long and bitter struggle that he won whatever power he had in his future life. It was here that he learned "to hold his will above him as his law", and to defy the world for the sake of his ideal. And then, too, this toil was the key that opened to him the treasure-house of a new art--which was music.

Until he was nearly out of college Thyrsis had scarcely heard any music at all. Church-hymns he had learned, and a few songs in school. But now in poetry and other books he met with references to composers, and to the meaning of great music; and the things that were described there were the things he loved, and he began to feel a great eagerness to get at them. As a first step he bought a mandolin, and set to work to teach himself to play, a task at which he wrought with great diligence. At the same time a friend had bought a guitar, and the two set to work to play duets. The first preliminary was the getting of the instruments in tune; and not knowing that the mandolin is an octave higher than the guitar, they spent a great deal of time and broke a great many guitar-strings.

As the next step, Thyrsis went to hear a great pianist, and sat perplexed and wondering. There was a girl next to him who sobbed, and Thyrsis watched her as he might have watched a house on fire. Only once the pianist pleased *him*--when he played a pretty little piece called somebody's "impromptu", in which he got a gleam of a "tune." Poor Thyrsis went and got that piece, and took it home to study it, with the help of the mandolin; but, alas, in the maze of notes he could not even find the "tune."

But if he could not understand the music, he could read books about it; he read a whole library--criticism of music, analysis of music, histories of music, composers of music; and so gradually he learned the difference between a sarabande and a symphony, and began to get some idea of what he went out for to hear. At first, at the concerts, all he could think of was to crane his neck and recognize the different instruments; he heard whole symphonies, while doing nothing but watching for the "movements," and making sure he hadn't skipped any. One heartless composer ran two movements into one, and so Thyrsis' concert came out one piece short at the end, and he sat gazing about him in consternation when the audience rose to go. Afterwards he read long dissertations about each symphony before he went, and he would note down the important points and watch for them. The critic would expatiate upon "the long-drawn dissonance *forte*, that marks the close of the working-out portion"; and Thyrsis would watch for that long-drawn dissonance, and be wondering if it was never coming--when suddenly the whole symphony would come to an end! Or he would read about a "quaint capering measure led off by the bassoons," or a "frantic sweep of the violins over a trombone melody," and he would watch for these events with eyes and ears alert, and if he found them-- *eureka*!

But such things could not last forever; for Thyrsis had a heart full of eagerness and love, and of such is the soul of music. And just then was a time when he was sick and worn--when it seemed to him that the burden of his life was more than he could bear. He was haunted by the thought that he would lose his long battle, that he would go under and go down; and then it was that chance took him to a concert which closed with the great "C-Minor Symphony."

Thyrsis had read a life of Beethoven, and he knew that here was one of the hero-souls--a man who had grappled with the fiends, and passed through the valley of death. And now he read accounts of this titan symphony, and learned that it was a battle of the human spirit with despair. He read Beethoven's words about the opening theme--"So knocks fate upon the door!" And a fierce and overwhelming longing possessed him to get at the soul of that symphony.

He went to the concert, and heard nothing of the rest of the music, but sat like a man in a dream; and when the time came for the symphony, he was trembling with excitement. There was a long silence; and then suddenly came the first theme--those fearful hammer-strokes that cannot be thought without a shudder. They beat upon Thyrsis' very heart-strings, and he sat appalled; and straight out he went upon the tide of that mighty music-passion--without knowing it, without knowing how. He forgot that he was trying to understand a symphony; he forgot where he was, and what he was; he only knew that gigantic phantoms surged within him, that his soul was a hundred times itself. He never guessed that an orchestra was playing a second theme; he only knew that he saw a light gleam out of the storm, that he heard a voice, pitiful, fearful, beautiful beyond utterance, crying out to the furies for mercy; and that then the storm closed over it with a roar. Again and again it rose; Thyrsis did not know that this was the "working-out portion" that had forever been his bane. He only knew that it struggled and fought his fight, that it pleaded and sobbed, and rose higher and higher, and began to rejoice--and that then came the great black phantom-shape sweeping over it; and the iron hammer-strokes of Fate beat down upon it, crushed it and trampled it into annihilation. Again and again this happened, while Thyrsis sat clutching the seat, and shaking with wonder and excitement. Never in his experience had there been anything so vast, so awful; it was more than he could bear, and when the first movement came to an end--when the soul's last hope was dead--he got up and rushed out. People who passed him on the streets must have thought that he was crazy; and afterwards, that day and forever, he lived all his soul's life in music.

As a result of this Thyrsis paid all his bank-account for a violin, and went to see a teacher.

"You are too old," the teacher said.

But Thyrsis answered, "I will work as no one ever worked before."

"We all do that," replied the other, with a smile. And so they began.

And so all day long, with fingers raw, and arms and back shuddering with exhaustion, Thyrsis sat and practiced, the spirit of Music beckoning him on. It was in a boarding-house, and there was a nervous old man in the next room, and in the end Thyrsis had to move. By the time he went away to the country, he was able to play a melody in tune; and then he would take some one that had fascinated him, and practice it and practice it night and day. He would take his fiddle every morning at eight and stride out into the forest, and there he would stay all day with the squirrels. They told him once how a new arrival, driving over in the hotel 'bus at early dawn, had passed an old Italian woman toiling up a hill and singing for dear life the "Tannhauser March." It chanced that the new arrival was a musician, and he leaned out and asked the old woman where she had learned it. And this was her explanation;

"Dey ees a crazy feller in de woods--he play it all day for tree weeks!"

Section 14. By this time Thyrsis had finished at college, passing comfortably near the bottom of his class, and had betaken himself to a university as a graduate student. He was duly registered for a lot of courses, and spent his time when he should have been at the lectures, sitting in a vacant class-room reading the book that had fascinated him last. His note-book began at that time to show two volumes a day on an average, and once or twice he stopped at night to wonder how it had actually been possible for him to read poetry fourteen hours a day for a whole week and not be tired.

He taught himself German, and that led to another great discovery--he made the acquaintance of Goethe. The power of that mighty spirit took hold of him, so that he prayed to him when he was lonely, and kept the photograph of the young poet in his pocket, to gaze at it as at a lover. The great eyes came to haunt him so that one night he awoke crying out, because he had dreamed he was going to meet Goethe.

In the catalog of the university there were listed a number of courses in "rhetoric and English composition". They were for the purpose of teaching one how to write, and the catalog set forth convincingly the methods whereby this was done. Thyrsis wished to know all there was to know about writing, and so ne enrolled himself for an advanced course, and went for an hour every day and listened to expositions of the elements of sentence-structure by Prof. Osborne, author of "American Prose Writers" and "The Science of Rhetoric". The professor would give him a theme, and bid him bring in a five-hundred word composition. Perhaps it was that Thyrsis was lacking in the play-spirit; at any rate he could not write convincingly on the subject of "The Duty of the College Man to Support Athletics." He struggled for a month against his own impotence, and then went to see his instructor.

"I think," he said, "I shall have to drop Course A."

The professor gazed over his spectacles at him.

"Why?"

"I don't think I am getting any good out of it."

"But how can you tell what good you are getting?"

"I don't seem to feel that I am," said Thyrsis, deprecatingly.

"It is not to be supposed that you would feel it," said the other--"not at this early stage. You must wait."

"But I don't like the method, sir."

"What's wrong with the method?"

Thyrsis was embarrassed. He was not sure, he said; but he did not think that writing could be taught. Anyway, one had first to have something worth saying--

"Are you laboring under the delusion that you know anything about writing?" demanded the professor. (He had written across Thyrsis' last composition the words, "Feeble and trivial".)

"Why, no," began the boy.

"Because if you are, let me disabuse your mind at once. There is no one in the class who knows less about writing than yourself."

"I think," said Thyrsis, "it's because I can't bring myself to write in cold blood. I have to be interested. I'm sure that is the trouble."

"I'm sure," said the other, "that the trouble is that you think you know too much."

"I'm sorry, sir," said Thyrsis, humbly. "I've tried my best---"

"It is my business to teach students to write. I've given my life to that, and I think I know something about it. But you think you know more than I do. That's all."

And so they parted. Thyrsis kept a vivid recollection of this interview, for the reason that at a later stage of his career he came into contact with Prof. Osborne again, and got another glimpse of the authoritarian attitude towards the art of letters.

Section 15. Thyrsis had not many friends at college, and none at all at the university. He had no time to make any; and besides, there was a certain facetious senior who had caught him hurrying through the corridors one day, declaring in excitement that---

"Banners yellow, glorious, golden,   On its roof did float and flow!"

But he had long ago ceased to hope for a friend, or to care what anybody thought about him; it was clear to him by this time that he had made himself into a poet, and was doomed to be unhappy. His mother had given up all hope of seeing him a bishop, and they had compromised upon a judgeship; but here at the university there was a law-school, and he met the students, and saw that this, too, could not be. These "lawyers" were not seeking knowledge for the love of it--they were studying a trade, by which they could rise in the world. They were not going out to do battle for truth and justice--they were perfecting themselves in cunning, so that they might be of help in money-disputes; they were sharpening their wits, to make them useful tools for the opening of treasure-chests. And this attitude to life was written all over their personalities; they seemed to Thyrsis a coarse and roistering crew, and he shrunk from them in repugnance.

He went his own impetuous way. He stayed at the university until he had taught himself French and Italian, as well as German, and had read all the best literature in those languages. And likewise he heard all the best music, and went about full of it day and night. By this time he had definitely beaten his devils, and had come to be master of himself; and though nobody guessed anything about it, there was a new marvel going on within him--he had, in a spiritual sense, become pregnant.

There were many signs by which this state might have been known. He went quite alone, and spoke to no man; he was self-absorbed, and walked about with his

eyes fixed on vacancy; he was savage when disturbed, and guarded his time un-
scrupulously. He had given up the very last of the formalities of life--he no longer
attended any lectures, or wore cuffs, and he would not talk at meal-times. He took
long walks at impossible hours, and he was fond of a certain high hill where the
storms blew. These things had been going on for a year; and now the book that had
been coming to ripeness in his mind was ready to be born.

It had its origin in the reading of history, and the fronting of old tyranny in its
cruel forms. Thyrsis had come to hate Christianity for many things by that time,
but most of all he hated it because it taught the bastard virtue of Obedience. Thyrsis
obeyed no man--he lived his life; and the fiery ardor with which he lived it was taking form in his mind as a personality. He was dreaming a hero who should be ***Resistance*** incarnate; the passionate assertion of man's right and of man's defiance.

It was in the days of ferocity in Italy, the days of the despot and the bravo;
and Thyrsis' hero was a minstrel, a mighty musician whose soul was free. And he
sung in the despot's hall, and wooed the despot's daughter. This was the minstrel of
"Zulieka"---

> "His ladder of song was slight,
>   But it reached to her window's height;
>   Each verse so frail was the silken rail,
>   From which her soul took flight."

Thyrsis went about quite drunk with the burning words with which the minstrel won the lady, and tore her free from the mockeries of convention, and that
divinity that doth hedge about a princess. He bore her away, locked tightly in his
arms, and all his own--into the great lonely mountains; and there lived the minstrel
and the princess, the lord and the lady of an outlaw band. But the outlaws were
cruel, and the minstrel sought goodness; and so there was a struggle, and he and
the lady went yet deeper into the black forest, where they dwelt alone in a hut, he
a prince of hunters and she a princess of love. But the outlaws led the despot to the
place, and there was a battle; the princess was slain, and the minstrel escaped in the
darkness. All night he roamed the forest, and in the morning he lay by the roadside
with a bow in his hand, and when the despot rode by he rose and drove the shaft

through his heart. Then they captured him, and tortured him, and he died with a song of mockery and defiance upon his lips.

Section 16. Now, when these things first came to Thyrsis, he whispered in awe that it would be a life-time before he could write them. And a year passed thus, while every emotion of his life poured itself into some part of that story, and every note of music that he heard came out of the minstrel's heart. At last the time came when he was so full of it that he could no longer find peace; when the wonder of it was such that he walked along the street laughing, and with tears in his eyes. Then he said to himself, "It must be done! Now! Now!" And he looked about him as a woman might, seeking some place for her labor.

That was in the late winter, when the professors at the university, and all his relatives and acquaintances, had given him up as a hopeless case. He had stopped all his writing for money--he had a hundred dollars laid by, and that would suffice him; and he was wandering about whispering to himself: "The spring-time! The spring-time! For it must be in the country!" When April had come he could stand it no longer--he must go! So he left all behind him, and set out for a place in the wilderness.

When he reached it, he found a lake that was all ice, and mountains that were all snow; the country people, who had never seen a poet, and knew not the subtle difference between inspiration and insanity, heard with wonder that he was going out into the woods. But he set out alone, through the snowy forest and along the lake-shore, to find some place far away, where he could build a hut, or even put up a tent; and when he was miles from the village, he came suddenly on a little wonderland that made his heart leap like the wild deer in the brake. Here was a dreamland palace, a vision beyond all thinking--a little shanty built of logs! It stood in a pretty dell, with a mountain streamlet dashing through it, and the mighty forest hiding it, and the lake spread out in front of it. It was all wet snow, and freezing rain, and mud and desolation; but Thyrsis saw the summer that was to be, and he sat down upon a stone and gazed at it, and laughed and sang for wonder and joy.

Then he fled back to the village, and found the owner of the earthly rights to this paradise, and hired it for a little gold; and then he moved out, in spite of the snow. At last his soul was free!

Twice a week they brought him provisions, and there he stayed. At first he nearly froze at night, and he had to write with his gloves on; but he did not feel the cold, because of the fire within. He climbed the mountains and yelled with the mad wind, and tramped through the bare, rocking forest, singing his minstrel songs. And all these days he walked with God, and there was no world at all save the world of nature. Millions of young-hearted things sprang up out of the ground to welcome him; the forests shook out their dazzling sheen, and the wild birds went mad in the mornings. All the time Thyrsis was writing, writing--thrilling with his ecstasy, and pouring out all his soul. He kept a little diary these days, and for weeks there was but one entry--"The book! The book!"

And then one day came a letter from his mother, saying that she was coming to the village nearby to spend the summer; also that Corydon's mother was coming, and that Corydon would be with her!

BOOK II
THE SNARE

The streamlet tinkled on. She sat, gazing about her at each familiar tree and rock. And meanwhile he was reading again from the book--

"Here, too, our shepherd-pipes we first assay'd!"

"Is that from 'Thyrsis'?" she asked. "Read me those lines that we used, to love so much."

And so he turned the page, and read again--

"A fugitive and gracious light he seeks,
  Shy to illumine; and I seek it, too.
    This does not come with houses or with gold,
  With place, with honor, and a flattering crew:
    'Tis not in the world's market bought and sold--
      But the smooth-slipping weeks
  Drop by, and leave its seeker still untired;
    Out of the heed of mortals he is gone,
    He wends unfollow'd, he must house alone;
  Yet on he fares, by his own heart inspired."_

Section 1. On the train Corydon was writing a letter to a friend, to say where she was going, and that Thyrsis was there. "I don't expect to see anything of him," she wrote. "He grows more egotistical and more contemptuous every day, and I cordially dislike him."

But when a man has spent three or four weeks with no company save the squirrels and the owls, there comes over him a mood of sociability, when the sight of a friendly face is an event. Thyrsis had now written several chapters of his book, and the first fury of his creative impulse had spent itself. So when Corydon stepped from the train, she found him waiting there to greet her; and he told her that he was laying in supplies for a feast, and that on the morrow she and her mother were to come out and see his fairy-palace and have a picnic dinner.

They came; and the May put on her finest raiment for their greeting. The sun shone warm and bright, and there was a humming and stirring in grass and thicket; one could feel the surge of the spring-time growth as a living flood. There was a glory of young green over the hill-sides, and a quivering sheen of white in the aspens and birches. Corydon clasped her hands and cried out in rapture when she saw it.

And Thyrsis, picturesque in his old corduroy trousers and his grey flannel shirt, played the host. He showed them his domestic establishment--wherein things were set in order for the first time since he had come. He told all his adventures: how the cold had crept in at night, and he had to fiddle to keep his courage up; how he had slept in a canvas-cot for the first time, and piled all the bedding on top, and wondered that he was cold; how he had left the pail with the freshly-roasted beef on the piazza, and a wild cat had carried off pail and all. He made fun of his amateur housekeeping-- he would forget things and let them burn, or let the fire go out; and he had tried living altogether on cold food, to the great perplexity of his stomach.

Then he gave a demonstration of his hard-won culinary skill. He boiled rice and raisins, and fried bacon and eggs; and they had fresh bread and butter, and jam and pickles, and a festive cake. And after they had feasted, Thyrsis stretched himself and leaned back against the trunk of a tree, and gazed up at the sky, quoting the words of a certain one-eyed Kalandar, son of a king, "Verily, this indeed is life! 'Tis pity 'tis fleeting!"

Afterwards he took Corydon for a walk. They climbed the hill where he came to battle with the stormwinds, and to watch the sunsets and the moon rising over the lake. And then they went down into the glen, where the mountain streamlet tumbled. Here had been wood-sorrel, and a carpet of the white trillium; and now there was adder's tongue, quaint and saucy, and columbine, and the pale dusty corydalis. There was soft new moss underfoot, and one walked as if in a temple.

Thyrsis pointed out a seat beside a deep bubbling pool. "Here's where I sit and write," he said.

"And how comes the book?" asked Corydon.

"Oh, I'm hammering at it--that's the best I can say."

"What is it?"

"Why--it's a story. I suppose it'll be called a romance, though I don't like the word."

Corydon pondered for a moment. "I wouldn't expect you to be writing anything romantic," she said.

Thyrsis, occupied with his own thoughts, observed, "I might call it a revolutionary romance."

"What is it about?"

He hesitated. "It happens in the middle ages," he said. "There's a minstrel and a princess."

"That sounds interesting," said Corydon.

Now in the period of pregnancy the artist's mood is one of secretiveness. But afterwards there comes a time for promulgation and rejoicing; and already there had been hints of this in the mind of Thyrsis. The great secret that he was cherishing-- what would be the world's reception of it? And now suddenly a wild idea came to him. He had heard somewhere that it is the women who read fiction. And was not Corydon a perfect specimen of the average middle-class young lady, and therefore of that mysterious potentiality, "the public", to which he must appeal? Why not see what she would think of it?

He took the plunge. "Would you like me to read it to you?" he asked.

"Why, certainly," she replied, and then added, gently, "If it wouldn't be a desecration."

"Oh, no," said Thyrsis. "You see, when it's been printed, all sorts of people will read it."

So he went back to the house and brought the precious manuscript; and he placed Corydon in the seat of inspiration, and sat beside her and read.

In many ways this was a revolutionary romance. Thyrsis had not spent any of his time delving into other people's books for "local color"; he was not relying for his effects upon gabardines and hauberks, and a sprinkling of "Yea, sires," and "prithees." His castle was but the vaguely outlined background of a stage upon which living hearts wrought out their passions. One saw the banquet-hall, with its tapestries and splendor, and the master of it, the man of force; there were swift scenes that gave one a glimpse of the age-long state of things--

> "Right forever on the scaffold,
>   Wrong forever on the throne."

There was a quarrel, and a cruel sentence about to be executed; and then the minstrel came. His fame had come before him, and so the despot, in half-drunken playfulness, left the deciding of the quarrel to him. He was brought to the head of the table, and the princess was led in; and so these two met face to face.

Here Thyrsis paused, and asked, "Are you interested?"

"Go on, go on," said Corydon.

So he read about his princess, who was the embodiment of all the virtues of the unknown goddess of his fancy. She was proud yet humble, aloof yet compassionate, and above all ineffably beautiful. And as for the minstrel--

> "The minstrel was fair and young.
>   His heart was of love and fire."

He took his harp, and first he pacified the quarrel, and then he sang to the lady. He sang of love, and the poet's vision of beauty; but most of all he sang of the free life of the open. He sang of the dreams and the spirit-companions of the minstrel, and of the wondrous magic that he wields--

> "Secrets of all future ages
>   Hover in mine ecstasy;
> Treasures never known to mortals
>   Hath my fancy hid for thee!"

He sang the spells that he would weave for her, the far journeys she should take--

"For thy soul a river flowing
   Swiftly, over golden sands,
 With the singing of the steersman
   Stealing into wonderlands!"

Section 2. This song was as far as Thyrsis had written, and he paused. Corydon was sitting with her hands clasped, and a look of enthrallment upon her face. "Oh, beautiful! beautiful!" she cried.

A thrill of pleasure went through the poet. "You like it, then?" he said.

"Oh, I like it!" she answered. And then she gazed at him, with wide-open eyes of amazement. "But you! You!" she exclaimed.

"Why not I?" he asked.

"How in the world did you do it? Where did you get it from?"

"It is mine," said Thyrsis, quickly.

"But I can't imagine it! I had no idea you were interested in such things!"

"But how could you know what I am interested in?"

"I see how you live--apart from everybody. And you spend all your time in books!"

Thyrsis suddenly recollected something which had amused him very much. Corydon had been reading "Middlemarch," and had told him that Dr. Casaubon reminded her of him. "And so I'm still just a bookworm to you!" he laughed.

"But isn't your interest in things always intellectual?" she asked.

"Then you suppose I'm doing this just as an exercise in technique?" he countered.

"It's taken me quite by surprise," said Corydon.

"We have three faculties in us," Thyrsis propounded--"intellect, feeling, and will; and to be a complete human being, we have to develop all of them."

"But you spend so much time piling up learning!"

"I need to know a great many things," he said. "I'm not conscious of studying anything I don't need for my purpose."

"What is the purpose?" she asked.

He touched the precious manuscript. "This," he said.

There was a pause.

"But you lose so much when you cut yourself off from the world," said Corydon. "And there are other people, whom you might help."

"People don't need my help; or at least, they don't want it."

"But how can you know that--if you never go among them?"

"I can judge by the lives they live."

"Ah!" exclaimed Corydon, quickly, "but people aren't to blame for the lives they live!"

"Why not?" he asked.

"Because--they can't help them. They are bound fast."

"They should break loose."

"That is easy for you to say," said Corydon. "You have no ties."

"I did have them--I might have them still. But I broke them."

"Ah, but you are a man!"

"What difference does that make?"

"It makes all the difference in the world. You can earn money, you can go away by yourself. But suppose you were a girl--shut up in a home, and told that that was your 'sphere'?"

"I'd fight," said Thyrsis--"I'd break my way out somehow, never fear. If one doesn't break out, it simply means that his desire is not strong enough."

Thyrsis had been surprised at the depth of Corydon's interest in his manuscript; he had not supposed that she would be so susceptible to anything of the imagination. And now he was surprised to see that her hands were clenched tightly, and that she sat staring ahead of her intently.

"Are you dissatisfied with your life?" he asked.

"Is there anything in it that I could be satisfied with?" she cried.

"I had no idea of that," he said.

"No," she replied; "that only shows how stupid you can be!"

"But--you never showed any signs--"

"Didn't you know that I was trying to prepare for college last year?"

"Yes; but you gave it up."

"What could I do? I had no help--no encouragement. I was groping like a blind person. And I told you about it."

"But I told you what to study," objected Thyrsis.

"Yes," said the girl; "but how could I do it? You know how to study--you've been taught. But I don't know anything, and I don't know how to find anything out. I began on the Latin, but I didn't even know how the words should be pronounced."

"Nobody else knows that," observed Thyrsis, somewhat inconsequently.

"It was all so dull and dreary," she went on--"everything they would have had me learn. I wanted things that had life in them, things that were beautiful and worth while--like this book of yours, for instance."

"I am really delighted that you like it," said Thyrsis, touched by that.

"Tell me the rest of it," she said.

Section 3. Thyrsis told his story at some length; in the ardor of her sympathy his imagination took fire, and he told it eloquently, he discovered new beauties in it that he had not seen before. And Corydon listened with growing delight and amazement.

"So that is the way you spend your time!" she exclaimed.

"That is the way," he said.

"And that is why you live like a hermit!"

"Yes, that is why."

"And you think that you would lose your vision if you went among people?"

"I know that I should."

"But how do you know?"

"I know because I have tried. You don't realize how hard I have to work over a thing like this. I have carried it in my mind for a year; I have lived for nothing else--I have literally had no other interest in the world. Every sentence I have read to you has been the product of work added to work--of one impulse piled upon another--of thinking and criticizing and revising. Just the little bit I have done has taken me a whole month, and I have hardly stopped to eat; it's been my first thought in the morning and my last at night. And when the mood of it comes to me, then I work in a kind of frenzy that lasts for hours and even days; and if I give up in the middle and fall back, then I have to do it all over again. It's like toiling up a mountain-side."

"I see," whispered Corydon. "And then, do you expect to have no human relationships as long as you live?"

Thyrsis pondered for a moment. "Did you ever read Mrs. Browning's poem, 'A Musical Instrument'?" he asked.

"No," she answered.

"It's a most beautiful poem," he said; "and it's hardly ever quoted or read, that I can find. It tells how the great god Pan came down by the river-bank, and cut one of the reeds to make himself a pipe. He sat there and played his music upon it--

'Sweet, sweet, sweet, O Pan!
  Piercing sweet by the river!
Blinding sweet, O great god Pan!
The sun on the hill forgot to die,
And the lilies reviv'd, and the dragon-fly
  Came back to dream on the river.

'Yet half a beast is the great god Pan,
  To laugh as he sits by the river,
Making a poet out of a man.
The true gods sigh for the cost and pain,--
For the reed which grows nevermore again
  As a reed with the reeds in the river.'"

Thyrsis paused. "Do you see what it means?" he asked.

"Yes," said Corydon, "I see."

"'Making a poet out of a man!' That is one of the finest lines I know. And that's the way I feel about it--I have given up all other duties in the world. If I can write one book, or even one poem, that will be an inspiration to men in the future--why, then I have done far more than I could do by a lifetime given to helping people around me."

"I never understood before," said Corydon.

"That is the idea the minstrel tries to voice to the princess. At first he pours out his soul to her; but then, when he finds that she loves him, he is afraid, and tries to persuade her not to come with him. He tells her how lonely and stern his life is; and she has been born to a gentle life--she has her station and her duty in the world. But the more he pleads the hardness of his life, the more she sees she must go with him. Even if the end be death to her, still she will be an inspiration to him, and give wings to his music. 'Be silent,' she tells him--'let me fling myself away for a song! To do one deed that the world remembers, to utter one word that lives forever--that is worth all the failure and the agony that can come to one woman in her lifetime!'"

Corydon sat with her hands clasped. "Yes," she said, "that is the way she would feel!"

"I'm glad to hear you say that," remarked the other. "I must make it real; and I've been afraid about it. Would she really go with him?"

"She would go if she loved him," said Corydon.

"If she loved him. But she must love his art still more."

"She must love *him,*" said Corydon.

Thyrsis shook his head. "It would not do for her to go with him for that," he said.

"Why not? Doesn't he love her?"

"Yes; but he is afraid to tell her so. They dare not let that sway them."

"I don't understand. Why not?"

"Because personal love is a limited thing, and comparatively an ignoble thing."

"I don't see how there can be anything more noble than true love between a man and a woman," declared Corydon.

"It depends on what you mean by 'true' love," replied Thyrsis. "If two people love each other for their own sakes, and go together, they soon come to know each other, and then they are satisfied--and their growth is at an end. What I conceive is that two people must lose themselves, and all thought of themselves, in their common love for something higher--for some great ideal, some purpose, some vision of perfection. And they seek this together, and they rejoice in finding it, each for the other; and so they have always progress and growth--they stand for something new to each other every day of their lives. To such love there is no end, and no chance of weariness or satiety."

"I had never thought of it just so," said the girl. "But surely there must be a personal love in the beginning."

"I don't know," he responded. "I hadn't thought about that. I'm afraid I'm impersonal by nature."

"Yes," she said, "that's what has puzzled me. Don't you love human beings?"

"Not as a rule," he confessed.

"But then--what is it you are interested in? Yourself?"

"People tell me that's the case. And there's a sense in which it's true--I'm wrapped up in the thought of myself as an art-work. I've a certain vision of the possibilities of my own being, and I'm trying to realize it. And if I do, then I can write books and communicate it to other people, so that they can judge it, and see if it's any better than the vision they have. It is a higher kind of unselfishness, I think."

"I see," said Corydon. "It's not easy to understand."

"No one understands it," he replied. "People are taught that they must sacrifice themselves for others; and they do it, blindly and stupidly, and never ask if the other person is worthy of the sacrifice--and still less if they themselves have anything worth sacrificing."

Corydon had clenched her hands suddenly. "How I hate the religion of self-sacrifice!" she cried.

"Mine is a religion of self-development," said Thyrsis. "I am sacrificing myself for what other people ought to be."

Section 4. They came back after a time, to the subject of love; and to the ideal of it which Thyrsis meant to set forth in the book. It was the duty of every soul to seek the highest potentiality of which it had vision; and as one did that for himself, so he did it for the person he loved. There could be no higher love than this--to treat the thing beloved as one's self, to be perpetually dissatisfied with it, to scourge it to new endeavor, to hold it in immortal discontent.

This was a point about which they argued with eager excitement. To Thyrsis, love itself was a prize to be held before the loved one; whereas Corydon argued that love must exist before such a union could be thought of. Her cheeks flushed and her eyes shone as she maintained the thesis that the princess could not go with the minstrel unless his love was given to her irrevocably.

"If you mean by love a sense of oneness in the pursuit of an ideal, then I agree with you," said Thyrsis. "But if you mean what love generally means--a mutual admiration, the worshipping of another personality--then I don't."

"And are lovers not even to be interesting to each other?" cried Corydon.

But the poet did not shrink even from that. "I don't think a woman could be interesting to me--except in so far as she was growing. And she must always know that if she stopped growing, she would cease to be interesting. That is not a matter of anybody's will, it seems to me--it is a fact of soul-chemistry."

"I don't think you will find many women to love you on that basis," said Corydon.

"I never expected to find but one," was Thyrsis' reply; "and I may not find even one."

She sat watching him for a moment. "I had never realized the sublimity of your egotism," she said. "It would never occur to you to judge anyone else by your own standards, would it?"

"That is very well put," laughed Thyrsis. "As a matter of fact, I have a maxim that I count all things lost in the world but my own soul."

"Why is that?"

"Because I can depend on my own soul; and I have not yet met anything else in life of which I can say that."

Again there was a pause. "You are as hard as iron!" exclaimed the girl.

"I am harder than anything you can find for your simile," he answered. "I know simply that there is no force existing that can turn me from my task."

"You might meet some woman who would fascinate you."

"Perhaps," he replied. "I have done things I'm ashamed of, and I've a wholesome fear of doing more of them. But I know that that woman, whoever she might be, would wake up some morning and find me missing."

Then for a while he sat staring at the eddies in the pool below. "I have a vision of another kind of woman," he said--"a woman to whom my ideal would be the same compelling force that it is to me--a living thing that would drive her, that she was both master of, and slave to, as I am. So that she would feel no fears, and ask no favors! So that she would not want mercy, nor ask pledges--but just give herself, as I give myself, and take the chances of the game. Don't you think there may be just one such woman in the world?"

"Perhaps," was the reply. "But then--mightn't a woman be sure of your ideal, but not of you?"

"As to that," said Thyrsis, "she would have to know me.

"As to that," said Corydon, "she would have to love you."

And Thyrsis smiled. "As in most arguments," he said, "it's mainly a matter of definitions."

Section 5. At this point there came a call from the distance, and Corydon started. "There is mother," she exclaimed. "How the afternoon has flown!"

"And must you go home now?" he asked.

"I'm afraid so," she replied. "We have a long row."

"I'm sorry," he said. "I wanted to advise you about books to read. You must let me help you to find what you are seeking."

"Ah," said Corydon, "if you only will!"

"I will do anything I can," he said. "I am ashamed of not having helped you before."

They had risen and started towards the house. "Can't you come to-morrow, and we can talk it over," he said.

"But I thought you were going to work," she objected.

"I can spare another day," he replied. "A rest won't hurt me, I know. And it's been a real pleasure to talk to you this afternoon."

So they settled it; and Thyrsis saw them off in the boat, and then he went back to the little cabin.

On the steps he stood still. "Corydon!" he muttered. "Little Corydon!"

That was always the way he thought of her; not only because he had known her when she was a child, but because this expressed his conception of her--she was so gentle and peaceable and meek. She was now eighteen, and he was only twenty, but he felt towards her as a grandfather might. But now had come this new revelation, that astonished him. She had been deeply stirred by his work--she had loved it; and this was no affectation, it was out of her inmost heart. And she was not really contented at all--she had quite a hunger for life in her!

It had been like an explosion; the barriers had been destroyed between them, and he saw her as she really was. And he could hardly believe it--all through the adventures that followed he would find himself standing in the same kind of daze, whispering to himself-- "Corydon! Little Corydon!"

He did not try to do any work that evening. He thought about her, and the problem of her life. She had stirred him strangely; he saw her beautiful with a new kind of beauty. He resolved that he would put her upon the way to some of the joy she sought.

She came early the next morning, and they sat by the lake-shore and talked. They talked about the things she needed to study, and how she should study them; about the books she had read and the books she was to read next. And from this they went on to a hundred questions of literature and philosophy and life. They became eager and excited; their thoughts took wings, and they lost all sense of time and place. There were so many things to be discussed!

Corydon, in spite of all her anti-clericalism, believed in immortality; she laid claim to intuitions and illuminations concerning it. And to Thyrsis, on the other hand, the idea of immortality was the consummation of all unfaith. To him life was a bubble upon the stream of time, a shadow of clouds upon the mountains; there was nothing about it that could be or should be immortal.

"The act of faith," he cried, "is to give ourselves into the arms of life, to take it as it comes, to rejoice in its infinite unfoldment, the 'plastic dance of circumstance'; to behold the budding flower and the new-born suns as equal expressions of the joy of becoming. But people are weak, they love themselves, and they set themselves up as the centre of existence!"

But Corydon was personal, and loved life; and she stood out that death was unthinkable--that she had the sense of infinity within her. Thyrsis strove to make her see that one was to wreak one's hunger for infinity at each moment, and not put it off to any future age; that life was a thing for itself, and needed no sequel to justify it. "It is a free gift, and we have no claim upon it; we must take it on the terms of the giver."

From that they came to religion. Thyrsis loved the forms of the old faiths, because of the poetry there was in them; and so he wrestled with Corydon's paganism. He tried to show her how one could read "Paradise Lost" and the English prayer-book, precisely as one read Virgil and Homer; to which Corydon answered that she had been to Sunday-school.

"But you once believed in Santa Claus!" he retorted. "And does that make you quarrel with him now? Every time you read a novel, don't you pretend to believe in people who never existed?"

He went on to show her how much she lost of the sublime and inspiring things of the past. He took the story of Jesus. It mattered not in the least if it was fiction or fact--it was there, as an achievement of the human spirit. He showed her the man of the gospels--not the stained-glass god with royal robes and shining crown, but the humble workingman, with his dream of a heaven nearby, and a father who loved his children without distinction. He went about among the poor and humble, the world's first revolutionist; teaching the supremacy of the soul--a doctrine which was to be as dynamite beneath the pillars of all established institutions. He lived as a tramp and an outcast, and he died the death of a criminal; and now those who had murdered him were using his doctrines to enslave the world!--All this was a new idea to Corydon, and she resolved forthwith that she would begin her readings with the New Testament.

Section 6. So it went, until Thyrsis looked up with a start, and saw that the shadows were falling. It was five o'clock, and they had not stopped to eat! Even so, they had no time to cook, but made a cold meal--and talked all the time they were eating.

Then Corydon said, "I must start for home."

"You won't want any supper," said Thyrsis. "Let's see the sunset first."

"But mother will be expecting me," she objected.

"She'll know you're all right," he replied.

So they climbed the hill, and sat and watched the sunset and the rising full moon. The air was clear, and the sky like opal, and the pale, pearly tints of the clouds were ravishing to behold. To Thyrsis it seemed that these colors were an image of the soul that was disclosed to him. He would have been at a loss for words to describe the extraordinary sense of purity that Corydon gave to him; it was not simply her maidenhood--it was something far more rare than that. Here was an utterly perfect human soul; a soul without speck or blemish--without a base idea, with no trace of a vanity, unaware what a pretense might be. The joy and wonder of life welled spontaneously in her, she moved to a noble impulse as a cloud moves before the wind. She was like a creature from the skies they were watching.

And here, in the silver moonlight, a memorable hour came to them. Thyrsis told her of his consecration, and why he lived his hermit-life. He had known for years that he was not as other men; and now every hour it was becoming clearer to him. He shrunk from the word, because it had been desecrated by the world; but it was Genius. More and more frequently there was coming to him this strange ecstasy, the source of which he could not guess; it was like the giving way of flood-gates within him--the pouring in of a tide of wonder and joy. It made him tremble like a leaf, it made him cry aloud and fall down upon the ground exhausted. And yet, whatever the strain might be, he never lost his grip upon himself; rather, all the powers of his mind seemed to be multiplied--it seemed as if all existence became one with his soul.

Never before had he uttered a word of this to anyone. No one could understand the burden it had laid upon him. For this was the thing that all the world was seeking, for the lack of which the world was dying; and it was his to give or to withhold, to lose or to save. He had to forge it and shape it, he had to embody it, to set it forth in images and symbols. And that meant a terrific labor, a feat of mental and emotional endurance quite indescribable. He must hold it, though it burned like fire; he must clutch it to his bosom, though it tore at his heart-strings.

"Sometimes," he said, "I fail and have to give up; and then I have nothing but a memory without words--or perhaps a few broken phrases that seem mere nonsense. Then I am like a man who has seen some loved one drowned or burned to death before his eyes. It is a thing so ineffable, so precious; and some power seeks to tear it away from me, to bear it into oblivion forever. I can't know, of course--it might come to some one else--or it might never come again. The feeling I have is like that of a mother for an unborn child; if I do not give it life, no one ever will. And don't you see--compared with that, what does anything else count? I would lie down and be crushed to pieces, if that would help; truly, I would suffer less than I suffer in what I try to do. And so, the things that other men care for--they simply don't exist for me. I must have a little money, because I have to have something to eat, and a place to work in. But I don't want position or fame--I don't shrink from any ridicule or humiliation. It seems like a mad thing to say, but I have nothing to do either with men's evil or with their good. I am not bound by any of their duties; I can't have any country or any home, I can't have wife or children--I can hardly even have any friends. Don't you see?"

"Yes," whispered Corydon, deeply moved, "I see."

"Look," he went on--"see all the vice and misery in the world--the cruelty and greed and hate. And see all the stupid and petty things, the narrow motives, the vanities and the jealousies! And all that is because people haven't this thing that has come to me; they don't know the possibilities of life, they lack the sense of its preciousness and sacredness. And they seek and seek--and go astray! Take drunkenness, for instance; that brings them joy, but it's a false scent, it leads them over a precipice. I've been down at the bottom of it--you know why I have to go there, and what I've seen. And that is where the best of men's faculties go--yes, it's literally true! The men who are dull and plodding, they are contented; it's the men who are adventurous and aspiring who come to that precipice. I walk down an avenue and see the lines of saloons with their gleaming lights, and that thought is like a scream of anguish in my soul; there came a phrase to me once, that I wanted to cry out to people--'the graveyards of your genius! the graveyards of your genius!'"

Corydon was gazing at his uplifted face. She said, "That is how Jesus must have felt, when he wept over Jerusalem."

"Yes," said Thyrsis. "It is a new religion trying to be born. Only nowadays they don't persecute you, they just ignore you. They don't hang you up on a cross and make you conspicuous and picturesque-- they ridicule you and let you starve. And that is what I face, you see. I've saved a hundred dollars--just barely enough to buy me food until I've written the book!"

"And other people have so much!" cried Corydon.

"So much--and no idea what to do with it. They just fling it away, in a drunken frenzy. And down below are the poor, who slave to make civilization possible. Such lives as they have to live--I can't ever get the thought out of my mind, not in any happiest moment! I feel as if I were a man who had escaped from a beleaguered city, and it all depended upon me to carry the tidings and bring relief. I'm their one hope, and if I fail them I'm a traitor, an accursed being! They are ignorant and helpless, and their cry comes to me like some great storm-wind of grief and despair. Oh, some day I mean to utter words that will reach them--I can't fail! I can't fail!"

"No!" whispered Corydon. "You must not fail!"

They sat in silence for a while.

"How I wish that I could help you!" she said.

"Who can tell?" he answered. "Perhaps you may. A true friend is a rare thing to find."

"I would do anything in the world to share in such a work."

"You really mean that? As hard as it is?"

"I would bear anything," she said. "I would go to the ends of the earth for it. I would fling away the whole world--just as you have done."

"Ah, but are you strong enough? Could you stand it?"

"I don't know that--I'm only a child. But I wouldn't mind dying."

And so it came. It came as the dawn comes, unheralded, unheeded--spreading wider, till the day is there. Months afterwards they talked about it, and Thyrsis asked, "When did I propose to you?"

"I don't think you ever proposed to me," she answered. "It just came. It had to come--there was no other way."

"But when did I first kiss you?" he asked.

"I don't know even that," she said, and pondered.

"Did I kiss you that night when we sat on the hill?" he asked.

"I wouldn't have known it if you had," said Corydon. "It was as natural for you to kiss me as it was for me to draw my breath."

Section 7. The moon was high when they went down the hill, and he rowed her home. They were silent with the awe that was upon them. They found the people at home in a panic, but they scarcely knew this--and they scarcely troubled to explain.

Then Thyrsis went home, and spent half the night roaming about in excitement. And early in the morning he was sitting on the edge of his canvas-cot, whispering to himself again, "Corydon! Little Corydon!"

He could not think of work that day, but set out to walk to the village by the lonely mountain-road; and half-way there he met the girl, coming in the other direction. There was a light of wonder in her eyes; and also there was perplexity. For all that morning she had been whispering to herself, "Thyrsis! Thyrsis!"

They sat by the roadside to talk it over.

"Corydon," he began, "I've been thinking about what we said last night, and it frightens me horribly. And I want to ask you please not to think about it any more. I could not take anyone else into my life--before God, I couldn't be so cruel. I have been shuddering at the thought of it. Oh please, please, run away from me--before it is too late!"

"Is that the way it seems?" she asked.

"Corydon!" he cried. "I am a tormented man! There can't be any happiness in the world for me. And you are so beautiful and so pure and so good--I simply dare not think of it! You must be happy, Corydon!"

"I have never yet been happy," she said.

"Listen," he went on--"there is a stanza of Walter Scott's that came to me this morning--an outlaw song. It seemed to sum up all my feeling about it:

"'Maiden! a nameless life I lead,   A nameless death I'll die;   The fiend whose lantern lights the mead   Were better mate than I!'"

Corydon sat staring ahead. "You can't frighten me away from you," she said, in a low voice. "It isn't worth your while to try. But let me tell you what I came to say. I'm so ignorant and so helpless--I didn't see how I could be of any use to you. And so I wanted to tell you that you must do whatever seemed best to you--just don't count me at all. You see what I mean--I'm not afraid for myself, but just for you. I couldn't bear the thought that I might be in your way. I felt I had to come and tell you that, before you went back to your work."

Now Thyrsis had set out with mighty battlements reared about him; and not all the houris and the courtesans of all the ages could have found a way to breach them. But before those simple sentences of Corydon's, uttered in her gentle voice, and with her maiden's gaze of wonder--the battlements crumbled and rocked.

And that was always the way of it. There were endless new explanations and new attitudes, new excursions and discoveries. They would part with a certain understanding, but they never knew with what view they would meet in the morning. They were swung from one extreme to the other, from certitude to doubt, from joy to dismay and despair. And so, day after day they would sit and talk, for uncounted hours. Corydon would come to the little cabin, or Thyrsis would come to the village, and they would wander about the roads or the woods, forgetting their meals, forgetting all the world. Once they wandered away into the mountains, and they sat until the dusk closed round them; they were almost lost that night.

"Of course," Thyrsis had been saying, "we should not be married like other men and women."

"No," said Corydon, "of course not."

"We should be brother and sister," he said.

"Yes," she assented.

"And it would not be real marriage--I mean, it would be just for the world's eyes."

"So I don't see how it could hinder you," Corydon added. "Whatever I did that was wrong, you would tell me. And then too, about money. I shouldn't be any burden; for I have twenty-five dollars a month of my own."

"I had no idea of that," said Thyrsis.

"I've only had it for a year," said Corydon. "An aunt left me nearly four thousand dollars. I can't touch the principal until I'm thirty, but I have the income, and that will buy me everything I need. And so it would be just as if you didn't have me to think of."

"I don't think the money side matters so much," was his reply. "It's only this summer, you see--until I've finished the book."

Section 8. The key to all the future was the book; but alas, the book was not coming on. How could one write amid such excitement? This was a new kind of wine in Thyrsis' blood. This was reality! And before it his dream-phantoms seemed to have dissolved into nothingness.

They would make a compact for so many days, and he would start to work; but he would find himself thinking of Corydon, and new problems would arise, and he would take to writing her notes--and finally realize in despair that he might as well go and see her.

Meantime Corydon would be wrestling with tasks of her own. They had talked over her development, and agreed that what she needed was discipline. And because Thyrsis had read her some of Goethe's lyrics, she had decided to begin with German. Thyrsis had wasted a great deal of time with German courses in college, and so he was able to tell her everything not to do. He got her a little primer of grammar, just enough to make clear the language-structure; and then he set her to acquiring a vocabulary. He had little books full of words that he had prepared for himself, and these she drilled into her brain, all day and nearly all night. She stopped for nothing but to eat--in the woods when the weather was fair and in her room when it rained, she studied words, words, words! And she made amazing progress--while Thyrsis was wrestling with his angels she read Grimm's fairy tales, and some of Heyse's "Novellen," and "Hermann and Dorothea," and "Wilhelm Tell."

But these were children's tasks, and her pilgrimage was one of despair. Above were the heights where Thyrsis dwelt, inaccessible, almost invisible; and how many years must she toil to reach them! She would come to him with tears in her eyes-- tears of shame for her ignorance and her stupidity. And then Thyrsis would kiss the tears away, and tell her how many brilliant and clever women he had met, who had the souls of dolls behind all their display of culture.

So Corydon would escape that unhappiness--but alas, only to fall into another kind. For she was a maiden, beautiful and tender, and ineffably precious to Thyrsis; and when they met, their hands would come together--it was as natural for them to embrace as for the flowers to grow. And this would lead to moods of weakness and satisfaction--not to that divine discontent, that rage of impatience which Thyrsis craved. It seemed to him that Corydon grew more and more in love with him, and more willing to cling to him; and he was savage because of his own complaisance. They would spend hours, exchanging endearments and whispering youthful absur- dities; and then, the next day, he would write a note of protest, and Corydon would be wild with misery, and would tear up his love-notes, and vow in tears that he should never touch her hand again. Now and then he would try to suggest to her that what she needed for the fulfillment of her life was not a madman like himself, but a husband who would love her and cherish her, as other women were loved and cherished; and there was nothing in all the world that galled her quite so much as this.

Section 9. There came a time when all these happenings could no longer be hid from parents. This unthinkable "engagement" had to be announced, and the furies of grief and rage and despair unchained. No one could realize the change that had come over Corydon--Cory-don, the meek and long-suffering, who now was turned to granite, and immovable as the everlasting hills. As for Thyrsis, all kinds of mad- ness had come from him, and were expected from him. But even he was appalled at the devastation which this thunderbolt caused.

"You have ruined your career! You have ruined your career!" was the cry that rang in his ears all day. And he knew what the world meant by this. Young men of talent who wished to rise in the world did not burden themselves with wives at the age of twenty; they waited until their careers were safe--and meantime, if they felt the need, they satisfied their passions with the daughters of the poor. And it was for some such "eligible man" as this that the world had been preparing Corydon; it was to save her for his coming that her sheltered life had been intended. Her beauty and tenderness would appeal to him, her innocence would bring a new thrill to his jaded passions; and when he offered his hand, there would be no whisper of what his past might have been, there would be no questions asked as to any vices or diseases he might bring with him. There would be trousseaus and flowers and wedding-cake, rice and white ribbons and a honeymoon-journey; and then an apartment in the city, or perhaps even a whole house, with a butler and a carriage--who could tell? With wealth pouring into the metropolis from North and West and South, such things fell often to beautiful and innocent maidens in sheltered homes.

And here was this one, flinging herself away upon a penniless poet who could not support her, and did not even propose to try! "Does he mean to get some work?" was the question; and gently Corydon explained that they intended "to live as brother and sister." And that capped the climax--that proved stark, raving madness, if it did not prove downright knavery and fraud.

In the end, being utterly baffled and helpless with dismay, the mothers turned upon each other; for to each of them, the virtues of her own offspring being so apparent, it was clear that this hideous tragedy must have come from the machi-nations of the other. One day Thyrsis and his mother, walking down a road, met Corydon and her mother, upon a high hill where the winds blew wildly; and here they poured out their grief, and hurled their impeachments against the storm. To Thyrsis they assumed heroic proportions, they towered like queens of tragedy; in after-history this was known as the Meeting of the Mothers, and he likened it to the great contest in the Nibelungenlied between Brunhild and Kriemhild.

Then, on top of it all, there came another calamity. In the boarding-house with Corydon lived some elderly ladies, who had a remarkable faculty for divining the evil deeds of other people. They had divined the evil deeds of Corydon and Thyrsis, and one of them was moved to come to Corydon's mother one day, and warn her lest others should divine them too. And so there was more agony; the discovery was made that Corydon had become a social outcast to all the maids and matrons of the summer population--a girl who went to visit a poet in his lonely cabin, and stayed until unknown hours of the night. And so there came to Thyrsis a note saying that Corydon must come no more to the cabin; and later in the day came Corydon herself, to bring the tidings that a telegram had come from the city, and that she and her mother were to leave the place the next day.

Thyrsis was aflame with anger, and was for going to the nearest parson and having the matter settled there and then. But Corydon dissuaded him from this.

"I've been thinking it over," she said, "and it's best that I should go. You must finish the book--everything depends upon that, and you know that if I came here now you couldn't do it. But if I go away, there'll be nothing to disturb you. I can study meantime; and when we meet in the city in the fall, everything will be clear before us."

She came and put herself in his arms. "You know, dear heart," she said, "it won't be easy for me to go. But I'm sure it's for the best!"

And Thyrsis saw that she was right, and so they settled it. She spent that day with him--their last day; and floods of tenderness welled up in their hearts, and the tears ran down their cheeks. It was only now that she was going that Thyrsis realized how precious she had become to him, and what a miracle of gentleness and trust she was.

They agreed that here, and not in the village, was the place for their parting. So they poured out their love and devotion, and made their pledges for the future; and towards sundown he kissed her good-bye, and put her in the boat, and stood watching until it was a mere speck down the lake. Then he went back to the house, with a great cavern of loneliness in his soul.

And in spite of all resolves, he was up with the dawn next day, and walking to the village--he must see her once again! He went to the depot with her, and upon the platform they said another farewell; thereby putting a seal upon Corydon's damnation in the eyes of the maids and matrons of the summer population.

BOOK III
THE VICTIM HESITATES

They had opened a wooden box which lay beside them.

"Ten years!" she said. "How they have faded!"

"And the creases are tight," said he; "they will be hard to read."

"Letters! letters!" she exclaimed--"some of them sixty pages long! How much would they make?"

"Perhaps a quarter of a million words," he said.

"What is to be done about it?"

"They must be selected, and then cut, and then trimmed and pruned."

"And will that leave any idea of it?"

He answered with a simile. "You wish to convey to a man how it feels to pound stone for twelve hours in the sun. The only way you could really do it would be to take him and let him pound for twelve hours. But he wouldn't stand for that."

"So you let him pound for one hour," said she, with a smile.

"I will put up a sign," he said--

'HERE BEGINS THE STONE-POUNDING!'

And then those who are interested will come in and try it; and the rest will peer through the fence and pass on."

To which she responded, "I would make the sign read,

'ADMISSION TO LOVERS ONLY!'"

MY THYRSIS!

Oh, if I might only stay in a convent until you are ready to take me! Since I left you I find myself possessed of cravings, which, if I indulged them, might bring me the fate of the Maid of Neidpath!

Truly I have known some miserable moments. But I am trying very hard to cultivate a happy, confident activity. The people here are aggressive, and I am afraid I have been rude, which I never like to be. I just succeeded in getting away from a young man who wanted to walk to the village with me. Do you know, it would drive me absolutely mad to talk to anyone now!

My soul has only one cry, and I could sometimes go out on the mountain-side and scream it aloud to the winds. I fear I shall be a trifle wild, in fact utterly in pieces, until you come, with that wonderful recipe of yours for binding me together, and making me complete. I think of you in your house, and wish to God I were there, or out in the desert even, if you were with me.

When I passed through the city I felt exactly as if I were in Hades. The glaring lights and the fearful rattle, the lazy, lounging men--I had dinner in a restaurant, in which all the people seemed to be feeding demons! It has been distinctly shown me why so many people have thought you a rude unmannerly boy! I don't know what people would think, if I had to be amongst them long.

I have begun so many letters to you in my mind, and oh, the times I have told myself how much I loved you! I have read your letters and slept with them under my pillow, like the veriest love-lorn maiden. But all my happy thoughts are gone at present. It is distracting to me to have to come into such close contact with people.

Oh, tell me, dearest one, what I shall have to do to control myself and preserve the peace of my soul, until I go to you forever? I must not long to see you, it prevents me from studying. If you might only come to me at one moment in the day, and give me one kiss, and then go away! You see, I am conducting myself in a very unwise manner--and it is necessary I should study! I should love to have an indomitable capacity for work, and eat only two meals a day, and never have to think about my body.

I want to tell you what I feel, how utterly and absolutely I am yours, and how any image that comes between you and me enrages me. If only you knew how I give myself up to you in thought, word, and deed!--My one reason for acting now, is that I may show you something I have done, my one thought is to be what you would wish me. No one, no one understands, or ever will, what is in your heart and in mine--to be locked there for ages. There I have placed all my power of love and religion and hope of the life that is to be. To you I give all my trust, all my worship, you are the one link that binds me to myself and to God. Without you I feel now that I should be a poor wanderer.

You give me my feeling of wholeness, of the possibility of completion, that I never had before. In my best and truest moments I know that with you I can be what I have hoped. With you before my eyes I have a grim resolution to conquer or die. The one thing I am sure of always is my love for you. It might be possible for you to stop loving me; but I, now that I have begun, shall continue to love you to the day I die--and after, I hope. I do not love you for what you can give me, I love you because you are you, I must love you now no matter what you are. I believe Shakespeare was right when he said that "love is not love which alters, when it alteration finds." I do not believe that a person can really love more than once.

I must go to my German again and leave you. Do you love me? Do you love me? Do you love me?

II

My dearest Corydon:

I received a letter from you before dinner, and as usual had one of my flights of emotion, and thought of many things to write to you. Now I am up on the mountain-side, trying to recall them. Dearest, you are, as always, more precious to me. I am glad to see that you are suffering some, and I think that it is well that you have to be away from me for awhile, to fight some of your own soul's battles. You see that I am in my stern humor; as convinced as ever that the soul is to be deepened only by effort, and that the great glory of life cannot be bought or stolen, or even given for love, but must be earned.

I will tell you what I have been doing since you left. I spent three whole days in the most unimaginable wretchedness; I had no hindrances like yours--only the most fearful burden of dullness and sloth, that had crept upon me and mastered me, during all the weeks that I had let myself be so upset and delayed. I cannot picture what I go through when I lose my self-command in that way, but it is like one who is tied down upon a railroad track and hears a train coming. He gets just as desperate as he pleases, and suffers anything you can imagine--but he does not get free. And always the book would be hanging before me, a kind of external conscience, to show me what I ought to have been.

Now I have gotten myself out of that, by an effort that has quite worn me out. When I found myself at work again, I felt a kind of savage joy of effort, a greater power than I ever knew before. In the reckless mood that I had got to, it seemed to me that I could keep so forever.

Now dearest, you must get the same unity in your life; you must concentrate all your faculties upon that--get for yourself that precious habit of being "instant in prayer", and "strenuous for the bright reward". As Wordsworth has it, "Brook no continuance of weak-mindedness!" Let it come to you with a pang that hurts you, that for one minute you have been idle, that you have admitted to yourself that life is a thing of no consequence, and that you do not care for it. I shall have to talk to you that way--perhaps not so often as I do to myself, because I do not think you are really in your heart such a very dull and sodden creature as I am.

I think the greatest trial we shall have will be our fondness for each other, and the possibility of being satisfied simply to hold each other in our arms. But we shall get the better of that, as of everything else; and that is not the problem now. You must learn to strive, learn to master yourself; you must prove your power so. Do not care how rude you have to be to those people; look upon the things about you as a kind of dream-world, and know that your own soul's life is the one real thing for you. And don't write any more about how circumstances hold you back. When you have got to work you will know that you are given your soul for no purpose but to fight circumstances; that they are the things to make you fight. When they are removed, as I know to my cost, there is still the same necessity of fighting; only it is like a horse who has to win a race without the spurs.

You must talk to yourself about this, night and day, until this desire is so awake in you that you can't go idle many moments without its rushing into your mind, and giving you a kind of electric shock. And when that happens you fling aside every thing else, every idea but the work that you ought to be doing, and put all your faculties upon that; and every time that you catch them wandering, you do the same thing again, and again. Some times when I become very keenly aware of myself, and of what a shallow creature I really am, it seems to me that it is only by wearing myself out in that grim and savage way that I can make myself even tolerable.

I **must** stop. Do you know that for five precious hours by my watch I have sat up here thinking about you and writing to you? Dear me--and I am tired, and frozen, for there is a cold wind. I shall have, I see, to prove some of **my** powers, by not writing letters to you when I should be at the book.

I see that it takes four or five days for letters to come and go between us; and so if we write often, our letters will be crossing. Four or five days is time enough for us to change our moods a dozen times, so our correspondence will be apt to be complicated!

III

MY DEAREST THYRSIS:

It has worried me somewhat to-day that you might be utterly disappointed in the letter I wrote you. It was a wild jumble of words, but I was fighting all sorts of uncomfortable things within me. To-day I have been anything but despairing, and have "gone at" the German. In fact, I quite lost myself in it, and believe I understand thoroughly the construction of the first poem. Wonderful accomplishment!

Your words, as I read them again, dear heart, are full of a great beauty and fire and energy, and I only hope you may keep them always. I believe that the possibility of the marriage we both desire, depends greatly if not entirely on **your** sternness. You must realize it.

I cannot tell with the proper conditions and training what energy I might be able to accumulate for myself, but in the meanwhile the thing that makes me most wretched is my utter incapacity at times, and my inability to share with you your work. In my weaker and more helpless moods, I ask myself with a pang, whether I ought to go with you at all, when I cannot help you. But I must stop fuming. I have come out of my mudpuddle for good and for all, and that is the main consideration. I don't intend to go back.

We must not think of each other in any way but as co-workers in a great labor; we must simply know that our love is rooted deeply, and the harder we work the more firm it will be. There is no reason why we should not go to the altar with just this sternness, and from now on preserve this attitude until the day when we have earned the right to consider what love means. Can you do it? I will prove to you that I can.

IV
MY DEAR THYRSIS:

I am trying very dreadfully, and go away alone and pound at the German as if my life depended upon it. I go to bed every night with a tight feeling in my head, but I do not mind, as I take it for a guarantee that I have not rested.

And oh, my dearest, dearest and best, I am trying not to think of you too much--that is too much in a way that does not help me to study. But I love you really, yes, truly, and I know I would follow you anywhere. I am not particularly joyful, but then I do not expect to be for a great many years.

V
DEAR THYRSIS:

Only a few words. I have been hovering to-day between spurts of hopeful energy, and the most indescribable despair. It positively freezes my heart, and I have been on the point of writing to you and telling you to relieve yourself of the responsibility of me. The reason is because it seems a perfectly Herculean task to read "Egmont". I have to look up words in the dictionary until I am absolutely so weary I care not about anything; and then I think of you, and what you are able to do, and at one word from you I would give up all idea of marrying you.

I tell you I am up and down in this mood. Great God, I could work all day and all night if I could do what you do, but to strain at iron fetters--a snail! Oh, I cannot tell you--I simply groan under it. At such times I have no more idea of marrying you than of journeying to the moon. I repeat to you, to be constantly choked back, while you are rapidly advancing, will kill me. I don't know what you will say to this, but it is intolerable, unendurable, to me. When I think of your ability and mine, I simply laugh about it --Thyrsis, it is simply ridiculous. I do not ask you to take me with you, Thyrsis.

Do you wonder at my writing all this? You would not if you understood. It is so hard for me to keep any joy in my heart, and I get tired of repeated failures, that is all. I thought I must write you this, and have it over with. This is the style of letter I have always torn up, but this time it goes. I think I will practice the piano now, and try to get some gladness into my soul again.

VI
MY DEAR, DEAR THYRSIS:
There is a dreadful sort of letter which I wrote you last night which I haven't sent you yet.

I have been studying, or trying to most of the day, and my mind has wandered most painfully. There were two days in which I seemed to have hold of myself, but with an effort that was a fearful strain. I must try so, that it almost kills me, if I wish to accomplish even a little of what I ought. The heat here is almost insupportable, it is stifling, and I spent an hour or so in the water this afternoon.

And the thought is always torture to me--that you are accomplishing so much more than I! I was thinking of your letters to-night, and I recalled some words that seemed to speak more of your love for me. Oh, Thyrsis, if your letters are fiery and passionate, is it for love of *me* that they are? I'm almost afraid at times, when I read your letters--when you tell me of the kind of woman you *want* to love.

I at present am certainly not she. And do you know that when we are married we shall be united forever? I don't know why I write you these things, they are not at all inspiring thoughts to me.

And yet I was able to go in swimming this afternoon, and forget everything and frolic around as happily as any water-baby!

VII
MY DEAR CORYDON:
I came off to write my poem, but I have been thinking about you, and I must write a long letter. It is one of the kind that you do not like.

In the first place, you complain of the contradictions in my letters. I am sorry. I live so, struggling always with what is not best in me, and continually falling down. Also, in this matter I am an utter stranger, groping my way; and there is an element of passion in it, a dangerous element, which leads me continually astray.

I can only say that in my ideal of love, which is utter love and spiritual love,

I think of living my life with you in entire nakedness of soul. Therefore, I shall always be before you exactly as I should be by myself. And I shall write you now exactly what I have been thinking, what is hard and unkind in it, as well as the rest. You will learn to know me as a man far from perfect, often going astray himself, often feeling wrong things, often leading you astray and making you wretched. But behind all this there is the thing often lost sight of, but always present--the iron duty that I have, and the force in me which drives me to it.

All this morning I have been thinking of my book, losing myself in it and filling myself with its glory. This afternoon I fell to thinking about us; and thoughts which have been lurking in my mind for a long time got the upper hand for the first time. They were that I did not love you as I ought to, that I could not; that the love which I felt was a thing from my own heart, and that it had carried me away because I was anxious to persuade myself I had found my ideal upon earth; that you *could* not satisfy the demands upon life that I made, and that if I married you it would be to make you wretched, and myself as well; that you had absolutely nothing of the things that I needed, and that the life which your nature required was entirely different from mine; that you had no realization of the madness that was driving me, could find and give me none of the power I needed; and that I ought to write and tell you this, no matter what it cost--that I owed it to the sacred possibility of my own soul, to live alone if I could live better alone. And when I had said these words, I felt a sense of relief, because they were haunting me, and had been for a long time.

How they will affect you I cannot tell, it depends upon deep your love for me is; certainly they mean for me that *my* love is not deep, that you have not made yourself necessary to me. I think that in that last phrase I put the whole matter in its essence--you have not *bound* yourself to me; I am always struggling to keep my love firm and right, to hold myself to you. The result is that there is no food for my soul in the thought of our love, in my thought of you; and therefore, I am continually dissatisfied and doubting, continually feeling the difference between the love I have dreamed and our love.

I tried to think the matter out, and get to the very bottom of it. The first thing that came to me on the other side was your absolute *truth*; your absolute devotion to what was right and noble in our ideal. So that, as I was thinking, I suddenly stopped short with this statement--"If you cannot find right love with that girl, it must be because you do not honor love, or care for it." And then I thought of your helplessness, of your lack of training and opportunity for growth; and I told myself how absurd it was of me to expect satisfying love from you--when all that I knew about in life, and thought of, was entirely unknown to you. I realized that I was a man who had tasted more or less of all knowledge, and had an infinite vision of knowledge yet before him, and an infinite hunger for it; and that you were a school-girl, with all of a school-girl's tasks on your hands. So I said to myself that the reason for the dissatisfaction was a fault of my own, that it had come from my own blindness. I had gone wrong in my attitude to you; I had failed in my sternness and my high devotion to perfection; I had contented myself with lesser things, had come down from my best self, and had failed to make you see what a task was before you, if you ever meant to know my best self. You perceive that this is a return to my old-time attitude; I am sorry if it makes you wretched, but I cannot help it. It is a surgical operation that must be borne. I shall not make it necessary again, I hope.

Now, dear Corydon, I am not trying to choose pleasant words in this letter, this is the way I talk to *myself*. And if anything good comes from our love, it will be because of this letter. I challenge what is noblest in you to rise to meet the truth of it. I should not care to write to you if I did not feel that it would.

You have had a possibility offered to you, and because you are very hungry for life you have clasped it to you, placed all your happiness in it. The possibility is the love of a man whose heart has been filled with the fire of genius. There are few men whom life takes hold of as it does me, who sacrifice themselves for their duty as I do, who demand *experience*--knowledge, power, beauty--as I do. There are very few men who will wrest out of existence as much as I will, or know and have as much of life. I am a boy just now, and only beginning to live; but I have my purpose in hand, and I know that if I am given health and life, there is nothing that men have known that I shall not know, nothing that is done in the world that I shall not do, or try to. I have a strong physique, and I labor day and night, and always shall. I shall always be hungry and restless, always dissatisfied with myself, and with everything about me, and acting and feeling most of the time like a person haunted by a devil. I make no apologies to you for the conceit of what I am saying; it is what I think of myself, without caring what other people think. I know that I have a tremendous temperament, tremendous powers hidden within me, and they have got to come out. When they do, the world will know what I know now.

Now Corydon, as you understand, I dream love absolute, and would scorn any other kind. I can master my passion, if it be that upon earth there is no woman willing or able to go with me to the last inch of my journey. I dream a life-companion to follow wherever my duty drives me; to feel all the desperateness of desire that I feel, to be stern and remorseless as I must be, wild and savage as I must be; to race through knowledge with me and to share my passion for truth with me; a woman with whom I need have no shame in the duty of my genius! As I tell you, if I marry you, I expect to give myself to you as your own heart; and then I think of the gentle and mild existence you have led!

It is very hard for me even to tell about my life, or to explain this thing that drives me mad. But I am writing this letter to you for the purpose of making clear to you that there are two alternatives before you, and that you must choose one or the other and stick by it, and bear the consequences. It is painful to me to think that I have fascinated you by what opportunities I have, even by what power and passion and talents I have, and filled you with a hunger for me--when really you do not realize at all what I am, or what I must be, and when what I have to do will terrify you. I write in the thought of terrifying you *now*, and making you give up this red-hot iron that you are trying to hold on to; or else to show you my life so plainly that never afterwards can you blame me, or shrink back except by your own fault.

You must not blame me for writing these words, for wondering if a woman, if *any* woman has power to stand what I need to do. And when I talk to you about giving me up, you must not think that is cold, but know that it is my faithfulness to my vision, which is the one thing to which I owe any duty in the world. Nor is it right that you should expect to be essential to me, when I have labored to be all to myself. You could become necessary to me in the years to come; if I marry you to-day I shall marry you for what you are to become, and for that *alone*--at any rate if I am true to myself.

If you are to be my wife you are to be my soul--to live my soul's life and bear its pain. You are to understand that I talk to you as I talk to myself, call you the names I call myself, and if you cry, give you up in disgust; that I am to deny you all pleasure as I do myself, and what God knows will be ten thousand times harder, let you take pleasure, and then spring up in the very midst of it--you know what I mean! That I am to be ever dissatisfied with you, ever inconsiderate of your feelings, and ever declaring that you are failing! That however much I may love you, I am to be your conscience, and therefore keep you--just about as you are now, miserable! You told me that you would gladly be whipped to learn to live; and this can be the only thing to happen to you.

You must understand why I act in this way. I am a weak and struggling man, with a thousand temptations; and when I marry you, you will be the greatest temptation of all. You are a beautiful girl, and I love you, and every instinct of my nature drives me to you; for me to live with you without kissing you or putting my arms about you, will remain always difficult. It will be so for you, as for me, and it will always be our danger, and always make us wretched. Your soul rises in you as I write this, and you say (as you've said before) that if I offered to kiss you after it, it would be an insult. But only wait until we meet!

This is the one thing that has become clear to me: just as soon as there comes the least thought of satisfaction in our love, just so soon does it cease to satisfy my best self. You cannot satisfy my best self, you do not even know it; and if it were a question of that, I should never dream of marrying you! I love you for this and for this alone--because you are an undeveloped soul, the dream of whose infinite possibilities is my one delight in the matter. I think that you are ***perfect*** in character, that you are truth itself; and therefore, no matter how helpless you may be, I have no fear of failing to make you "all the world to me", provided only that I am not false to my ideal. You must know from what I have written before that I ***can*** love, that I do know what love is, and that you may trust me. I am not trying to degrade passion--I simply see how passion throws the burden on the woman, and therefore it is utterly a crime with us--the least thought of it! I ought to consider you as a school-girl, really just that; and instead of that I write you love letters!

I tell you there is nothing more hateful for me to look back upon than that childish business of ours, that time when we went upstairs that we might kiss each other unseen. I tell you, it revolts my soul, from love and from you! I should be perfectly willing to take all the blame--I do; only I have led you to like that (or to act as if you did) and I must stop it. Can you not understand how hateful it is to me to think of making you anything that I should be disgusted with?

I expect you to read over this letter until you realize that it is, every word of it, completely true and noble, and until you can write me so. You and I are to feel ourselves two school-children and live just so. It is not usual for school-children to marry, but that we dare upon the strength of our purpose, and in defiance of all counsel, and of every precedent. We are to feel that we owe our duty to our ideal; and that simply *because* of the strength and passion of our love for each other, we demand perfection, each of the other. My setting this stern challenge before you is nothing but my determination to give you my right love, to demand that you be a perfect woman.

I promise you therefore no quarter; I shall make no sacrifice of my ideal for your sake. As I wrote you, I mean to be absolutely one with you, and I expect you to be the same. You shall have (if you wish it) all of my soul--I shall live my life with you and think all my thoughts aloud--study to give you *everything* that I have. And God only, who knows my heart, knows what utter love for you lies in those words, what utter trust of you--how I think of you as being purity and holiness itself. To offer to take any other being into my soul, to lay bare all the secret places of it to its gaze, all the weaknesses as well as all the strength, and all that is vain as well as all that is sacred! You cannot know how I feel about my heart, but this you may know, that no one else has had a glimpse of it, you are the first and the last; and so sure am I of you that I dare to say it, *all* my life will I live in your presence, and trust to your sympathy and truth--and feel that I am false to love if I do not. If there were anything in my heart so foul that I feared to speak of it, I should give you that first, as the sacrifice of love; or any vanity or foible--such things are really hardest to have others know, so great is our conceit.

If I could talk to you to-night, I should do just as I did up on the hill in the moonlight--frighten you, and make you wonder if there was *any* woman who wished to bear such a burden; and perhaps the saddest thing of all to me is that I do not bear it--instead I bear the gnawing of a conscience bitter and ashamed of itself. And could you bear *that* burden? For Corydon, as I look at myself to-night, I am before God, a coward and a dastard! I have not done my work! I have not borne the pain He calls me to bear, I have not wrested out the strength He put in my secret heart! And here I am chattering, *talking* about work to you! And these things are like a nightmare to me; they turn all my life's happiness to gall. And you are taking upon yourself this same burden--coming to help me to get rid of it. Or if you do not wish to, for God's sake, and mine, and yours, don't come near me--you have come too near as it is! Can you not see that when I am face to face with these fearful things--and you come and ask me to give my life to you, to worship you with the best faculties I possess--that I have no right to say yes?

You once told me you were happy because I called you "mein guter Geist, mein bess'res Ich"; well, you are not in the least that. The name that I give you, and that you may keep, is "the beautiful possibility of a soul". Remember a phrase I told you at the very beginning of our love, of the peril of "ceasing to love perfection and coming to love a woman." And read Shelley's sad note to "Epipsychidion"!

VIII

Dear Corydon:

You tell me in your last letter that you are leaving all who love you; and you ask "How do you know that because you love beauty, you will love *me*?"

I have been thinking a good deal about this; I do not believe, Corydon, that a man more haunted by the madness of desire ever lived upon earth than I. And when I get at the essence of myself, I do not believe that I am a kind man; I think that a person with less patience for human hearts never existed, perhaps with less feeling. There is only one thing in the world that I can be sure of, or that you can, my fidelity to my ideal! I know that however often I may fail or weaken, however many mistakes I may make, my hunger for the things of the soul will *never* leave me, and that night and day I shall work for them. I do not believe I have the right to promise you anything else, I have no right to dream of anything else; this is not my pleasure, as I feel it, it is a frenzy, it is that to which some blind and nameless and merciless impulse drives me. And I may try to persuade myself all my life that I love you, Corydon, and nothing else, and want nothing else; and all the time in the depths of my heart I hear these words from my conscience--"You are a fool." I love power, I love life, and seek them and strive for them, and care for nothing else and never have; and nothing else can satisfy me. And I cannot give any other love than this, any other promise.

IX

My dear Corydon:

I have been taking a walk this morning, thinking about us, and that I had treated you fearfully. The whole truth of it all is this--that I am so raw and so young and so helpless (and you are as much, if not more so) that I cannot, to save my life, be sure if my love for you is what it ought to be, or even if I could love any one as I ought. And I am so wretchedly dissatisfied! Do you know that for two weeks I have been trying to write a passage of my book--and before God, I ***cannot!*** I have not the power, I have not the life!

Dear Corydon, it comes to me that you are ***miserable*** to be in love with me-- that I had no right to put this burden on your shoulders. I would say better things if I could, but I think that our marriage will be a setting out across a wild ocean in the dark! It is for you to be the heroine, to dare the voyage if you choose. These sound like wild words, but they are the truth of my life, and I dare not say any others. Can a girl who has been brought up in gentleness and sweetness, in innocence of life and of pain--can she say things, feel things like these?

X

Thyrsis:

God did not endow me with your tongue, or else it would not be the great effort it is to me to tell you some of the thoughts that have rushed through my mind in the last hour.

It is an hour since I began to read your letter of Horrible Truth. Now it seems to me it might have been in the last year, in the last century. Actually I feel like a stranger to myself; and my movements are very slow. First, I will tell you that I believe in God, oh, so implicitly--this thought gives me infinite hope. I long to let you know as much of my heart as I can, if I am to be your life-companion, as I firmly believe I am to be. I have such a strange calmness now, and I imagine that I must feel very much the way Rip Van Winkle did when he awoke. I want to try to show you my heart--it is right that I should try, is it not?

Know that I have placed much faith and trust in you, in anything that you did. If you opened one door to me and told me it led to the great and permanent truth, I believed you absolutely. If you hauled me back and put me through an opposite one, telling me that there my road lay, I believed you with equal faith. Now, now, at the end of an hour, I am, through you, convinced of one door, the only and true entrance; and I am as sure as I am that the sun is shining at this moment, that nothing in God's world can ever again make me lose sight of it. I have found that *you* can lose sight of it, Thyrsis,--something shows me that I have in the last month been more right than you. Yes, I have, Thyrsis, though you may not know it. And the reason I couldn't stay right was because I am not strong enough to grasp my good impulses, and keep hold of them: because I have not enough faith in the soul within me.

I will try to tell you what I have felt since reading your letter. All is so disgustingly calm in me now. But listen, I believe I have had a little glimpse this afternoon of what it is to *feel*; and because of that knowledge I now am not afraid to tell you that I claim something of God and life--that I can get it if you can. This has been very strong in me at moments, but, as I tell you, I have not yet learned to hold my glimpses of truth--they seem to come to me, and as quickly disappear.

I began to read your letter, and I cannot describe to you the convulsion that came over me. It seemed that I had the feeling of an empty skull on a desert; such a feeling--you can never have it! All the horror and despair! I tried to form my thoughts and tell myself it was not true. I tried to pray, and I did pray--out loud--and asked God to give me strength to read the letter.

I tried to use all the penetration I was capable of, to find out one thing, whether you were purely and unreservedly sincere in it. I wondered whether you really wished to live your life alone, but could not find the courage to tell me so. I firmly believe that no failure in the future, no disgust or helplessness, could ever bring me the complete anguish of those moments.

Can you realize what such a thing meant to me, Thyrsis?

Last spring, I had succeeded in bringing myself into an almost complete state of coma--I saw that I could do nothing, and because I would not endure such profitless pain I drugged myself to sleep. And you, you fiend, waked me up; and may your soul be thrice cursed if you have only pulled the doll to pieces ***to see what it was made of!*** Know, you that have a soul which says it lives and suffers--that I can't go to sleep again! There is no joy for me in mother or father, in friends or admiration--I can tolerate nothing that I tolerated before you came with your cursed or blessed fire!

Also, if you do not marry me, or if I do not find some man who has your strength and desire for life, and who will take me and help me to learn, I shall die without having lived.--And I cried out in misery--only forty-two years, only forty-two little years, and I shall be an old woman of sixty! Only forty-two years in which to learn to live!

I believe if I had you here now I could almost strangle you. We may kill each other some day. I sometimes feel that there is nothing that will give me any relief, that I cannot breathe, I cannot support my body. But these are foolish and unprofitable feelings--and I believe I will yet be saved, if not by you, perhaps by myself. I think some heavenly aid came to me to-day. I asked for it, I simply said it *must* come--and now I am able to bear myself and look around me, and say that the secret of my liberation is not death but life.

Please realize, Thyrsis, that I know you do not need me, that I cannot either entertain you or help you. My dear, do you not know that I have been conscious of this from the very beginning--and it has been this thought that has often made me worry, and doubt, and question. And then I have told myself that you had found *something* in me to love; and that I also was very hungry to know about life and God; and that if you loved me enough to believe I was not dross, we might, with our untiring devotion--well, we might be right in going with each other. And now--would you rather I should tell you I will not marry you, be my desire, or effort, what it may? I do not know--even though I want to live so terribly. I have no word, no proof to give!

And now, Thyrsis, I have no more strength to write. I only wish I had some power to make you know what I have felt this afternoon--I think if I could, you would have no more doubt of me. And I believe it is my God-given right not to doubt myself.

I will write no more--I have written enough to make you answer one of two things. "Come with me," or, "I would rather go alone." I know which one it will be, even now in my wretchedness. The sky is so blue this evening, and everything is so beautiful--and I am trying so hard to be right, to feel strong and confident!

XI

Dear Thyrsis:

I have just arisen. I woke in the middle of the night, and there was a spectre sitting by my bedside to frighten me; he succeeded at first, but I managed finally to get rid of him, and to find some peace. Many of your sentences came to me, and I was able to get behind the words, and I saw plainly that the letters were just what you should have written, and that they could not but benefit me. They have accomplished their purpose, I believe--they are burned into my soul, and have placed me rightly in our relation. I shall simply never trust the permission you may give me, in the future, to rest or be satisfied. I shall only hate you, for the pain of some of your words I shall *never* forget.

The memory of the first two pages of your letter will always put me in mortal terror of you. For the rest, I am very grateful, and I will try to show you how I love your ideal. I can never repay you as long as I live for letting me come with you. Oh Thyrsis, I am sure that I will never think or care whether you love me or not, if only I may go with you and learn how to strive!

I tore up all your love-letters this morning. I kept the last letter--though I do not think I could bear to read it over. I should be afraid of again going through with that despair. Oh, I beg for the time when I shall be obliged to waste none of my minutes--and when I shall have no opportunity of writing you! What *time* I have spent over your letters and mine!

XII

Dear Thyrsis:

I am restlessly waiting for the supper-bell to ring, and my head is aching intensely, and I am generally topsy-turvy. Alas! alas! the distance that separates us and our understanding!

I received a letter to-day while I was studying--but said I would not open it for a week, that I wanted strength to study. Well, I studied all the afternoon and found it none too easy. When I came home, I thought perhaps it was better to read your letter, which I grimly did.

Do you know, you are keeping me on the rack, literally on the rack, and my flesh and blood do not seem to be able to stand it--my body seems to be the organ that first fails me, my brain is never so tired as my body. I love to think that you are not less merciful to me than you would be to yourself, I feel that you could not have used more cruel whips to yourself. Do you suppose that any disgust, scolding, or malediction to me could, as your wife, hurt me, as your doubt of me hurts me now?

And I just begin to read your letter again, and I tell you, you are a fool. You say you do not know whether you could love any one as you ought--well, I, with all my weakness, know whether *I* can love, and I love you a thousand times more than you have given me cause to. And you are so *hungry!* Will you always starve because you are blind? As to being *satisfied,* how could you be? But you say you will love me as much as I deserve. How much do I deserve--do you know? I sometimes cry out against you and long to get hold of you. If you have genius, why doesn't it give you some inkling whether you are a man with a heart, not only a stupid boy? And then I see it all plainly, or think I do, and know that you are trying so hard to be right towards us, because you think you love me the way other people love; and you know if I am weak, it would degrade your genius; and you cannot be sure of my character or strength. You cannot know whether I realize the life I am selecting--you have found it hard, and you have every reason to think that I will find it ten times harder; and you love me in a way that is not the highest,--but yet you love me enough, thank God, to tell me the whole truth!

I have come to a pass where I can say to myself with truth, that I do not care how much or how little you love me. That depends upon *you*, as well as myself. I believe the time will come, when you will love me as you ought, and I say this in perfect calm conviction, in all my weakness, and with all my maudlin habits clinging to me. Strangely enough your doubt of me has made me rise up in arms to champion my cause, or else I should lie down forever in the dust, and deny my God.

I wonder whether it is my love for you that makes me believe? I cling to you, as a mother might cling to her child; I cling to you as the embodiment, the promise, of all I will ever find true in life. I look to live in you, to fulfil all my possibilities in you, and if you die or forsake me, all my hope is gone, and I am dead. This is a letter in which I have no scorn or doubt, or ridicule of myself, as formerly.

And then you ask me, "Can a girl brought up in gentleness and sweetness, and innocence of life and of pain, can she say things, feel things like these?" It is the gentleness and sweetness and innocence that are galling to me. I can tolerate no more of them. They have warped me, they have given me no chance. But I have had some pain in my life, and since I have known you I have known more about pain and what it brings, and leaves.--And now I am feeling ill, and I cannot control that. Oh, God!

XIII

Dearest Corydon:

I have a chance to finish the first part of my book to-day, and save myself from Hades; and here I am writing to you--just a line. (Of course it turned out to be six pages!)

Your last letter was very noble; I can only say to you, that the treatment which makes you upbraid me is not done for *my* sake; that the life which I live is not lived for *my* sake. You say perhaps you are better than I; it is very possible--I often think so myself; but that is nothing to the point. I should be very wretched if I sat down to think what I am. Oblige me by being better than my ideal--if you can! You must understand, dearest, that behind all that I am doing, there is truth to the soul; and that truth to the soul is love, and the only love. I am seeking for nothing but the privilege of treating you as myself; and rest assured, that if I treat you any differently it will be better than I treat myself! There is no peril in our life except that!

Some day you will understand that I can sometimes feel about myself that I am utterly hateful, utterly false, utterly shallow and *bad*; and that to get away from myself would be all that I desire in life. I cannot imagine my having such opinion of you; but some dissatisfaction--just a little--I may have. Only let us love perfection, you and I, with all our souls, and I think our love for each other may safely be allowed to take care of itself. Remember the two ships in Clough's poem, which parted, but sailed by the compass, and reached the same port.

I shall spend no more time comforting you about this.

And dear Corydon, when you are angry at my doubting your power, and say that I do not know you, I can only reply--Why of course I don't, and neither do you. You find your own self out little by little--why get angry with me because I don't know it until you tell me? You are a grown woman compared to what you were three months ago; and this character that you ask me to know--well, it takes years of hard labor to prove a character.

XIV

Dearest Corydon:

Do you ever realize how much *faith* in you I have? As utterly different is your whole life, as if you had been in another world; and through all the wilderness that I have travelled, I hope to drag you. But I cannot carry you, or take you; I must trust in the frenzy of your grip upon me. There is nothing else you could have that I would trust. You might be wonderfully clever and wonderfully wise--and I could do nothing with you. Do you remember Beethoven's saying, that he would like to take a certain woman, if he had time, and marry her and break her heart, so that she might be able to sing?

Ah dear heart, I wish you could read in my words what I feel! I wonder if I am dreaming when I live in this ideal of what a woman's love can be--so complete and so utter a surrender, so complete a forgetting, a losing of the self, so complete a living in another heart! I am not afraid to ask just this from a woman--from you! For I have enough heart's passion to satisfy every thirst that you may feel. Ah, Corydon, I want you! I am drunk with the thought of *making* a woman to love. I wonder if any man ever thought of that before! Artists go about the world with the great hunger of their hearts, and expecting to find by chance another soul like the one they have spent years in making beautiful and swift and strong; but has anyone ever thought that instead of writing books that no one understands, he might be making another kind of an artwork--one that would be alive, and with sacred possibilities of its own?

XV

DEAR THYRSIS:

Your last letters have been very beautiful. I see one thing--though you inform me that you believe you are a hard man, your natural gentleness and sympathy of heart would be the ruin of both of us in the future if I would permit it. But I think you can trust me, not ever as long as I live to lead you into weakness. My desperateness, before I received your letter saying that I might come with you, was rather dreadful; it made me doubt myself, for it was so difficult to keep myself from going to pieces. I have been wicked enough, to wonder whether I could ever make you feel as I felt for two days--if I could only bring to your heart that one pang, the only real one I ever felt in my life! But it taught me one thing, that the only road toward realization of life and one's self is through suffering. I found out that I could bear, for it seems to me as I look back at that horrible nightmare, that it was almost by a superhuman effort I was able to read the letter at all. But enough of that!

I think I have effectually cured myself of any weak yearning for your love. I go to you in gratefulness, knowing what I lack and what you need. Anything my love can do for you, it shall do. It may have some power--I sometimes think that it could have more than you realize.

I suppose every woman has thought that the man she loved was her very life, but I do not think it of you, I simply *know* it. I must go with you, whether I loved you or not.

Meanwhile my love has assumed a strength to me that I never felt before. I don't know how my wild and incoherent letters have affected you, but there were many times when I longed to get hold of you, literally, and simply shake into you some recognition of my soul. Oh, I am afraid you couldn't get away from me; the more merciless you are to me, the wilder I get.

I am possessed by so many opposite moods and influences. I am afraid of you a little. I never know what you are going to do to me.

I feel, I cannot help but feel, that I am part of your life, now, you could not neglect me any more than you could your own soul. I consider you just as responsible for mine as you are for your own. I say this with no doubts, but know that it is true, and you must know it.

XVI

DEAR THYRSIS:

You certainly have a wonderful task in store for me, and I pray God to give me strength for it. I can see very plainly that you expect to find the essence of my soul better than yours, because it seems that you are making my task harder than yours.

Do you know, I have actually found myself asking, at times, with a certain defiant rage--if you were actually going to give love to your princess before you had made her suffer! So far you have not made her suffer at all. I had become quite excited over this idea --though perhaps I had no right to. I suppose it is all right, because she is an imaginary person, and you can endow her with all the perfections you please. She is triumphant and thrilling, and worthy of love--whereas I am just little Corydon, whom you have known all your life, and who is stupid and helpless, and impossible to imagine romances about! Is that the way of it?

XVII

MY DEAREST THYRSIS:

A long letter has just come to me. I always receive your letters with many palpitations, and by the time I get through reading, my cheeks are flaming. It is too bad it takes letters so long to go to and fro.

I have finally come to bear the attitude towards myself, that I would to a naughty child. I will have no nonsense, and all my absurdities and inefficiencies **must** be cured. I think I have come to know myself a little better within the last few days. I know that I have no right to quick victories, or any happiness at all, even your love. I tell you truly, if it were only possible, I would go away this minute--do you hear?--oh! to some lonely place, and then I would do something with myself. I want to be alone, alone--I want to be face to face with myself, and God, if possible! I have come to the conclusion that I can do anything I must do. I think (I am not sure) I could give you up, if I were obliged to, and go away by myself and try alone. If I do not have you, I must have solitude.

XVIII

MY DEAREST CORYDON:

Thinking about my work this morning, and how hard it was, and how much strength it would take, my thoughts turned to you, and I discovered, as never before, just how I like to think of you. It seemed to me that you were part of the raw material that I had to use; that I had mastered you, and was going to make you what you had to be. And there woke in my heart at those words a fierceness of purpose that I had never felt in my life before--I was quite mad with it; and you cried out to escape me, but I would not let you go, but held you right tightly in my arms. And so--I do not mean to let you go! I shall bear you away with me, and make you what

I wish. And the promise of marriage that I make you is just this: not that I love you--I do not love you; but what I wish the woman to be whom I am to love--that I will make you!

And do not ever dare to ask me for any other promise, for you will not get it. You will come with this.

XIX
MY THYRSIS:

I had an *iron grip* at my heart just now, as I was trying to study. I had a foreboding of something--and then I came home and found your letter telling me I was yours, and I *must.* At last I may go to you the way I wish! My love, my love, I do not care what you are, or what you do to me, as long as I may go with you.

How I laugh at myself as I say it! You have mastered me to worship your *life*--not you. I shall not work for your love, I shall work to live. Our love will be one of the incidents of our life. Meanwhile, I may go with you, that is all that I say--I sing it. I may go with you, not to happiness, but to necessity!

And now that cursed German! It hangs over my head like a sword of Damocles I have heard of--though I don't know why it was held over his head!

You think our love was settling into the cooing state! Dear me, Thyrsis, I hope I will not always have to yell to you over a foggy ocean!

XX
DEAR THYRSIS:

Can you imagine what it must be to be shut up in a little room on a rainy night, with the children and people screaming under your window? That is my position now.

I find myself hard to manage at times. I want to become discouraged or melancholy or disgusted, but I drive myself better than I used to. I even was happy a little for a few moments to-night. I was playing one of my piano-pieces, and I found myself imagining all sorts of things. But this happens very seldom, and only lasts for a moment. I often wonder at myself. Two months ago I did not love you one particle; I love you now, so that--so that it is impossible for me to do anything else. In fact I did not realize how much I loved you until that terrible moment when I read you did not love me. I saw how impossible it will be to cease to love you, no matter what you do to me. I do not know *why* it is; I simply know it is, and perhaps some day I may teach *you* how to love. I do not imagine you know how very well, at present--no, Thyrsis, I don't.

I know your true self now, and I love it better than ever I loved the other. I say it with a certain grimness. I know you, your real self, and I love it.

Know, oh, my Beloved, that in the last three months you have grown to me from a boy into a man, into my husband! When I think of you as you were at first you seem a child compared to what you are now.

XXI
DEAREST LOVE:

Last night, as I went to sleep, I was thinking of you and our problem, and there were all sorts of uncertainties; but one thing I have to tell you, my Corydon--that it came to me how sweet and true, and how pure and good you have been; and I loved you very, very much indeed. I thought: I should like to tell her that, and ask her always to be so noble and unselfish. Can you not realize how all your deficiencies are as nothing to me, in the sight of that one unapproachable perfection? For my Corydon is all devotion and love, and pure, pure, maiden goodness! And there is quite a whole heart full of feeling for you in that, and I wish I had you here to tell you.

XXII
MY CORYDON:

I am coming more and more to realize myself, and what is the single faculty I have been given. I think of a dear clergyman friend I used to have, and I realize what a *loving* heart is--what it is to delight in a human soul for its own sake, and to be kind to it, fond of it. And I know that there could not be a man with less of that than I have. Certainly I know this, I never did love a soul for its own sake, and don't think I could. I love beauty, and truth, and power, and I hate everything else, if it come across my way. If I had to live the life of that clergyman friend I should be insane in a month. I see this as something very hateful; but there is only one thing I can do, to see that I hate my own self more than I hate any other self--and work, work, for the thing I love.

You asked me once to tell you if your death would make any difference to me. If you were to die to-morrow I should feel that a sacred opportunity was gone out of my life, that all my efforts must have less result forever after. But I do not think I should stop working a day.

I love you because you are something upon which I may exert the force of my will. I honestly believe that the truest word, the nearest to my character, I ever spoke. If I care about you it is for one thing, and one only--because you are a soul hungry for life, because you are capable of sacrifice and high effort, because you are sensitive and eager. I love you and honor you for this; I take you to my bosom, I give all my life to your service; and I shall make you a perfect woman, or else kill you.

You must understand what I want; I want no concrete thing, no dozen languages to throw you into despair. I want effort, effort, *effort!* That's all. And I believe that you might be a stronger soul than I at this moment, if only you chose to hunt yourself out and fight! That is truly what I feel about you, and that is why I love you.

XXIII

DEAREST THYRSIS:

I have no more to say, my precious one; I bow in joy before your will, your certainty, your power. Let it be so, I shall adore you as I so long to do.

You are giving me all I could ask for. What more could I wish from you, dear Thyrsis, than to know you will never leave my side? I will try not to do any more bemoaning of my shortcomings. To-night I reached a wonderful security and almost sublimity, until I could have fallen on my face and praised God for His mercy. I talked out loud to myself, I exhorted myself, I explained to myself what is my beauty and possibility in life--the *reason* for which I was born. I was quite lifted out of myself, by a conviction that came like a benediction, that the essence of my soul was good and pure, and that if anybody upon earth had the power to reach God, it was myself.

Dear God, *how* I have spent the years of my life! like an imbecile! But you--if you take me, I shall go mad--I shall love you like a tigress! I shall implore you to invent any way that will enable me to realize life! Oh, if you take me, how madly I shall love you! I fancy myself seeing you now, and I don't know what I should do--I love you so dreadfully! I think of you, and everything about you seems so wondrously beautiful to me!

I almost have a feeling that I have no right to love you so much. Oh, tell me, do you want me to love you as I can? Already you seem part of me, mine--mine! And it is wonderful how you help me.

XXIV

Thyrsis:

I spent the whole day in the park without a bite to eat, because I did not want to take the trouble to come home after it, and I only had five cents. I have tried, oh, tried to control myself and make myself saner. I am seized with occasional fits of the horrors, and of wild cravings for you, until I could scream. It is so unbearable, and I almost want to die. Oh, but I do *not* want to die! My imagination has become so fevered in the last few days--if I do not see you soon, I know not what will become of me!

I have never loved you so wildly--though I have always longed for you. I sometimes feel now as if my brain were utterly wrecked. I know not what is the matter; I gasp, when I think of you. I am convinced of heaven and hell almost in the same breath--experience each in rapid succession. One touch of your hand and one look, I think would cure me. I seem as if in a thunder-storm--pitchy blackness with flashes of light--and in the flashes I see you, my beloved!

XXV

Thyrsis:

I am atrociously weary of being able to depend upon myself not at all; but oh, how marvellously sweet and good you are to me! I shall never be able to pay you for your help!

Dear Heaven, what a cup of bitterness I have drunk, since I last saw you! Dearest, you have really torn me to pieces, unwittingly. But now I am healed, and I may go on in your blessed sight, with my terrors gone forever.

And then I actually wonder if you have an earthly form! It will be very strange to see you and touch you, I sometimes wake up with a start at the thought of it!

XXVI

Thyrsis:

Here I am, the most restless and miserable and uncomfortable and pining of creatures--a very Dido! Are you satisfied, now that you have made it almost impossible for me to put my mind on anything but you, you? I spend hours reading one page of my book.

I was reading peaceably just now, and I suddenly thought how I would feel if I saw you coming in at the door. I started and could hardly believe that I will really see you--in something besides visions. When night comes I usually get fidgety, and can hardly realize I do not need to worry over phantoms. Then I go on with "Classicism and Romanticism in Music," and I think of you--and read a line and think of you! You see, it doesn't do for me to be too intense, for I just devour myself, and that is all. My only idea of a vent is to knock my head against something.

I suppose it is the inevitable result of caring for someone you cannot see. Here I might be studying now, but what do I do? I go around seeking rest--and I write you a dozen times a day, and use up all the stamps in the house.

Oh well, I dare say if you wished me to love you, you have accomplished your purpose most successfully. There is nothing in life but you, and to suddenly acquire a new self is most startling, and something hard to believe. Thyrsis, I simply cannot realize that I may go to you and find peace and security.

XXVII

MY DEAREST CORYDON:

I have just a few words to say. I have two weeks left in which to shake off my shoulders the fearful animal that has been tearing me. *For just three weeks to-day,* not a line written!

The task seems almost beyond my powers. God, will people ever know how I have worked over this book!

But unless you develop some new doubt, or I persist in writing letters, I ought to get it done now. I shall see you as soon as I have finished, and meantime I shall write no letters.

XXVIII

DEAR THYRSIS:

I would give a great deal to let you know how I have struggled and suffered.

I have had almost *more* than I could bear--the more horrible because the more unreasonable. You must know it. If it disturbs you, please put the letter away until a favorable time. I account my trouble greatly physical--I have never been in such a nervous state. The murky despair that has come over me--that I have writhed and struggled in, as in the clutches of some fiend! It seems to me I have experienced every torment of each successive stage of Dante's Inferno. I know what is the emotion of a soul in all the bloom and hope of youth, condemned *to die*.

I woke up in the middle of the night last night--and felt as if a monster sat by to throw a black cloth over me and smother me. I got up and shook myself, and my heart was beating violently.

I managed to get myself free. This morning I am better. God in Heaven only knows--I would rather be torn limb from limb, yes, honestly, than endure the blackness of soul that I have had through all these years of strife and failure by myself.

Dearest Thyrsis:

Perhaps if I have written to you a few words, I shall be able to put my mind on study--as so far I have not done. I actually to-night have been indulging in all sorts of romantic moods about you. I felt in a singing mood, and when I came up from dinner I put on a beautiful dress, just for fun, and I looked quite radiant. I dreamed of you, and imagined that you were at my feet, in true Romeo fashion--and I was your Juliet. I imagined--I couldn't help thinking of this, and I knew I ought to be doing something else! Oh, but how I want a poor taste of joy! You were my Romeo to-night--you were beautiful and young and loving; and well, I had one dream of youth and happiness before my miseries begin.

I have felt that we were very near to each other lately. You have shown me the tenderness of your heart, and I love you quite rapturously. I love your goodness, your sympathy--perhaps when I see you I can tell you!

XXIX
DEAREST THYRSIS:

I received a postal just now, saying that you were coming soon. I had my usual queer faintness. It was like receiving word from the dead--it seemed such centuries---aeons--since I heard from you! I send you this batch of notes I have written you at various times, a sort of mental itinerary, for my mind has traveled into all sorts of queer places, back and forth. I tell you that without your continual influence, I am lost in doubt and uncertainty. Please try to understand these notes and my fits of love and fear.

XXX
DEAR THYRSIS:

I am in one of my cast-iron moods, this morning--in a fighting mood, I do not care with whom or what. You, even you, have not altogether understood me--you have often given me a dog's portion. I have been a slave, a cowering kitten before you, and you (unwittingly I know) have done much to destroy all my courage and hope and love--by what you call making me aware of your higher self. Fortunately I *know* what your higher self is, quite as well as you do, if not a little better--and I know that it is the self that most strengthens my love and courage, the self that most fills me with life. I have a right to life as well as you, and a right to the love in you that most inspires me. I feel I am capable of judging this, in spite of all my lack of education, and my inability to follow you in your intellectual life.

I have thought lately that you were able to make yourself believe that you were anything you wished to think yourself. Whenever you wring my heart and deprive me of strength, I shall go somewhere alone, and when I have controlled myself, come back to you.

You say you are master--but it must be master of the right. I want strength, and why you should think it right ever to have helped to throw me into more despair, I do not know. The reason I have written all this is because such ideas have come to me lately, and a fear that sometimes you might resort to your unloving methods, with the thought of its being right. I tell you I would rather stay at home, than ever go through with some of the pangs you have cost me, in what you called your higher moods. You must not gainsay me, that I am also capable of respecting high moods and bowing before them; but it would seem to me that they are only high if they are a source of inspiration and joy to me.

Because we love each other, would that be any reason why we must dote upon each other, or sink from our high resolves? I cannot see why our love for each other should not always be a means of our reaching our higher selves. You need not answer this letter--but when you come back, tell me whether what I say impresses you as being right or wrong--if there is not some justification in it. But perhaps I should wait. I have no right to disturb you now.

XXXI

THYRSIS:

I woke up this morning with the feeling that I did not love you. That same thing has happened to me two or three times, and I do not understand it.

It must be because at the present moment you do not love *me!* You are writing your book, and telling yourself that you cannot love me as you ought! Is this so? It is only a surmise on my part, and I do not know, but I should not be surprised if you were. I only know that the one thing that can bring us together is love, and I do not love you now. Perhaps you can explain it to me. I write this absolutely without emotion.

I tell you there have been things horribly wrong about you. You have done anything but inspire love in my heart--you have never seen me with love in my heart. Until lately, I never have felt any love for you; before, I simply compelled myself to think I loved you, because my life seemed to depend upon it. There have been many times when, as I look back, you seem to me to have been base.

Well may you preach, while you are alone, and are monarch of yourself. I shall have to have more of a chance than has ever come to me, before I will bear your displeasure or your exhortations. If you come to me and speak to me of the high, proud self that I must reach, every vestige of love for you will leave my heart, and I would as soon marry a stone pillar!

Great Heaven, what strange moods I have! I picture our meeting each other, unmoved by love; you determined, energetic, indifferent to all things, myself included; and I disappointed, but with a hardness in my heart--no tears!

I am indulging now in the most lifeless and gloomy of broodings; if you do not come back to me, the only soul I can love, if you are not joyful and strong, sincere, sympathetic, and loving, all of these--I shall know it is a farce for me to ever hope to gain any life with *you*. I do not believe that any woman can grow without love, and a great deal of it. Why do you suppose I am writing all this--I, who have felt such deep and true love for you? I have no courage--the dampness of the day has settled into my soul--and I shall be joyless until there is no more cursed doubt of you and your love for me.

XXXII

Dear Corydon: Against resolutions, I am writing to you again. I thought of you--there is a boat up the lake to-day with some hunters, and if I finish this letter, I can send it in by them as they pass. I have many things to tell you, and you must think about them.

This is one of my paralyzing letters. It will reach you Monday. I can't tell where I may be then. I have been wrestling with the end of the book, and I am wild with rage at my impotence. The fact has come to me that no amount of will is enough, because all my life is cowardly and false. I have found myself wanting *to sneak through this work*, and come home and enjoy myself; and you can't sneak with God, and that's all. I cannot come home beaten, and so here I am, still struggling--and with snow on the ground, and the shack so cold that I sit half in the fire-place.

I think of you, and at times when my soul is afire, I imagine I can do anything. I see that you are helpless, but I think that I can change your whole being, and *make* you what I wish. But then that feeling dies out, and I think of you as you *are*, and with despair. I do not allude to any of your "deficiencies"--music, learning, and other stuff. I mean your life-force, or your lack of it. I see that you have learned nothing of the unspeakable, unattainable thing for which I am panting. And it has come to me that I dare not marry you, that I should be binding my life to ruin. My head is surging with plans, and a whole infinity of future, and I simply cannot carry any woman with me on this journey.

As I say this, I see the tears of despair in your eyes. I can only tell you what I am--God made me for an *artist,* not a *lover!* I have not deep feelings--I do not care for human suffering; I can *work,* that is all. Art is no respecter of persons, and neither am I--I labor for something which is not of self, and requires denial of self. And as I think about you, the feeling comes to me that it is not this you want, that I should make you utterly wretched if I married you. You love *love;* you do not wish to fling yourself into a struggle such as my life must be. I see that in all your letters --your terror of this highest self of mine. If you married me, you would have to fight a battle that would almost kill you. You would have to wear your heart out, night and day--you would have to lose yourself and your feelings--fling away everything, and live in self-contempt and effort. You would have to know it--I can't help it-- that I love life, and that to human hearts I owe no allegiance; that to me they are simply impatience and vexation.

Do you want such a life? If you can learn to love it for what it is--a wild, un-natural, but royal life--very well. If you are coming to me with pleading eyes, se-cretly wishing for affection, and in terror of me when you don't get it, then God help you, that is all!

You are a child, and you can not dream what I mean. But every day I learn something more of a great savage force of mine, that will stand out against the rest of this world, that is burning me up, that is driving me mad. One of two things it will do to you--it will make you the same kind of creature, or it will tear the soul out of you. Do you understand that? And nothing will stop it--it cares for nothing in the world but the utterance of itself! And if you wish to marry me, it will be with no promise of mine save to wreak it upon you! To take you, and make you just such a creature, kill or cure--nothing else! Not one instant's patience--but just one insis-tent, frantic demand that you succeed--and fiery, writhing disgust with you when you do not succeed--disgust that will make you scream--and make you live! Do you understand this--and do you get any idea of the temper behind this? And how it seems to you, I don't know--it is the only kind of truth I am capable of; I shall sim-ply fling naked the force of my passionate, raging will, and punish you with it each instant of your life--until you understand it, and love it, and worship it, as I do.

Now, I don't know what you will think about this letter--and I don't care. It is here--and you must take it. It does not come to you for criticism, any more than it would come for criticism to the world. It will rule the world. If I marry you I must live all my soul before you, and you must share it; if you think you can do this without first having suffered, having first torn loose your own crushed self, you are mistaken. But remember this--I shall demand from you just as much fire as I give; you may say you *cannot*, you may weep and say you cannot--I will gnash my teeth at you and say you *must*.

Perhaps I'm a fool to think I can do this. At any rate, I don't want to do anything else; I am a fool to think of doing anything else, and you to let me.

I *cannot* be false to my art without having a reaction of disgust, and you cannot marry me, unless you understand that. When I sat down to this letter I called myself mad for trying to tie my life to yours. Now I am interested in you again. You may wish to make this cast still; and oh, of course I shall drop back as usual, and you'll be happy, and I'll be your "Romeo"!

Ugh--how I hated that letter! *"Romeo"* indeed! Wouldn't we have a fine sentimental time--you with your prettiest dress on, and I holding you in my arms and telling you how much I loved you!

XXXIII

MY DEAR THYRSIS:

I shall be your wife. This thought takes hold of me firmly and calmly, and I have no tears, nor fright, nor uncertainty. I suffered, of course, while I read your letter, and my self-control toppled, but no "tears of despair" came into my eyes. I am not despairing--I shall be your wife, and I shall feel that for many years one of my greatest efforts will be to prevent you from becoming my "Romeo." I am very weak and human, and you become that easily--do you know it?

Rejoice, I have gained my self-control, and well, I am going to be your wife. Or else (it comes to me quite as a matter of course, without any feeling of it being unnatural or unusual) I shall not care to live. But after all, I do not fear that I shall die--I shall be your wife. You may even gainsay it, you may *even* tell me I shall ruin your life, you may *even* tell me that you refuse to take me--but sooner or later I shall be your wife. I say it with perfect certainty, and almost composure.

It is unfortunate that at such a time as this I cannot see you--it is quite cruelly wicked. There is so much to say, not all in *your* favor either. Some day I shall learn to bring out and keep before me that higher self of yours, which *now* I do not fear. I also have a higher self, though it does not show itself very often. It is a self which can meet that self of yours without flinching, but which loves it, and stretches out its arms to it--which knows that without that self of yours it cannot, **will** not live. It is hard to realize such a thing, but I beseech you no longer, I am going with you. You see now, I have no fear of your not taking me--I simply have no fear of this.

If I had, I could not write you this way. But you have been the means of showing me I **can** awaken, and that I was not meant to live the life of the people around me. Chance tried hard to put me to sleep forever, but you have roused me. Dear me, how I smile to myself at my confidence! But I am so sure--this feeling would not be in my heart if it had no meaning! I was not meant for this life I am leading. I am not afraid because I have no proof that I am a genius, and no prospect of being one at present. I do not know whether what you have must come as an inspiration direct from God, I do not know whether I am **capable** of winning any of this life that you are seeking; but I do know this--I'm going to have the chance to try, and you are going to give it to me. Do you suppose I could tell you that I am willing to stay at home and let you leave me?

I have not even any fear now of your wishing to leave me. Why, I wouldn't hold my life at a pennyworth if you were out of it!

"You are my only means of breathing, you fool," I thought. I sometimes wonder how you could think of leaving me, when I feel as I do at present. I ask myself why it is that you know nothing of it, and why it does not make you put out your hand in gladness to me--how you could write me that all my letters showed you I did not want to struggle to lead your life!

My words are failing me now--this is probably the reason you know nothing about me.

Besides, when I have written you before this, I have been worrying and doubting and afraid. I am none of these now; and I do not believe I am deluding myself--in fact I **know** I am not. **I shall be your wife.** It is indeed a pity I cannot talk to you now--yes, a very great pity. It is also rather incomprehensible, that you can imagine leaving me **now.** And all my letters have told you that I wish to be petted and cuddled, did they? If you were here, I do not know that it would do any good to give my feelings vent, it would profit me nothing to strike you, and what could I do? I cannot hate you--it is not natural that one should hate one's husband.

Some day, oh, **some** day, I tell myself--you will no lonnger play and trifle with me and my soul!

Did you really think you are going to put me to sleep again? Surely my life is something; and you have given me some reason for its existence. I can hardly tell you what I wish to say; people run in and out, and I am bothered--I suppose this is one of my tasks. But do you not see that you have taken the responsibility of a soul into your hands? I cannot live without you. What is it--do creatures go around the world struggling and saying they must live, and are they only pitiful fools for trying?

And are you one of God's chosen ones? Will you tell me, "Corydon, you simply cannot live my life--you are not fit?" Dear Thyrsis, I actually believe that if you should tell me that now, I should laugh with joy, for I would see that I had gained one victory, that of proving to you your own weakness and stupidity. And I should not let you discourage me. I should throw my arms around your neck, and cling to you until you had promised to take me. After all, it is a small boon to ask the privilege of trying to live, it cannot but be a glory to you to help me; and if I do not make you waste your time or money, how can I hinder you?

Ask yourself how you have treated me--have I not suffered a little? Though I may have been miserably weak, have I not now a little courage? Why do the moments blind you so, that you can speak to me as though I were a sawdust doll?

There is only one thing that I will let myself do. I know that you are strong and brave, and that I can be if I go with you; and I am going with you--there simply is no other alternative--for I love you! Yes, dear, I saw it very plainly as I read your letter to-day. I seem to feel very differently about it all now. I know we *cannot* sit still and love each other--this costs me no pang. You need not love me one bit; I may simply belong to you, we may simply belong to each other.

I see how I fall into blindness of the high things at home. How almost impossible it is for me to do anything, while I have the earthly ties of love! I study--but how? How is it possible to live the physical life of other people--to be sympathetic and agreeable and conciliatory, and gain anything for your own soul? How is such a creature as myself to get what it wants, unless it goes away where there are no contrary and disturbing influences--where it has no ties, no obligations? The souls that have won, how did they do it-- did they go alone, or did they stay in the parlor and serve tea?

Such thoughts as these would make me grovel at your feet, if need be, in an agony of prayer. The means, I cry--and you are the means! What is there for me, then, but to beseech you to have faith in me? I suppose, as yet, you have little or no cause--though once or twice I have risen to you, even though perhaps you did not know it. I am almost happy now--for I feel that this *useless* strife is at an end, this craving and wondering if you wish to leave me. And for all that, I despise you, too-- for your blind and wanton cruelty in wishing to crush what you have created! How do you expect God to value your soul, when you so lightly value mine?

But after all, will it help me to beseech you? The thing I honor in you is your desire to be right--and I know that you will act toward me as your sense of right prompts you. You will act toward me as you feel you *must* do, to be true. Yes, be true to yourself, please; I am happy to trust in yourself so. If you believe that I will mar your life, I do not wish to go I with you. I do not know why, but I feel that something has come to me to prevent my despair from returning; I shall take care of my soul--there *must* be something for me in this life. I have a feeling that perhaps you will think I am writing this last mute acceptance of your will, without knowing what I am doing. But I *know* that I shall struggle without you, I shall not die.

And I wish that you would do one thing--see me as soon as you can; let it be early in the morning, and it shall be decided *on that day* whether I am to marry you or not. I shall leave you, not to see you again--or knowing that I am to be your wife. I am sick unto death of fuming and sighing, tears and fears.

What will you do, Thyrsis? I cannot write any more.

I unfold the letter again. *What, in the name of God, are you going to do?*

BOOK IV
THE VICTIM APPROACHES

A silence had fallen upon them. She sat watching where the light of the sun flickered among the birches; and he had the book in his hand, and was turning the pages idly. He read--
"I know these slopes; who knows them if not I?"
And she smiled, and quoted in return--

"Here cam'st thou in thy jocund youthful time,
  Here was thine height of strength, thy golden prime!
  And still the haunt beloved a virtue yields."

Section 1. It was early one November afternoon, in his cabin in the forest, that Thyrsis wrote the last of his minstrel's songs. He had not been able to tell when it would come to him, so he had made no preparations; but when the last word was on the paper, he sprang to his feet, and strode through the snow-clad forest to the nearest farm-house. The farmer came with a wagon, and Thyrsis bundled all his belongings into his trunk, and took the night-train for the city.

He came like a young god, radiant and clothed in glory. All the creatures of his dreams were awake within him, all his demons and his muses; he had but to call them and they answered. There was a sound of trumpets and harps in his soul all day; he was like a man half walking, half running, in the midst of a great storm of wind.

He had fought the good fight, and he had conquered. The world was at his feet, and he had no longer any fear of it. The jangling of the street-cars was music to him, the roar and rush of the city stirred his pulses--this was the life he had come to shape to his will!

And so he came to Corydon, glorious and irresistible. His mind was quite made up--he would take her; he was master now, he had no longer any doubts or fears. He was thrilled all through him with the thought of her; how wonderful it was at such an hour to have some one to communicate with--some one in whose features he could see a reflection of his own exaltation! He recollected the words of the old German poet--

"Der ist selig zu begrussen Der ein treues Herze weiss!"

He went to Corydon's home. In the parlor he came upon her unannounced; and she started and stared at him as at a ghost. She did not make a sound, but he saw the pallor sweep over her face, he saw her tremble and sway. She was like a reed shaken by the wind-- so fragile and so sensitive! He got a sudden sense of the storm of emotion that was shaking her; and it frightened him, while at the same time it thrilled him strangely.

He came and took her hands in his, and gently touched her cheek with his lips. She stared at him dumbly.

"It's all right, sweetheart," he whispered. "It's all right." And she closed her eyes, and it seemed as if to breathe was all she could do.

"Come, dearest," he said. "Let us go out."

And half in a daze she put on her hat and coat, and they went out on the street. He took her arm to steady her.

"Well?" she asked.

"It's all right, dearest," he said.

"You got my letter?"

"Yes, I got it. And it was a wonderful letter. It couldn't have been better."

"Ah!"

"And there's no more to be said. There's no refusing such a challenge. You shall come with me."

"But Thyrsis! Do you *want* me to come?"

"Yes," he said, "I want you."

And he felt a tremor pass through her arm. He pressed it tightly to his side. "I love you!" he whispered.

"Ah Thyrsis!" she exclaimed. "How you have tortured me!"

"Hush, dear!" he replied. "Let's not think of that. It's all past now. We are going on! You have proven your grit. You are wonderful!"

They went into the park, and sat upon a bench in the sun.

"I've finished the book!" he said. "And in a couple more days it'll be copied. I've a letter of introduction to a publisher, and he wrote me he'd read it at once."

"It seems like a dream to me," she whispered.

"We won't have to wait long after that," he said. "Everything will be clear before us."

"And what will you do in the meantime?" she asked.

"Mother wants me to stay with her," he said. "I've only got ten dollars left. But I'll get some from the publisher."

"Are you sure you can?" she asked.

"Oh, Corydon!" he cried, "you've no idea how wonderful it is--the book, I mean. You'll be amazed! It kept growing on me all the time--I got new visions of it. That was why it took me so long. I didn't dare to appreciate it, while I was doing it--I had to keep myself at work, you know; but now that it's done, I can realize it. And oh, it's a book the world will heed!"

"When can I see it, Thyrsis?"

"As soon as it's copied--the manuscript is all a scrawl. But you know the minstrel's song at the end? My Gethsemane, I called it! I found a new form for it--it's all in free verse. I didn't mean it to be that way, but it just wrote itself; it broke through the bars and ran away with me. Oh, it marches like the thunder!"

He pulled some papers from his coat-pocket. "I was going over it on the train this morning," he said. "Listen!"

He read her the song, thrilling anew with the joy of its effect upon her. "Oh, Thyrsis!" she cried, in awe. "That is marvellous! Marvellous! How could you do it?"

And yet, for all the delight she expressed, Thyrsis was conscious of a chill of disappointment, of a doubt lurking in the background of his mind. It was inevitable, in the nature of things--how could the book mean to any human creature what it had meant to him? Seven long months he had toiled with it, he had been through the agonies of a child-birth for it. And another person would read it all in one day!--It was the old, old agony of the artist, who can communicate so small a part of what has been in his soul.

Section 2. He wanted to talk about his book, but Corydon wanted to talk about him. She had waited so long, and suffered so much--and now at last he was here! "Oh, Thyrsis!" she cried. "There's just no use in my trying--I can't do anything at all without you!"

"You won't have to do it any more," he said. "We shall not part again."

"And you are sure you want me? You have no more doubts?"

"How could I have any doubts--after that letter. Ah, that was a brave letter, Corydon! It made me think of you as some old Viking's daughter! That is the way to go at the task!"

"And then I may feel certain!" she said.

"You may stop thinking all about it," he replied. "We'll waste no more of our time--we'll put it aside and get to work."

They spent the day wandering about in the park and talking over their plans. "I suppose it'll be all right now that I'm with you," said Thyrsis. "I mean, there's no great hurry about getting married."

"Oh, no!" she answered. "We dare not think of that, until you have money."

"How I wish we didn't have to get married!" he exclaimed.

"Why?" she asked.

"Because-why should we have to get anybody else's permission to live our lives? I've thought about it a good deal, and it's a slave-custom, and it makes me ashamed of myself."

"But don't you believe in marriage, dear?"

"I do, and I don't. I believe that a man who exposes a woman to the possibility of having a child, ought to guarantee to support the woman for a time, and to support the child. That's obvious enough--no one but a scoundrel would want to avoid it. But marriage means so much more than that! You bind yourself to stay together, whether love continues or whether it stops; you can't part, except on some terms that other people set down. You have to make all sorts of promises you don't intend to keep, and to go through forms you don't believe in, and it seems to me a cowardly thing to do."

"But what else can one do?" asked Corydon.

"It's quite obvious what *we* could do. We don't intend to be husband and wife;

and so we could simply go away and go on with our work."

"But think of our parents, Thyrsis!"

"Yes, I know--I've thought of them. But if every one thought of his parents, how would the world ever move?"

"But, dearest!" exclaimed Corydon, "if we didn't marry, they'd simply go out of their senses!"

"I know. But then, they might threaten to go out of their senses if we *did* marry? And would that work also?"

"We must be sensible," said the girl. "It means so much to them, and so little to us."

"Yes, I suppose so," he answered. "But all the same, I hate it; when you once begin conforming, you never know where you'll stop."

" *We* shall know," declared the other. "Whatever we may have to do to get married, we shall both of us know that neither would ever dream of wishing to hold the other for a moment after love had ceased. And that is the essential thing, is it not?"

"Yes," assented Thyrsis. "I suppose so."

"Well, then, we'll make that bargain between us; that will be *our* marriage."

"That suits me better," he replied.

She thought for a moment, and then said, with a laugh, "Let us have a little ceremony of our own."

"Very well," said he.

"Are you ready for it now?" she inquired. "Your mind is quite made up?"

"Quite made up."

She looked about her, to make sure that no one was in sight; and then she put her hand in his. "I have been to weddings," she said. "And so I know how they do it.--I take thee, Thyrsis, to be the companion of my soul. I give myself to thee freely, for the sake of love, and I will stay so long as thy soul is better with me than without. But if ever this should cease to be, I will leave thee; for if my soul is weaker than thine, I have no right to be thy mate."

She paused. "Is that right?" she asked.

"Yes," he said, "that is right."

"Very well then," she said; "and now, you say it!"

And she made him repeat the words--"I take thee, Corydon, to be the companion of my soul. I give myself to thee freely, for the sake of love, and I will stay so long as thy soul is better with me than without. But if ever this should cease to be, I will leave thee; for if my soul is weaker than thine, I have no right to be thy mate."

"Now," she exclaimed, with an eager laugh--"now we're married!" And as he looked he caught the glint of a tear in her eyes.

Section 3. But the world would not be content to leave it on that basis. When they parted that afternoon, it was with a carefully-arranged program of work--they were to visit each other on alternate days and go on with their German and music. But in less than a week they had run upon an obstruction; there was no quiet room for them at Corydon's save her bedroom, and one evening when Thyrsis came, she made the announcement that they could no longer study there.

"Why not?" he asked.

"Well," explained Corydon, "they say the maid might think it wasn't nice."

She had expected him to fly into a rage, but he only smiled grimly. "I had come to tell you the same sort of thing," he explained. "It seems you can't visit me so often, and you're never to stay after ten o'clock at night."

"Why is that?" she inquired.

"It's a question of what the hall-boy might think," said he.

They sat gazing at each other in silence. "You see," said Thyrsis, at last, "the thing is impossible--we've got to go and get married. The world will never give us any peace until we do."

"Nobody has any idea of what we mean!" exclaimed Corydon.

"No idea whatever," he said. "They've nothing in them in anyway to correspond with it. You talk to them about souls, and they haven't any. You talk to them about love, and they think you mean obscenity. Everybody is thinking obscenity about us!"

"Everybody but our parents," put in Corydon.

To which he answered, angrily, "They are thinking of what the others are thinking."

But everybody seemed to have to think something, and that was the aspect of the matter that puzzled them most. Why did everybody find it necessary to be thinking about it at all? Why did everybody consider it his business? As Thyrsis phrased it--"Why the hell can't they let us alone?"

"We've got to get married," said she. "That's the only way to get the best of them."

"But is that really getting the best of them?" he objected. "Isn't that their purpose--to make us get married?"

This was a pregnant question, but they did not follow it up just then. They went on to the practical problem of where and when and how to accomplish their purpose.

"We can go to a court," said he.

"Oh, no!" she exclaimed. "We'd have to meet a lot of men, and I couldn't stand it."

"But surely you don't want to go to a church!" he said.

"Couldn't we get some clergyman to marry us quietly?"

"But then, there's a lot of rigmarole!"

"But mightn't he leave it out?" she asked.

"I don't know," he said. "They generally believe in it, you see."

He decided to make an attempt, however.

"Let's go to-morrow morning," he said. "I'm going over to have the sound-post set in my violin, and that'll take an hour or so. Perhaps we can finish it up in the meantime."

"A good idea," said Corydon. "It'll give me to-night to tell mother and father."

Section 4. So behold them, the next morning, emerging from the little shop of the violin-dealer, and seeking for some one to fasten them in the holy bonds of matrimony! They were walking down a great avenue, and there were many churches--but they were all rich churches. "I never thought about it before," said Thyrsis. "But I wonder if there are any poor churches in the city!"

They stopped in front of one brown-stone structure that looked a trifle less elaborate. "It says Presbyterian," said Corydon, reading the sign. "I wonder how they do it."

"I don't know," said he. "But he'd want a lot of money, I'm sure."

"But mightn't he have a curate, or something?"

"Goose," laughed Thyrsis, "there are no Presbyterian curates!"

"Well, you know what I mean," she said--"an assistant, or an apprentice, or something."

"I don't know," said he. "Let's go and ask."

So, with much trepidation, they rang the bell of the parsonage on the side-street. But the white-capped maid who answered told them that the pastor was not in, and that there were no curates or apprentices about.

They went on.

"How much do you suppose they charge, anyway?" asked Thyrsis.

"I don't know--I think you give what you can spare. How much money have you?"

"I've got eight dollars to my name."

"Have you got it with you?"

"Yes--all of it."

"I get my twenty-five to-morrow," she added.

"Do you really get it?" he asked. "You can depend on it?"

"Oh yes--it comes the middle of each month."

"I've heard of people getting incomes from investments, and things like that, but it always seemed hard to believe. I never thought I'd meet with it in my own life."

"It's certainly very nice," said Corydon.

"Where does it come from?"

"There's a trustee of the estate who sends it. It's Mr. Hammond."

"That bald-headed man I met once?"

"Yes, he's the one. He's quite a well-known lawyer, and they say I'm fortunate to have him."

"I see," said Thyrsis. "I'll have to look into it some day. You know you have to endow me with all your worldly goods!"

They went on down the avenue, and came to a Jewish temple with a gilded dome. "I wonder how that would do," said Corydon.

"I don't think it would do at all," said Thyrsis. "We'd surely have to believe something there."

So they went on again. And on a corner, as they stopped to look about them, a strange mood came suddenly to Thyrsis. It was as if a veil was rent before him--as if a bolt of lightning had flashed. What was he going to do? He was going to bind himself in marriage! He was going to be trapped--he, the wild thing, the young stag of the forest!

"What is it?" asked Corydon, seeing him standing motionless.

"I--I was just thinking," he said.

"What?"

"I was afraid, Corydon, I wondered if we were sure--if we realized--"

"If we *realized!*" she cried.

"You know--it'll be forever--"

"Why, Thyrsis!" she exclaimed, in horror.

And so he started, and laughed uneasily. "It was just a queer fancy that came to me," he said.

"But how *could* you!" she cried.

"Come, dearest," he said, hurriedly--"it's nothing. It seems so strange, that's all."

In the middle of the block they came to another church. "Unitarian!" he exclaimed. "Oh, maybe that's just the thing!"

And so they went in, and found a friendly clergyman, Dr. Hamilton by name, to whom they explained their plight. They answered his questions--yes, they were both of age, and they had told their parents. Also, with much stammering, Thyrsis explained that his worldly goods amounted to eight dollars.

"But--how are you going to live?" asked Dr. Hamilton.

Thyrsis was tempted to mention the masterpiece, but he decided not to. "I'm going to earn money," he said.

"Well," responded the other, "I suppose it's all right. I'll marry you."

And so the sexton was called in for a witness, and the clergyman stood before them and made a little speech, and said a prayer, and then joined their hands together and pronounced the spell. The two trembled just a little, but answered bravely, "I do," in the proper places, and then it was over. They shook hands with the doctor, and promised to come hear one of his sermons; and with much trepidation they paid him two dollars, which he in turn paid to the sexton. And then they went outside, and drew a great breath of relief. "It wasn't half as bad as I expected," the bridegroom confessed.

Section 5. Thyris invested in a newspaper, and as they went back to get the violin they read the advertisements of furnished rooms. In respectable neighborhoods which they tried they found that the prices were impossible for them; but at last, upon the edge of a tenement district, they found a corner flat-house, with a saloon underneath, where there were two tiny bedrooms for rent in an apartment. The woman, who was a seamstress, was away a good deal in the day, and Corydon learned with delight that she might use the piano in the parlor. The rooms were the smallest they had ever seen, but they were clean, and the price was only fifty cents a day--a dollar and a half a week for Thyrsis' and two dollars for Corydon's, because there was a steam-radiator in it.

There was a racket of school-children and of streetcars from the avenue below, but they judged they would get used to this; and having duly satisfied the landlady that they were married, and having ascertained that she had no objection to "light housekeeping," they engaged the rooms and paid a week's rent in advance.

"That leaves us two and a half to start life on!" said Thyrsis, when they were on the street again. "Our housekeeping will be light indeed!"

They walked on, and sat down in the park to talk it over.

"It's not nearly so reckless as it would seem," he argued. "For I have to earn money for myself any-how. And then there's the book."

"When will you hear about it?"

"I called the man up the day before yesterday. He said they were reading it."

"Have you said anything to him about money?"

"Not yet."

"Will they pay something in advance?"

"They will, I guess, if they like the story. I don't know very much about the business end of it."

"We mustn't let them take advantage of us!" exclaimed Corydon.

"No, of course not. But I hate to have to think about the money side of it. It's a cruel thing that I have to sell my inspiration."

"What else could you do?" she asked.

"It's something I've thought a great deal about," said he. "It kept forcing itself upon me all the time I was writing. Here I am with my vision--working day and night to make something beautiful and sacred, something without taint of self. And

I have to take it to business-men, who will go out into the market-place and sell it to make money! It will come into competition with thousands of other books--and the publishers shouting their virtues like so many barkers at a fair. I can hardly bear to think of it; I'd truly rather live in a garret all my days than see it happen. I don't want the treasures of my soul to be hawked on the streets."

"But how else could people get them?" asked Corydon.

"I would like to have a publishing-house of my own, and to print my books with good paper and strong bindings that would last, and then sell them for just what they cost. So the whole thing would be consistent, and I could tell the exact truth about what I wrote. For I know the truth about my work; I've no vanities, I'd be as remorseless a critic of myself as Shelley was. I'd be willing to leave it to time for my real friends to find me out--I'd give up the department-store public to the authors who wanted it. And then, too, I could sell my books cheaply, so that the poor could get them. I always shudder to think that the people who most need what I write will have it kept away from them, because I am holding it back to make a profit!"

"We must do that some day!" declared Corydon.

"We must live very simply," he said, "so we can begin it soon. Perhaps we can do it with the money we get from this first book. We could get everything we need for a thousand dollars a year, and save the balance."

The other assented to this.

"I've got the prospectus of my publishing-house all written," Thyrsis went on. "And I've several other plans worked out--people would laugh if they saw them, I guess. But before I get through, I'm going to have a reading-room where anyone can come and get my books. It'll be down where the poor people are; and I'm going to have travelling libraries, so as to reach people in the country. That is the one hope for better things, as I see it--we must get ideas to the people!"

Thus discoursing, they strolled back to the home of Thyrsis' mother, and he went in to get his belongings together. Corydon went with him; and as they entered, the mother said, "There's an express package for you."

So Thyrsis went to his room, and saw a flat package lying on the bed. He stared at it, startled, and then picked it up and read the label upon it. "Why--why!--" he gasped; and then he seized a pair of scissors and cut the string and opened it. It was his manuscript!

With trembling fingers he turned it over. There was a letter with it, and he snatched it up. "We regret," it read, "that we cannot make you an offer for the publication of your book. Thanking you for the privilege of examining it, we are very truly yours." And that was all!

"They've rejected the book!" gasped Thyrsis; and the two stared at each other with consternation and horror in their eyes.

That was a possibility that had never occurred to Thyrsis in his wildest moment. That anyone in his senses could reject that book! That anyone could read a single chapter of it and not see what it was!

"They only had it five days!" he exclaimed; and instantly an explanation flashed across his mind. "I don't believe they read it!" he cried. "I don't believe they ever looked at it!"

But, read or unread, there was the manuscript--rejected. There was no appeal from the decision; there was no explanation, no apology--they had simply rejected it! It was like a blow in the face to Thyrsis; he felt like a woman whose love is spurned.

"Oh the fools! The miserable fools!" he cried.

But he could not bring much comfort to his soul by that method. The seriousness of it remained. The publishing-house was one of the largest and most prosperous in the country; and if they were fools, how many more fools might there not be among those who stood between him and the public? And if so, what would he do?

Section 6. So these two began their life under the shadow of a cloud. At the very first hour, when they should have been all rapture, there had come into the chamber of their hearts this grisly spectre--that was to haunt them for so many years!

But they clenched their hands grimly, and put the thought aside, and moved their worldly goods to the two tiny rooms. When they had got their trunks in, there was no place to sit save on the beds; and though Corydon had cast away all superfluities for this pilgrimage, still it was a puzzle to know where to put things.

But what of that--they were together at last! What an ecstasy it was to be actually unpacking, and to be mingling their effects! A kind of symbol it was of their spiritual union, so that the most commonplace things became touched with meaning. Thyrsis thrilled when the other brought in an armful of books to him--all this wealth was to be added to his store! He owned no books himself, save a few text-books, and some volumes of poetry that he knew by heart. Other books he had borrowed all his life from libraries; and he often thought with wonder that there were people who would pay a dollar or two for a book which they did not mean to read but once!

Also there were a hundred trifles which came from Corydon's trunk, and which whispered of the intimacies of her life; the pictures she put upon her bureau, the sachet-bags that went into the drawer, the clothing she hung behind the door. It disturbed him strangely to realize how close she was to be to him from now on.

And then, the excursion to the corner-grocery, and the delight of the plunge into housekeeping! A pound of butter, and some salt and pepper, and a bunch of celery; a box of "chipped beef", and a dozen eggs, and a quart of potatoes; and then to the baker's, for rolls and sponge-cakes--did ever a grocer and a baker sell such ecstasies before? They carried it all home, and while Corydon scrubbed the celery in the bath-room, Thyrsis got out his chafing-dish and set the beef and eggs to sizzling, and they sat and sniffed the delicious odors, and meantime munched at rolls and butter, because they were so hungry they could not wait.

What an Elysian festivity they made of it! And then to think that they would have three such picnics every day! To be sure, the purchases had taken one half of Thyrsis' remaining capital; but then, was it not just that spice of danger that gave the keen edge to their delight? What was it that made the sense of snugness and intimacy in their little retreat, save the knowledge of a cold and hostile world outside?

The next morning Thyrsis took his manuscript to another publisher, and then they went at their work. Corydon laughed aloud with delight as they began the German--for what were all its terrors now, when she had Thyrsis for a dictionary! They fairly romped through the books. In the weeks that followed they read "Werther" and "Wilhelm Meister" and "Wahlverwandschaften"; they read "Undine" and "Peter Schlemil" and the "Leben eines Taugenichts"; they read Heine's poems, and Auerbach's and Freitag's novels, and Wieland's "Oberon"--is there anybody in Germany who still reads Wieland's "Oberon?" Surely there must somewhere be young couples who delight in "Der Trompeter von Sekkingen," and laugh with delight over "der Kater Hidigeigei!"

Also they went at music. Corydon had been taught to play as many "pieces" as the average American young lady; but Thyrsis had tried to persuade her to a new and desperate emprise--he insisted that there was nothing to music until one had learned to read it at sight. So now, every day when their landlady had gone out, he moved his music-stand into the little parlor, and they went at the task. Thyrsis proposed to achieve it by a *tour de force*--the way to read German was to read it, and the way to read music was to read music. He would set up a piece they had never seen before, and they would begin; and he would pound out the time with his foot, and make Corydon keep up with him--even though she was only able to get one or two notes in each bar, still she must keep up with him. At first this was agony to her--she wanted to linger and get some semblance of the music; but Thyrsis would scold and exhort and shout, and pound out the time.

And so, to Corydon's own amazement, it was not many weeks before she found that she was actually reading music, that they were playing it together. In this way they learned Haydn's and Mozart's sonatas, they even adventured Beethoven's trios, with the second violin left out. Then Thyrsis subscribed to a music-library, and would come home twice a week with an armful of new stuff, good and bad. And whenever in all their struggles with it they were able to achieve anything that really moved them as music, what a rapture it brought them!

Section 7. This was indeed the nearest they could ever come to creative achievement together; this was the one field in which their abilities were equal. In all other things there were disharmonies--they came upon many reefs and shoals in these uncharted matrimonial seas.

Thyrsis was swift and impatient, and had flung away all care about external things; and here was Corydon, a woman, with all a woman's handicaps and disabilities. She was like a little field-mouse in her care of her person--she must needs scrub herself minutely every morning, and have hot water for her face every night; her hair had to be braided and her nails had to be cared for--and oh, the time it took her to get her clothes on, or even to get ready for the street! She would struggle like one possessed to accomplish it more quickly, while Thyrsis chafed and growled and agonized in the next room. There was nothing he could do meantime--for were they not going to do everything together?

Then there was another stumbling-block--the newspapers! Thyrsis had to know what was going on in the world. He had learned to read the papers and magazines like an exchange-editor; his eye would fly from column to column, and he would rip the insides out of one in two or three minutes. To Corydon it was agony to see him do this, for it took her half an hour to read a newspaper. She besought him to read it out loud--and was powerless to understand the distress that this caused him. He stood it as long as he could, and then he took to marking in the papers the things that she needed to know; and this he continued to do religiously, until he had come to realize that Corydon never remembered anything that she read in the papers.

This was something it took him years to comprehend; there were certain portions of the ordinary human brain which simply did not exist in his wife. She had lived eighteen years in the world, and it had never occurred to her to ask how steam made an engine go, or what was the use of the little glass knobs on the telegraph-poles. And it was the same with politics and business, and with the thousand and one personalities of the hour. When these things came up, Thyrsis would patiently explain to her what she needed to know; and he would take it for granted that she would pounce upon the information and stow it away in her mind--just as he would have done in a similar case. But then, two or three weeks later, the same topic would come up, and he would see a look of sudden terror come into Corydon's eyes--she had forgotten every word of it!

He came, after a long time, to honor this ignorance. People had to bring some real credentials with them to win a place in Corydon's thoughts; it was not enough that they were conspicuous in the papers. And it was the same with facts of all sorts; science existed for Corydon only as it pointed to beauty, and history existed only as it was inspiring. They read Green's "History of the English People" in the evenings; and every now and then Corydon would have to go and plunge her face into cold water to keep her eyes open, The long parliamentary struggle was utter confusion to her--she had no joy to watch how "freedom slowly broadens down from precedent to precedent." But once in a while there would come some story, like that Of Joan of Arc--and there would be the girl, with her hands clenched, and hot tears in her eyes, and the fires of martyrdom blazing in her soul!

These were the hours which revealed to Thyrsis the treasure he had won--

the creature of pure beauty whose heart was in his keeping. He was humbled and afraid before her; but the agony of it was that he could not dwell in those regions of joy with her--he had to know about stupid things and vulgar people, he had to go out among them to scramble for a living. So there had to be a side to his mind that Corydon could not share. And it did not suffice just to tolerate the existence of such things--he had to be actively interested in them, and to take their point of view. How else could he hold his place in the world, how could he win in the struggle for life?

This, he strove to persuade himself, was the one real difficulty between them, the one thing that marred the perfection of their bliss. But as time went on, he came to suspect that there was something else--something even more vital and important. It seemed to him that he had given up that which was the chief source of his power--his isolation. The center of his consciousness had been shifted outside of himself; and try as he would, he could never get it back. Where now were the hours and hours of silent brooding? Where were the long battles in his own soul? And what was to take he place of them--could conversation do it, conversation no matter how interesting and worth while? Thyrsis had often quoted a saying of Emerson's, that "people descend to meet." And when one was married did not one have to descend all the time?

He reasoned the matter out to himself. It was not Corydon's fault, he saw clearly; it would have been the same had he married one of the seraphim. He did not want to live the life of any seraph--he wanted to live his own life. And was it not obvious that the mere physical proximity of another person kept one's attention upon external things? Was not one inevitably kept aware of trivialities and accidents? Thyrsis had an ideal, that he should never permit an idle word to pass his lips; and now he saw how inevitably the common-place crept in upon them--how, for instance, their conversation had a way of turning to personality and jesting. Corydon was sensitive to external things, and she kept him aware of the fact that his trousers were frayed and his hair unkempt, and that other people were remarking these things.

Such was marriage; and it made all the more difference to an author, he reasoned, because an author was always at home. Thyrsis had been accustomed, when he opened his eyes in the morning, to lie still and let images and fancies come trooping through his mind; he would plan his whole day's work in that way, while his fancy was fresh and there was nothing to disturb him. But now he had to get up and dress, thus scattering these visions. In the same way, he had been wont to walk and meditate for hours; but now he never walked alone. That meant incidentally that he no longer got the exercise he needed--because Corydon could never walk at his pace. And if this was the case with such external things, how much more was it the case with the strange impulses of his inmost soul! Thyrsis was now like a hunter, who starts a deer, and instead of putting spurs to his horse and following it, has to wait to summon a companion--and meanwhile, of course, the deer is gone!

From all this there was but one deliverance for them, and that was music. Music was their real interest, music was their religion; and if only they could go on and grow in it--if only they could acquire technique enough to live their lives in it! This would take years, of course; but they did not mind that, they were willing to work every day until they were exhausted--if only the world would give them a chance! But alas, the world did not seem to be minded that way.

Section 8. Thyrsis had waited a week, and then written the second publisher, and received a reply to the effect that at least two weeks were needed for the consideration of a manuscript. And meantime his last penny was gone, and he was living on Corydon's money. It was clear that he must earn something at once; and so he had to leave her to study and practice in her own room, while he cudgelled his brains and tormented his soul with hack-work.

He tried his verses again; but he found that the spring had dried up in him. Life was now too sombre a thing, the happy spontaneous jingles came no more. And what he did by main force of will sounded hollow and vapid to him--and must have sounded so to the editors, who sent them back.

Then he tried book-reviewing; but oh, the ghastly farce of book-reviewing! To read futile writing and sham writing of a hundred degrading varieties--and never dare to utter a truth about them! To labor instead to put one's self in the place of the school-girl reader and the tired shop-clerk reader and the sentimental married-woman reader, and imagine what they would think about the book, and what they would like to have said about it! To take these little pieces of dishonesty to an office, and sit by trembling while they were read, and receive two dollars apiece for them if they were published, and nothing at all if one had been so lacking in cunning as to let the editor think that the book was not worth the space!

However, Thyrsis had cunning enough to earn the cost of his room and his food for two weeks more. Then one day the postman brought him a letter, the inscription of which made his heart give a throb. He ripped the envelope open and read a communication from the second publisher:

"We have been interested in your manuscript, and while we do not feel that we can undertake its publication, we should like an opportunity to talk with you about it."

"What does *that* mean?" asked Corydon, trembling.

"God knows," he answered. "I'll go and see them this morning."

When he came back, it was to sink into a chair and stare in front of him with a savage frown. "Don't ask me!" he said, to Corydon. "Don't ask!"

"Please tell me!" cried the girl. "Did you see them?"

"Yes," said Thyrsis--"I saw a fat man!"

"A fat man!"

"Yes--a fat man. A fat body, and a fat mind, and a fat soul."

"Please tell me, Thyrsis!"

"He said my book wouldn't sell, because the public had got tired of that sort of thing."

"That sort of thing!"

"It seems that people used to buy 'historical romances', and now they've stopped. The man actually thought my book was one of that kind!"

"I see. But then--couldn't you tell him?"

"I told him. I said, 'Can't you see that this book is original--that it's come out of a man's heart?' 'Yes,' he said, 'perhaps. But you can't expect the public to see it.' And so there you are!"

Thyrsis sat with his nails dug into his palms. "It's just like the book-reviews!" he cried. "He knows better, but that doesn't count--he's thinking about the public! And he's got to the point where he doesn't really care--he's a fat man!"

"And so he'll not publish the book?"

"He'll not have anything more to do with me. He hates me."

"*Hates* you?"

"Yes. Because I have faith, and he hasn't! Because I wouldn't stoop to the indignity he offered!"

"What did he offer?"

"He says that what the public's reading now is society novels--stories about up-to-date people who are handsome and successful and rich. They want automobiles and theatre-parties and country-clubs in their novels."

"But Thyrsis! You don't know anything about such things!"

"I know. But he said I could find out. And so I could. The point he made was that I've got passion and color--I could write a moving love-story! In other words, I could use my ecstasy to describe two society-people mating!"

There was a pause. "And what did you do with the manuscript?" asked Corydon, in a low voice.

"I took it to another publisher," he answered.

"And what are you going to do now?"

"I've been to see the editor of the 'Treasure Chest.'"

The "Treasure Chest" was a popular magazine of fiction, a copy of which Thyrsis had seen lying upon the table of their landlady. He had glanced through the first story, and had declared to Corydon that if he had a stenographer he could talk such a story at the rate of twenty thousand words a day.

"And did the editor see you?"

"Yes. He's a big husky 'advertising man'--he looks like a prize-fighter. He said if I could write, to go ahead and prove it. He pays a cent for five words--a hundred dollars for a complete serial. He pays on acceptance; and he said he'd read a scenario for me. So I'm going to try it."

"What's it to be about?" asked Corydon.

"I'm going to try what they call a 'Zenda' story," said Thyrsis. "The editor says the readers of the 'Treasure Chest' haven't got tired of 'Zenda' stories."

And so Thyrsis spent the afternoon and evening wandering about in the park; and sometime after midnight he wrote out his scenario. The advantage of a "Zenda" story was that, as the adventures happened in an imaginary kingdom, there would be no need to study up "local color". As for the conventional artificial dialect, he could get it from any of the "romances" in the nearby circulating library. He did not dare to take the scenario the next day, but waited a decent interval; and when he returned it was to report that the story was considered to be promising, and that he was to write twenty thousand words for a test.

Section 9. So Thyrsis shut himself up and went to work. Sometimes he wrote with rage seething in his heart, and sometimes with laughter on his lips. This latter was the case when he did the love-scenes--because of the "passion and color" he bestowed upon the fascinating countess and the clever young American engineer. He could have written the twenty thousand words in three days; but he waited ten days, so that the editor might not think that he was careless. And three days later he went back for the verdict.

The editor said it was good, and that if the rest was like it he would accept the story. So Thyrsis went to work again, and finished the manuscript, and put it away until time enough had elapsed. And meanwhile came a letter from the literary head of the third publishing-house, regretting that he could not accept the book.

It was such a friendly letter that Thyrsis went to call there, and met a pleasant and rather fine-souled gentleman, Mr. Ardsley by name, who told him a little about the problems he faced in life.

"You have a fine talent," he said--"you may even have genius. Your book is obviously sincere--it's *vecu,* as the French say. I suspect you must have been in love when you wrote it."

"In a way," said Thyrsis, flushing slightly. He had not intended that to show.

The other smiled. "It's overwrought in places," he went on, "and it tends to incoherency. But the main trouble is that it's entirely over the heads of the public. They don't know anything about the kind of love you're interested in, and they'd laugh at it."

"But then, what am I to do?" cried Thyrsis.

"You'll simply have to keep on trying, till you happen to strike it."

"But--how am I to live?"

"Ah," said Mr. Ardsley, "that is the problem." He smiled, rather sadly, as he sat watching the lad. "You see how *I've* solved it," he went on. "I was young once myself, and I tried to write novels. And in those days I blamed the publishers--I thought they stood in my way. But now, I see how it is; a publisher is engaged in a highly competitive business, and he barely makes interest on his capital; he can't afford to publish books that won't pay their way. Here am I, for instance--it's my business to advise this house; and if I advise them wrongly, what becomes of me? If I take them your manuscript and say, 'It's a real piece of work,' they'll ask me, 'Will it pay its way?' And I have to answer them, 'I don't think it will.'"

"But such things as they publish!" exclaimed the boy, wildly.

And Mr. Ardsley smiled again. "Yes," he said. "But they pay their way. In fact, they save the business."

So Thyrsis went out. He saw quite clearly now the simple truth--it was not a matter of art at all, but a matter of business. It was a business-world, and not an art-world; and he--poor fool--was trying to be an artist!

For three days more he toiled at his pot-boiler; and then, late at night, he went out to get some fresh air, and to try to shake off the load of despair that was upon him. And so came the explosion.

Perhaps it was because the wind was blowing, and Thyrsis loved the wind; it was a mirror of his own soul to him, incessant and irresistible and mysterious. And so his demons awoke again. He had gone through all that labor, he had built up all that glory in his spirit--and it was all for naught! He had made himself a flame of desire--and now it was to be smothered and stifled!

He had written his book, and it was a great book, and they knew it. But all they told him was to go and write another book--and to do pot-boilers in the meantime! But that was impossible, he could not do it. He would win with the book he had written! He would make them hear him--he would make them read that book!

He began to compose a manifesto to the world; and towards morning he came home and shut himself in and wrote it. He called it "Business and Art;" and in it he told about his book, and how he had worked over it. He told, quite frankly, what the book was; and he asked if there was anywhere in the United States a publisher who published books because they were noble, and not because they sold; or if there was a critic, or booklover, or philanthropist, or a person of any sort, who would stand by a true artist. "This artist will work all day and nearly all night," he wrote, "and he wants less than the wages of a day-laborer. All else that ever comes to him in his life he will give for a chance to follow his career!"

Then Corydon awoke, and he read it to her. She listened, thrilling with amazement.

"Oh, Thyrsis!" she cried. "What are you going to do with it?"

"I'm going to have it printed," he said, "and send it to all the publishers; and also to literary men and to magazines."

"And are you going to sign your name to it?" she cried.

"I've already signed my name to it," he answered.

"And when are you going to do it?"

"As soon as the book comes back from the next publisher."

Then he sat down to breakfast; and afterwards, without resting, he finished the pot-boiler, and took it to the editor. After a due interval he went again, trembling and faint with anxiety. He had sold only one book-review, and he was using Corydon's money again. People who hated him had predicted that he would do just that, and he had answered that he would die first!

He came home, radiant with delight. "He says he'll take it!" he proclaimed. "Only I've got to do a new ending for the fourth installment--he wants something more exciting. So I'm going to have the countess caught in a burning tower!"

And he wrote that, and went yet again, and came home with a hundred dollars buttoned tightly in his inside vest-pocket. He was like a man who has escaped from a dungeon. The field was clear before him at last! His manifesto was going out to the world!

BOOK V
THE BAIT IS SEIZED

They sat, gazing down the slope of the little vale. She was turning idly the pages of the book, and she read to him--

"Lovely all times she lies, lovely to-night!--
  Only, methinks, some loss of habit's power
    Befalls me wandering through this upland dim.
  Once pass'd I blindfold here, at any hour;
    Now seldom come I, since I came with him."

"It was here we first read the poem," he said. "Every spot brings back some line of it."

"Even the old oak-tree where we used to sit," she smiled--

"Hear it, O Thyrsis, still our tree is there!"

Section 1. Thyrsis was half hoping that the next publisher would decline the manuscript; and he was only mildly stirred when he got a letter saying that although the publisher could not make an offer for the book, one of his readers was so much interested in it that he would like to have a talk with the author. Thyrsis replied that he was willing; and to his surprise he learned that the reader was none other than that Prof. Osborne, who in the university had impressed upon him his ignorance of the art of writing.

He paid a call at the professor's home, and they had a long talk. There was nothing said about their former interview. Evidently the other recognized that Thyrsis had succeeded in making good his claim to be allowed to hew his own way; and Thyrsis was content with that tacit surrender.

They talked about the book. The professor first assured him that it would not sell, and then went on to explain to him why; and so they came to a grapple.

"The thing is sincere, perhaps even exalted," said Prof. Osborne; "but it's over-strained and exaggerated."

"But isn't it alive?" asked Thyrsis.

The other pondered; he always spoke deliberately, choosing his words with precision. "Some people might think so," he said. "For myself, I have never known any such life."

"But what's that got to do with it?" cried Thyrsis.

"It has much to do with it--for me. One has to judge by what one knows--"

"But can't one be taught?"

The professor meditated again. "I have lived forty-five years," he said, "and you have lived less than half that. I imagine that I have read more, studied more, thought more than you. Yet you ask me to submit myself to your teaching!"

"No, no!" cried Thyrsis, eagerly. "It is not as if it were a matter of learning--of scholarship--of knowledge of the world. There is an intensity of experience that is not dependent upon time; in the things of the imagination--in matters of inspiration--surely one does not have to be old or learned."

"That might be true," admitted the other, hesitatingly.

"You read the poetry of Keats or Shelley, for instance. They were as young as I am when they wrote it, and yet you do not refuse to acknowledge its worth. Is it just because they are dead, and their poems are classics?"

So these two wrestled it out. Thyrsis could bring the other to the point of acknowledging that there might be genius in his work, but he could not bring him to the point of *doing* anything about it. The poet went away, seeing the situation quite clearly. Prof. Osborne was an instructor; it was his business to know; and if he should abdicate before one of his pupils, then what would become of authority? He had certain models, which he set before his class; these models constituted literature. If anyone might disregard them and proceed to create new models according to his own lawless impulse--then what anarchy would reign in a classroom! Under such circumstances, it was remarkable that the professor had even been willing to admit of doubts; as Thyrsis walked home he clenched his hands and whispered to himself, "I'll get that man some day!"

Section 2. The road now lay clear before Thyrsis, and accordingly he set grimly to work. He had his document printed upon a long slip of paper, and got several packages for Corydon to address. And one evening they took them out and dropped them into the mailbox. "And now we'll see!" he said.

They soon saw. When he came in for lunch the next day, Corydon came to the door, in great excitement. "S-sh!" she whispered. "There's a reporter here!"

"A reporter!" he echoed.

"Yes--a woman."

"What does she want?"

"She wants an interview about the book."

"Where is she from?"

"She's from the 'Morning Howl'. She's read the circular."

"But I never sent it there!"

"I know; but she says a friend gave it to her. She knows all about it."

So Thyrsis went in, like a lamb to the slaughter. He was new to interviews, and he yielded to the graces of the friendly and sympathetic lady. Yes, he would be glad to tell about his book; and about where and how he had written it, and all the hopes he had based upon it.

"And your wife tells me you've just been married!" said the lady, with a winning smile, and she proceeded to question him about this. They had become good friends by that time, and Thyrsis told her many things that he would not have told save to a charming lady. And then she asked for his picture, explaining that she could give so much more space to the "story" if she had one. And then she begged for a picture of Corydon, and was deeply hurt that she could not have it.

She prolonged the interview for an hour or so, and came back again and again in the effort to get this picture of Corydon. Finally she rose to go; but out in the hall, as she was bidding them good-bye, she suddenly exclaimed that she had left her gloves, and went back and got them, and then hurried away. And it was not until an hour or two later that Thyrsis made the horrible discovery that the photograph of Corydon which had stood upon his bureau was standing upon his bureau no longer!

So next morning, there were their two photographs upon the second page of the 'Morning Howl', and a, two-column headline:

"YOUTHFUL GENIUS OFFERS HIMSELF FOR SALE!"

Thyrsis rushed through this article, writhing with horror and dismay. The woman had made him into what they called a "human interest" feature. There was very little about his book, but there was much about the picturesque circumstances under which he had written it. There was a description of their personal appearance-- of Corydon's sweet face and soulful black eyes, and of his broad forehead and sensitive lips. There was also a complete description of their domestic *menage*, including the chafing-dish and the odor of lamb-chops. There was a highly diverting account of how they had "eloped" with only eight dollars in the world; together with all the agonies of their parents, as imagined by the sympathetic lady.

They had been butchered to make a holiday for the readers of a yellow journal! "This is a wonderfully interesting world," the paper seemed to say--"well worth the penny it costs to read about it! Here on the first page is Antonio Petronelli, who cut up his sweetheart with a butcher-knife, and packed her in a trunk. And here are seven people burned in a tenement-house; and an interview with Shrike, the plunger, who made three millions out of the wheat-corner. But most diverting of all are these two little cherubs who ran away and got married, and now want the world to support them while they write masterpieces of literature!"

And could not one see the great public devouring the tale--the Wall Street clerks in the cars, and the shop-girls over their sandwiches and coffee, and the loungers in the cafes of the Tenderloin! Could not one picture their smiles--not contemptuous, but genial, as of people who have learned that it is indeed an interesting world, and well worth the penny it costs to read about it!

Section 3. Corydon shed tears of rage over this humiliation, and she wrote a letter full of bitter scorn to the newspaper woman. In reply to it came a friendly note to the effect that she had done the best thing in the world for them--that when they knew more about life and the literary game, they would recognize this!

The tangible results of the adventure were three. First there came a letter, written on scented note-paper, from a lady who commended their noble ideals and wished them success--but who did not sign her name. Second, there came a visit from a brother poet--a man about forty years of age, shabby and pitiful, with watery, light blue eyes and a feeble straggly moustache, and a manner of agonized diffidence. He stood in the doorway and shifted from one foot to the other, and explained that he had read the article, and had come because he, too, was an un-recognized genius. He had written two volumes of poetry, which were the great-est poetry ever produced in English--Milton and Shakespeare would be forgotten when the world had read these volumes. For ten years he had been trying to find some publisher or literary man to recognize him; and perhaps Thyrsis would be the man.

He came in and sat on the bed and unwrapped his two volumes--several hun-dred typewritten pages, elaborately bound up in covers of faded pink silk. And Thyrsis read one and Corydon the other, while the poet sat by and watched them and twisted his hands nervously. His poetry was all about stars and blue-bells and moonlight, about springtime and sighing lovers, about cold, rain-beaten graves and faded leaves of autumn--the subjects and the images which have been the stock in trade of minor poets for two thousand years and more. Thyrsis, as he read, could have marked fifty phrases which were feeble imitations of things in Tennyson and Longfellow and Keats; and he read for half an hour, in the vain hope of finding a single vigorous line.

This interview was a very painful one. He could not bear to hurt the poor crea-ture's feelings, and he did not know how to get rid of him. The matter was made still more difficult by the presence of Corydon, who did not know the models, and therefore thought the poetry was good. She let the visitor go on to pour out his heart; until at last came a climax that Thyrsis had been expecting all along. The man explained that he was a bookkeeper, out of work, and with a wife and three children on the verge of starvation; and then he tried to borrow some money from them!

The third result was the important one. It was a letter from a publishing-house.

"We are on the lookout for vital and worth-while books," it read, "and we are not afraid to venture. We have been much interested in the account of your work, and we should be very glad if you would give us a chance to read it immediately."

Thyrsis had never heard of this publishing-house, but that did not chill his delight. He hurried downtown with the manuscript, and came back to report. The concern was lodged in two small rooms in an obscure office-building. The manager, a Mr. Taylor, was a man not particularly prepossessing in appearance, but he was a person of intelligence, and was evidently interested in the book. Moreover he had promised to read it at once.

And that same week came the reply--a reply which set the two almost beside themselves with happiness. "I have read your manuscript," wrote Mr. Taylor. "And I have no hesitation in pronouncing it a work of genius. In fact, I am not sure but what it is the greatest piece of literature it has ever been my fortune as a publisher to come upon. It is vital, and passionately sincere, and I will stake my reputation upon the prophecy that it will be an instantaneous success. I hope that we may become the publishers of it, and will be glad if you will come to see me at once and talk over terms."

Thyrsis read this aloud; and then he caught Corydon in his arms, and tears of joy and relief ran down her cheeks.

He went to see the publisher, and for ten or fifteen nunutes he listened to such a panegyric upon his book as made his cheeks burn. Visions of freedom and triumph rose before him--he had come into his own at last. An then Mr. Taylor proceeded to outline his business proposition--and as Thyrsis realized the nature of it, it was as if he had been suddenly plunged into an Arctic sea. The man wanted him to pay one-half the cost of the plates of his book, and in addition to guarantee to take one hundred copies at the wholesale price of ninety cents per copy!

"Is that--is that customary in publishing?" asked the other.

"Not always," Mr. Taylor replied; "but it is our custom. You see, we are an unusual sort of publishing-house. We do not run after the best-sellers and the trash--we publish real books, books with a mission and a message for the world. And we advertise them widely --we make the world heed them; and so we feel justified in asking the author to help us with a part of the expense. We pay ten per cent. royalty, of course, and in addition the author has the hundred copies of his book, which he can sell to friends and others if he wishes."

"What would it cost for my book?" Thyrsis asked.

And the man figured it up and told him it could be done for about two hundred and fifty dollars. "I'll make it two hundred and twenty-five to you," he said--"just because of my interest in your future."

But Thyrsis only shook his head sadly. "I wish I could do it," he said, "but I simply haven't the money--that's all."

And so he took his departure, and carried his manuscript to another publisher, and then went home, crushed and sick.

Section 4. But the more Thyrsis thought of this plan, the more it came to possess him. If he could only get that book printed, it could not fail to make its impression! He had thought many times in his desperation of trying to publish it himself; and if he did that, he would have to pay the cost of the plates, of the printing and everything; whereas by this method he could get it for much less, and would have a hundred copies which he could send to critics and men of letters, in order to make certain of the book's being read.

When the manuscript came back from the next publisher, with a formal note of rejection, Thyrsis made up his mind that he would concentrate his efforts upon this plan. So he got down to another pot-boiler.

An old sea-captain had told him a story of some American college boys who had stolen a sacred idol in China. Thyrsis saw a plot in that, and the editor of the "Treasure Chest" considered it a "bully" idea. So he toiled day and night for a couple more weeks, and earned another hundred dollars. And then he did something he had never done in his life before--he went to some relatives to beg. He pleaded how hard he had worked, and what a chance he had; he would pay back the money out of the first royalties from the book--which could not possibly fail to earn the hundred dollars he asked for.

Besides this, he had some money left from his first story; and so he went to Mr. Taylor, who was affable and enthusiastic as ever, and paid his money and signed the contracts. He was told that his book would be ready for the spring-trade; which meant that he would have to possess his soul in patience for three months. Meantime he had forty dollars left--upon which he figured that he could have eight weeks of uninterrupted study.

But alas, for the best-laid plans of men! It was on a Tuesday morning that he paid out his precious two hundred and twenty-five dollars; and on the next Thursday morning, as he was glancing through the newspapers, he gave a cry of dismay.

"Corydon," he called. "What's the name of that lawyer, your trustee?"

"John C. Hammond," she replied.

"He shot himself in his office yesterday!" exclaimed Thyrsis; and he read her the account, which stated that Hammond had been speculating, and was believed to have lost heavily in the recent slump in cotton.

Corydon was staring at him with terror in her eyes. "What does it mean?" she cried.

"I don't know," said Thyrsis. "We'll have to inquire!"

They went out and telephoned to Corydon's father, and Thyrsis got hold of a college friend, a lawyer, and the four went to the office of the dead man. It was weeks before they became sure of the whole sickening truth, but they learned enough on that first day to make them fairly certain. John C. Hammond had got rid of everything--not only his own funds, but the funds belonging to the eight or ten heirs of the estate. The house in which he lived and everything in it was held in the name of his wife; and so there was not a penny to pay Corydon her four thousand dollars!

The girl was almost prostrated with misery; she vowed that she would go back to her parents, that she would go to work in an office. And poor Thyrsis could only hold her in his arms and whisper, "It doesn't matter, dear--it doesn't matter! The book will be out in the spring, and I can do pot-boilers for two!"

Section 5. But in the small hours of the night Thyrsis lay awake in his little room, and the soul within him was sick with horror. He was trapped--there was no use trying to dodge the fact, he was trapped! His powers were waning hour by hour, his vision was dying within him; every day he knew that he was weaker, that the grip of circumstance was tighter upon him. Ah, the hideous cruelty of the thing--it was like a murder in the night-time, like a torturing in some secret dungeon! He was burning up with his inward fires--there was a new book coming to ripeness within him, a book that would be greater even than his first one. And he could not write it, he could not even think about it! And there was the soul of Corydon calling to him, there were all the heights of music and poetry--and instead of climbing, he must torture his brain with hack-writing! He must go down to the editors, and fawn and cringe, and try to get books to review; he must study the imbecilities of the magazines and watch out for topics for articles; he must rack his brains for jokes and jingles--he, the master of life, the bearer of a new religion, the proud, high-soaring eagle, whose foot had never known a chain!

When such thoughts came to him, he would dig his nails into the palms of his hands, he would grit his teeth and curse the world. No, they should not conquer him! They should never bend him to their will! They might starve him, they might kill him--they might kill Corydon, also, but he would never give up! He would fight, and fight again, he would struggle to the last gasp--he would do his work, though all the powers of hell rose up to stop him!

One thing became clear to him that night, they could not afford two rooms. They must get along with one, and with the dollar and a half one at that. The steam-radiator had proved a farce, anyway--there was never any steam, and they had had to use gas-heaters. And now, what things Corydon could not get into his room, she would have to send back to her parents. The cost of the other room was the price of a book-review, and that sometimes meant a whole day of his precious time.

He talked it over with his wife, and she agreed with him. And so they under-went the humiliation of telling their landlady, and they obtained permission to keep Corydon's trunk in the hall, as there was no place for it in the tiny room. Such things as would not go upon the little dressing-stand, or hang behind the door, they put into boxes and shoved under the bed. And now, when midnight came, Thyrsis would go out for a walk while Corydon went to bed; and then he would come in and make his own bed upon the floor, with a quilt which the landlady had given them, and a pair of blankets they had borrowed from home, and his overcoat and some of Corydon's skirts when it was cold. Sometimes it would be very cold, and then he would have to sleep in his clothing; for there was no room save directly under the window, and they would not sleep with the window down. In the morning Corydon would turn her face to the wall while Thyrsis washed and dressed; and then he would go out and walk, while she took her turn.

And so he parted with the last shred of his isolation. He had to do all his work now with his wife in the room with him. And though she would sit as still as a mouse for hours, still he could not think as before; also, when she was worn out at night, he had to stop work and let her sleep. Under such circumstances it was small wonder that he was sometimes nervous and irritable; and, of course, there could be nothing hid between them, and when he was out of sorts, Corydon would be plunged into a bottomless pit of melancholy.

Then the strain and worry, and the night and day toil, began to have effects upon their health. Thyrsis had a strong constitution, but now he began to have headaches, and sometimes, if he worked on doggedly, they grew severe. He blamed this upon their heater; he knew little about hygiene, but he had studied physics, and he knew that a gas-heater devitalized the air. They had tried living in the room without heat, but in mid-winter they could not stand it. So on moderate days they would sit with the window up and their overcoats on; and when it was too cold for this, they would burn the heater for an hour or so, and when they began to feel the effects of the poisons, they would go out and walk for a while and let the room air.

But then again, Thyrsis wondered if the headaches might not be due to the food he was eating. They were anxious to economize on food; but they did not know just how to set about it. Thyrsis had read the world's literature in English, French and German, in Italian, Latin and Greek; but in none of that reading had he found anything about the care of his own body. Such subjects had not been taught at school or college or university, and he knew of no books about them. Both he and Corydon had come from families which had the traditions of luxurious living, brought down from old days when there were plenty of negro servants, and when the ladies had been skilled in baking and preserving, and the men with chafing-dish and punch-bowl. At his grandfather's table Thyrsis had been wont to see a great platter of fried chicken at one end, and a roast beef at the other, and a cold ham on a side table; and he had hot bread three times a day, and cake and jam and ice-cream- -and he had been taught to believe that such things were needed to keep up one's working-powers.

But now he had read how Thoreau had lived upon corn-meal mush; and he and Corydon resolved to patronize the less expensive foods. The price of meat and eggs and butter in the winter-time was in truth appalling; so they would buy potatoes and rice and corn-meal and prunes and turnips. They paid the landlady for the use of her gas-range, and would cook a sauce-pan full of some one of these things, and fill up with it three times a day. Then, at intervals, some one would invite them out to dinner; and because they were under-nourished they would gorge themselves-- which was evidently not an ideal method of procedure. So in the end Thyrsis made up his mind to consult a physician about it; and this was a visit he never forgot--for it led directly to the most momentous events of his whole lifetime.

Section 6. The doctor announced that he had a little dyspepsia, and gave him a bottle full of a red liquid that would digest his food. Also he warned him to eat slowly, and to rest after meals. And Thyrsis, after thanking him, had started to go; when the doctor, who was an old friend of both families, asked the question, "How's Corydon?"

"She's pretty well," said Thyrsis.

"And are you expecting any children yet?" asked the other, with a smile.

Thyrsis started. "Heavens, no!" he said.

"Why not?" asked the doctor.

"We aren't going to have any."

"But why? Are you preventing it?"

Thyrsis hesitated a moment. "We're not living that way," he said.

The doctor stared at him. "Come here, boy," he said, "and sit down."

Thyrsis obeyed.

"Now tell me what you mean," said the other.

"I mean that we--we're just brother and sister," said Thyrsis.

"But--why did you get married?"

"We got married because we wanted to study."

"To study what?"

"Well, everything--music, principally."

"And how long do you expect to keep that up?"

"Oh, for a good many years--until we've accomplished something, and until we've got some money."

And the doctor sank back and drew his breath. "I don't wonder your stomach's out of order!" he said.

"What do you mean?" asked Thyrsis.

But the man did not answer that question. Instead he asked, "Don't you realize what you'll do to Corydon?"

"What?"

"You'll wreck her whole life--her health, to begin with."

"But how, doctor? She's perfectly happy. It's what we both want to do."

"But doesn't she love you?"

"Why, yes--but not that way."

The doctor smiled. "How do you know?" he asked.

"Because--she's told me so."

"And if it was otherwise--do you think she'd tell you that?"

"Why, of course she would."

"My boy," said the man, "she'd die first!"

Thyrsis was staring at him, amazed.

"Let me tell you a little about a good woman," said the other. "I've been married for thirty years--really married, I mean; we've got five children. And in all those thirty years my wife has never made an advance of that sort to me!"

After which the doctor went on to expound his philosophy of sex. "Love is just a little thing to you," he said; "you've got your books and your career. And you want it to be the same with Corydon--you've succeeded in persuading her that that's what she wants also. You're going to make her a copy of yourself! But you simply can't do it, boy--she's a woman. And a woman's one interest in the world is love--it's everything in life to her, the thing she's made for. And if you deprive her of love, whole love, I mean, you wreck her entirely. Just now is the time when she ought to be having her children, if she's ever to have any--and you're trying to satisfy her with music and philosophy!"

"But," cried Thyrsis, horrified, "I know she doesn't feel that way at all!"

"Maybe not," said the other. "Her eyes are not opened. It's your business to open them. What are you a man for?"

"But--she's all right as she is---"

"Isn't she nervous?"

"Why, yes--perhaps---"

"Isn't she sometimes melancholy? And doesn't she like you to kiss her? Doesn't she show she's happy when you hold her in your arms."

Thyrsis sat mute.

"You see!" said the other, laughing. "The girl is in love with you, and you haven't sense enough to know it."

Again Thyrsis could find no words. "But if we had a child it would ruin us!" he cried, wildly. "I've not a cent, and my whole career's at stake!"

"Well," said the other, "if it's as bad as that, don't have any children yet."

"But--but how *can* we?"

"Don't you know how to control it?"

Thyrsis was staring at him, open-eyed. "Why, no!" he said.

"Good lord!" laughed the other. "Where have you been keeping yourself?"

And then the doctor proceeded to explain to him the "artificial sterilization of marriage." No whisper of such a thing had ever come to the boy before, and he could hardly credit his ears. But the doctor spoke of it as a man of the world, to whom it was a matter of course; he went into detail as to the various methods that people used. And when finally Thyrsis rose to leave he patted him indulgently on the shoulder, and laughed, "Go home to your wife, my boy!"

Section 7. The effect of this conversation upon Thyrsis was alarming to him. At first he tried to put the thing aside, as being something utterly inconceivable between him and Corydon. But it would not be put aside.

The doctor had planted his seed with cunning. If he had told Thyrsis that he was doing harm to himself, Thyrsis would have said that it was not true, and stood by it; for he knew about himself. But the man had made his statements about Corydon--and how could he be sure about Corydon?

The crucial point was that it set him to thinking about her in this new way; a way which he had not dreamed of previously. And when once he had begun to think about her so, he found he could not stop. For hitherto in his life, whenever he had thought of passion it had been as a temptation; he had known that it was wrong, and all that was best in him had risen up to oppose it. But now all that was changed--the image of Corydon the doctor had called up was one that broke down all resistance, and left him at the mercy of his impulses.

These impulses awoke--and with a suddenness and force that terrified him. He thought of her as his wife, and this thought was like a rush of flame upon him. His manhood leaped up, and cried aloud for its rights. He discovered, almost instantly, that he loved her thus, that he desired her completely. This was true now, and it had been true from the beginning; he had been a fool to try to persuade himself otherwise. What else had been the meaning of the passionate protests in his letters to her? Of the images he had used--of carrying her away in his arms, of breaking her to his will? And she loved him, too--she desired him completely! Why else had it been that those passages were precisely the ones that satisfied her? Why was it that she was always most filled with joy when he was aggressive and masterful?

Ah God, what an inhuman life it was they had been living all these months! In that inevitable proximity--shut up in a little room! And with the most intimate details of her life about him--with her kisses always upon his lips, her arms always about him, the subtle perfume of her presence always in his senses! Was it any wonder that they were nervous and restless--always sinking into tenderness, and exchanging endearments, and then starting up to scourge themselves?

He went home, and there was Corydon preparing supper. He went to her and caught her in his arms and kissed her. "I love you, sweetheart!" he whispered. And as she yielded to his embraces, he kissed her again and again, upon her lips and upon her cheeks and upon her neck. Ah, she loved him--else how could she let him kiss her like that!

But it was not so quickly that the inhibitions of a lifetime could be overcome. A sudden fear took hold of Thyrsis. What was he doing? No, she must have no idea of this--at least not until he had reasoned it out, until he had made up his mind that it was right.

So he drew back--and as he did so he noticed in her eyes a look of surprise. He did not often greet her in that way!

"I'm hungry as a bear," he said, to change the subject; and so they sat down to their supper.

Thyrsis had important writing to do that evening, and he tried his best, but he could not put his mind upon anything. He was all in a ferment. He pleaded that he had to think about his work, and went out for a long walk.

A storm was raging, and the icy gale beat upon him. It buffeted him, it flung him here and there; and he set himself to fight it, he drove his way through it, lusty and exultant. And music surged within him, lusty and exultant music. All the pent-up passion of his lifetime awoke in him, the blood ran hot in his veins; from some hidden portion of his being came wave after wave of emotion, sweeping him away--and he spread his wings to it, he rose to the heights upon it, he laughed and sang aloud in the glory of it. He had known such hours in his own soul's life, but never anything like it with Corydon. He cried out, what a child he had been! He had taken her, he had sought to shape her to his will; and he had failed, she was not yet his--and all because he had left unused the one great power he had over her, the one great hold he had upon her. But now it would be changed--she should have him! And as he battled on with the elements there came to him Goethe's poem of passion:

"Dem Schnee, dem Regen,   Dem Wind entgegen!"

Section 8. So for hours he went. But when he had come home, and stood in the vestibule, stamping the snow from him, there came a reaction. It was Corydon he had been thinking of--Corydon, the gentle and innocent! How could he say such things to her? How could he hint of them? Why, he would fill her with terror! It was not to be thought of!

He went upstairs, and found that she was asleep. So he crept into his little bunk; but sleep would not come to him. The image of her haunted him. He listened to her breathing--he was as close to her as that, and still she was not his!

It was nearly day before he slept, and so he awoke tired and restless. And then came rage at himself--he went out and walked again, and stormed and scolded. He would not permit this, he had work to do. And he made up his mind that he would not allow himself to think about the matter for three days. By that time the truth would be clearer to him; and he meant to settle this question with his reason, and not with his blind desire.

He adhered to his resolution firmly. But when the three days were past, and he tried to think about it, it was only to be swept away in another storm of emotion. It seemed that the more tightly he pent this river up, the fiercer was its rush when finally it broke loose. For always his will was paralyzed by that suggestion that he might be doing harm to Corydon!

At last he made up his mind that he must speak to her; and one afternoon he came and knelt beside her and put his arms about her. "Sweetheart," he said, "I've something to ask you about."

Now to Corydon the mind of Thyrsis was like an open book. For days she had known that something was disturbing him. But also she had known that he was not ready to tell her. "What is it?" she asked.

"It's something very important," he said.

"Yes, dear."

"You know, I went to see the doctor the other day."

"Yes."

"And he told me--he thinks we are doing each other harm by the way we are living."

"What way, Thyrsis?"

"By not being really married. He says you are suffering because of it."

"But Thyrsis!" she cried, in astonishment. "I'm not!"

"He says you wouldn't know it, Corydon. It would keep you nervous and up-set."

"But dear," she said, "I'm perfectly happy!"

"Are you sure of it?"

"Perfectly sure."

"And--and if it was ever otherwise--you would tell me?"

"Why, yes."

"And are you sure of *that*?"

She hesitated; and when she tried to answer, her voice was a whisper--"I think so, dear."

There was a pause. "Thyrsis," she exclaimed, suddenly, "I would have a child!"

"No, you needn't," he said; and he told her what the doctor had said.

It was quite as new to her as it had been to him, and even more startling. "I see," she said, in a low voice.

"Listen, Corydon," he whispered, "do you think you love me at all that way?"

"I don't know," she answered. "I never thought of such a thing."

"Do you think you could learn to love me so?"

"How can I tell, Thyrsis? It's so strange to me. It--it frightens me."

He looked up at her; and he saw that a flush was mottling her throat, and spreading over her cheeks. He saw the wild look in her eyes also; and he turned away.

"Very well, dearest," he said. "I don't want to disturb you."

So he tried to go back to his work. But he could not do his real work at all. He could practice the violin or read German with Corydon, but when he tried to plan his new book--that involved turning his thoughts loose to graze in a certain pasture, and they would not stay in that pasture, but jumped the fence and came back to her. And so he found himself taking more long journeys, in which he walked in the midst of the storm of his desire.

So, of course, all the former naturalness was gone between them. No longer could they kiss and toy with one another as children in a fairy-world. They had suddenly become man and woman--fighting the age-long duel of sex. They would talk about the question; and the more they talked about it, the more it came to dominate the thoughts of both of them; and this broke down the barriers between them--Thyrsis became bolder, and more open in his speech. He lost his awe of her maidenhood and her innocence--he wooed her, he lured her on; he rejoiced in his power to agitate her, to startle her, to speak to her about secret things. He would clasp her in his arms and shower his kisses upon her; and she would yield to him, almost fainting with bliss--and then shrink from him in sudden alarm.

Then he would go out into the night and battle again with the wintry winds. That frightened shrinking of hers puzzled him. Everything was so strange to him; and how could he be sure what was right? He wanted to do what was right, with all his soul he wanted it; if he were to do wrong, or to make her think less of him, he could never forgive himself all his life. But then would come the wild surge of his longing, and his man's power would cry out within him. It was his business to overcome her shrinking, to compel her to yield. The question of the doctor rang in his ears as a taunt--"Why are you a man?" Why *was* he a man?

Section 9. In the end these emotions reached a point where Thyrsis could no longer bear them. They were a torment to him, they deprived him of all rest and sleep. One afternoon he had held her a long time in his arms, and it hurt him; he turned away, and put his hands to his forehead. "Dearest," he cried, "I can't stand this any longer!"

"Why?" she asked. "What do you mean?"

"I mean it's just tearing me to pieces!"

She stared at him in fright. "Thyrsis!" she exclaimed. "You are unhappy!"

He sunk down upon the bed and hid his face in his arms. "Yes," he whispered, "I am unhappy!"

And so, all at once, he broke down her resistance. What had swayed him had been the thought of her suffering; and the thought of his suffering now conquered her.

Only she did not take days to debate it. She fled to him instantly, and wrapped her arms about him.

"Thyrsis," she whispered, "listen to me! I had no idea of that!"

"No, sweetheart," he said. "I'm sorry--I'm ashamed of myself--"

"No, no!" she cried, vehemently. "Don't say that! I love you, Thyrsis! I love you, heart and soul!"

He turned and gazed at her with his haggard eyes.

"I will do anything for you," she rushed on. "You shall have me! I will be your wife!"

Then, however, as he clasped her to him, there came once more the shrinking. "Only give me a little time, dear," she whispered. "Let me get used to it. Let it come naturally."

But the only way he could have given her time would have been to go away. Here he was, in her room--with every reminder of her about him, with every incitement to his desire. And he had but two things to choose between--to go out and walk and think about her, or to come home and sit with her and talk about their love.

They had their supper, and then again she was in his arms. He told her about this trouble--he showed how the love of her was consuming him. Far into the night they sat talking, and he poured out his heart to her, he bore her with him to the mountain-tops of his desire. He took down a book of Spenser's, and read her the "Epithalamium"; he read her Shelley's "Epip sychidion," which they both loved. All the power of Thyrsis' genius was turned now to passion, and the hidden forces of him were revealed as never had they been revealed to her before. He became eloquent; he talked to her as he had lived with himself; he awed her and frightened her, as he had that evening upon the hill-top. Then at last, as the tide of his feeling swept him away again, he clasped her to him tightly, and hid his face in her neck. "I love you! Oh, I love you!" he cried.

She had sunk back and closed her eyes. "My Thyrsis!" she whispered.

"You love me?" he asked. "You are quite sure?"

"I am quite sure!" she said.

He kissed her; again and again he kissed her, until he had made sure of her desire. Then suddenly, he began with trembling fingers to unfasten the neck of her dress.

For a moment she did not comprehend what he meant. Then she gave a start. "Thyrsis!" she cried.

And she sprang up, staring at him with fright in her eyes.

"What is it?" he asked.

"Thyrsis!" she gasped. "What--what were you going to do?"

And at her question, shame swept over him. He was horrified at himself. How could he find words to tell her what he had been going to do?

He turned away with a moan, and put his hands over his face. "Oh God, I can't stand this!" he exclaimed.

Suddenly he went to his hat and coat. "I must go out!" he said.

"What do you mean?" cried Corydon.

"I mean I've got to go somewhere!" he replied. "I can't stand it--I can't stay here."

"Thyrsis!" she cried, wildly. And she sprang to him and flung her arms about him. "No, no!" she cried. "No!"

"But what am I to do?"

"Wait! Wait!"

And she pressed him tightly to her. "Thyrsis!" she whispered. "Can't you un derstand? Don't be so stupid, dear!"

"Stupid!"

"Yes, sweetheart--can't you see? I'm only a child! And it's so strange! It frightens me! Try to realize how I feel!"

"But what am I to do?"

"Do? Why you must **make** me, Thyrsis!" And as she said this she hid her face upon his shoulder and sobbed. "You are a man, Thyrsis, you are a man, and I am only a girl! Do what you want to! Don't pay any attention to me!"

And those words to Thyrsis were like the crashing of a peal of thunder. He clutched her to him, with a force that crushed her, that made her cry out. The soul of the cave-man awoke in him--he lifted his mate in his arms and bore her away to a secret place.

"Put down the light," she whispered, and he did this. And then again he began to unfasten her dress.

She submitted at first, she let him have his way. But later, when his hands touched the soft garment on her bosom, he felt a sharp tremor pass through her.

"Thyrsis!" she whispered.

"What is it?" he asked.

"Wait dear, wait!"

"Why wait?" he cried.

"Just a moment--please, dear!"

But he answered her--"No! Not a moment! No!"

She clung to him, trembling, pleading. "Please, dearest, please! I'm afraid, Thyrsis."

But nothing could stop him now. She was his--his to do what he pleased with! And he would bend her to his will! The voice of his manhood shouted aloud to him now, and it was like the clashing of wild cymbals in his soul.

He went on with what he was doing. She shrunk away from him, but he followed her, he held her fast.

Then she began to sob--"Oh Thyrsis, wait--spare me! I can't bear it! No, Thyrsis--no!"

But he answered her, "Be still! I love you! You are mine." And for every sob and every shudder and every moan of fear he had but one response--"I love you! You are mine!"

He knew that he loved her now--and he knew what his love meant. Before this they had been strangers; but now he would penetrate to the secret places, to the holy of holies of her being.

Never in all his life had Thyrsis known woman. To him woman had been the supreme mystery of life, a creature of awe and sacredness--not to be handled, scarcely even to be thought about. Now the awful ban was lifted, the barriers were down; what had been hidden was revealed, what had been forbidden was permitted. So all the chained desire of a lifetime drove him on; it was almost more than he could bear. The touch of her warm breasts, the faint perfume of her clothing, the pressure of her soft, white limbs--these things set every nerve of him a-tremble, they turned a madness loose in him. A blinding whirl of emotion seized him, he was like a leaf swept away in a gale; his words came now in wild sobs, "I love you! I love you!"

So with quivering fingers he stripped her before him; and she crouched there, cowering and weeping. He took her in his arms; and that clasp there was no misunderstanding, for all the mastery of his will was in it. Nor did she try to resist him--she lay still, but shaking like a leaf, and choking with sobs. And so it was that he wreaked his will upon her.

Section 10. And then came the reaction--the most awful experience of his life. Thyrsis was sitting upon the bed, and staring in front of him, dazed. He was exhausted, faint, shuddering with horror. "Oh, my God, my God!" he whispered.

What had he done? Corydon, the gentle and pure--she had trusted herself to him, and how had he treated her? He had tortured her, he had defiled her! Oh, it was sickening; brutal, like a butchery! He sunk down in a heap, moaning, "My God! I can't bear it! I can't bear it!"

And then a strange thing happened--the strangest of all strange things! An unforeseeable, an unimaginable thing!

Corydon had started up, and was listening; and now suddenly he felt her arms stealing about him. "Thyrsis!" she whispered. "Thyrsis!"

"Oh, what shall I do?" he sobbed.

"What's the matter?"

"Oh, it was so horrible! horrible!"

"Thyrsis!" she panted, swiftly. "Don't say that!"

"How could I have done it?" he rushed on. "What a monster I am!"

"No! no!" she cried. "You don't understand, I love you! Don't you know that I love you?"

And she tightened her clasp about him, she stole into his arms again. "Forgive me!" she whispered. "Please, please--forgive me, Thyrsis!"

He stared at her, dazed. "Forgive *you*?"

"I had no right to behave like that!" she cried. "I was afraid--I couldn't control myself. But oh, Thyrsis, I love you!"

And she pressed herself upon him convulsively; she was troubled no longer. "Yes!" she panted. "Yes! I don't mind it any more! I am yours! I am yours! You may do whatever you please to me, Thyrsis--I love you!"

She covered him with kisses--his face, his neck, his body. She drew him down to her again, whispering in ecstasy, "***My husband!***"

He was lost in amazement. Could this be Corydon, the gentle and shrinking? No, she was gone; and in her stead this creature of desire--tumultuous and abandoned! She was like some passion-goddess out of the East, shameless and terrible and destroying! She was like a tigress of the jungle, calling in the night for its mate. She locked him fast in her arms--she was swept away in a whirlwind of emotion, as he had been swept before. And all her being rose up in one song of exultation--"Mine! Mine! Mine! Mine!"

"Ah, Thyrsis!" she cried. "My Thyrsis! I belong to you now! You can never escape me now! You can never leave me--my love, my love!"

And as Thyrsis listened to this song, his passion died. Reason awoke again, and a cold fear struck into his heart! What was the meaning of *this?*

Long hours afterward, as she lay, half-asleep, in his arms, she felt him give a sudden start and shudder.

"What is it?" she asked.

"Nothing," he said--"I just happened to think of something. Something that frightened me."

"What was it?"

"I was thinking, dear-- *suppose I should become domestic!*"

BOOK VI
THE CORDS ARE TIGHTENED

She had been reading in the little cabin, and a hush had fallen upon them.

"Yes, thou art gone! And round me too the night In ever-nearing circle weaves her shade."

"Gone!" she said, and smiled sadly. "Where is he gone?"

And she turned the page and read again--

"But Thyrsis nevermore we swains shall see;
  See him come back, and cut a smoother reed,
  And blow a strain the world at last shall heed--
For Time, not Corydon, hath conquer'd thee!"

Then, after a pause, she added, "How often I have remembered those words! And how pitiful they are, when I remember them!"

Section 1. It was a tiny cupboard of a room in a tenement. They sat upon their bed to eat, and they hid their soiled dishes beneath it. Dirty children screamed upon the avenue in front, and frowsy-headed women and wolfish men caroused in the saloon below. Yet here there came to them the angel with the flame-tipped wings, and here they dreamed their dream of wonder.

In the glory of their new-found passion all life became transfigured to them; they discovered new meaning in the most trivial actions. There was no corner so obscure that they might not come upon the young god hidden; they might touch his warm, tender flesh, and hear his silvery laughter, and thrill with the wonder of his presence. They spoke a new language, full of fire and color; they read new meanings in each other's eyes. The slightest touch of hand upon hand, or of lips to lips, was enough to dissolve them in tenderness and delight.

They rejoiced in the marvel of each other's being--in the glory of their bodies, newly revealed. To Thyrsis especially this was life's last miracle, a discovery so fraught with bliss as to be a continual torment. The incitements that were hidden in the softness and the odor of unbound and tumbled hair; the exquisiteness of maiden breasts, moulded of marble, rosy-tipped; the soft contour of snowy limbs, the rhythmic play of moving muscles--to dwell amid these things, to possess them, was suddenly to discover in reality what before had only existed in the realm of painting and sculpture.

Corydon also, in the glow of his delight, of his rapture and his ravening desire, discovered anew the wonder of herself, and came to a new consciousness of her beauty. She would stand and gaze before her, with her hands upon her breasts, and her head flung back and her eyes closed in ecstasy, so that he might come to her and kiss her--might kiss her again and again, might touch her with his lover's hands and clasp her with his lover's arms.

In most of these things she was his teacher. For Corydon was one person, in body, mind and soul; in her there were no disharmonies, no warring elements. His friend the doctor had set forth his idea of "a good woman"; but Corydon's goodness proved to be after no such pattern. Now that she was his, she was his; she belonged to him, she was a part of him, and there could be no thought of a secret shame, of any reserves or hesitations. Her body was herself, and it was joy to her; it was joy the more, because she could give it for love; and she sought for new ways to utter the completeness of her giving.

She was like a little child about it--so free, so spontaneous, so genuine; Thyrsis marvelled at her utter naturalness. For himself, in the midst of these things, there was always a sense of the strange and the terrible, a sense of penetrating to forbidden mysteries; but Corydon laughed in the sunlight of utter bliss--and she laughed most at him, when she found that her simple language had startled him.

For the maiden out of ancient Greece was now become a lover! And so she was revealed to Thyrsis--she who might have marched in the Panathenaic processions, with one of the sacred vessels in her hands, or run in the Attic games, bare-limbed and fearless. So he learned to think of her, singing in the myrtle groves Of Mount Hymettus, or walking naked in the moonlight in Arcadian meadows.

So he thought of her all through her life, whenever a moment of joy came to her--whenever, for instance, she found her way to the water. They had dressed her in long skirts and put her in a drawing-room--but Corydon had got to the water in spite of them; and all that any Nereid had ever known, that she had known from the time the waves first kissed her feet.

And so it was also with love; she was born to be a priestess of love's religion. She had waited for this hour--that she might take his hand, and lead him into the temple, and teach him the ritual. It was a ministry that she entered upon with the joy of all her being. "Ah, let me teach you how to love!" she would cry. "Ah, let me teach you how to love!"

Love was to her an utter blending of two selves, the losing of one's personality in another's; it meant the forgetting of one's self, and all the ends of self. And Thyrsis marvelled at the glory that came upon her, at each new rapture she discovered. All the language of lovers was known to her, all the songs of lovers were upon her lips:

> "Du bist mir ewig,
>   Bist mir immer--
> Erb und Eigen
> Ein und All!"

Such was her woman's gift: precious beyond all treasures of earth, and given without price or question. And Thyrsis trembled as he realized it; he lived upon his knees before her, and floods of tenderness welled up in his heart. How utterly she trusted him, how completely she belonged to him! And what could he do to show himself worthy of it--this most wonderful dream of his life come true--

> "If someone should give me a heart to keep,
>   With love for the golden key!"

Yet, amid all these raptures, Thyrsis was haunted by ghosts of doubt. Would he be able to do what his heart yearned to do? Love meant so much to her--and could it mean that much to him? Why could it not be to him the complete thing it was to her--why must he argue and wonder and fear?

For Thyrsis' ancestors had not dallied in Arcadian meadows. They had come from the wilds of Palestine and the deserts of Northern Africa; they had argued and wondered and feared in Gothic cloisters, in New England meeting-houses; and the shadow of their souls hung over him still. He could not love love as Corydon loved it, he could not trust it as she trusted it. It could never seem to him the utterly natural thing--there was always a fear of pollution, a hint of satiety, a thrill of shame. Directly the first fires of passion had spent themselves, these anxieties came to him; he remembered how in his virgin youth he had thought of passion--as of something strange and uncomfortable, even grotesque, suggesting too closely a kinship with the animals. So he noticed that his feelings always waned before Corydon's. She wished him to linger--love meant so much to her!

Then too, the code of passion was all unknown to him. What was right and what was wrong? When should one yield to desire, and when should one restrain it? To Corydon such questions never came--to her there was no such possibility as excess; she was complete and perfect, and nature told her. If there were temptations and restraints and regrets, they were for Thyrsis; and he had to keep them for his own secret, he could ask no help from her. For he discovered immediately that with his proud imperiousness, he could not endure to have Corydon refuse herself to him. So this laid a new burden upon him, an appalling one. For were they not always together--her lips always calling him, the impulse towards her always with him?

There was another circumstance--the means they had to take to prevent the consequences of their love. From the very first, Thyrsis had shrunk from the thought of this; but it was only later that he realized how much it repelled him. It offended all his sense of economy and purpose; it was something done, and at the same time undone--and so it had in it the essence of all futility and wrongness. It took from passion its meaning and its excuse; and yet he could not say this to Corydon; and he knew also that he could no longer do without her. He was bound--bound fast! And every hour his chains would become tighter; what was now spontaneous joy would become a habit--a thing like eating and sleeping, a new and humiliating necessity of the flesh!

Section 2. Such were their problems. They might have solved them all, perhaps--had they only had time. But others came crowding upon them, others still more insistent and perplexing. The world was pressing them, jealous of their dream of delight.

Their little fund of money was gone, and so Thyrsis went back to his hack-work. All day he sat by the window and slaved at it, while Corydon lay upon the bed and read, or wandered about the park by herself. Thyrsis' burden was twice as heavy now, for he had to earn for two; and when in the ecstasies of love she cried out to him that she was his forever, the cruel mockery of circumstance translated this to mean that he would forever have to earn for two!

He wrote more book-reviews, and peddled them about; sometimes he was forced to exchange them for books he reviewed, and then to sell the books for twenty or thirty cents apiece. He wrote up some ideas for political cartoons, and got three dollars for one of them. He wrote a parody upon a popular poem, and got six dollars for that. He met a college friend, just returned from a trip in the Andes, and he patiently collected the material for a narrative, and sold it to a minor magazine for fifteen dollars.

And meanwhile he toiled furiously at another pot-boiler, a tale of Hessians and Tories and a red-cheeked and irresistible revolutionary heroine, to fill the insatiable maw of the readers of the "Treasure Chest." On one occasion, when everything went wrong, Corydon took the half-dozen solid silver coffee-spoons and the heavy gold-plated berry-spoon which had constituted her outfit of wedding-presents, and sold them to a nearby jeweler for two dollars and a quarter.

But through all this bitter struggle they looked forward to a glorious ending. In April the book would be out--and then they would be free! They would go away to the country--perhaps to the little cabin of last summer! Ah, how they dreamed of that cabin, how they hungered for it! They pictured it, covered in snow, with the ice-bound brook in front of it--both the cabin and the brook asleep, and dreaming of the spring-time.

Thyrsis was dreaming of it also, with tears in his eyes and a mighty passion in his heart; for his new book was calling to him--he had to fight hard to keep it from taking possession of his thoughts and driving the pot-boilers out of the temple.

There came the joyful excitement of reading the proofs of his book; also of inspecting the cover-design, and the sample of the paper, and the "dummy". And then--it was two weeks from now! Then it was only ten days--then only one week. And finally the raptures of the first sample copy!

It was time the publishers had begun to advertise it, and Thyrsis went to see Mr. Taylor about the matter. Mr. Taylor was vague in his replies. Then came publication-day, and still no advertisements; and Thyrsis called again, and insisted and expostulated, and learned to his consternation that they were not going to advertise it; the season was a bad one, the firm had met with unexpected expenses, and so on. When Thyrsis reminded them of their promises, and threatened and stormed, Mr. Taylor informed him quietly that there was nothing in the contract about advertising.

So Thyrsis went home, and tried to forget his rage in the work of disposing of his hundred copies. He had prepared himself for the possibility of everything else failing, but here he had a plan whereby he felt that his deliverance was assured. He had made up a list of a hundred of the best-known men of letters in the country--college presidents and professors, editors and clergymen, novelists and poets and critics; and he had done more hack-work, and earned the twenty dollars it would take to send to each of them a copy of the book, together with his manifesto, and a little type- written note. This, he felt, would make certain of the book's being read; and once let the book be read by the real leaders of the country's thought, and his siege would be at an end!

So the packages went to the post-office, freighted with the burden of his hopes and longings. And two or three times a week Thyrsis went to see his publishers, and find out how the book was going. He was never able to ascertain just what they were doing with it, or how they expected to sell it; Mr. Taylor would tell him vaguely that it was doing fairly well--the season was "slow", and he must give the book time to "catch on".

And then came the reviews. A clipping-bureau had written, offering to furnish them at five cents apiece; and this was moderate, considering that there were only a dozen altogether. Most of these were from unimportant out-of-town papers, whose book-reviews are written by the high-school nieces and the elderly maiden-aunts of the publishers. Of the metropolitan newspapers and literary organs, only three noticed the book at all; and two of these gave perfunctory mention, evidently made up from the publisher's statement on the cover.

The third writer had connected the book with the interview in the "Morning Howl", and he wrote a burlesque review of it, in which he hailed it as the "Great American Novel". His method was to retell the story, quoting the most highly-wrought passages, with just enough comment to keep it in the vein of farce. To Thyrsis this mockery came like a blast of fire in the face; he did not know that it was the regular method of the newspaper--a method by means of which it had made itself known as the cleverest and most readable paper in the country.

Section 3. All this was the harder for him, because it came at a black and spectral hour of his life. It was not enough that the book was falling flat, and that all their hopes were collapsing; a new and most terrible calamity befell them. For three months now they had been dissolved in the bliss of their young dream of love; and now suddenly had come a thunderbolt, splitting the darkness about them, and revealing the grim hand of Fate closing down!

For several years of her life Corydon had carried a trying burden--once each month she would have to lie down for three or four days and be a semi-invalid. And last month this had not happened; the time had come and gone, and she was as well as ever. She had told Thyrsis about it, and how it disturbed her; it might mean nothing, it had happened several times before to her; but then again--it might mean that she had conceived.

The idea had been too frightful to contemplate, however, and they had put it aside. It was not possible--the doctor had told them how to prevent it; he had told them that "everybody" did it, and that they could feel safe.

But now came the second month; and Corydon, filled with a vague terror, waited for the day. And horrible beyond all telling--the day came and went once more! And two days came--three days! And so finally Corydon went to see the doctor.

When she came home again, and entered the room, Thyrsis saw it all in her face, without her uttering a word. He went sick, all at once; and Corydon sank down upon the bed.

"Well?" he asked, in a hoarse voice.

"It's true," she said.

"And what did he say?"

"He said--he said I was in splendid shape, and that I would have a fine baby!"

And Thyrsis stared at her, and then suddenly burst into wild laughter, and hid his head in his arms. Such was their mood that she could not feel sure whether he was laughing or crying.

Now, indeed, they were facing the reality of life. All the problems with which they had ever wrestled were as child's play to this problem; they could sit and read the deadly terror in each other's eyes. Corydon's lip was trembling, and her face was white and drawn and old. So swiftly had fled her young dream of joy!

"Thyrsis," she said, in a low voice, "it means ruin!"

"Yes," he answered.

And she clenched her hands tightly. "I will kill myself first!" she whispered. "I will not drag you down!"

He made no reply.

"Listen, Thyrsis," she went on. "There is only one thing to be thought of. I must get rid of it."

"Get rid of it?" he echoed. "How?"

"I don't know," she said. "But women often do it."

"I've heard of it," he replied. "But isn't it dangerous?"

"I don't know," she said, "and I don't care."

There was a pause.

"Why don't you ask the doctor?" he inquired.

"The doctor? There was no use us asking him, Thyrsis."

"Why not?"

"Because--he doesn't understand. He likes babies. That's his business."

They argued this. But in the end Thyrsis resolved that he must see the doctor himself. He must see him if it was only to pour out his anguish. It was the doctor's fault that this fearful accident had befallen them!

But the boy soon saw that it was as Corydon had said, there was nothing to be gained in that quarter. Babies were indeed the doctor's business; they were the business of the whole world, from his point of view. People got married to have babies; they were in the world to have babies, and anything else was just nonsense. Nowadays babies were the only excuse that people had for living--their morality began and ended with them. Moreover, babies were fine in themselves; they were beautiful and fat and jolly. The pagan old gentleman sang a very paean in praise of babies--the more of them there were, the more laughter upon earth.

Also, having them was the business of women--that, and not reading German poetry and playing the piano. They all made a little fuss at the outset, but then they submitted, and they soon found that Nature knew more than they. Babies completed women's lives, they settled their nerves; they gave them something to think about, and saved them from hysteria and extravagance and sentimentalism, and all the rest of the ills of the hour.

Then the doctor fixed his keen eyes upon him. "Are you and Corydon thinking about an abortion?" he demanded.

"I--I don't know," stammered Thyrsis. The word sounded ugly.

"I got that impression from her," said the other. "And now let me tell you--if you do that, it'll be something you'll never forgive yourself for as long as you live. In the first place, you may lose your wife. It's a very dangerous thing, and a woman is seldom the same after it. You might make it impossible for her ever to have a child again, and so blast her whole life. You'll have to trust her in the hands of some vile scoundrel--you understand, of course, that it's a crime?"

"I suppose so," said Thyrsis.

"It's a crime not only against the law--it's a crime against God. And it's the curse of our age!"

There was a pause.

"What's the matter with Corydon, anyway?" demanded the doctor.

"She's so young!" cried Thyrsis.

"Nonsense! She's nineteen now, isn't she? And she couldn't be in better condition."

"But she's so undeveloped--mentally, I mean."

"There's nothing in the world will develop her like maternity. And can't you see that she wants the baby?"

"Wants it!" shouted Thyrsis.

"Why, of course! She's dead in love with you, boy. And she wants the baby! Why shouldn't she have it?"

"If I could only make you understand--" protested Thyrsis, feebly.

"Yes!" exclaimed the doctor. "That's what they all say! Not a day passes that some woman doesn't sit in this office and say it! Each case is different from any other case that ever was or could be. They tell me how much they suffer, and what a state their nerves are in, and how busy they are, and how poor they are--their social duties, and their artistic duties, and their religious duties, and their philanthropic duties! And they weep and wring their hands, and tell me agonizing stories, and they offer me any sum I could ask--many a time I might earn a thousand dollars by something that wouldn't take me ten minutes, if only I didn't have a conscience!--Go away, boy, and get those ideas out of your head!"

Section 4. So Thyrsis went away, with a new realization of the seriousness of his position, with a new sense of the grip in which he was fast. It was a conspiracy of Nature, a conspiracy of all the world! It was a Snare!

All through this love-adventure, even when most under the sway of his emotions, Thyrsis' busy mind had been groping and reaching for an understanding of it. Little by little this had come to him--and now the picture was complete. He had beheld the last scene of the panorama; he had got to the moral of the tale!

He had been the sport of cosmic forces, of the blind and irresistible reproductive impulse of Nature. Step by step he had been driven, he had played his part according to the plan. He had hesitated and debated and resolved and decided--thinking that he had something to do with it all! But now he looked back, and saw himself as a leaf swept along by a torrent. And all the while the torrent had known its destination! He had had many plans and many purposes, but always Nature had had but one plan and one purpose--which was the Child!

Twelve months ago Thyrsis had been a boy, carefree and happy, rapt in his dream of art; and now here he was, a married man, with the cares of parenthood on his shoulders! If anyone had told him that a trick could be played upon him, he would have laughed at them. How confident he had been--how certain of his mastery of life! And now he was in the Snare!

Dismayed as he was, Thyrsis could not but smile as he realized it. The artist in him appreciated the technique of the performance. How cunningly it had all been managed--how cleverly the device had been hidden how shrewdly the bait had been selected!

He went back over the adventure. What a fuss he and Corydon had made about it! What a vast amount of posturing and preluding, of backing and filling! And how solemnly they had taken it--how earnestly they had believed in the game! What

convictions had weighed upon them, what exaltations had thrilled them--two pitiful little puppets, set here and there by unseen hands! Rehearsing from prologue to
curtain the age-long drama, the drama of Sex that had been played from the beginning of the world!

He marvelled at the prodigality that Nature had displayed--at the treasures she
had squandered to accomplish her purpose! She would create a million eggs to make
one salmon; and she had created a million emotions to make one baby! What poems
she had written for them--what songs she had composed for them! She had emptied
the cornucopiae of her gifts into their lap! She had strewn the pathway with roses
before them, she had filled their mouths with honey, and their ears with the sound
of sweet music; she had blinded them, she had stunned them, she had sent them
drunken and reeling to their fate!

And the elaborate set of pretenses and illusions that she had invented for them!
The devices to lull their suspicions--the virtues and renunciations, the humilities
and the consecrations! Corydon had been frightened and evasive; Nature had made
him suffer, so as to break her down! And he had been proud and defiant; and so
Corydon, the meek and gentle, had been turned into a heroine of revolt! Nay, worse
than that; those very powers and supremacies that he had thought were his protec-
tion--were they not, also, a part of the Snare? His culture and his artistry, his visions
and his exaltations--what had they been but a lure for the female? The iris of the
burnished dove, the ruff about the grouse's neck, the gold and purple of the butterfly's wing! Even his genius, his miraculous, ineffable genius--that had been the
plume of the partridge, the crowning glory before which his mate had capitulated!

These images came to Thyrsis, until he burst into wild, sardonic laughter. He
saw himself in new and grotesque lights; he was the peacock, spreading his gor-
geousness before a dazzled and wondering world; he was the young rooster, strutting before his mate, and thrilling with the knowledge of his own importance! He
was each of the barnyard creatures by turn, and Corydon was each of the fascinated
females. And somewhere, perhaps, stood the farmer, smiling complacently--for
should there not be somewhere a farmer in this universal barnyard?

But then, the laughter died; for he thought of Maeterlinck's "Life of the Bee",
and shuddered at the fate of the male-creature. He was a mere accident in the
scheme of Nature--she wasted all his splendors to accomplish the purpose of an

hour. And now it had been accomplished. He had had his moment of ecstasy, his dizzy flight into the empyrean; and now behold him falling, disembowelled and torn, an empty shell!

But no--it was not quite that way, Thyrsis told himself, after further reflection. In the human hive the male creature was not only the bearer of the seed he was also the worker. And so there was one more function he had to perform. All those fine frenzies of his, his ideals and his enthusiasms--they had served their purpose, and would fade; but before him there was still a future--a drab and dreary future of perpetual pot-boiling!

He recalled their bridal-night. All that had puzzled him in it and startled him-- how clear it was now! Corydon had shrunk from him, just enough to lure him; and then, suddenly, her whole being had seemed to change--she had caught him, and held him fast. For he had accomplished her purpose; he had gotten her with child! And so he must stand by her--he must bring her food, that she might give the child life! And for that purpose she would hold him; for that she would use every art of which she was mistress--the whole force of her being would go into it!

She would not know this, of course; she would do it blindly and instinctively, as she had done everything so far. She would do it by those same generous and beautiful qualities that had made him hers! Therein lay the humor of his whole adventure--there lay the deadly nature of this Snare. The cords of it were woven out of love and tenderness, out of ecstasy and aspiration; and they were wound about his very heart-strings, so that it would kill him to pull them loose. And he would never pull them loose--he saw that in a sudden vision of ruin! She would be noble to the uttermost limit of nobleness. She would threaten to destroy herself--and so he would save her! She would bid him cast her away--and so he would stand by her to the end! And the end would be simply the withering and shrivelling of those radiant qualities which he called his genius--qualities which were so precious to him, but about which Nature knew nothing!

So grim an aspect had life come to wear to this boy of twenty-one! He stripped all the flesh of illusion from its fair face, and saw the grinning skull beneath. And he mocked at himself, because of all those virtues by which he had been caught--and which yet he knew were stronger than his will. Through faith and love he had been made a captive; and through faith and love would he waste away and perish!

Section 5. Meantime, Corydon was prosecuting an inquiry into these matters upon her own account, and getting at quite other points of view. There were some, it seemed, who took this game less seriously than she and Thyrsis; and these managed to go free--they broke the cords of the Snare, they slipped between the fingers of the hand of Fate. Corydon had heard a certain scientist refer to man as "Nature's insurgent son"; and now came the discovery that Nature had insurgent daughters also.

Being in an "interesting condition," Corydon was entitled to the confidences of the married women acquaintances of the family. They were eager to know all about her, and what she was going to do; and they told her their own experiences. She brought these to Thyrsis, who was thus admitted to a view of the inner workings of the "race-suicide" mill.

It was as the doctor had said; each one of these middle-class ladies considered herself a special case, but their stories all seemed to fit together. Nature's boundless and irrational fecundity was an exceedingly trying feature of the life of middle-class ladies. In the first place, the having of babies was a tedious and painful matter. One became grotesquely disfigured, and had to hide away and sever all social relationships. One lost one's grace and attractiveness, and hence the power to hold one's husband. And then, there were all the cares and the inconveniences of children. What was one to do with them, in a city where the best hotels and apartment-houses barred them out?

Then, too, even supposing the best of intentions--there was the cost of living. At present prices it was impossible for a man who had only a salary to support more than one or two children; and with prices increasing as they were, one could not be sure of educating even these. And meanwhile, the Nature of Things had apparently planned it that a woman should bear a child once a year for half her life-time!

So all these middle-class ladies used devices to prevent conception. But these were not always successful--husbands were frequently inconsiderate. And so came the abortion-business, which the doctor had described as the curse of the age.

Now and then one could accomplish the thing by some of the innumerable drugs that were advertised for the purpose. But these always made one ill, and seldom did anything else. Corydon met one young person, the wife of a rising stockbroker, who had presented her husband with twins in the first year of their marriage, and who declared that she was apparently designed to populate all the tenements in the city. This airy and vivacious young lady lay back in her automobile and prattled to Corydon, declaring that she was "always in trouble." She had tried to coax her family physician in vain, and had finally gone elsewhere. She had got quite used to the experience. All that troubled her nowadays was how to make excuses to her friends. one could not have "appendicitis" forever!

But there was another side to the matter. There was one woman who had had a hemorrhage; and another whose sister had contracted blood-poisoning, and had died in agony. There were even some who pleaded and exhorted like the doctor, and talked about the thing's being murder. All of which arguments and fears Corydon brought to her husband, to be pondered and discussed.

They spent whole days wandering about in the park in agony of soul. They had one brief month in which to decide the question--the question of life or death to the possible child. Truly here, once more, was an issue to which Thyrsis might apply the words af Carlyle--

"Choose well, your choice is
Brief and yet endless!"

Section 6. This was also the month in which the fate of the book was decided. Each day, as he went for the mail, Thyrsis' heart would beat high with expectation; and each day he would be chilled with bitter disappointment. He was still hoping for a real review, or for some signs of the book's "catching on". Nor did he finally give up until he chanced to have a talk about it with his friend, Mr. Ardsley; who explained to him that here, too, he had fallen into a trap.

His "publishers" were not really publishers at all. They did not make their profit by selling books--they made it out of authors. There were many vain and foolish people who wrote books which they were anxious to see in print, so that they might be known as literary lights among their friends. Many of them had money, and would buy a number of copies; and the "publishers" had the expenses guaranteed in advance and so would make a profit upon the sale of even one or two hundred copies. All this being well known, the reviews never paid any attention to the announcements of this concern, nor did "the trade" handle their books. As for Thyrsis' volume, they had printed it very cheaply--it was to be doubted if it had cost them what he had paid them. And they had even published it as a "net price" book--thereby taking three cents more off the royalty to which he was entitled!

Mr. Ardsley had declared that he would be lucky if his book sold three hundred copies; and so he felt that it was quite a tribute to the merits of his work when, after six months more of waiting, he received a royalty statement from the concern showing a sale of seven hundred and forty-three copies, and enclosing a check for eight-nine dollars and sixteen cents. This check Thyrsis paid over to his rich relative, and a week or two later, when he sold a short story, he sent the balance of the hundred dollars that he owed. And so he figured that the privilege of writing his first book and offering it to the hundred great men of letters of the country, had cost him the sum of one hundred and thirty-five dollars and eighty-four cents!

Meantime, of course, Thyrsis was hearing from these great men of letters. When he counted up at the end he found that he had received replies from sixteen of them; whether the other eighty-four received his book, or what they did with it, he never knew. Of these sixteen, six wrote formal acknowledgements, and two others said that they found nothing to appeal to them in his book; so there were left eight who gave him comfort, Several of these were among the really vital men of the time, as Thyrsis found out later, when he came to read their books, and to know them as something other than newspaper names. Several of them wrote him long and really helpful criticisms of his work, recognizing the merits he knew it had, and pointing out defects which he was quick to acknowledge. Four of them even told him that he had undoubted genius, and predicted great things for him. But that was as far as any of them went. They wrote their opinions, and there they stopped, as if at a blank wall. No one among them seemed to feel that he could take any action upon his opinion, however favorable; not one comprehended that what the boy was groping for was neither praise nor blame, but a chance for life. Not one had any advice of a practical sort to offer; not one had any personal or human thing to say; not one even asked to see him! And lest this should be due to oversight, or to false delicacy, Thyrsis wrote, in his desperation, and reminded them that the "genius" they recognized was being killed by starvation. To this, one did not reply, and another advised him to take up newspaper work, as "a means of getting in touch with the public"!

It was a ghastly thing to the boy as he came to realize it--this utter deadness and coldness of "the world". Thyrsis himself was all afire with love--with love, not only for his vision and his art, but for all humanity, and for humanity's noblest dreams. His friends were poets and sages of past time, men of generous faith and quick sympathies; and in all the world of the living, was there not one such man to be found? Was there nothing left upon earth but critical discernment and epistolary politeness?

The question pursued him still more, after the one interview which resulted from all this correspondence. There was a distinguished Harvard professor who had told him that he had rare powers and must go on; and hearing that the professor was in New York, Thyrsis asked the privilege of calling.

It was in one of the city's most expensive hotels--for the professor had married a rich wife, and was what people called "socially prominent". The other did not know this; but it seemed an awful thing to him that anyone should be sitting in a brocaded silk-covered chair in a palace of luxury like this, while possessed of the knowledge that his genius was starving.

"You tell me to go on, professor," he said. "But how *can* I go on?"

The professor was fingering his gold eyeglasses and studying his visitor.

"You must get some kind of routine work," he declared--"enough to support you. You can't expect to live by your writing."

"But if I do that, I can't write!" cried Thyrsis.

"You'll have to do the best you can," said the other.

"But I can't do *anything!* The emotions of it eat me all up. I daren't even let myself think about my work when I have to do other things."

"I should think," commented the professor, "that you would find you are still more hindered by the uncertainties of hack-work."

"I do find that," the boy replied. "That is just what is the matter with me."

"I'm afraid you'll be forced to a compromise in the end."

"But I won't! I won't!" cried Thyrsis, wildly. "I will starve first!"

The other said nothing.

"Or I will beg!" added Thyrsis.

The other's look clouded slightly--as the boy, with his quick sensitiveness, noted instantly. "Of course," said the professor, "if you are not ashamed to do that--"

"But why should I be ashamed? Greater men than I have begged for their art."

"Yes. I know that. And naturally--I honor that feeling in you. If you have that much fervor--why, of course, you will do it. But I'm afraid you'll find it a humiliating experience."

"I wouldn't expect to find it a picnic," answered Thyrsis, and took his departure--having perceived that the professor's leading thought was a fear lest he should begin his begging that day.

So there it was! There was the eminent critic, the writer of exquisite appreciations of literature! The darling of the salons of Boston--which called itself the Athens of America and the hub of the universe! A man with a brain full of all the culture of the ages--and with the heart of a mummy and the soul of a snob! He had approved of Thyrsis' consecration with his lips--because he did not dare to disapprove it, because the ghosts of a thousand paupers of genius had stood over him and awed him into silence. But in his secret heart he had despised this wan and haggard boy who threatened to beg; and the boy went out of the palace of luxury, feeling like an outcast rat.

Section 7. From this interview Thyrsis went to meet Corydon in the park; and after he had told her what had happened, they began one more discussion of their great problem. This had to be the final one; for the month of respite had passed, and the time for action was come!

Through their long arguments, Thyrsis had gradually come to realize that the decision rested with him. Corydon was in his hands; she had become a burden upon him, and she would rather she were dead; and so he had to take the responsibility and issue the command. So through many an hour while Corydon slept he had marshalled the facts and tested them, hungering with all his soul for knowledge of the right.

To bring a child into the world would shatter every plan they had formed. And yet, again and again, he forced himself to face the idea. They had always meant to have children ultimately; and now the gift was offered--and suppose they rejected it, and it should never be offered again! However unpropitious the hour might be, still the hour was here--the task was already one-third done. And if there were cares and responsibilities, expenses and pains of child-birth--at least they would be for a child; whereas, in the other case, there were also cares and responsibilities, expenses and pains--and for naught!

Throughout all this long pilgrimage of love, Thyrsis had been struck by the part which blind chance had played. It was blind chance that had brought Corydon to the country where he had gone. It was blind chance that he had read his book to her. And then--the chance that he had gone to see a doctor about diet! And that dark accident in the night, that had opened the gates of life to a new human soul! And now, strangest of all--the chance by which this last issue was to be decided! By a walk in the park, and a casual meeting with a nurse-maid!

"God knows I want to do what is right!" Thyrsis had said. "But I just don't know what to say!"--And then they sat down upon a bench, and the nurse-maid came and sat beside them.

It was five or ten minutes before Thyrsis noted what was going on. He was lost in his sombre brooding, his eyes fixed upon vacancy; when suddenly he heard Corydon exclaim: "Isn't he a little love!" He turned to look.

The nurse-maid was in charge of a carriage, and in the carriage was a baby; and the baby was smiling at Corydon, and Corydon was smiling back. She was poking her finger at it, and it was catching at the finger with its chubby paws. "Isn't he a little love!" Corydon repeated.

Thyrsis stared at her. But then, quickly, he hid his thought. He even pretended to be interested.

"Isn't he pretty?" she asked him.

Now as a matter of fact he seemed to Thyrsis to be quite conspicuously ugly. He had red hair, and a flat nose, and was altogether lacking in aristocratic attributes. But Thyrsis answered promptly, "Yes, dear," and continued to watch.

And Corydon continued to play. Apparently she knew something about babies--how to amuse them and how to handle them, and had even heard rumors about how to feed them. She was asking questions of the nurse-maid, and displaying interest--Thyrsis would have been no more amazed had he found her in converse with a Chaldean astrologer. For a full quarter of an hour she had managed to forget her agonies of spirit, and to play with a baby!

They got up to go. "You like babies, don't you, dearest?" asked Thyrsis, as they walked.

"Why, yes," she said.

And then there was a silence, while he pondered. Here, he perceived in a flash, was the great hand of Nature again!

Since the first day of their marriage Thyrsis had been haunted by the sense of a dark shadow hanging over them, of a seed of tragedy in their love. He had his great task to do, and Corydon could not do it with him. The long road of his art-pilgrimage stretched out before him; and some day he must take his staff and go.

And now here, of a sudden, was the solution of the problem! The answer to the riddle of all their disharmonies! Let Corydon have her baby--and then he might have his books! As he pondered, there came to him the words of the old doctor--"She wants that baby!"

So before he reached home, his mind was made up. Cost what it might, she should have the baby. But he would not tell her his reason--that must be a secret between himself and Mother Nature. And then it seemed to him that he could hear Mother Nature laughing behind her curtain--and laughing not only at Corydon, but at him. He recalled with a twinge all his earlier cynicism, his biological bitterness; he had taken up the burden of his virtues again!

Section 8. In many ways this decision, once arrived at, was a relief to them. It lifted the weight of a great fear from their lives; it gave them six months more of respite--and in six months, what might not Thyrsis be able to do? He had been toiling incessantly at his hack-work, and had saved nearly ninety dollars, which would be enough to keep them going until his new book was written.

This book was now fairly seething in him. A wonderful thing it was to be, far beyond his first; in the beauty of it and the glow of it he was forgetting all his disappointments, all the mockeries of fate and the hardness of the world. If only he could get *this* book done, then surely he would be saved, then surely men would be forced to give him a chance!

So he waited not a moment after the decision was made; he even blamed himself for having waited so long. From the "higher regions" there had come a windfall in the shape of two railroad-passes; and a couple of days later they stepped out upon the depot-platform of a little town upon the shore of Lake Ontario.

Oh, the joy of being in the country again! The smell of the newly-plowed earth, the sight of the spring-time verdure; and then the first glimpse of the lake, with its marvellous clear-green water, and the fresh cold breeze that blew from off it! There was challenge and adventure in that air--Thyrsis thought of argonauts and old sea-rovers, and his soul was stirred to high resolves. He took deep breaths of delight, and clenched his hands, and imagined that he was at his book already.

They found a second-hand tent which could be bought for eight dollars; four dollars more would pay for the lumber, and so they would live rent-free for the next five months! They went far down the shore of the lake, looking for a place to camp, and picked out a rocky headland, a mile from the nearest farmhouse, and completely out of sight of all the world. The rich woman who owned it was in Europe, but the agent gave permission; and then Thyrsis looked at his watch and made a wild suggestion--"Let's get settled this afternoon!"

"Why, it's nearly three o'clock!" cried Corydon. "It'll be dark!"

"There'll be a moon," he replied, "and we can work all night if want to."

"But suppose it should rain!"

"I don't see any signs of it. And what's the use of spending a night in the town, and wasting all that money?"

And so it was decided. They went to the store and purchased their housekeeping equipment. What a sense of power and prosperity it gave them as they made their selection--two canvas-cots and two pairs of blankets, a lamp and an oil-can and a tiny oil-stove, two water- buckets and an axe and a wash-basin, a camp-stool and a hammock and a box full of groceries! They got a team to carry all this, in addition to their lumber and their trunks. They stopped at a farm-house, and arranged to get their milk and eggs and bread and vegetables, and also to borrow a hammer and saw; and then till after sundown Thyrsis toiled at the building of the platform and the cutting of stakes and poles for the tent.

Corydon fried some bacon and heated a can of corn, and they had a marvellous and incredible supper. Afterwards they raised the tent, and she held the poles erect while Thyrsis tied the guy-ropes. They had been advised to choose a sheltered place, back in the woods; but they were all for adventure and a view of the water, and so they were out on the open point. There were pine-trees, however, and Thyrsis had strong ropes with which to anchor the tent fast. When he finished, about ten o'clock at night, he stood off and admired the job by the light of the moon, and declared that a storm might tear the tent to pieces, but could never blow it over.

They hauled in their trunks and the rest of their belongings, and set up the cots and spread the blankets. Then by the light of the oil-lamp they gazed about.

"Oh, Thyrsis," she cried, "isn't it glorious!"

"It's our home," he said. "A home we made all for ourselves!"

"And a home without a landlady!" she added.

"And with no saloon underneath!" said he. "And no street-cars and no scream-ing children in front of it!"

Instead there was the night with its thousand eyes, and the lake, with the moon-fire flung wide across it, and the pine-trees singing in the wind.

"Brr! it's cold!" exclaimed Corydon.

"We'll have to sleep with our clothes on for a while," said he. And yet they laughed aloud in glee. "It's all we want!"

"It's all we ever could want!" declared Corydon. "Oh, let's work hard and earn money enough, so that we can stay here beneath the open sky, and not have to go back into slavery!"

Then, in the morning, the joy of a plunge in the icy lake, and of a run in the woods, and of breakfast eaten in the warm sunlight! There was much work still to be done; Thyrsis had to build a stand of shelves and a table for the tent, and a table and a bench outside; and then all their belongings had to be unpacked and set in order. Such fun as they had laying out the imaginary partitions in their house; two bedrooms and a library, a kitchen and a pantry--and all outdoors for a living-room!

They would count this the beginning of their love; at last they were free to love, and to be happy as they chose. There was no longer anyone to criticize them scarcely anyone to know about them; their only contact with the world was when they went for the mail and for provisions. They learned that the washer-woman who came for their clothes was ashamed for the poverty in which they lived, and that some of the neighbors suspected them of being oil-smugglers; on two occasions came sheriffs from distant counties to compare Thyrsis with the photographs and descriptions of long-sought bank-burglars and murderers. But although Thyrsis had often declared that he would rob a bank to secure his freedom to work, he had not yet done it, and so these experiences only added piquancy to their adventure.

It was a life such as might have been lived in the Garden of Eden. They cooked and ate and studied out doors, in a sunny glade when it was cool, and in the shade of a great oak-tree when it was warm. They wandered about in the forest, they bathed naked in the crystal lake--diving from the rocky headland, and afterwards standing upon it and drying themselves in the sun. Corydon was now free to fling away the conventionalities which had hampered her in the city; by way of signalizing her enfranchisement she cut short her hair--that untamed, rebellious hair which had taken so long to dry and to braid and to keep in order!

So they lived, in daily touch with the great heart of Nature. They saw the sun rise on one side of the rocky headland, and set upon the other; they watched the great storms sweep across the lake, and the lightnings stab into the water. Sometimes, at night, the gale would shake their tent until they could not be sure if it was wind or thunder; but the stays held fast, and they slept untroubled. And then the storm would pass, and in the morning there would be the lake, sparkling in the sunlight; and the sky, clear as crystal, with the white gulls wheeling about, and grey-blue herons standing near the shore.

There were bass to be caught from the rocky point. "So we must have at least one meal of fish every day," declared Thyrsis.

"I'm willing," said Corydon--"if you'll catch them."

"And then, there are lots of squirrels about."

"Squirrels!" cried she.

"Yes. I can knock one over with a stone now and then--you'll see."

"But, Thyrsis! To eat them!"

"Did you ever taste one?" he laughed.

"But it's cruel!" she exclaimed; and he thought to himself, How like the little Corydon of old!

"Wait till I've skinned him and fried him in bacon grease," he answered.

And even so it proved. Corydon was troubled by the crisp little toes turned up in the air, but when these had been cut off, she yielded to the allurements of odor and taste. "I'm nothing but a digesting machine nowadays!" she lamented.

To which Thyrsis replied in the words of the village-girl in "Faust," "'She feeds two when she eats!'"

They had been obliged to give up their attempt to live on prunes and turnips. For the doctor had warned them that Corydon must have plenty of "good nourishing food"; and this warning was backed up by all her women acquaintances--and also by Corydon's own inner voices. The appetite that she developed was appalling to them--not only as to quantity but as to quality. She would find herself unable to eat anything they had in their pantry, and with a craving for the wildest and most impossible things; or she would not know what she wanted--and would travel to the store and gaze about at the provisions, until a sudden illumination came. Sometimes she would be so hungry for it that she could not wait to get home, but would sit down by the road-side and devour the contents of the market-basket. To these cravings she yielded religiously, because she had been told that they represented vital needs of her system. Some one had told her an appalling tale about a pregnant woman who had been possessed by a desire for bananas; and because she had not gratified it, the baby when born had cried for five weeks--until they had fed it a banana!

These strange experiences lent new interest to their intimacy. They went through all the journey of maternity together. Pretty soon the changes in her body began to be noticeable; and day by day they would watch these. How wonderful it all was, how incredible! Thyrsis would sink upon his knees before her, and clasp his arms about her and laugh "She's going to have a little baby!" And Corydon would blush and protest; she did not like to be teased about it--she was still only half reconciled to it. "I'm only a child myself!" she would cry. "I've no education--nothing! And I'm not fit for it!" Then he would have to comfort her, telling her that life was long, and that the child would be something to study.

They discussed the weighty question of the name which they should give the child. In this, as in other matters, they were without precedents and limitations, and they found that excess of freedom is sometimes an embarrassment. They were impelled towards literary reminiscence; and Thyrsis soon realized that this was a matter in which the sensuous temperament would have to have its way. "After all," argued Corydon, "to you a name is a name. If you can call the baby and have it answer, isn't that all you care about?"

"Yes," he assented, "I suppose so; if the name's too unhandy for calling, I can have a nickname."

To Corydon, on the other hand, a name was a vital thing; a child that was lovely under one name might be unendurable under another. She had been reading Ossian, and the poems of the neo-Celtic enthusiasts; so after much pondering and consultation she announced that Cedric and Eileen were the two names from which they would choose.

Section 9. Many moods of tenderness came to them. He loved to fondle her, to exchange endearments with her. They gave each other foolish names, after the fashion of lovers the world over; and they would go on to modify these names, and add prefixes and suffixes, until the most ingenious philologist could not have figured out where the names had started. They made new words, also; they invented a whole language for use in these times of illumination, and which Thyrsis denoted by the name of "dam-fool talk".

One was always discovering new qualities in Corydon. She had as many moods as the lake by which they lived, and it seemed to him that with each mood her whole personality changed--she would even look like another being. There was the every-day Corydon, demure, and rather silent; and then there was the Corydon who lived in the arms of Nature--who swam in the water, a sister of the mermaids, and made herself drunken with the sunlight; and then would come a mood of mischief, and laughter would break from her, and her wit would be such that Thyrsis would sigh for a stenographer. She would make herself a Grecian costume out of a sheet, and dance to music of her own making; or she would put trinkets upon her forehead, and be a gypsy-queen--she could be anything that was wild and exotic and unpremeditated. She had dances for that mood also--she would laugh and caper as merrily as any young witch. But then, again, there would come the Corydon of melancholy and despair; her features would shrink up, her face would become peaked and pitiful, she would seem like a child of ten. Sometimes Thyrsis could laugh her out of such a mood by telling her of her "beady black eyes"; and she did not like to desecrate her eyes.

And now there was a new Corydon--the Corydon who had been chosen of the Lord, the worker of a miracle. This gave new awe to her presence, it set a crown upon her forehead. One morning, in mid- summer, they had come out from their bath, and she stood upon the rock in the sunshine; and suddenly he saw her give a start, and stand transfixed, staring in front of her.

"What is it?" he asked.

Her voice thrilled as she whispered, "Thyrsis! It moved!"

"Moved?" he echoed.

"I felt the child move!" she cried.

And so he came and put his hands upon her body, and together they stood waiting, breathless, as if listening for a far-off sound.

"There! There!" she cried. "Did you feel it?"

Yes, he had felt it. And in all his life had he ever felt anything stranger? The first sign of the new life that was to be--the first hail out of the darkness of nonentity! And truly, to hear that hail was to be rapt into regions of wonder unspeakable!

It was to be a new human soul; a creature like themselves, with a mind of its own, and a sense of responsibility--It would be a man or a woman, independent, self-creating, and knowing naught about this strange inception. And yet, it would be their life also; they had caused it--but for them it would never have been! Blindly, unwittingly, following the guidance of some power greater than themselves, they had called it into being. And in some mysterious and incredible way it would share their qualities; it would be a blending of their natures, a symbol of their union, of the strange fire that had blazed up in them and fused them together. Truly, had they not come here to the essence of love, that great blind force which had ruled and guided all things from Time's beginning?

They had come to the very making of life, it seemed. And yet, they wondered--were they really there? This new soul that was to be--had they in truth created it? Or had it existed before this? And whence did it come? If it was really the dignified and divine thing that it would someday imagine itself to be, was it not uncanny that it should have come thus--a nameless, half-human, half-animal thing, kicking inside the body of a woman?

It was Being, in all its ineffable mystery, its monstrous and unendurable strangeness. They lived face to face with it, they saw a thousand aspects of it. Sometimes Corydon would be obsessed with the sense of the sheer weight she carried; a burden fastened upon her and not to be got rid of--an imposition and torment to her. Then again, she would see herself in grotesque and even comical lights--as akin to all the animals, a cousin of the patient cow. And then would come a moment of sudden wonder, when she would be transfigured, a being divine, conferring the boon of life upon another.

It was in this last way that Thyrsis thought of her. There was about her a sense of brooding mystery, as of one who walks in the midst of supernatural presences.

She would sit for hours gazing before her, like Joan of Arc listening to her voices; and he would be touched with awe, and would kiss her tenderly and with reverence.

This brought new meanings into their love, new meanings into his life; he would clench his hands and vow afresh his battle with the world. How hideous a thing it was that at this time she should be tormented by fears of want and failure! That she should have to go without comforts, that she should even fear to ask for necessities --because she knew how fast his little store of money was going! Other women had children, and they did not have to be haunted by the doubt if it was right to have them, if there would be any place for them in the world. And some of these were selfish and idle women, too--and yet they had everything they needed! And here was Corydon, beautiful and noble, the very soul of devotion--Corydon must be harrowed and tortured! He did not really mind the world's treatment of himself, but for this treatment of her--ah, someday the world should pay for that! Someday it should do penance for its mockery and its blindness, that had been a blasphemy against the holy spirit itself!

At such times as this he would put his arms about her, and try to whisper something of the pity and grief that filled his heart. He would try to tell her how much he really loved her, how utterly he was devoted to her. Some day she should have her rights, some day he would repay her for all that she had dared for him. And then the tears would come into Corydon's eyes, and she would answer that she feared nothing and cared about nothing, so long as she had his love.

Section 10. After these things, Thyrsis would go at his book again. He would go at it doggedly, desperately. He had scarcely taken time to get settled in the tent and to get their housekeeping regime under way, before he had heard the call of the book and wandered away to wrestle with it. The writing of it was a matter of life and death with him now--of life and death, not only for himself, and for Corydon, but for the unborn soul as well. His money would last him only six or eight weeks, and then he would have to take to pot-boiling again. So every hour was precious; this time there could be no blundering permitted.

Thyrsis was not writing now about minstrels and princesses; he was not painting enraptured pictures of joy and love. The pain of life had become too real to him. His six months of contact with the world had filled him with bitterness; and he was forging a sharp spear, that he could drive into the heart of folly and stupidity.

It was the story of Hathawi, the dreamer, which he had come upon in a Hindoo legend. "The Hearer of Truth," was to be the title of the book; and for it Thyrsis was working out a new style. In the original it had been a fanciful tale; but he meant to take it over to the world of everyday reality, to give it the atmosphere of utter verihood. He meant to use a style of biblical simplicity, bare of all ornament, dealing with the most elemental things. And this might seem easy, but in reality it was the hardest thing in the world--it was like blank verse. One might toil all day for a single phrase into which to pack one's meaning.

He wished to show Hathawi from the beginning; the solitary child, the seer of life's mystery, who went away into a lonely place to brood. He dwelt in the high mountains, where the lightning played and the storm-winds shook him; he disciplined his will by fasting and prayer, so that the self in him died, and he could perceive eternal things, and aspects of being that are hidden. He went into the forests and dwelt with the wild things, and learned to understand their language--not only their beauty and their power, which are plain; not only their fears and their hatreds, which are painful to discover; but also their love, which is deepest of all. He learned to know the life which is in lifeless things--in water and air and fire; the joys and sorrows of the flowers, and the venerable wisdom of great trees, and the worship which is in the floods of sunlight. And having learned these things, Hathawi came back into the world.

He found that he was able to read the souls of men, but at first he could not believe what he read--it was so terrible, and so far from nature. He preferred to stay among the poor, because they were closer to the heart of things, and their falsehoods were simple. But he discovered that the evil and misery of men's life came from above, and so he went into the "great world" to dwell.

And everywhere he went, men's innermost thoughts were revealed to him, and to themselves through him. He acted upon men and women like wine--an impulse seized them to speak the truth, the truth that they had hidden even from their own hearts. Afterwards, when they realized what they had done, they hated Hathawi and feared him; but they said nothing, because each thought that the secret was his own.

But then, as his power grew, Hathawi began to reveal men in more public ways, and a scandal arose. There was whispered a story of a great statesman who had declared at a banquet what was his real work in the world; and one day a bishop arose in his cathedral and said that he taught the dogmas of his church, because they were necessary to keep the people in subjection. Then came the famous episode of a policeman who bade the prisoner go free and arrested the judge instead. Other policemen were called upon to hinder their comrade, but they declared that he was right; and then newspaper reporters, when ordered to write about it, avowed that they would write only what they believed. After which came a convention of one of the great political parties; and the presidential candidate made a speech, outlining his actual beliefs, and so destroyed his party. This, of course, was a national calamity, for all statesmen declared that the people could not be deceived by one party; and then, too, it was reported that Hathawi meant to attend the convention of the other party!

Because of this they shut him up in jail, charging him with being a vagrant, which he undoubtedly was. But he won over all the jailers and the prisoners to his doctrine, and so the jail was emptied. Moreover, it was found that some of those who loved him most truly had come to share his power of hearing truth. The madness was spreading everywhere; agitators were busy among the people, and public safety was threatened. So a certain very rich man, who in Hathawi's presence had vowed himself a wolf, engaged an assassin to strike him down in broad daylight upon the street.

Then in order to suppress the disturbance, they spirited the body away and burned it, and scattered the ashes. But this was a bad thing for them to do, for the ashes became seeds of the new contagion, and all through the great city, in the strangest and most unaccountable way, men would suddenly begin to speak the truth. And, of course this made business impossible--the merchants and traders had to move away; and how was it possible to preserve authority, when sooner or later all the lawyers and the judges and the politicians would speak truth? So the people arose and declared that they were weary of lies, and they erected a statue of Hathawi at one of the places where his ashes had fallen, and declared that every candidate for office must make his speeches there. After that it was a long time before there were any officials elected--because no man could be found to whom prominence and power were not more precious than public welfare. But meanwhile the people thrived exceedingly.

Finally, however--the climax of the story--the news of all this had spread to other nations, and the rulers of these nations perceived that it was anarchy, and could by no means be permitted--their own people were threatening to rise. It must be clearly shown that a state without a government would be plundered by enemies; and so they prepared to plunder it. And so arose a great agitation in Hathawi's home-state, and men called for a dictator, and for preparations of defence. But the followers of Hathawi cried out, saying, "Let us submit! Let us open our city to these men, and let them do their will--for the power of the truth is greater than even they." And so it was decided.

When the hostile rulers heard of this a great fear took possession of them. They remembered the fate of certain famous diplomatists they had already sent over; and they dared not trust themselves near the statue of the Hearer of Truth. So their plans of invasion came to naught; and among their own people there was laughter and bitter mockery; and behold, one morning, a statue of Hathawi which some one had set up in a public-square! Here the lovers of truth gathered by thousands, and the soldiers who were sent to shoot them laid down their arms and joined them; and so, all over the world, was the end of the dominion of the lie.

Section 11. Such was the outline of Thyrsis' story. He judged that it might be a very great story, or a comparatively commonplace one--it all depended upon the power with which it was visioned. He must get into himself and wrestle the thing out. This was to be his act of creation--his baby!

It was the first time since his marriage that Thyrsis had tried really to do what he called work. All things else had been mere echoes of the work he had done the previous summer; but now he had to do something new, something that was an echo of nothing else. Every day that he faced the task, his agony and despair of soul grew greater; for he found that he *could* not do the work. He could not even begin to do it--he could not even try to do it! He was helpless, bound hand and foot!

It was not his fault, it was not Corydon's fault; it was a tragedy inherent in the very nature of things--in the two natures that were in himself. There was the man, who loved a woman, and hungered to see her happy; and there was the artist, to whom solitude was the very breath of life. To write this book--to write it really--he would have to spend weeks of brooding over it, thinking about nothing else day and night; he would have to shape his whole existence to that end to be free from every distracting circumstance, from everything that called him out of himself. And how could he hope for such a thing, while he was living in a tent with another person?

Thyrsis had his artist's standard of perfection. Of course, he could never actually be satisfied with what he did; but at least he could feel that it was the best he was equal to--he could get a real and honest sense of exhaustion for himself. But now, the moment that he faced the problem fairly, he saw he could never get that real and honest sense of exhaustion again. He was dragged up to the issue and forced to face it instantly. The pressure of circumstances upon him was overwhelming; and he had to make up his mind to do something he had never done before--instead of really writing his books, to do the best he could with them!

Yet, inevitable as this was, and clearly as he saw it, he could not make up his mind to it. In reality, he never did make up his mind to it. He did it, and in his inmost heart he knew that he was doing it; but all the time he was trying to deny it, was wrestling with agony and despair in his soul in the effort to do something else.

He would go away in the morning and try to think about the book; and just when he would get started, it would be time for dinner, and there would be the image of Corydon waiting for him. And so he would go home, and go back in the afternoon--and when he had got started again, it would be dark. The next day, having explained his trouble, he would take his lunch away with him; but in the forenoon there would come a drenching thunder-storm, and he would have to go back again. Or he would try to work in the tent at night; and the wind would howl and blow the lamp so that he could not put his mind on anything. Nor did it avail him to rail at himself, to tell himself that he was a fool for being at the mercy of such mishaps. It was none the less a fact that he was at the mercy of them, and that he could no longer give himself up to the sway of his imagination.

And always there was Corydon, yearning for his companionship. It had always been their idea that they should do the work together; so completely would they be fused in the fire of love, that she would share his soul states and write parts of his books. But now that idea had to be abandoned; and this was *her* tragedy.

"I have to sit and think of my health!" she would exclaim.

"It isn't your health, dear," he would plead; "it's the health of the child!"

"I know that. But then, am I always to sit at home and be placid, while you go away to wrestle with the angels?"

"Not always, Corydon," he said. "This will pass--"

"If I do," she cried, "I only stay to wrestle with the demons. And is that so very good for a pregnant woman?"

"My dear!" he protested.

"It's just as I said!" she went on. "I ought not to have had the child! I'm only a school-girl, with a school-girl's tasks. And I try and try, but I can't help it--everything within me rebels at the cares of mother-hood."

"That's one mood, dear," he said. "But you know that's not true always."

"It's all the clearer to me," she insisted, "since we've had to give up our music. I can't work at the piano any more--I may never be able to."

"But even if you could, Corydon, I couldn't afford to get you one now."

"No, of course not. And you have to give up your violin!"

"Much time I have to practice it in our present plight!"

"I know--I know! But don't you see, we lose our last hope of growing together? I've a vision that haunts me all the time--you going away to do your work, and staying for longer and longer periods--and I sitting at home to mind the baby!"

Day after day he would come back, and she would ask him how the book was going; and he would have to answer that it was not going at all. Then, in his desperation, he would make up his mind to write what he could--to be content with this glimpse of one scene, and with that feeble echo of what he knew the next scene ought to be; and he would bring the result to Corydon, and would discover with a secret pang that she did not know the difference. But then he would ask himself--how could she know the difference? The difference did not exist! His vision of the thing had existed in himself, and in himself alone; if he never uttered it, the world would never know what it might have been--and would never care. Ah, what a future was that to look forward to--to filling the ears of the world with lamentations concerning the books that he might have written! And all the time knowing that the ears of the world were deaf to every sound he made!

Section 12. He thought that he realized the bitterness of this tragedy all at once; but the real bitterness was that he had to realize more and more of it every day. It was a tragedy he had to live in the house with. He had to watch it working itself out in all the little affairs of life; he had to see it manifesting itself in his own soul, and in the soul of Corydon, and even in the soul of the child. Worst of all to him, the artist, he had to see it working itself out in what he wrote--in book after book that went out to represent him to the world, and that did not represent him at all, but only represented the Snare in which he had been caught! It was one of the facts about this Snare, that there was no merciful Keeper to come and put the victim out of his misery with a blow upon the head; that he was left alone, to writhe and twist and tear himself to pieces, and to perish of slow exhaustion. It was not a murder --it was a crucifixion!

He could not have told for whom his heart bled most, for himself, or for Corydon. Here she was, with her grim problems and her bitter necessities; needing advice and comfort, needing companionship--needing a husband! And she had married an artist--a reed that would grow "nevermore again as a reed with the reeds by the river!" That could not grow, even if it had wanted to! For it was quite in vain that the world cried out to him to settle down and become as other men; he could not. The thing that was tearing at his vitals would continue to tear; the only choice he had was between self-expression and madness.

So, wrung as his heart was, he had to go away and as he could. If he yielded to his desire and stayed by her, then the book would not be written in time; and so all their hopes would be gone--they would never win their freedom then! And he would explain this to her; with their relentless devotion to the truth, they would talk it all out between them. They would trace every cord and knot of the Snare. And Corydon would grant that he was right, and that she must submit. He must stay away all day--and all night, if need be--till the book was done.

Not that they were always able to settle their problems in the cold light of reason. Sometimes Thyrsis, with his artist's ups and downs, would be nervous and irritable; he would manifest impatience over trifles, and this would give rise to tragedies. There was a vast amount of fetching and emptying of water to be done for their little establishment; and sometimes a man who was carrying the destinies of the human race in his consciousness was not as prompt as he might have been in attending to these humble tasks. And moreover, the water all had to be dipped up from the lake; and sometimes, when it was stormy, it was a difficult matter to get it as free from specks as was needed for the ablutions of a fastidious young lady like

Corydon.

"If you'd only take a little trouble!" she would say.

"Trouble!" he would exclaim. "Do you think I enjoy hearing you complain about it?"

"But Thyrsis, this is dirtier than ever!"

"I know it. The wind is blowing harder."

"But if you'd only reach out a little ways---"

"I reached out till I nearly fell into the water!"

"But Thyrsis, how can I ever wash my face?"

And so it would go. Thyrsis would be absorbed in some especially important mental operation, and it would be a torment to him to have such things forced upon his attention. Corydon, it seemed to him, was always at the mercy of externals; and she was forever dragging him out of himself, and making him aware of them. The frying-pan was not clean enough, or his hair was unkempt; his trousers were ragged or his coat was too small for him. Was life always to consist of such impertinences as this?

And so Thyrsis, in a sudden burst of rage, gave the water-bucket a kick which sent it rolling down the bank, and then strode away to his work. But unfortunately his work was not of a sort which he could do with angry emotions in his soul. And so very soon remorse overcame him. He returned, to find that Corydon had rushed out to the end of the point, and flung herself down upon the rocks in hysterics. And this, of course, was not a good thing for a pregnant woman, and so he had to set to work to soothe her.

But alas, to soothe her was never an easy task, because of her sensitiveness, and her exalted ideals of him. However humbly he might apologize and beg forgiveness, there would remain her grief that it had been possible for a quarrel to occur between them. She would drive him nearly wild by debating the event, and rehearsing it again and again, trying to justify herself to him, and him to himself. Thyrsis was robust, he wanted to let the past take care of itself; he would tell her of all the worries that were harassing him, and would plead with her to grant him the privilege of any ordinary human creature, to manifest annoyance now and then. And Corydon would promise it--she would promise him anything he asked for; but this was a boon it did not lie within the possibility of her temperament to grant.

He could be angry at fate and at the world, and could rage and storm at them all he pleased; but he could never be harsh with Corydon without inflicting upon her pain that wrecked her, and wrecked him into the bargain.

Perhaps, he thought, it was her condition that accounted for this morbidness. She was liable to fits of depression, and to mysterious illness--nausea and faintness and what not. Also, she had been told weird tales about prenatal influences; and he, not having been educated in such matters, could not be sure what were the facts. So, whenever she had been unhappy, there was the possibility that she had done some irreparable harm to the child! And that made more problems for an over-worked and sensitive artist.

He soon saw that he had to suppress forever the side of him that was stern and exacting. Such things had a place in his own life, but no longer in Corydon's. In-stead, he would see how she suffered, and his heart would be wrung, and he would come back again and again to comfort her, and to tell her how he loved her, how he longed to do what was right. He would set before her the logic of the situation, so that if things went wrong she might realize that it was neither his fault nor hers--that it was the world, which kept them in this misery, and shut them up to suffer together. So it was, all through their lives, that their remorseless reason saved them; they would find in the analysis and exposition of the causes of their own unhappi-ness the one common satisfaction they had in life.

Section 13. These were the circumstances of the writing of "The Hearer of Truth". It was completed in six weeks, and it did not satisfy its author, the finish-ing of it brought him no joy. But that, though he did not realize it, was the one circumstance in its favor--the less it satisfied him, the more chance there was that the world would know what it was about.

He had the manuscript copied, and then he sent it off to a magazine in Boston, whose editor had been one of his hundred great men, and had promised to read the new manuscript at once. Meantime Thyrsis sent for some books to review, and got to work at another plot to be submitted to the editor of the "Treasure Chest". For their own treasure-chest was now all but empty, and one could not live forever upon blueberries and fish.

Day by day they waited; and at last, one fateful afternoon, the farmer came with some provisions and their mail. There was a letter from Boston, and Thyrsis opened it and read as follows:

"I have read your manuscript, 'The Hearer of Truth', and I wish to tell you of the very great pleasure it has given me. It is noble and fine, and amazingly clever as well. I must say frankly that I was astonished at the qualities of maturity and restraint it shows. I think it quite certain that we shall wish to use it as a serial; but before I can say anything definite, the manuscript will have to be read by my associates. In the meantime I wished to tell you personally how highly I think of your work."

Thyrsis read this, and then, without a word, he passed it on to Corydon. As soon as the farmer's back was turned, the two fell into each other's arms, and all but wept. It was victory, beyond all question. The magazine might pay as much as five hundred dollars for the serial rights--and with that start, they would surely be safe. Besides that, it would mean recognition for Thyrsis--the world would have to discuss his work!

Doing pot-boilers was easy after such a triumph as that. They even treated themselves to holidays--they purchased a quart of ice-cream on one day, and hired a boat and went picnicking on another. Thyrsis got out his fiddle once again, and even became so reckless as to inquire about the price of a "practice-clavier" for Corydon. Also he began inquiring as to the cost of houses; when they got the money they would build themselves a little cabin here--a cabin just the size of the tent, but with a room upstairs where Thyrsis could do his work. After that they would be free from all the world--they would never go back to be haunted by the sight of

"Sorrow barricadoed evermore   Within the walls of cities."

Section 14. So a month passed by; and Thyrsis wrote again to the editor, and was told that they were still discussing the story. And then, after two more weeks, there came another letter; and this was the way it read:

"I am sorry to have to tell you that the decision has been adverse to using your story. My own opinion of it has not changed in the least; but I have been unable to induce my associates to view it in the same light. They seem to be unanimous in the opinion that your work is too radical for us to put to the front. We have a very conservative, fastidious, and sophisticated constituency; and this is one of the limitations by which we are bound. I am more than sorry that things have turned out so, and I trust I need hardly say that I shall be glad to read anything else that you may have to submit to us."

And there it was! "A conservative, fastidious, and sophisticated constituency!" Thyrsis believed that he would never forget that phrase while he lived. Could one get up a thing like that anywhere in the world save in Boston?

It was a bitter and cruel disappointment--the more so because it had taken six weeks of his precious time. But there was nothing to be done about it save to send off the manuscript to another magazine. And when it had come back from there he sent it to another, and to yet another--paying each time a total of eighty cents to the express-company, a sum which was very hard for him to spare. To make an ending at once to the painful episode, he continued to send it from one place to another, until "The Hearer of Truth" had had the honor of being declined by a total of fifteen magazines and twenty-two publishing-houses. The pilgrimage occupied a period of nineteen months--after which, to Thyrsis' great surprise, the thirty-eighth concern offered to publish it. And so the book was brought out, with something of a flourish, and met with its thirty- eighth rejection--at the hands of the public!

BOOK VII
THE CAPTURE IS COMPLETED

The shadow of a dark cloud had fallen upon the woods, and the voices of the birds were strangely hushed.

"There is a spell about this place for me," she said, and quoted--

"Here came I often, often in old days--
Thyrsis and I, we still had Thyrsis then!"

"Where is Thyrsis now?" she asked; and he smiled sadly, and responded:

"Ah me! this many a year
My pipe is lost, my shepherd's holiday!
Needs must I lose them, needs with heavy heart
Into the world and wave of men depart!"_

Section 1. They returned to the city early in October--not so much because they minded the cold in the tent, as because their money was gone, and it was not easy to do hack-work at a distance. One had to be on the spot, to interview the editors, to study their whims and keep one's self in their minds; otherwise some one else got the work.

So Thyrsis came back to his "world"; and he found this world up in arms against him. All the opposition that he had ever had to face was nothing to what he faced now. Society seemed to have made up its collective mind that he should give in; and every force it could use was brought to bear upon him--every person he knew joined in the assault upon him.

He was bound to admit that they had all the arguments on their side. He had gone his own obstinate way, in defiance of all advice and of all precedent; and now he saw what had come of it--exactly what every common-sense person had foreseen. He and Corydon had tried their "living as brother and sister"--and here she was with child! And that was all right, no one proposed to blame him for it; it was what people had predicted, and they were rather pleased to have their predictions come true--to see the bubble of his pretenses burst, and to be able to point out to him that he was like all other men. What they wanted now was simply that he should recognize his responsibility, and look out for Corydon's welfare. Living in tenement-rooms and in tents, like gypsies and savages, was all right by way of a lark; it was all very picturesque and romantic in a novel; but it would not do for a woman who was about to become a mother. Corydon had been delicately reared. She was used to the comforts and decencies of life; and to get her in her present plight and then not provide these things for her would be the act of a scoundrel.

All through his life the world had had but one message for Thyrsis: "Go to work!" From the world's point of view his languages and literatures, his music and writing were all play; to "work" was to get a "position". And now this word was dinned into his ears day and night, the very stones in the street seemed to cry it at him--"Get a position! Get a position!"

As chance would have it, the position was all ready. In the higher regions they were preparing to open a branch of a great family establishment abroad, and Thyrsis was invited to take charge of it. He would be paid three thousand dollars a year at the start, and two or three times as much ultimately; and what more could he want? He knew nothing about the work, but they knew his abilities--that if he would undertake it, and give his attention to it, he would succeed. He would meet people of culture, they argued, and be broadened by contact with men; as for Corydon, it would make her whole life over. Surely, for her sake, he could not refuse!

Thyrsis had foreseen just such things. He had braced himself to meet the shock, and the world found him with his hands clenched and his jaws set. There was no use in arguing with him, he had but one answer--"No! No! No!" He would not take that position, and he would not take any other position--neither now, nor at any future time. He was not a business-man, he was an artist; and an artist he would remain to the end. It might as well be understood at the outset; there was nothing that the world could do or say to him that would move him one inch. They might starve him, they might kill him, they might do what they could or would--but never would he give in.

"But--what are you going to do?" they cried.

He answered, "I am going to write my books."

"But you have already written two books, and nothing has come of them!"

"Something may come of them yet," he said. "And if it doesn't, I shall simply go on and write another, and another, and another. I shall continue to write so long as I have the strength left in me; I shall be trying to write when I die."

And so, while they argued and pleaded and scolded and wept, he stood in silence. They could not understand him--he smiled bitterly as he realized how impossible it was for them to understand even the simplest thing about him. There was the dapper corporation lawyer and his exquisite young wife, who came to argue about it; and Thyrsis asked them not to tell Corydon why they had come. He saw them look at each other significantly, and he could read their thought--that he was afraid of his wife's importunities. And how could he explain to them what he had really meant--that if they had told Corydon they had come to persuade him to give up his art, Corydon would probably have found it impossible to be even decently polite to them!

Section 2. So Thyrsis went away, carrying the burden of the scorn and contempt of every human soul he knew. It was in truth a dark hour in his life. He was at his wit's end for the bare necessities. He had reached the city with less money in his pocket than he had had the year before; and all the ways by which he had got money seemed to have failed him at once. All the editors who published book-reviews seemed to have a stock on hand; or else to know of people whose style of writing pleased their readers better. And none of them seemed to fancy any ideas for articles that Thyrsis had to suggest.

Worst of all, the editor of the "'Treasure Chest" turned down the pot-boiler which he had been writing up in the country. He would not say anything very definite about it--he just didn't like the story--it had not come up to the promise of the scenario. He hinted that perhaps Thyrsis was not as much interested in his work as he had been before. It seemed to be lacking in vitality, and the style was not so good. Thyrsis offered to rewrite parts of the story; but no, said the editor, he did not care for the story at all. He would be willing to have Thyrsis try another, but he was pretty well supplied with serials just then, and could not give much encouragement.

Corydon had yielded to her parents and gone to stay with them for a while; and Thyrsis had got his own expenses down to less than five dollars a week--including such items as stationery and postage on his manuscripts. And still, he could not get this five dollars. In his desperation he followed the cheap food idea to extremes, and there were times when an invitation to an honest meal was something he looked forward to for a week. And day after day he wandered about the streets, racking his brains for new ideas, for new plans to try, for new hopes of deliverance.

In later years he looked back upon it all--knowing then the depth of the pit into which he had fallen, knowing the full power of the forces that were ranged against him--and he marvelled that he had ever had the courage to hold out. But in truth the idea of surrender did not occur to him; the possibility of it did not lie in his character. He had his message to deliver. That was what he was in the world for, and for nothing else; and he must deliver what he could of it.

He would go alone, and his vision would come to him. It would come to him, radiant, marvellous, overwhelming; there had never been anything like it in the world, there might never be anything like it in the world again. And if only he could get the world to realize it--if only he could force some hint of it into the mind of one living person! It was impossible not to think that some day that person would be discovered--to believe otherwise would be to give the whole world up for damned. He would imagine that chance person reading his first book; he would imagine the publishers and their advisers reading "The Hearer of Truth"--might it not be that at this very hour some living soul was in the act of finding him out? At any rate, all that he could do was to try, and to keep on trying; to embody his vision in just as many forms as possible, and to scatter them just as widely as possible. It was like shooting arrows into the air; but he would go on to shoot while there was one arrow left in his quiver.

Section 3. Thyrsis reasoned the problem out for himself; he saw what he wanted, and that it was a rational and honest thing for him to want. He was a creative artist, engaged in learning his trade. When he had completed his training, he would not work for himself, he would work to bring joy and faith to millions of human beings, perhaps for ages after. And meantime, while he was in the practice-stage, he asked for the bare necessities of existence.

Nor was it as if he were an utter tyro; he had given proof of his power. He had written two books, which some of the best critics in the country had praised. To this people made answer that it was no one's business to look out for genius and give it a chance to live. But with Thyrsis it was never any argument to show that a thing did not exist, if it was a thing which he knew *ought* to exist. He looked back over the history of art, and saw the old hideous state of affairs--saw genius perishing of starvation and misery, and men erecting monuments to it when it was dead. He saw empty-headed rich people paying fortunes for the manuscripts of poems which all the world had once rejected; he saw the seven towns contending for Homer dead, through which the living Homer begged his bread. And Thyrsis could not bring himself to believe that a thing so monstrous could continue to exist forever.

There was no other department of human activity of which it was true. If a man wanted to be a preacher, he would find that people had set up divinity-schools and established scholarships for which he could contend. And the same was true if he wished to be an engineer, or an architect, or a historian, or a biologist; it was only the creative artist of whom no one had a thought--the creative artist, who needed it most of all! For his was the most exacting work, his was the longest and severest apprenticeship.

Brooding over this, Thyrsis hit upon another plan. He drew up a letter, in which he set forth what he wanted, and stated what he had so far done; he quoted the opinions of his work that had been written by men-of-letters, and offered to submit the books and manuscripts about which these opinions had been written. He sent a copy of this letter to the president of each of the leading universities in the country, to find out if there was in a single one of them any fellowship or scholarship or prize of any sort, which could be won by such creative literary work. Of those who replied to him, many admitted that his point was well taken, that there should have been such provision; but one and all they agreed that none existed. There were rewards for studying the work of the past, but never for producing new work, no matter how good it might be.

Then another plan occurred to him. He wrote an anonymous article, setting forth some of his amusing experiences, and contrasting the credit side of the "pot-boiling" ledger with the debit side of the "real art" ledger. This article was pictur-esque, and a magazine published it, paying twenty-five dollars for it, and so giving him another month's lease of life. But that was all that came of it--there was no rich man who wrote to the magazine to ask who this tormented genius might be.

Then Thyrsis, in his desperation, joined the ranks of the begging letter-writers. He would send long accounts of his plight to eminent philanthropists--having no idea that the secretaries of eminent philanthropists throw out basketsful of such let-ters every day. He would read in the papers of some public-spirited enterprise--he would hear of this man or that woman who was famous for his or her interest in helpful things--and he would sit down and write these people that he was starving, and implore them to read his book. In later years, when he came to know of some of these newspaper idols, it was a comfort to him to feel certain that his letters had been thrown away unread.

Also he begged from everybody he met, under whatever circumstances he met them. If by any chance the person might be imagined to possess money, sooner or later would come some hour of distress, when Thyrsis would be driven to try to borrow. On one occasion he counted it up, and there were forty-three individuals to whom he had made himself a nuisance. With half a dozen of them he had actu-ally succeeded; but always promising to return the money when his next check came in--and always scrupulously doing this. There was never anyone who rose to the understanding of what he really wanted--a free gift, for the sake of his art. There was never anyone who could understand his utter shamelessness about it; that fervor of consecration which made it impossible for a man to humiliate him, or to insult him--to do anything save to write himself down a dead soul.

People were quite clear in their views upon this question; a man must earn his own way in the world. And that was all right, if a man were in the world for himself. But what if he were working for humanity, and had no time to think about himself? Was that truly a disgraceful thing? Take Jesus, for instance; ought he to have kept at his carpenter's trade, instead of preaching the Sermon on the Mount? Or was it that his right to preach the Sermon was determined by the size of the col-lection he could take among the audience?

And then, while he pondered this problem of "earning one's own way," Thyrsis was noting the lives of the people who were preaching it. What were *they* doing to earn the luxuries they enjoyed? Even granting that one recognized their futile benevolence as justifying them personally--what about the tens of thousands of others who lived in utter idleness, squandering in self-indulgence and ostentation huge fortunes of which they had never earned a penny? The boy could not go upon the streets of the city without having this monstrous fact flaunted in his face in a thousand forms. So many millions for folly and vice, and not one cent for his art! This was the thing upon which he was brooding day and night--and filling his soul with an awful bitterness which was to horrify the world in later years.

Section 4. He might not come to see Corydon in her home; but she would meet him in the street, and they would walk in the park, a pitiful and mournful pair. They had to walk slowly, and often he would have to help her, for her burden had now become great. She had altered all her dresses, and she wore a long cape, and even then was not able to hide the disfigurement of her person. They would sit upon a bench in the cold, and talk about the latest aspects of his struggle, what he was doing and what he hoped to do. Corydon would bring him the opinions of a few more members of the bourgeois world, and they would curse this world and these people together. For there was no more thought of giving up on Corydon's side than there was on his; it was not for nothing that he had talked to her upon the hill-top in the moonlight.

Meanwhile, however, time was passing, and the prospect of her approaching confinement hung over them like a black thunder-cloud. It came on remorselessly, menacingly. The event was due about Christmas time, and there must be some money then--there must be some money then! But where was it to be found?

Thyrsis had tried another story for the "Treasure Chest," but the editor had not liked his plot. Also he was taking "The Hearer of Truth" from one place to another; but with less and less hope, as he learned from various editors and publishers how radical and subversive they considered it. He took it now mechanically, as a matter of form--making it his rule always to count upon rejection, so that he might never be disappointed.

One of Corydon's rich friends had told her of a certain famous surgeon, and Corydon had gone to see him. He had a beautiful private hospital, and his prices were unthinkable; but he had seemed to be interested in her, and when she told him her circumstances, he had said that he would try to "meet her halfway." But even with the reductions he quoted, it would cost them nearly a hundred and fifty dollars; and how could Thyrsis get such a sum? Even if the surgeon were willing to wait--what prospect was there that he could ever get it?

This again was the curse of their leisure-class upbringing. They did not know how poor women had their babies, and they shrunk from the thought of finding it out. Corydon had met this man, and had been impressed by him; and Thyrsis realized, even if she did not, that she had got her heart set upon the plan. And if he did not make it possible, and then anything were to go wrong with her, how would he ever be able to forgive himself? This event would come but once, and might mean so much to them.

So he said to himself that he would "raise the money". But the days passed and became weeks, and the weeks became months, and there was no sign of the raising. And then suddenly came one of those shafts of sunlight through the clouds--one of those will-o'-the-wisps that were forever luring Thyrsis into the swamps. Another editor liked "The Hearer of Truth"; another editor said that it was a great piece of literature, and that he would surely use it! So Thyrsis went to the great surgeon and told him that he would be able to pay him in a little while; and the arrangement was made for Corydon to come. And then the editor put the "great piece of literature" away in his desk, and forgot all about it for a month--while Thyrsis waited, day by day, in an agony of suspense.

The appointed time had come--the day when Corydon must go to the hospital; and still the editor had not reported, and there was only fifteen or twenty dollars, earned by weeks of verse-writing and reviewing. So in desperation Thyrsis made up his mind to give up his violin. He had paid ninety dollars for it three years before; and now, after taking it round among the dealers, he sold it for thirty-five dollars.

So, to the very gateway of life itself, Thyrsis was hounded by these spectres of want; even to the hospital they came, and followed him inside. Here was a beautiful place, a revelation to him of the possibilities of civilization and science. But it was all for the rich and prosperous, it was not for him; he felt that he had no business to be there.

What a contrast it all made with the tenement-room in which he had to house! Here were glimpses to be had of rich women, soft-skinned and fair, clad in morning-gowns of gorgeous hue; here were baskets of expensive fruits and armfuls of sweet-scented flowers; and here was he with his worn clothing and his haggard face, his hungry stomach and still hungrier heart! Must not all these people know that he had had to ask for special rates, and then for credit on top of that? Must they not all know that he was a failure--that most worthless of all worthless creatures, the man who cannot support his family? What did it mean to them if he had written master-pieces of literature--what would it avail with them that he was the bearer of a new religion! Thyrsis had heard too much of the world's opinion of him; he shrunk from contact with his fellow-creatures, reading an insult into every glance. He was like a dog that has been too much beaten, and cringes even before it is struck.

Section 5. But these thoughts were for himself; he did not whisper them to Corydon. However people might despise him, they did not blame her, and there was no need of this bitterness in her cup. Corydon was beautiful--ah God, how beautiful she looked, lying there in the snowy bed, with the snowy lace about her neck and arms! How like the very goddess of motherhood she looked, a halo of light about her forehead. She, too, must have flowers, to whisper to her of hope and joy; and so he had brought her three pitiful little pinks, which he had purchased from a lame girl upon the corner. The tears started into Corydon's eyes as she saw these-- for she knew that he had gone without a part of his dinner in order to bring them to her.

Everybody had come to love her already, he could see. How gentle and kind they were to her; and how skillfully they did everything for her! His heart was full of thankfulness that he had been able to bring her to this haven of refuge. And resolutely he put aside all thoughts of his own humiliation--he swept his mind clear of everything else, and went with her to face this new and supreme experience of her life.

"You will stay with me?" she had pleaded; and he had promised that he would stay. She could not bear to have him out of her sight at all, and so they made him a bed upon the couch, and he spent the night there; and through the next day he sat with her and read to her. But now and then he would know that her thoughts had wandered, and he would look at her and see her eyes wide with fear. "Oh, Thyrsis," she would whisper, "I'm only a child; and I'm not fit to be a mother!"

He would try to comfort her and soothe her. But in truth, he too was full of fears and anxieties. He had felt the dome-like shape within her abdomen, which they said was the head of the child; and he could not conceive how it was ever to be got out. But they told him that the thing had happened before. There was nothing for either of them to do but to wait;

They were in the hands of Nature, who had brought them thus far, who had had her will with them so utterly. And now her purpose was to be revealed to them--now they were to know the wherefore of all that they had done. They were like two children, travelling through a dark valley; they walked hand in hand, lifting their eyes to the mountain-tops, and seeking the first signs of the coming light.

Section 6. Outside, whenever they opened the window, they could hear the noise of the busy city; and it seemed so strange that street-cars should jangle on, and news-boys shout, and tired men hurry home to their dinners--while such a thing as this was preparing. Thyrsis gave utterance to the thought; and the doctor, who was in the room, smiled and responded, "It happens twice every second in the world!"

This was the house-physician, who was to take charge of the case; a young man, handsome and rather dapper. He went about his work with an air of its being an old story to him--an air which was at once reassuring and disturbing. The two sat and watched him, while he made his preparations.

He had two white-gowned nurses with him, and he spoke to them for the most part in nods. One of them was elderly and grey-haired, and apparently his main reliance; the other was young and pretty, and her heart went out to Corydon. She sat by the bedside and confided to her that she was a pupil, and that this was only her third "case".

"Will it hurt me much?" the girl asked, weakly.

And then suddenly, before there was time for an answer, she turned white, and clutched Thyrsis' hand with a low cry.

"What's the matter?" he whispered.

Her fingers closed upon his convulsively, and she started up, crying aloud.

The doctor was standing by the window, opening a case of instruments. He did not even turn.

"Doctor!" Thyrsis cried, in alarm.

He put the case down and came toward the bed. "I guess there is nothing wrong," he said, with a slight smile. He laid his hand upon the shuddering girl.

"It is all right," he said, "I shall examine her in a few moments."

He turned away, while Thyrsis and the young nurse held Corydon's hand and whispered to her soothingly.

She sank back and lay tossing from side to side, moaning; and meantime the doctor went quietly on, arranging his basins and bottles, and giving his orders. Then finally he came and made his examination.

"She is doing very well," he said, "and now, Miss Mary, I have an engagement for the theatre for this evening. I think there will be no need of me for some hours."

Thyrsis started, aghast. "Doctor!" he cried.

"What is it?" asked the other.

"Something might happen!" he exclaimed.

"I shall be only two or three blocks away," was the reply--"They will send for me if there is need."

"But this pain!" cried Thyrsis, excitedly. "What is she to do?"

The man stood by the bedside, washing his hands. "You cannot have a child-birth without pain," he said. "These are merely false pains, as we call them; the real birth-pains may not come for hours--perhaps not until morning. There are membranes which have to be broken, and muscles which have to be stretched--and there is no way of doing it but this way."

He stood with his hand on the doorknob. "Do not be worried," he said. "Whatever happens, the attendant will know what to do."

"The theatre!" It seemed so strange! To be sure, it was unreasonable--if a man had several cases each week to attend to, he could not be expected to suffer with each one. But at least he need not have mentioned the theatre! It gave one such a strange feeling of isolation!

Section 7. However, he was gone, and Thyrsis turned to Corydon, who lay moaning feebly. It was like a knife cutting her, she said; she could not bear to lie down, and when she tried to sit up she could not endure the weight of her own body. She found it helped her for Thyrsis to support her, and so he sat beside her, holding her tightly, while she wrestled with her task. The nurse fanned her brow, on which the sweat stood in drops.

Thyrsis' position strained every muscle in his body; it made each minute seem an hour. But he clung there, till his head reeled. Anything to help her--anything, if only he could have helped her!

But there was no help; she was gone alone into the silent chamber of pain, where there comes no company, no friend, no love. His spirit cried out to her, but she heard him not--she was alone, alone! Is there any solitude that the desert or the ocean knows, that is like the solitude of suffering?

It would come over her in spasms, and Thyrsis could feel her body quiver; it would be all he could do to hold her. And minute after minute, hour after hour, it was the same, without a moment's respite--until she broke into sobbing, crying that she could not bear it, that she could not bear it! She clutched wildly at Thyrsis' hand, and her arms shook like a leaf.

He ran in fright for the elder nurse, who had left the room. She came and questioned Corydon, and shook her head. "There is nothing to be done," she said.

"But something is wrong!" Thyrsis cried. He had been reading a book, and his mind was full of images of all sorts of accidents and horrors, of monstrosities and "false presentations." "You must send for the doctor," he repeated, "I know there **must** be something wrong!"

"I will send for the doctor if you wish," was the reply. "But you must order it. The birth has not yet begun, you know--when it does the character of the pains will change altogether, and she will know. Meantime there is nothing whatever for the doctor to do."

"He might give her an opiate!" Thyrsis exclaimed.

"If he did," said the woman, "that would stop the birth. And it must come."

So they turned once more to the task. Thyrsis bore it until it seemed to him that his body was on fire; then he asked the nurse to take his place. He reeled as he tried to walk to the sofa; he flung himself down and lay panting. Outside he could still hear the busy sounds of the street--the world was going on its way, unknowing, unheeding. There came a chorus of merry laughter to him--his soul was black with revolt.

He went back to his post, biting his lips together.

She was only a child--she was too tender; it was monstrous, he cried. Why, she was being torn to pieces! She writhed and quivered, until he thought she was in convulsions. And then, little by little, all this faded from his thoughts; he had his own pain to bear. He must hold her just so, with the grip of a wrestler; his arms ached, and his temples throbbed, and he fought with himself and whispered to himself--he would stay there until he dropped.

Would the doctor never come? It was preposterous for him to leave her like this. The time passed on; he was wild with impatience, and suddenly Corydon sank back and burst into tears. He could stand it no more, and sent for the nurse again.

"You must send for the doctor!" he cried.

"He has just come in," the woman answered; "I heard him close the door."

The doctor entered the room, softly. He was perfectly groomed, clad in evening-dress, and with his gloves and his silk hat in his hand. Thyrsis hated him at that moment--hated him with the fury of some tortured beast. He was only an assistant; and were not assistants notoriously careless? Why had the great surgeon himself not come to see to it?

"How does she bear it?" he said, to the nurse; and he took off his overcoat and coat, and rolled up his sleeves, while she reported progress. Then he felt Corydon's pulse, and after washing his hands, made another examination. Thyrsis watched him with his heart in his mouth.

He rose without saying anything.

"Has it presented?" the nurse asked.

"Not yet," he said, and turned to look at the temperature of the room.

It was so, then--there was nothing to be done! Thyrsis was dazed--he could hardly believe it. He had never dreamed it could be anything like this.

"How long is this to last, doctor?" he cried. "She is suffering so horribly!"

"I fear it will be until morning," he said--"it is a question of the rigidity of certain muscles. But you need not be alarmed, she is doing very well."

He spoke a few words to the patient, and then turned towards the door. "I shall sleep in the next room," he said to his assistant; "you may call me at any time."

Section 8. So the two went apart again; and the leaden-footed hours crept by, and the girl still wrestled with the fiend. The young nurse was asleep on the couch, and the elder sat dozing in her chair; the two were alone--all alone! One of the window-shades was raised, and Thyrsis could see far over the tops of the buildings. Somewhere out there was another single light, where perhaps some other soul counted the fiery pulses of torture. A death--or another birth, perhaps! The doctor had said it happened twice every second!

Thyrsis was unskilled in pain, and perhaps he bore it ill; he feared that the nurses thought so too--that Corydon called too often for something, or cried out too much in mere aimless misery.

But the time sped on, and at last a faint streak of day appeared in the sky, and the shadows began to pale in the room. Thyrsis started, realizing that it was morning. He had given up the morning, as a thing that would never come again. He insisted upon sending for the doctor, who came, striving not to yawn, but to look pleased. Once more he shook his head; there was nothing to do.

The street began to waken. The milkman came, his cans rattling; now and then he shouted to his horse, or whistled, or banged upon a gate. Then the sun came streaming into the room. The newsboys began to call--the young nurse woke up and began to straighten her hair. The elder nurse also opened her eyes, but did not stir; she seemed to challenge anyone to assert that she had ever been asleep.

"Perhaps, Miss Mary," ventured the young nurse, timidly, "we had best prepare the patient."

Corydon seemed to rest a little easier now, and they carried her and laid her on the couch. They made the bed, with many sheets and with elaborate care; and then they brought her back and dressed her, putting a short gown upon her, and drawing long white bags over her limbs. Ah, how white she was, and what fearful lines of suffering had been graven into her forehead!

She lay in a kind of stupor, and Thyrsis, exhausted, began to doze. He knew not how long a time had passed--it had been an hour, perhaps two, when suddenly he opened his eyes and sat up with a bound galvanized into life by a cry from Corydon. She had started forward, grasping around her wildly, uttering a series of rising screams. He clutched her hand, and stared around the room in fright.

They were alone. He leaped up; but the nurse ran into the room at the same instant. She gazed at the girl, whose face had flushed suddenly purple; she came to her, and took her hand.

"You feel some pain?" she asked.

Corydon could not speak, but she nodded; a moment later she sunk back with a gasp.

"A kind of bearing-down pain?" said the nurse. "Different from the other?"

Corydon gasped her assent again.

"That is the birth," the nurse said. "The doctor will be here in a moment."

Again the horrible spasm seized the girl, and brought her to a sitting posture; again her hand clutched Thyrsis' with a grip like death, and again the veins on her forehead leaped out. Like the surging of an ocean billow, it seemed to sweep over her; and then suddenly she screamed, and sank back upon the pillow.

Thyrsis was wild with alarm; but the doctor entered, placid as ever. "So they've come?" he said.

Nothing seemed to disturb him. He was like a being out of another region. He took off his coat and bared his arms; he put on a long white apron, and washed his hands elaborately again, and then once more examined his patient. His face was opposite to Thyrsis, and the latter watched his expression, breathless with dread. But the doctor only said, "Ah, yes."

He turned to Corydon. "These pains that you feel," he said, "are from the compressing of the womb. Don't let them frighten you--everything is just as it should be. You will find that you can help at each pang by holding your breath; just as soon as you cry out, it releases the diaphragm, and the pressure stops, and the pain passes. You must bear each one just as long as you can. I don't want you to faint, of course--but the longer the pressure lasts, the sooner it will all be over."

The girl was staring at him with her wild eyes--she looked like a hunted creature in a trap. It sounded all so very simple--but the horror of it drove Thyrsis mad. Ah, God, it was monstrous--it was superhuman--it was a thing beyond all thinking! It wrung all his soul, it shook him as the tempest shakes a leaf--the sight of this awful agony.

It was like the sudden closing of a battle; the shock of squadrons, the locking of warriors in a grip of death. There was no longer time for words now, no longer time for a glance about him; the spasms came, one after another, relentless, unceasing, inevitable--each trooping upon the heels of the last; they were uncounted--uncountable--piling upon one another like waves upon the sea, like the gusts of a raging storm. And this girl, this child, that he had watched over so hungrily, that was so tender and so sensitive--it was like wild horses tearing her apart! The agony would flame up in her, he would see her body turn rigid, her face flush scarlet, her teeth become set and her gums fleshed. The muscles would stand out in her cheeks, the perspiration start upon her forehead. She would grip Thyrsis' hand until all the might of both his arms was not enough to match her.

On the other side of the bed knelt the young nurse, wrestling with the other hand; and Thyrsis could see her face flush too, each time--until at last a cry seem to tear its way from the girl's throat, and would sink back, faint and white.

It was a new aspect of life to Thyrsis, a new revelation of being; it was pain such as he had never dreamed it was horror the like of which was unknown in his philosophy. All the suffering of the night was nothing to a minute of this; it came upon her with the rush of a flood of waters--it seized her--instant, insistent, relentless as the sweep of the planets. Thyrsis had been all unprepared for it; he cried out for time to think--to realize it. But there was no time to think or to realize it. The thing was here--now! It glared into his eyes like a fiend of hell; it was fiery, sharp as steel--and it had to be seized with the naked hands!

The pangs came, each one worse than the last. They built themselves up in his soul in a symphony of terror; they lifted him out of himself, they swept him away beyond all control, like a leaf in the autumn wind. He had never known such a sensation before--his soul seemed whirled into pieces. His feeling was apart from his action; he could not control his thoughts; he was going mad! He loved her so--she was so beautiful; and to see her thus, in the grip of horror!

He tried to get hold of himself again--he talked to himself, pinning his attention on the task of his hands. Perhaps maybe it was his fancy--it did not really hurt her so! Maybe--

He spoke to her, calling to her, in between the crises. She turned her eyes upon him, looking unutterable agony; she could not speak. And then again came the spasm, and she reared herself to meet it. She seemed to loom before his eyes; she was no longer human, but in her agony transfigured. She was the suffering of being, made flesh; a figure epic, colossal, worthy of an Angelo; the mighty mother herself, the earth-mother, from whose womb have come the races!

And then--"Perhaps she would be more comfortable with another pillow," said the doctor, and the spell was broken.

Corydon shook her head with swift impatience. This was her conflict, the gesture seemed to say. They had only to let her alone--she had no words to spare for them.

"How long does this last?" Thyrsis asked, his voice trembling. The doctor made a motion to him to be silent--evidently he did not wish Corydon to hear the answer to that question.

Section 9. For the girl's soul was rising within her; perhaps from the deeps of things there came comfort to her, from the everlasting, universal motherhood of life. Nature must have told her that this at least was pain to some purpose; something was being accomplished. And she shut her jaws together again, and closed with it--driving, driving, with all the power of her being. A feeling of awe stole over Thyrsis as he watched her--a feeling the like of which he had never known in his life before. She was a creature consecrated, made holy by suffering; she was the sacredness of life incarnate, a thing godlike, beyond earth. It came as a revelation, changing the whole aspect of life to him. It was hard to realize--that woman, woman who endured this, was the same being that he had met in the world all his life--laughing and talking, careless and commonplace. This--this was woman's *fate*! It was the thing for which woman was made, and the lowest, meanest of them might have to bear it! He swore vows of reverence and knighthood; he fell upon his knees before her, weeping, his soul white-hot with awe. Ah what should he do that he might be worthy to live upon the earth with a woman?

And this was no mere fine emotion; there was no room for imagination in it--the reality exceeded all imagination. Overwhelming it was, furious, relentless; his thoughts strove to roam, but it seized him by the hair and dragged him back. Here-- *here!*

She was wrung and shaken with her agony, her eyes shut, her face uplifted, her muscles turned to stone. And the minutes dragged out into hours--there was no end to it--there was no end to it! There was no meaning--it was only naked, staring terror. It beat him up again and again; he would sink back exhausted, thinking that he could feel no more; but it dragged him up once more--to agony without respite! The caverns of horror were rent open; they split before his eyes--deeper, deeper--in vistas and abysses from which he shrunk appalled. Here dwelt the furies, despair and madness--here dwelt the demon-forces of being, grisly phantoms which come not into the light of day. Their hands were upon him, their claws were in his flesh; and over their chasms he shuddered--he scented the smoke of that seething pit of life, whose top the centuries have sealed, and into which no mortal thing may gaze and live.

Life--life--here was life, he felt. What had he known of it before this?--the rest was pageantry and sham. Beauty, pleasure, love--here they were in the making of them--here they were in the real truth of them! Raw, naked, hideous it was; and it was the source of all things else! His being rose in one titan throb of rebellion. It was monstrous--it was unthinkable! He wanted no such life--he had no right to it! Let there be an end of it! No life that ever was could be worth such a price as this! It was a cheat, a horror--there could be no justice in such a thing! There could be no God in it--it was oppression, it was wrong! He thought of the millions that swarmed on the earth--they had all come from this! And it was happening every hour--every second! He saw it, the whole of it--the age-long agony, the universal birth-pang of being. And he hated it, hated it with a wild, raging hatred--he would have annihilated it with one sweep of his arm.

And yet--there was no way to annihilate it! It was here--it was inevitable. And it was everlasting--it was an everlasting delusion, an everlasting madness. It was a Snare!

Yes, he came back to the thought--that was the image for it! It mattered not how much you might cry out, you were in it, and it held you! It held you as it held Corydon, in throb after throb of torment. She moaned, she choked, she tossed from side to side; but it held her. It seemed to him that the storm of her agony beat upon her like the tempest upon a mountain pine-tree.

Section 10. The doctor's hands were red with blood now, like a butcher's. He bent over his work, his lips set. Now and then he would speak to the young nurse, whom he was teaching; and his words would break the spell of Thyrsis' nightmare.

"You can see the head now," he said once, turning to the boy.

And Thyrsis looked; through the horrible gaping showed a little patch, the size of a dollar--purplish black, palpitating, starting forward when the crises shook the mother. "And that is a head!" he whispered, half aloud.

"But how can it ever get out?" he cried suddenly with wildness.

"It will get out," the doctor answered, smiling. "Wait--you will see."

"But the baby will be dead!" he panted.

"It is very much alive," replied the other. "I can hear its heart beating plainly."

All the while Thyrsis had never really believed in the child--it was too strange an idea. He could think only of the woman, and of her endless agony. Every minute seemed a life-time to him--the long morning had come and gone, and still she lay in her torment. He was sick in body, and sick in soul; she had exerted the strength of a dozen men, it seemed to him.

But now her strength was failing her, he was certain; her moans were becoming more frequent, her protests more vehement. The veins stood out on the doctor's forehead as he worked with her--muscular, like a pugilist. Gigantic, he seemed to Thyrsis--terrible as fate. Time and again the girl screamed, in sudden agony; he would toil on, his lips set. Once it was too much even for him--her cries had become incessant, and he nodded to the nurse, who took a bottle from the table, and wetting a cloth with it, held it to Corydon's face. Then she shouted aloud, again and again--wildly, and more wildly, laughing hysterically; she began flinging her arms about--and then calling to Thyrsis, as her eyes closed, murmuring broken sentences of love, "babbling o' green fields." It was too much for the boy--there was a choking in his throat, and he rushed from the room and sank down upon a chair in the hall, crying like a child.

After a while he rose up. He paced the hall, talking to himself. He could not go on acting in this way--he must be a man. Others had borne this--he would bear it too; he would get himself together. It would all be over before long, and then how he would be ashamed of himself!

He went back. "It is the chloroform that makes her do that," said the young nurse, soothingly. "She is out of pain when she cries out so."

Corydon was coming back from her stupor; the strife began again. She cried out for its end, she could bear no more. "Help me! Help me!" she moaned.

The head was the size of a saucer now--but each time that she screamed it would go back. Thyrsis stood up to get the strength to grip her hand; her face stared up into the air, looking like the face of a wolf. And still there was no end--no end!

There was an hour more of that--the room seemed to Thyrsis to reel. Corydon was crying, moaning that she wished to die. There was now in sight a huge, bulging object--black, monstrous--rimmed with a band of bleeding, straining flesh, tight like the top of a drum. The doctor was bent over, toiling, breathless.

"No more! No more!" screamed the girl. "Oh, my God! my God!"

And the doctor answered her, panting: "Once more! once more! Now! now!" And so on, for minute after minute; luring her on, pleading with her, promising her, lying to her--"Once more! Once more! This will be the last!" He called to her, he rallied her; he signalled to Thyrsis to help him--to inspire her, to goad her to new endurance.

And then another titan effort, and suddenly--incredibly--there burst upon Thyrsis' sight an apparition. Sick at heart, numb with horror, dazed--he scarcely knew what it was. It happened so swiftly that he had hardly time to see; but something leaped forth something enormous, supernatural! It came--it came--there seemed never to be an end to it! He started to his feet, staring, crying out; and at the same moment the doctor lifted the thing aloft, with a cry of exultation. He held it dangling by one leg. Great God! It was a man!

A man! A thing with the head of a man, the body of a man, the legs and arms, the face of a man! A thing hideous--impish--demoniac! A thing purple and dripping with blood--ghastly--unthinkable-- monstrous--a spectre of nightmare dreams!

And suddenly the doctor lifted his hand and smote it; and the mouth of the thing opened, and there came forth a purplish froth--and then a cry! It was a sound like a tin-pan beaten--a sound that was itself a living presence, an apparition; a thing superhuman, out of another world--like the wailing of a lost spirit, terrifying to every sense! With Thyrsis it was like the falling down of towers within him--his whole being collapsed, and he sunk down upon the bed, sobbing, choking, convulsed.

Section 11. When he looked up again the elder nurse had the baby in her arms; and there was a wan smile on Corydon's face.

The doctor's hand was in the ghastly wound, and he was talking to the young nurse, giving her instruction, in a strange, monotonous tone. "The placenta," he was saying, "often has to be removed; we do it by twisting it round and round--very gently, of course. Then it comes--so!"

There came a rush of blood, and Thyrsis turned away his head.

"Give me the basin," said the doctor. "There!--And now the next thing is to see that the uterus contracts immediately. We assist it by compressing the walls, thus. It must be tightly bandaged."

Thyrsis had turned to see the child. He looked at it, and clenched his hands to

control his emotions. Yes, it was a man! it was a man! Not a monster, not a demon-
-a baby!

His boy! himself! God, what a ghastly thing to realize! It had his forehead, it
had his nose! It was a caricature of himself! A caricature grotesque and impish, and
yet one that no human being could mistake--a caricature by the hand of a master!

And it was a living thing! It had power of motion--it twisted and writhed, it
bent its arms and legs! It winked its eyelids, it opened and shut its mouth, it breathed
and made sounds! And it had feeling, too! It had cried out when it was struck!

Gently, with one finger, he touched it; and the contact with its flesh sent a
shudder through every nerve of him. His child! His child! And a living child! A
creature that would go on; that would eat and sleep and grow, that would learn to
make sounds, and to understand things! That would come to think and to will! That
would be a man!

"Is it--is it all right?" he asked the nurse, in a trembling whisper.

"It's a magnificent boy," she said. And then she struck a match, and held the
light in front of its eyes; and the eyes turned to follow the light. "He sees!" she
said.

Yes, he could see! And Thyrsis had already heard that he could speak! What
could it not do--this marvellous object! It was Nature's supreme miracle--it was the
answer to all the riddles, the solution of all the mysteries! It was a vindication of
the subterfuges, a reward for the sacrifices, a balm for the pain! It was the thing for
which all the rest had been, it was the crown and consummation of their love--it
was Life's supreme shout of triumph and exultation!

The nurse was holding the child up before Corydon; and she was gazing at it,
she was feeding her eyes upon it. And oh, the smile that came upon her face--the
ineffable smile! The pride, and the relief, and the beatific happiness! This thing she
had done--it was her act of creation! Her battle that had been fought, her victory
that had been won; and now they brought her the crown and the guerdon! To
Thyrsis there came suddenly the words of Jesus: "A woman when she is in travail
hath sorrow, because her hour hath come; but as soon as she is delivered of the
child, she remembereth no more the anguish, for joy that a man is born into the
world." And he sunk down beside the bed, and caught the woman's hand in his, and
began to sob softly to himself.

Section 12. Later on he went into the street. Evening was come again--for twenty-two hours that siege had lasted! And the boy had eaten nothing since noon of the day before, and he was weak and dizzy.

But how strange the world seemed to him all at once! Peopled with phantom creatures, that came he knew not whence, and went he knew not whither! Creatures of awe and horror, who came out of chaos, and went back into annihilation! Who were flung here and there by cosmic forces, played with by tragic destinies! And all of them without any sense of the perpetual marvel of their own being! They ate and dressed and slept, they laughed and played and worked, they hated and loved and got and spent, with no thought of the wonder of their lightest breath, with no sense of the terrors that ringed them about--the storms that swept them hither and thither, the million miracles that were wrought for them every instant of their lives!

He went into a restaurant, and sat down; and in the seat beside him, close at his elbow, was a man. He was a fat man--eating roast pork, and apple-sauce, and mashed potatoes, and bread. And Thyrsis looked at him with wondering eyes. "Man," he imagined himself saying, "do you know how you came into this world? A thing impish, demoniac--purple and dripping with blood--a spectre of nightmare dreams?"

"W-what?" the man gasped.

"And you know nothing of the pain that it cost! You have no sense of the strangeness of it! You never think what your coming meant to some woman!"

And then--in the seat opposite was a woman; and Thyrsis watched her.

"You!" he thought, "a woman! Can it be that you know what you are? The fate that you play with--the power that dwells in you! To create new life, that may be handed down through endless ages!"

Thyrsis did not say these things; they were what he wanted to say--what he thought that he ought to say. But then he reminded himself that these things were forbidden; these mighty facts of child-birth, of life-creation--they might not be spoken about! They must be kept hidden, veiled with mystery--if one wished to refer to them, he must employ metaphors and polite evasions.

And as Thyrsis sat and thought about this, he clenched his hands. Some day the world would hear about it--some day the world would think about it! Some day people would behold life--would realize what it was and what it meant. They did not realize it now--else how could it be that women, who bore the race with so much pain and sorrow, should be drudges and slaves, or the ornaments and playthings of men? Else how could it be that life, which cost such a fearful price, should be so cheap upon the earth? For every man that lived and walked alive, some woman had had to bear this agony; and yet men were pent up in mines and sweat-shops, they were ground up in accidents in factories and mills--nay, worse than that, were dressed up in gaudy uniforms, and armed with rifles and machine-guns, and marched out to slaughter each other by tens and hundreds of thousands!

So, as he walked the streets that night, Thyrsis made a vow. Some day he would put before the world this vision that had come to him, some day he would blast men's souls with it. He would shake them with this horror, he would thrill them with this sense of the infinite preciousness and holiness of life! He would drive it into them like a barbed arrow--that never afterwards in all their lives would they be rid of. Never afterwards would they dare to mock, never afterwards would they be able to rest until these things had been done away with, until these horrors had been driven from the earth.

PART II
Love's Captivity

BOOK VIII
THE CAPTIVE BOUND

They sat with the twilight shadows about them. Memories too poignant assailed them, and her hand trembled as it lay upon his arm.

"How strange it was!" she whispered. "Have we kept the faith?"

"Who knows?" he answered; and in a low voice he read--

"And long the way appears, which seem'd so short
To the less practised eye of sanguine youth;
And high the mountain-tops, in cloudy air,
The mountain-tops where is the throne of Truth,
Tops in life's morning-sun so bright and bare!"_

Section 1. This was a golden hour in Thyrsis' life. The gates of wonder were flung open, and all things were touched with a new and mystic glow. He scarcely realized it at the time; for once he was too much moved to think about his own emotions, the artist was altogether lost in the man. Even the room in which he lodged was relieved of its sordidness; it was a thing that men had made, and so a part of the mystery of becoming. He yearned for some one to whom he could impart his great emotion; but because of the loneliness of his life he could find no one but the keeper of his lodging-house. Even she became a human thing to him, because of her interest in the great tidings. If all the world loved a lover, it loved yet more one through whom the supreme purpose of love had been accomplished.

Thyrsis went each day to the hospital, to watch the new miracle unfolding itself; to see the Child asserting its existence as a being with a life of its own. He could never tire of watching it; he watched it asleep, with the faint heaving of its body, and the soft, warm odor that clung to it; he watched its awakenings--the opening of its eyes, and the sucking movements that it made perpetually with its lips. They had dressed it up now, and hid some of its strangeness; but each morning the nurse would undress it, and give it a bath; and then he marvelled at the short crooked legs, and the tiny red hands that clutched incessantly at the air, and the strange prehensile feet, that carried one back to distant ages, hinting at the secrets of Nature's workshop. Sometimes they would permit him to hold this mystic creature in his arms--after much exhortation, and assurance that his left arm was properly placed at the back of its head. One found out in this way what a serious business life really was.

Corydon lay back among her pillows and smiled at these things. Most wonderful it was to him to see how swiftly she recovered from her ordeal, how hourly the flush of health seemed to steal back into her cheeks. He became ashamed of the memory of his convulsive anguish and his blind rebellions. He saw now that her pain had not been as other pain; it was a constructive pain, a part of the task of her life. It was a battle in which she had fought and conquered; and now she sat, throned in her triumphal chariot, acclaimed by the plaudits of a multitude of hopes and joys unseen.

There came the miracle of the milk. Incessantly the Child's lips moved, and its hands groped out; it was an embodied demand for new experience--for life, it knew not what. But Nature knew, and had timed the event to this hour. And Thyrsis watched the phenomenon, marvelling--as one marvels at the feat of engineers, who tunnel from opposite sides of a mountain, and meet in the centre without the error of an inch.

It was in accordance with the impression which Corydon made upon him, as a dispenser of abundance, a goddess of fruitfulness, that there should have been more milk than the Child needed. The balance had to be drawn off with a little vacuum-pump; and Thyrsis would watch the tiny jets as they sprayed upon the glass bulb.

The milk was rich and golden-hued; he tasted it, with mingled wonder and shuddering.

These procedures filled the room with a warm, luscious odor, as of a dairy; they were eminently domestic procedures, such as in fancy he had been wont to tease her about. But he had few jests at present--he was in the inner chambers of the temple of life, and hushed and stilled with awe. The things that he had witnessed in that room were never to be forgotten; each hour he pledged himself anew, to the uttermost limits of his life. The voice of skeptic reason was altogether silent in him now. And also he was interested to observe that all protest was ended in Corydon; the impulses of motherhood had now undisputed sway in her.

Section 2. BUT even in such an hour of consecration, the sordid world outside would not leave him unmolested. It was as if the black clouds had parted for a moment, while the sunlight poured through; and now again they rolled together. The great surgeon, who had told Thyrsis that he would wait for his money, professed now to have forgotten his agreement. Perhaps he had really forgotten it--who could tell, with the many things he had upon his mind? At any rate, Corydon found herself suddenly confronted with a bill, which she was powerless to pay; with white cheeks and trembling lips she told Thyrsis about it--and so came more worry and humiliation. The very food that she ate became tasteless to her, because she felt she had no right to it; and in a few days she was begging Thyrsis to take her away.

So he helped to carry her downstairs, and back to her parents' home; and then he returned to his own lonely room, and sat for hours in the bitter cold, with his teeth set tightly, and the nails dug into the palms of his hands. It so happened that just then the editor was beginning to change his mind about "The Hearer of Truth"; and so he had new agonies of anxiety and disappointment.

Again he might not come to see Corydon; and this led to a great misfortune. For she could not do without him now, her craving for him was an obsession; and so she left her bed too soon, and climbed the stairs to his room. Again and again she did this, in spite of his protests; and when, a little later, the doctors found that she had what they called "womb-trouble", they attributed it to this. Perhaps it was not really so, but Corydon believed it, and through all the years she laid upon it the blame for innumerable headaches and backaches. Thus an episode that might have been soon forgotten, stayed with her, as the symbol of all the agonies of which her life was made.

She would come, bringing the baby with her; and they would lay it upon the bed, and then sit and talk, for hours upon hours, wrestling with their problems. Later on, when Corydon was able, they would go to the park, craving the fresh air. But in midwinter there were few days when they could sit upon a bench for long; and so they would walk and walk, until Corydon was exhausted, and he would have to help her back to the room.

Thyrsis in these days was like a wild animal in a cage; pacing back and forth and testing every corner of his prison. But they never thought of giving up; never in all their lives did that possibility come into their discourse. And doggedly, blindly, they kept on with their studies. Corydon mastered new lists of German words, and they read Freitag's "Verlorene Handscrift" together, and von Scheffel's "Ekkehard", and even attempted "Iphigenie auf Tauris"--though in truth they found it difficult to detach themselves to quite that extent from the world of every-day. It is not an easy matter to experience the pure *katharsis* of tragedy, with a baby in the room who has to be nursed every hour or two, and who is liable to awaken at any moment and make some demand.

He was such an intricate and complicated baby, with so many things to be understood--belly-bands and diapers and irrational length of skirts. Sometimes, when Corydon was quite exhausted, the attending to these matters fell to Thyrsis, who became for the time a most domestic poet. He once sent an editorial-room into roars of merriment by offering to review a book upon the feeding of infants. But he told himself that even the hilarious editors had been infants once upon a time; and he had divined that there were secrets about life to be learned, and great art-works to be dreamed, even amid belly-bands and diapers. Also, Thyrsis would brave a great deal of ridicule in order to be paid a dollar for the reading of a book that he really wanted to read. For books that one wanted to read came so seldom; and dollars were so difficult to earn!

It seemed as if the task grew harder every week. He went without cuffs, and wore old and frayed collars, and washed his solitary necktie until it was threadbare, and lived upon prunes and crackers, and gave up the gas-stove in his room--and still he could scarcely manage to get together the weekly rent. He studied the magazines in the libraries, and racked his wits for new ideas to interest their editors. He haunted editorial-rooms until his presence became a burden, and he brought new agonies and humiliations upon himself. He would part from Corydon in the afternoon, and shut himself in his room; and sitting in bed to keep warm, he would work until midnight at some new variety of pot-boiler. After which he would go out to walk and clear his brain--and even then, exhausted as he was, his vision would come to him again, wonderful and soul-shaking. So he would walk on, and go back to write until nearly dawn at something he really loved.

Section 3. It was so that he wrote his poem, "Caradrion". It was out of thoughts of Corydon, and of the tears which they shed in each other's presence, that this poem was made. Thyrsis had a fondness for burrowing into strange old books, in which one found the primitive wonder of the soul of man, first awakening to the mystery of life. Such a book was Physiologus, with his tales of strange beasts and magic jewels. "There is a bird called Caradrion", Thyrsis had read.... "And if the sick man can be healed, Caradrion goes to him, and touches him upon the mouth, and takes his sickness from him; and so the man is made well." And out of this hint he had fashioned the legend of the two children who had grown up together in "the little cot, fringed round with tender green"; one of them Cedric, and one Eileen-- for he had given the names that Corydon preferred.

They grew "unto the days of love", so the story ran--

"And Cedric bent above her, stooping light,
To press a kiss upon her tender cheek.
And said, 'Eileen, I love thee; yea I love,
And loved thee ever, thou my soul's delight.'

So time sped on, until there came

"To Cedric once a strange unlovely thought,
That haunted him and would not let him be.
'Eileen,' he said, 'there is a thing called death,
Of which men speak with trembling at the lips;
And I have thought how it would be with me
If I should never gaze upon thee more.'"

So Cedric went to find out about these matters; he sought a
witch--"the haggard woman, held in awe."

"He found her crouching by a caldron fire;
 Far gleams of light fled through the vault away.
 And tongues of darkness flickered on the wall.
 Then Cedric said, 'I seek the fate to know'.
 And the witch laughed, and gazed on him and sang:

'Fashioned in the shadow-land,
    Out into darkness hurled;
 Trusted to the Storm-wind's hand,
    By the Passion-tempest whirled!
        Ever straining,
        Never gaining,
        Never keeping,
            Young or old!
        Whither going
        Never knowing,
        Wherefore weeping,
            Never told!
 Rising, falling, disappearing,
 Seeking, calling, hating, fearing;
 Blasted by the lightning shock,
 Trampled in the earthquake rock;
 Were I man I would not plead
 In the roll of fate to read!'

"Then Cedric shuddered, but he said again,
 'I seek the fate,' and the witch waved her hand;
 And straight a peal of thunder shook the ground,
 And clanged and battered on the cavern walls,

Like some huge boulder leaping down the cliff.
And blinding light flashed out, and seething fire
Shattered the seamy crags and heaving floor."

And so in a vision of terror Cedric saw the little vale, and the cot "fringed round with tender green"; and upon the lawn he saw Eileen, lying as one dead.

"And Cedric sprang, and cried, 'My love! Eileen!'
And on the instant came a thunder-crash
Like to the sound of old primeval days,
Of mountain-heaving shock and earthquake roar,
Of whirling planets shattered in the dark."

And so, half wild with grief and despair, Cedric wandered forth into the world; and after great suffering, the birds took pity upon him, and gave him advice--that he should seek Caradrion.

"'Caradrion?' cried Cedric, starting up,
'Speak swiftly, ere too late, where dwelleth he?'
'Ah, that I know not,' spake the little voice,
'Yet keep thy courage, seek thou out the stork,
The ancient stork that saw from earliest days,
Sitting in primal contemplation lost,
Sphinx-like, seraphic, and oracular,
Watching the strange procession of men's dreams.'"

But the stork was cruel and would not heed him, and led Cedric a weary chase through the marshes and the brakes. But Cedric pursued, and finally seized the bird by the throat, and forced the secret from him--

"'Fare southward still,
Fronting the sun's midnoon, all-piercing shaft,
Unto the land where daylight burns as fire;

Where the rank earth in choking vapor steams,
And fierce luxurious vegetation reeks.
So shalt thou come upon a seamed rock,
Towering to meet the sun's fierce-flashing might,
Baring its granite forehead to the sky.
There on its summit, in a cavern deep,
Dwells what thou seekest, half a bird, half man,
Caradrion, the consecrate to pain.'"

Then came the long journey and the search for the seamed rock.

"'Twas night; and vapors, curling, choked the ground,
And the rock writhed like flesh of one in pain.
But Cedric mounted up to find the cave,
Crying aloud: 'I seek Caradrion.'
And so, till from the cavern depth a voice:
'Come not, except to sorrow thou be born.'
And Cedric, panting, stretched his shrunken arms:
'Another's sorrow would I change to joy,
And mine own joy to sorrow; help thou me.'
To which the voice, sunk low, replied: 'Come thou.'
And Cedric came, unfearing, in the dark,
And saw in gloomy night a form in pain,
With wings stretched wide, and beating faint and fast.
'Art thou Caradrion?' he murmured swift,
And echo gave reply, 'Caradrion'."

So Cedric told of his errand, and pleaded for help; he heard the
answer of the voice:

"'Yea, I can save her, if thou be a soul
  That can dare pain and face the rage of fate;
  A soul that feareth not to look on death.'

'Speak on,' said Cedric, shaking, and he spoke:
'This is my law, that am Caradrion,
Whose way is sorrow and whose end is death;
That by my pain some fleeting grace I win,
Some joy unto another I can give.
Far through this world of woe I seek, and find
Some soul crushed utterly, and steeped in pain;
And when it sleeps, I stoop on silent wing,
And with a kiss take all its woe away--
Take it for mine, and then into this cave
Return alone, the blessing's price to pay.'
Then up sprang Cedric. 'Nay,' he,' cried, 'then swift,
Ere life be gone!' But once more spake the voice:
'Nay, boy, my race is run, my power is spent;
This hope alone I give thee, as thou wilt;
Whoso stands by and sees my heart-throb cease,
Who tastes its blood, my power and form are his,
And forth he fares in solitary flight,
Caradrion, the consecrate to pain.
And so my word is said; now hide thee far
In the cave's night, and wrestle there in prayer.'
But Cedric said, 'My prayer is done; I wait.'
So in the cave the hours of night sped by,
And sounds came forth as when a woman fights
In savage pain a life from hers to free."

Then in the dawn a dark shadow flew from the cave, and sped across the blue, and came to the little vale, where Eileen lay dying, as he had seen her in the vision in the "haggard woman's" cavern.

"Then Cedric sprang, and cried, 'My love! Eileen!'
And Eileen heard him not; nor knew he wept.--
For mighty sorrow burst from out his heart,

And flooded all his being, and he sunk,
And moaned: 'Eileen, I love thee! Yea, I love,
And loved thee ever; and I can not think
That I shall never gaze upon thee more.
My life for thine--ah, that were naught to give,
Meant not the gift to see thee nevermore!
Never to hear thy voice. Nay, nay, Eileen,
Gaze on me, speak to me, give me but one word,
And I will go and never more return.'
But Eileen answered not; he touched her hand,
And she felt nothing. Then he whispered, low,
'Oh, may God keep thee--for it must be done--
Guard thee, and bless thee, thou my soul's delight!
And when thou waken'st, wilt thou think of me,
Of Cedric, him that loved thee, oh so true?
Nay, for they said thou shouldst no sorrow know,
And that would be a sorrow, yea, it would.
And must thou then forget me, thou my love?
And canst not give me but one single word,
To tell me that I do not die in vain?
Gaze at me, Eileen, see, thy love is here,
Here as of old, above thee stooping light,
To press a kiss upon thy tender lips.--
Ah, I can kiss thee--kiss thee, my Eileen,
Kiss as of yore, with all my passion's woe!'
And as he spoke he pressed her to his heart,
Long, long, with yearning, and he felt the leap
Of molten metal through his throbbing veins;
His eyes shot fire, and anguish racked his limbs,
And he fell back, and reeled, and clutched his brow.
An instant only gazed he on her face,
And saw new life within her gray cheek leap,
And her dark eyelids tremble. Then with moan,

And fearful struggle, swift he fled away,
That she might nothing of his strife perceive.
And then, reminded of his gift of flight,
He started from the earth, and beat aloft,
Each sweep of his great wings a torture-stroke
Upon his fainting heart. And thus away,
With languid flight he moved, and Eileen, raised
In new-born joy from off her couch of pain,
Saw a strange bird into the distance fade."

And so Cedric went back to the seamed rock, and there he heard a voice calling, "I seek Caradrion!" And as before he answered,

"Come not, except to sorrow thou be born!"

And again, in the cave--

   "The hours of night sped by.
And sounds came forth as when a woman fights
In savage pain, a life from hers to free.

But Eileen dwelt within the happy vale,
Thinking no thought of him that went away."

Section 4. This had come so very easily to Thyrsis that he could not believe that it was good. "Just a little story," he said to Corydon, when he read it to her, and he was surprised to see how it affected her--how the tears welled into her eyes, and she clung to him sobbing. It meant more to her than any other thing that he had written; it was the very voice of their tenderness and their grief.

Then Thyrsis took it to the one editor he knew who was a lover of poetry, and was surprised again, at this man's delight. But he smiled sadly as he realized that the editor did not use poetry--they did not praise so recklessly when it was a question of something to be purchased!

"The poem is too long for any magazine," was the verdict, "and it's not long enough for a book. And besides, poetry doesn't sell." But none the less Thyrsis, who would never take a defeat, began to offer it about; and so "Caradrion" was added to the list of stamp-consuming manuscripts, and set out to see the world at the expense of its creator's stomach.

So there was one more wasted vision, one more futile effort--and one more grapple with despair, in the hours when he and his wife sat wrapped in a blanket in the tenement-room. Corydon was growing more nervous and unhappy every day, it seemed to him. There were, apparently, endless humiliations to be experienced by a woman "whose husband did not support her". Some zealous relative had suggested to her the idea that the "hall-boys" might think she was not really married; and so now she was impelled to speculate upon the psychology of these Ethiopian functionaries, and look for slights and disapproval from them!

Thyrsis, from much work and little sleep, was haggard and wild of aspect; the cry of the world, "Take a position!" rang in his ears day and night. The springs of book-reviews had dried up entirely, and by sheer starvation he was forced to a stage lower yet. A former college friend was editing a work of "contemporary biography", and offered Thyrsis some hack-writing. It meant the carrying home of huge bundles of correspondence from the world's most brightly-shining lights, and the making up of biographical sketches from their eulogies of themselves. With every light there came a portrait, showing what manner of light it was. As for Thyrsis, he did his writing with the feeling that he would like to explore with a poniard the interiors of each one of these people.

For nearly three months now an eminent editor had been trying to summon up the courage to accept "The Hearer of Truth". He had written several letters to tell the author how good a work it was; and now that it was to be definitely rejected, he soothed his conscience by inviting the author to lunch. The function came off at one of the most august and stately of the city's clubs, a marble building near Fifth Avenue, where Thyrsis, with a new clean collar, and his worn shoes newly shined, passed under the suspicious eyes of the liveried menials, and was ushered before the eminent editor. About the vast room were portraits of bygone dignitaries; and there were great leather-upholstered arm-chairs in which one might see the dignitaries of the present--some of them with little tables at their sides, and decanters and soda and cracked ice. They went into the dining-room, where everyone spoke and ate in whispers, and the waiters flitted about like black and white ghosts; and while Thyrsis consumed a cupful of cold ***bouillon***, and a squab ***en casserole***, and a plate of what might be described as an honorific salad, he listened to the soft-voiced editor discussing the problem of his future career.

The editor's theme was what the public wanted. The world had existed for a long time, it seemed, and was not easily to be changed; it was necessary for an author to take its prejudices into consideration--especially if he was young, and unknown, and--er--dependent upon his own resources. It seemed to Thyrsis, as he listened, that the great man must have arranged this luncheon as a stage-setting for his remarks--planning it on purpose to light a blaze of bitterness in the soul of the hungry poet. "Look at me," he seemed to say--"this is the way the job is done. Once I was poor and unknown like you--actually, though you might not credit it, a raw boy from the country. But I had taste and talent, and I was judicious; and so now for thirty years I have been at the head of one of the country's leading magazines. And see--by my mere word I am able to bring you here into the very citadel of power! For these men about you are the masters of the metropolis. There is a rich publisher--his name is a household word--and you saw how he touched me on the shoulder. There is an ex-mayor of the city--you saw how he nodded to me! Yonder is the head of one of the oldest and most exclusive of the city's landed families--even with him I am acquainted! And this is power! You may know it by all these signs of mahogany furniture, and leather upholstery, and waiters of reverential deportment. You may know it by the signs of respectability and awesomeness and chaste abundance. Make haste to pay homage to it, and enroll yourself in its service!"

Thyrsis held himself in, and parted from the editor with all courtesy; but then, as he walked down Fifth Avenue, his fury burst into flame. Here, too, was power--here, too, the signs of it! Palaces of granite and marble, arid towering apartment-hotels; an endless vista of carriages and automobiles, with rich women lolling in them, or descending into shops whose windows blazed with jewels and silver and gold. Here were the masters of the metropolis, the masters of life; the dispensers of patronage--that "public" which he had to please. He would bring his vision and lay it at their feet, and they would give him or deny him opportunity! And what was it that they wanted? Was it worship and consecration and love? One could read the answer in their purse-proud glances; in the barriers of steel and bronze with which they protected the gates of their palaces; in the aspects of their flunkeys, whose casual glances were like blows in the face. One could read the answer in the pitiful features of the little errand-girl who went past, carrying some bit of their splendor to them; or of the ragged beggar, who hovered in the shelter of a side-street, fearing their displeasure. No, they were not lovers of life, and protectors; they were parasites and destroyers, devourers of the hopes of humanity! Their splendors were the distilled essence of the tears and agonies of millions of defeated people--their jewels were drops of blood from the heart of the human race!

Section 5. So, with rage and bitterness, Thyrsis was gnawing out his soul in the night-time; distilling those fierce poisons which he was to pour into the next of his works--the most terrible of them all, and the one which the world would never forgive him.

There came another episode, to bring matters to a crisis. In the far Northwest lived another branch of Thyrsis' family, the head of which had become what the papers called a "lumber-king". One of this great man's radiant daughters was to be married, and the family made the selecting of her trousseau the occasion for a flying visit to the metropolis. So there were family reunions, and Thyrsis was invited to bring his wife and call.

Corydon voiced her perplexity.

"What do they want to see *us* for?" she asked.

"I belong to their line," he said.

"But--you are poor!" she exclaimed.

"I know," he said, "but the family's the family, and they are too proud to be snobbish."

"But--why do they ask me?"

Thyrsis pondered. "They know we have published a book," he said. "It must be their tribute to literature."

"Are they people of culture?" she asked.

"Not unless they've tried very hard," he answered. "But they have old traditions--and they want to be aristocratic."

"I won't go," said Corydon. "I couldn't stand them."

And so Thyrsis went alone--to that same temple of luxury where he had called upon the college-professor. And there he met the lumber-king, who was tall and imposing of aspect; and the lumber-queen, who was verging on stoutness; and the three lumber-princesses, who were disturbing creatures for a poet to gaze upon. It seemed to Thyrsis that he had been dwelling in the slums all his life--so sharp was the shock which came to him at the meeting with these young girls. They were exquisite beyond telling: the graceful lines of their figures, the perfect features, the radiant complexions; the soft, filmy gowns they wore, the faint, intoxicating perfumes that clung to them, the atmosphere of serenity which they radiated. There was that in Thyrsis which thrilled at their presence--he had been born into such a world, and might have had such a woman for his mate.

But he put such thoughts from him--he had made his choice long ago, and it was not the primrose-path. Perhaps he was over-sensitive, acutely aware of himself as a strange creature with no cuffs, and with hardly any soles to his shoes. And all the time of these women was taken up by the arrival of packages of gowns and millinery; their conversation was of diamonds and automobiles, and the forthcoming honeymoon upon the Riviera. So it was hard for him not to feel bitterness; hard for him to keep his thoughts from going back to the lonely child-wife wandering about in the park--to all her deprivations, her blasted hopes and dying glories of soul.

The family was going to the matinee; as there was room in their car, they asked Thyrsis to go with them. So he watched the lumber-king (who had refused to lend him money, but had offered him a "position") draw out a bank-note from a large roll, and pay for a box in one of Broadway's great palaces of art. And now--having been advised so often to study what the public wanted--now Thyrsis had a chance to recline at his ease and follow the advice.

"The Princess of Prague", it was called; it was a "musical comedy"; and evidently exactly what the public wanted, for the house was crowded to the doors. The leading comedian was said by the papers to be receiving a salary of a thousand dollars a week. He held the center of the stage, clad in the costume of a lieutenant of marines, and winked and grinned, and performed antics, and sang songs of no doubtful significance, and emitted a fusillade of cynical jests. He was supposed to be half-drunk, and making love to a run-away princess--who would at one moment accept his caresses, and then spurn him coquettishly, and then execute an unlovely dance with him. In between these diverting procedures a chorus would come on, a score or so of highly-painted women, hopping and gliding about, each time clad in new costumes more cunningly indecent than the last.

From beginning to end of this piece there was not a single line of real humor, a spark of human sentiment, a gleam of intelligence; it was a kind of delirium tremens of the drama. To Thyrsis it seemed as if a whole civilization, with all its resources of science and art--its music and painting and costumes, its poets and composers, its actors, singers, orchestra, and audience--had all at once fallen victims to an attack of St. Vitus' dance. He sat and listened, while the theatre full of people roared and howled its applause; while the family beside him--mother and father and daughters--laughed over jokes that made him ashamed to turn and look at them. In the end the realization of what this scene meant--not only the break-down of a civilization, but the trap in which his own spirit was caught--made him sick and faint all over. He had to ask to be excused, and went out and sat in the lobby until the "show" was done.

The family found him there, and the bride-to-be inquired if he "felt better"; then, looking at his pale face, an idea occurred to her, and after a bit of hesitation, she asked him if he would not stay to dinner. In her mind was the conflict between pity for this poor boy, and doubt as to the fitness of his costume; and Thyrsis, having read her mind in a flash, was divided between his humiliation, and his desire for some food. In the end the baser motive won; he buried his pride, and went to dinner.--And so, as the fates had planned it, the impulse to his next book was born.

Section 6. There came another guest to the meal--the rector of the fashionable church which the family attended at home. He was a young man, renowned for the charm of his oratory; smooth-shaven, pink-and-white-cheeked, exquisite in his manners, gracious and insinuating. His ideas and his language and his morals were all as perfectly polished as his finger-nails; and never before in his life had Thyrsis had such a red rag waved in his face. But he had come there for the dinner, and he attended to that, and let Dr. Holland provide the flow of soul; until at the very end, when the doctor was sipping his *demi-tasse*.

The conversation had come, by some devious route, to Vegetarianism; and the clergyman was disapproving of it. That made no difference to Thyrsis, who was not a vegetarian, and knew nothing about it; but how he hated the arguments the man advanced! For that which made the doctor an anti-vegetarian was an attitude to life, which had also made him a Republican and an Imperialist, a graduate of Harvard and a beneficiary of the Apostolic Succession. Because life was a survival of the fittest, and because God had intended the less fit to take the doctor's word as their sentence of extermination.

The duty of animals, as the clergyman set it forth to them, was to convert plant-tissue into a more concentrated and perfect form of nutriment. "The protein of animal flesh," he was saying, "is more nearly allied to human tissue; and so it is clearly more fitted for our food."

Here Thyrsis entered the conversation. "Doctor Holland," he said, mildly, "I should think it would occur to you to follow your argument to its conclusion."

The other turned to look at him. "What conclusion?" he asked.

"I should think you would become a cannibal," Thyrsis replied.

And then there was silence at the table. When Dr. Holland spoke again it was to hurry the conversation elsewhere; and from time to time thereafter he would steal a puzzled glance at Thyrsis.

But this the boy did not see. His thoughts had gone whirling on; here, in this elegant dining-room, the throes of creation seized hold of him. For this was the image he had been seeking, the phrase that would embrace it all and express it all--the concentrated bitterness of his poisoned life! Yes, he had them! He had them, with all their glory and their power! They were Cannibals. *Cannibals*!

So, when he set out from the hotel, he did not go home, but walked instead for uncounted hours in the park. And in those hours he lived through the whole of his new book, the unspeakable book--"The Higher Cannibalism"!

In the morning he told Corydon about it. She cried in terror, "But, Thyrsis, nobody would publish it!"

"Of course not," said he.

"But then," she asked, "how can you write it?"

"I shall write it," he said, "if I have to die when I get through". So he shut himself up in his room once more.

Section 7. A famous scientist began the story--reasoning along the lines of Dr. Holland's argument. The grass took the inorganic matter, and made it into food; the steer ate the grass, and carried it to the next stage; and beyond that was one stage more. So the scientist began making experiments--in a quiet way, of course. He reported the results before a learned scientific body, but his colleagues were so scandalized that the matter was hushed up.

The seed had been sown, however. A younger man took up the idea, and made researches in the South Seas--substantiating the claim that those races which took to anthropophagy had invariably supplanted the others. The new investigator printed his findings in a book which was circulated privately; and pretty soon he was called into consultation by the master-mind of the country's finance--the richest man in the world. This man was old and bald and feeble; and now suddenly there came to him a new lease of life--new health and new enthusiasm. It was given out that he had got it by wandering about bare-footed in the grass, and playing golf all day-- an explanation which the public accepted without question. No one remarked the fact that the old man began devoting his wealth to the establishing of foundling asylums; nor did any one think it suspicious that the younger generation of this multi-millionaire should rise so suddenly to power and fame.

But there began to be strange rumors and suspicions. There were young writers, who had developed a new technique, and had carried poetic utterance to undreamed of heights; and in this poetry were cryptic allusions, hints of diabolic things. A Socialist paper printed the menu of a banquet given by these "Neo-Nietzscheans", and demanded to know what one was to understand by *filet de mouton blanc*, and wherein lay the subtle humor of *pate de petit bete*. And at last the storm broke--a youth scarcely in his teens published a book of poems in which the dread secret was blazoned forth to the world with mocking defiance. There were frantic attempts to suppress this book, but they failed; and then a prosecuting officer, eager for notoriety, placed the youth upon trial for his life. And so the issue was drawn.

The public at large awakened to a dazed realization of the head-way which the new idea had made. It had become a cult of the ruling-class, the esoteric religion of the state; everywhere its defenders sprang up--it seemed as if all the intellectual as well as the material power of the community was under its spell. To oppose it was not merely bad form--it was to incur a stigma of moral inferiority, to be the victim of a "slave-ethic".

With the scientific world, of course, its victory was speedy; the new doctrine was in line with recognized evolutionary teaching. The great names of Darwin and

Spencer were invoked in its support; and, of course, when it came to economic science, there could be no two opinions. Had *laissez-faire* ever meant anything, if *laissez-faire* did not mean this?

At the very outset, the country was startled by the publication of a book by a college professor, famed as a leading sociologist, in which the case was presented without any attempt at sophistication. It was a fact, needing no attestation, that the mass of mankind had always lived in a state of slavery. At the present hour, under the forms of democracy, there were a quarter of a million men killed every year in industry, and half a million women living by prostitution, and two million children earning wages, and ten million people in want; and in comparison with these things, how humane was the new cult, how honest and above-board, how clean and economical! For the first time there could be offered to the submerged tenth a real social function to be performed. Once let the new teaching be applied upon a world-wide scale, and the proletariat might follow its natural impulse to multiply without limit; there would be no more "race-suicide" to trouble the souls of eminent statesmen.

And this at the time when the attention of the community was focussed upon the new *cause celebre*! When the public prints were filled with an acrimonious discussion as to the meaning of the instructions given to the jury. If anyone chose to will his body to a purchaser, said the judge, and then go and commit suicide, there was no law to prevent him; and, of course, the subsequent purposes of the purchaser had nothing to do with the point at issue. This was a matter of taste--here the learned justice rapped for order--a matter of prejudice, largely, and the question at issue was one of law. There was no law controlling a man's dietetic idiosyncrasies, and it was to be doubted if constitutionally any such law would stand--certainly not in a federal court, unless it chanced to be a matter of interstate commerce.

In their bewilderment and dismay, the people turned to the Church. Surely the doctrines of Christianity would stand like a barricade against this monstrous cult. But already within the Church there had been rumors and disturbances; and now suddenly a bishop arose and voiced his protest against this attempt "to drag the Church into the mire of political controversy." It must be made perfectly clear, said the bishop, that Christianity was a religion, and not a dietetic dogma. Its purpose was to save the souls of men, and not to concern itself with their bodies. It had been stated that we should have the poor always with us; which made clear the futility of attempting to change the facts of Nature. Also it was certain that the founder of Christianity had been a meat-eater; and though there might be more than one interpretation placed upon his command concerning little children---

There we might leave Thyrsis with the established Church. He had it just where he wanted it, and he shook it until its smoothly-shaven pink and white cheeks turned purple, and the ***demi-tasse*** went flying out of its beautifully manicured fingers! And while he did it he laughed aloud in hideous glee, and in his soul was a cry like the hunting-call of the lone gray wolf, that he had heard at midnight in his wilderness camp. So far a journey had come the little boy who had been dressed up in scarlet and purple robes, and had carried the bishop's train at the confirmation service! And so heavy a penalty did the church pay for its alliance with "good society"!

Section 8. Thyrsis paid a week's living expenses to have this manuscript copied; and then he took it about to the publishers. First came his friend Mr. Ardsley, who had become his chief adviser. When Thyrsis went to see him, Mr. Ardsley drew out an envelope from his desk, and took from it the opinion of his reader. "'What in the world is the matter with this boy?'" he read. "That's the opening sentence."

And then he fixed his eyes upon the boy. "What in the world *is* the matter?" he asked.

Thyrsis sat silent; there was no reply he could make. He was strongly tempted to say to the man, "The matter is that I am not getting enough to eat!"

But already Thyrsis himself had judged "The Higher Cannibalism" and repudiated it. It was born of his pain and weakness, and it was not the work he had come into the world to do. So at the end he had placed a poem, which told of a visit from his muse, after the fashion of Musset's "Nuits"; the muse had been sad and silent, and in the end the poet had torn up the product of his hours of despair, and had renewed his faith with the gracious one.

Meantime the long winter months dragged by, and still there was no gleam of hope. For Corydon it was even harder than for her husband. He at least was expressing his feelings, while she could only pine and chafe, without any sort of vent. Her life was a matter of colorless routine, in which each day was like the last, except in increased monotony. She tried hard not to let him see how she suffered;

but sometimes the tears would come. And her unhappiness was bad for the child, which in the beginning had been robust and magnificent, but now was not growing properly. Thyrsis would have ridiculed the idea that nervousness could affect her milk; but the time came when, in later life, he saw the poisons of fatigue and fear in test-tubes, and so he understood why the child had not been able to lift its head until it was a year old, and had then been well on the way to having "rickets."

All their life was so different from the way they had dreamed it! The dream still lured them; but its voice grew fainter and more remote. How were they to keep it real to themselves, how were they to hold it? Their existence was made up of end-less sordidness, of dreary commonplace, that opposed them with its passive inertia where it did not actively attack them. "Ah, Thyrsis!" Corydon would cry to him, "this will kill us if it lasts too long!"

For one thing, they no longer heard any music at all--She was not strong enough to practice the piano; and his violin was gone. Here in the great city an end-less stream of concerts and operas and recitals flowed past; and here were they, like starving children who press their faces against a pastry-cook's window and devour the sweets with their eyes. Thyrsis kept up with musical and dramatic progress by reading the accounts in the papers and magazines; but this was a good deal like slak-ing one's thirst with a mirage. He used to wonder sometimes if he were to write to these great artists--would they invite him to hear them, or would they too despise him? He never had the courage to try.

Once in the course of the long winter some one presented Corydon with two tickets to the opera, and they went together, in a state of utter bliss. It was an un-usual experience for Thyrsis, for their seats were in the orchestra, and hitherto he had always heard his operas from the upper rows in the fifth balcony, where the air was hot and stifling, and the singers appeared as a pair of tiny arms that waved, and a head (frequently a bald head) that emitted a thin, far-distant voice. This had become to him one of the conventions of the opera; and now to discover the singers as full-sized human beings, with faces and legs and loud voices, was very disturbing to his sense of illusion.

Also, alas, they had not been free to select the opera. It was "La Traviata"; and there was not much food for their hungry souls in this farrago of artificiality and sham sentiment. They shut their eyes and tried to enjoy the music, forgetting the gallant young men of fashion and their fascinating mistresses. But even the music, it seemed, was tainted; or could it be, Thyrsis wondered, that he could no longer lose himself in the pure joy of melody? Many kinds of corruption he had by this time learned about; the corruption of men, and of women, and of children; the corruption of painting and sculpture, of poetry and the drama. But the corruption of music was something which even yet he could not face; for music was the very voice of the soul--the well-spring from which life itself was derived. Thyrsis thought, as he and Corydon wandered about in the foyers of this palatial opera-house, was there anywhere on earth a place in which heaven and hell came so close together. A place where the lust and pride of the flesh displayed themselves in all their glory; and in contrast with the purest ecstasies the human spirit had attained! He pointed out one rich dowager who swept past them; her breasts all but jostling out of her corsage as she walked, her stomach squeezed into a sort of armor-plate of jewels, her cheeks powdered and painted, her head weighted with false hair and a tiara of diamonds, her face like a mask of pride and scorn. And then, in juxtaposition with that, the **Waldweben** and the **Feuerzauber**, or the grim and awful tragedy of the Siegfried funeral-march! There were people in this opera-house who knew what such music meant; Thyrsis had read it in their faces, in that suffocating top-gallery. He wondered if some day the demons that were evoked by the music might not call to them and lead them in revolt, to drive the money- changers from the temple once again!

Section 9. Another editor was reading "The Hearer of Truth," and a publisher was hovering on the brink of venturing "The Higher Cannibalism"; and so the two had new hopes to lure them on. When the spring-time had come, they would once more escape from the city, and would put up their tent on the lake-shore! They spent long afternoons picturing just how they would live--what they would eat, and what they would wear, and what they would study. As for Cedric--so they had called the baby--they saw him playing beneath the big tree in front of the tent. And what fun they would have giving him his bath on the little beach inside the point!

"I'll fix up a clothes-basket for him to sleep in!" declared Thyrsis.

"Nonsense, dear!" said Corydon. "I've told you many times before--we'll **have** to have a crib for him!"

"But why?" cried he; and there would follow an argument which gave pain to his economical soul.

Corydon declared herself willing to do her share in the matter of saving money; but it seemed to him that whenever he suggested a concrete idea, there would be objections. "We can get up at dawn," he would say, "and save the cost of oil."

"Yes," she would answer.

"And we can do our own laundry," he would continue. But immediately another argument would begin; it was impossible to persuade Corydon that diapers could be washed in cold water, even when one had the whole of the Great Lakes for a washtub.

They would go on to contemplate the glorious time when they would have money enough to build a home of their own, that could be inhabited in winter as well as in summer; Corydon always referred to it with the line from "Caradrion"--"the little cot, fringed round with tender green." It would be fine for the baby, they agreed--he should never have to go back to the city again. Thyrsis had a vision of him as he would be in that home: a brown and freckled country boy, with what were known, in the dialect of "dam-fool talk", as "yagged panties and bare feets".

But Corydon would protest at that picture. "It's all right," she said, "to put up with ugliness if you have to. But what's the use of making a fetish of it?"

"It wouldn't be ugliness," replied he. "It would be Nature! 'Blessings on thee, little man!'"

"That's all very well. But I want Cedric to have curls--"

"Curls!" he cried. "And then a Fauntleroy suit, I suppose!"

"No--at least not while we're poor. But I want him to look decent----"

"If you have curls, then you'll want a nurse-maid to brush them!"

"Nonsense, Thyrsis! Can't a mother take care of her child's own hair?"

"*Some* mothers can--they have nothing better to do. But if you were going in for the hair-dresser's art, why did you cut off your own?"

And so would come yet new discussions. "You'll be wanting me to maintain an establishment!" Thyrsis would cry, whenever these aesthetic impulses manifested themselves. He seemed to be haunted by that image of an establishment. All married men came to it in the end--there seemed to be something in matrimony that predisposed to it; and far better adopt at once the ideals and habits of the gypsies, than to settle into respectability with a nurse-maid and a cook!

Thyrsis was under the necessity of sweeping clean his soul, because of all the luxury and wantonness he saw in this metropolis, and the madness to which it goaded his soul. Some day fame would come to him, he knew--wealth also, perhaps; and oh, there must be one man in all the city who was not corrupted, who did not learn extravagance and self-indulgence, who practiced as well as preached the life of faith! And so, again and again, he and Corydon would renew the pledges of their courtship-days--pledges to a discipline of Spartan sternness.

Poor as he was, Thyrsis still found time to figure over the things he meant to do when he got money: the publishing-house that was to bring out his books at cost, and the free reading-rooms and the circulating libraries. Also, he wanted to edit a magazine; for there was a great truth which he wished to teach the world. "We must make these things that we have suffered count for something!" he would say to Corydon, again and again. "We must use them to open people's eyes!" He was thinking how, when at last he had escaped from the pit, he would be in a position to speak for those others who were left behind. Men would heed him then, and he could show them how impossible it was for the creative artist to do his work, and at the same time carry on the struggle for bread. He would induce some rich man to set aside a fund for the endowment of young writers; and so the man who had a real message might no longer have to starve.

Thyrsis had by this time tried all the world, and he knew that there was no one to understand. Just about now he was utterly stranded, and had to borrow money for even his next day's food. And oh, the humiliations and insults that came with these loans! And worse yet, the humiliations and insults that came without any loans! There was one rich man who advanced him ten dollars; Thyrsis, when he returned it, sent a check he had received from some out-of-town magazine--and in return was rebuked by the rich man for failing to include the "exchange" on the check. Thyrsis wrote humbly to inquire what manner of thing the "exchange" on a check might be; and learned that he was still in the rich man's debt to the sum of ten cents!

His case was the more hopeless, he found, because he was a married man. The world might have pardoned a young free-lance who was willing to "rough it" and take his chances for a while; but a man who had a wife and child--and was still prating about poetry! To the world the possession of a wife and child meant self-indulgence; and when a man had fallen into that trap, he simply had to settle down and take the consequence. How could Thyrsis explain that his marriage had not been as other men's? How could he hint at such a thing, without proving himself a cad?

Section 10. The work of "contemporary biography" had come to an end; there followed weeks of seeking, and then another opening appeared--Mr. Ardsley offered him a chance to do some manuscript-reading. This was really a splendid opportunity, for the work would not be difficult, and the payment would be five dollars for each manuscript. Thyrsis accepted joyfully, and forthwith carried off a couple of embryo books to his room.

It was a new and curious occupation, which opened up to him whole worlds whose existence he had not previously suspected. Through his review-writing he had become acquainted with the books that had seen the light of day; now he made the startling discovery that for every one that was born, there were hundreds, perhaps thousands, that died in the womb. He could see how it went--the hordes of half-educated people who read books and were moved to write something like them. Each manuscript was a separate tragedy; and often there would be a letter or a preface to make certain that one did not miss the sense of it. Here would be a settlement-worker, burning with a message, but unable to draw a character or to write dialogue; here would be a business-man, who had studied up the dialect of the region where he spent his summer vacations, and whose style was so crude that one winced as he turned the pages; here would be a poor bookkeeper, or a type-writer, or other cog in the business machine, who had read of the fortunes made by writers of fiction, and had spent all his hours of leisure for a year in composing a tale of the ***grand monde***, or some feeble imitation of the sugar-coated "historical romance" of the hour.

Sometimes as he read these manuscripts, a shudder would come over Thyrsis; how they made him realize the odds in the game of life! These thousands and tens of thousands panting and striving for success; and he lost in the throng of them! What madness it seemed to imagine that he might climb over their heads--that he had been chosen to scale the heights of fame! Their letters and prefaces sounded like a satire upon his own attitude, a ***reductio ad absurdum*** of his claims to "genius". Here, for instance, was a man who wrote to introduce himself as America's first epic poet --stating incidentally that he was an inspector of gas-meters, and had a wife and six children. His poem occupied some six hundred foolscap sheets, finely bound up by hand; it set forth the soul-states of a Byron from Alabama--an aristocratic hero who was refused by the lady of his heart, and voiced his anger and perplexity in a long speech, two lines of which stamped themselves forever upon the mind of the reader---

"But I! he cried. My limbs are straight,
My purse well-filled, my veins all F. F. V.!"

As a method of earning one's living, this was almost too good to be true. The worse the manuscripts were the easier was his task; in fact, when he came upon one which showed traces of real power and interest he cursed his fate, for then it might take several days to earn his five dollars. But for the most part the manuscripts were bad enough, and he could have earned a year's income in a week, if only there had been enough of them. So he made a great effort to succeed at the work, and filled his reports with epigrams and keen observations, carefully adapted to what he knew was Mr. Ardsley's point of view. He allowed time for these devices to be effective, and then paid a visit to find out about the prospects.

"Mr. Ardsley," he began, "I am going to try to meet you half way with a book."

"Ah!" said the other.

"I want to write a novel that you can publish. I believe that I can do it."

Mr. Ardsley warmed immediately. "I have always been certain that you could," said he. He went on to expound to Thyrsis the ethics of opportunism--how it would not be necessary to be false to his convictions, to write anything that he did not believe--but simply to put his convictions into a popular form, and to impart no more than the public could swallow at the first mouthful.

Thyrsis told him the outline of a plot. He would write a story of the struggles of a young author in the metropolis--not such a young author as himself, a rebel and a frenzied egotist, but a plain, everyday young author whom other people could care about. He had the "local color" for such a tale, and he could do it without too much waste of time. Mr. Ardsley thought it an excellent idea.

After which Thyrsis came, very cautiously, to the meat of the matter. "I want to get away into the country to write it," he said; "and so I wanted to ask you about the manuscripts you are sending me. Have you found my work satisfactory?"

"Why, yes," said the other.

"And do you think you can send them through the summer?"

"I presume so. It depends upon how many come to us."

"You--you couldn't arrange to let me have any more of them?"

"Not at present," said Mr. Ardsley. "You see, I have regular readers, whose work I know. I'll send you what I have to spare."

"Thank you," said Thyrsis. "I'll be glad to have all you can give me."

So he went away; and in the little room he and Corydon had an anxious consultation. He had been getting about twenty dollars a month; which was not enough for the family to exist upon. "Our only hope is a new book," he declared; and Corydon saw that was the truth. "Each week that I stay here is a loss," he added. "I have to pay room-rent."

"But can you stand tenting out in April?" asked she.

"I'll chance it," he replied--"if you'll say the word."

She saw that her duty was before her; she must nerve herself and face it, though it tore her heartstrings. She must stay and take care of the baby, while he went away to work!

He sat and held her hands, and saw her bite her lips and fight to keep back the tears in her eyes. Their hearts had grown together, so that it was like tearing their flesh to separate them. They had never imagined that such a thing could come into their lives.

"Thyrsis," she whispered--"you'll forget me!"

He pressed her hands more tightly. "No, dear! No!" he said.

"But you'll get used to living without me!" she cried. "And it's the time in my life when I need you most!"

"I will stay, dearest, if you say so."

She exclaimed, "No, no! I must stand it!"

And seeing her grief, his heart breaking with pity, a strange impulse came to Thyrsis. He took her hands in his, and knelt down before her, and began to pray. It had been years since he had thought of prayer, and Corydon had never thought of it in her life. It came from the deeps of him--a few stammering words, simple, almost childish, yet exquisite as music. He prayed that they might have courage to keep up the fight, that they might be able to hold their love before them, that nothing might ever dim their vision of each other. It was a prayer without theology or metaphysics--a prayer to the unknown gods; but it set free the well-spring of tenderness and pity within them; and when he finished Corydon was sobbing upon his shoulder.

BOOK IX
THE CAPTIVE IN LEASH

They were standing on the hill-top, watching the last glimmer of the sinking moon. As the faint perfume of the clover came to them upon the warm evening wind, she sighed, and whispered--

"Too rare, too rare, grow now my visits here!
   'Mid city noise, not as with thee of yore,
      Thyrsis! in reach of sheep-bells is my home!"

She paused.
"Go on," he said, and she quoted--

"Then through the great town's harsh, heart-wearying roar,
  Let in thy voice a whisper always come,
    To chase fatigue and fear:
  Why faintest thou? I wandered till I died.
    Roam on! The light we sought is shining still."_

Section 1. Thyrsis made his plans and packed his few belongings. There came another pass from the "higher regions", and he took the night-train once more, and came to the little town upon the shores of Lake Ontario. Once more the sun shone on the crystal-green water, and the cold breeze blew from off the lake. There was still snow in the ravines of the deep woods, but Thyrsis got his tent out of the farmer's barn, and patched up the holes the mice had gnawed, and put it up on the old familiar spot.

It was strange to him to be there without Corydon. There were so many things to remind him of her--a sudden memory would catch him unawares, and stab him like a knife. There was the rocky headland where they had swam, and there was the pine-tree that the lightning had splintered, one day while they were standing near. When darkness came, and he was unpacking a few old things that they had left up in the country, his loneliness seemed to him almost more than he could bear; he sat by the little stove, holding a pair of her old faded slippers in his hands, and felt his tears trickling down upon them.

But it took him only a day or two to drive such things out of his mind. There was no time for sentiment now--it was "Clear ship for action!" For once in his life he was free, and had a chance to work. He was full of his talk with Mr. Ardsley, and meant to do his best to be "practical." And so behold him wandering about in the water-soaked forests, or tramping the muddy roads, or sitting by his little stove while the cold storms beat upon the tent--wrestling with his unruly Pegasus, and dragging it back a hundred times a day to what was proper, and human, and interesting!

The neighbors had warned him that it was too early for tenting, but Thyrsis had vowed he would stand it. And now, as if to punish him for his defiance, there was emptied out upon him the cave of all the winds; for four weeks there were such storms of rain and sleet and snow as the region had never known in April. There were nights when he sat wrapped in overcoats and blankets, with a fire in the stove; and still shivering for the gale that drove through the canvas. There came one calm, starlit night when he lay for hours almost frozen, and sat up in the morning to find a glass of water at his bedside frozen solid. Thirteen degrees the thermometer showed, according to the farmer; and oh, the agony of getting out of bed, and starting a fire with green wood! In the end Thyrsis poured in half a can of kerosene, and got the stove red-hot; and then he turned round to warm his back, and smelled smoke, and whirled about to find his tent in a blaze!

With a bucket of water and a broomstick he beat out the fire, and went for a run to warm up. But when he came back there was more wind, so that he could not keep warm in the tent, and more rain, so that he could not find shelter in the woods. In the end he discovered a ruined barn, in a corner of which he would sit, wrapped in his blankets and writing with cold fingers.

Perhaps all these mishaps had something to do with the refusal of his ideas to flow. But apparently it was in vain that Thyrsis tried at any time to work at things that were interesting to other people. Perhaps he could have worked better at them, if there had not been so many things that were interesting to *him*. He would find himself confronted with the image of the society clergyman, or of the sleek editor in his club, or some other memory out of the world of luxury and pride. And each day came the newspaper, with its burden of callousness and scorn; and perhaps also a letter from Corydon, with something to goad him to new tilts with the enemies of his soul.

So, before long, almost without realizing it, he was putting the "interesting" things aside, and girding himself for another battle. His message was still undelivered; and in vain he sought to content himself by blaming the world for this. Until he had forced the world to hear him, he had simply not yet done his work. He must take his thought and shape it anew--into some art-work finer, stronger, truer than he had yet achieved.

Day after day he pondered this idea--eating with it and walking with it and sleeping with it; until at last, of a sudden, the vision came to him. It came late at night, while he was undressing; and he sat for five or ten minutes, with his shirt half off, as if in a trance. Then he put the shirt on again, and went out to wander about the woods, laughing and talking to himself.

"Genius surrounded by Commercialism"--that was his theme; and it would have to be a play. Its hero would be a young musician, a mere boy, a master of the demon-voices of the violin; he would be rapt in his vision, and around him a group of people who would be embodiments of the world and all its forces of evil. One by one they came trooping before Thyrsis' fancy, with all their trappings of pomp and power, their greatness and their greed--sinister and cruel figures, but also humorous, very creatures of the spirit of comedy! Yes, he had a comedy this time--a real comedy!

Section 2. In this hour, of course, Thyrsis forgot all about the "plot" he had outlined to Mr. Ardsley, and about his promises to be "practical." Something arose within him, imperious and majestic, and swept all this out of the way with one gesture of the hand. He dropped everything else and plunged into the play. Never yet in his life had anything taken hold of him to such an extent; it drove him so that he forgot to eat, he forgot to sleep. He would work over some part of it until he was exhausted--and then, without warning, some other part would open out in a vista before him, and he would spring up in pursuit of that. Characters and episodes and dialogue, wild humor, scalding satire, grim tragedy--they thronged and jostled and crowded one another in his imagination.

"The Genius" was the title of the play. Its protagonist had come home after completing his education in Vienna; and there was the family gathered to greet him. Mr. Hartman, the father, was a wholesale grocer--a business large enough to have brought wealth, but painfully tainted with "commonness". Then there was Mrs. Hartman, stout and tightly-laced, who had studied the science of elegance while her husband studied sugar. There was the elder son, who under his mother's guidance had married well; and Miss Violet Hartman, who was looking up to the perilous heights of a foreign alliance.

Only of late had the family come to realize what an asset to their career this "Genius" might be. They had humored him in his strange whim to devote his life to fiddling; money had been spent on him freely--he brought home with him a famous Cremona instrument for which three thousand dollars had been paid. But now it was dawning upon them that this was an "ugly duckling"; he was to make his *debut* in the metropolis, where an overwhelming triumph was expected; and then he would return to the home city in the middle West, and would play at *musicales*, which even the most exclusive of the "*elite*" must attend.

There was also the great Prof. Reminitsky, the teacher who had made Lloyd, and had come to New York with him; and there was the Herr Prof. von Arne, of the University of Berlin, a world-renowned psychiatrist, author of "The Neurosis of Inspiration". The Herr Professor had come to America to make some studies for his forthcoming masterpiece on the religious mania; and he was glad to see his old friend Reminitsky, whose seventeen-year-old musical prodigy was most interesting material for study.

Prof. Reminitsky was the world's greatest authority in the art of tearing the human soul to pieces by means of horse-hair rubbed with resin and scraped over the intestines of a pig. There were no tricks of finger-gymnastics and of tone-production that he had not mastered. As for the emotions produced thereby, he felt them, but in a purely professional way; that is, the convictions he had concerning them related to their effects upon audiences, and more especially upon the score or two of critical experts whose psychology had been his life-study. But having studied also the psychology of youth, he knew that his ***protege*** must needs have other convictions concerning his performances. This was his supreme greatness--that he understood the paranoia of enthusiasm, and used this understanding to tempt his pupils to new heights of achievement.

In all of which, of course, his friend von Arne was a great help to him. Von Arne had dug through a score of great libraries, and had travelled all the world over, frequenting cafes and salons, monasteries and prayer-cells, prisons and hospitals and asylums--wherever one might get new glimpses of the extraordinarily intricate phenomena of the aberration called "Genius". He had several thousand cases of it at his finger-tips--he had measured its reaction-times and calculated its cephalic index, and analyzed its secretions and tested it for indecan. He knew trance and clairvoyance, auto-suggestion and telepathic hallucination, epilepsy and hysteria and ecstasy; and over the head of any disputatious person he would swing the steam-shovel of his erudition, and bury the unfortunate beneath a wagon-load of Latin and Greek derivatives.

Also, there was Moses Rosen, the business-manager. Moses was short, and wore a large diamond ring, and he also was a specialist in the phenomena of "Genius". He studied them from the point of view of the box-office, and his tests were quite as definite as those of the psychological laboratory. There came to Moses an endless stream of prodigies, all of them having long hair and picturesque aspects, and talking rapidly and rolling their eyes; the problem was to determine which of them had the faculty of true Genius, which not only talked rapidly and rolled its eyes, but also had the power of causing money to flow in through a box-office window.

In this case Moses felt that the prospects were good; the only trouble being that the prodigy intended to render a ***concerto*** by a strange composer--a stormy and unconventional thing which would annoy the critics. Moses suggested something that was "classic"; and agreed with Mrs. Hartman that there ought to be something corresponding to "good form" in music.

Section 3. So all these strange creatures were poking and peering and smelling about the "Genius"; and meanwhile, there came at intervals faint strains of music from a distant room. At last Lloyd Hartman entered; beautiful, pale and sensitive--a haunted boy, and the most haunting figure that had yet come to Thyrsis' imagination. Also, it was the hardest piece of work he had ever undertaken; for the character had come to him, not as a formula or a collection of phrases, but as an intuition, a part of his own soul; and he would work out a scene a score of times, finding words to phrase it, and then rejecting them. By what speeches could he give his sense of the gulf that lay between Lloyd and the people about him? For this boy could not cope with them in argument, he would have no mastery of the world of facts. He must be without any touch of sophistication, of cynicism; and yet, when he spoke to them, it must be clear that he knew them for different beings from himself. He would go with them meekly; but one would feel that it was because his path lay in their direction. When the point came that their ways parted, he would go his own way; and just there lay the seed of the tragi-comedy.

The family gathers about him, and he answers their questions. He will wear the kind of tie that his sister prefers, and they may set any date they please for the *musicales* at home. He hears the "copy" which Moses has prepared for his advertisements; and then he sits, absent-minded, while they talk about him. Music is in his thoughts, and gradually it steals into his aspect and the gestures of his hand. They watch him, and a pall comes over them: until at last the mother exclaims that he makes her nervous, and leads the family off.

Then Miss Arnold is announced--Helena Arnold, who has been recommended as accompanist at the great concert. She is young and beautiful; and the two go into the next room to play, while the professors remain to talk over this new complication.

Prof. von Arne, of course, lays especial emphasis upon the sex-element in psychopathology; he and Reminitsky have talked the subject out many years ago, and adopted a definite course of action. The abnormalities incidental to sex-repression were innumerable, and for the most part destructive; but there could be no question that all the more striking phenomena of the neurosis called "Genius" were greatly increased in their intensity by this means. So, in dealing with his pupils, and especially with a prodigy like young Hartman, Prof. Reminitsky would call into service all the paraphernalia of religious mysticism; teaching his pupil to regard woman as the object of exalted adoration, a being too holy to be attained to even in thought. And now, of course, when the proposed accompanist turns out to be a decidedly alluring young female, it is necessary to take careful heed.

Meanwhile from the distance come bursts of wild music; and at last Helena returns--pale, and deeply agitated. "It is that ***concerto!***" she says, and then asks to be excused from talking. Lloyd comes, and stands by the door watching her. When his teacher begins to open business negotiations, he asks him abruptly to leave them alone.

Helena asks, "Who wrote that music?" He tells her a ghastly story of a titan soul who starved in a garret and shot himself, crushed by the mockery of the world.

"I might have saved him!" the boy exclaims. "I was so busy with the music I forgot the man!"

They talk about this epoch-making ***concerto***, and how Lloyd means to force it upon the public. "And you shall play it with me!" he exclaims. "You are the first that has ever understood it!"

"I cannot play it!" she protests; to which he answers, "It was like his voice come back from the grave!" And so we see these two souls cast into the crucible together.

Section 4. The second act showed the aftermath of the great concert, and took place in the drawing-room of the Hartman family's apartment, at four o'clock in the morning. We see Moses and the two professors, who have not been able to tear themselves away; dishevelled, ***distrait***, wild with vexation, they pace about and lament. Failure, utter ruin confronts them--the structure of their hopes lies in the dust! They blame it all on "that woman"--and members of the family concur in this. It was she who kept Lloyd to his resolve to play that mad ***concerto;*** and then, to cast aside all the master had taught them, all the results of weeks of drilling--and to play it in that frantic, demonic fashion. Now the men await the morning papers, which will bring them the verdict of "the world"; and they shudder with the fore-knowledge of what that verdict will be.

Lloyd and Helena enter. They have been walking for hours, and have not been thinking of "the world". They listen, half-heeding, to the protests and laments; they could not help it, they explain--the music took hold of them.

The two professors go off to get the papers, and Moses goes into the next room to rest; after which it becomes clear to the audience that Lloyd and Helena are fighting the sex-duel.

"You do not care about people," she is saying, sombrely.

To which his reply is, "It is not to be found in people."

"And yet from people it must come!" she insists.

He answers, "They do not even know what I mean; and they have no humility."

"It is a problem," Lloyd continues, after a pause. "Shall one go on alone, or wait and bring others with him?--You have brought that problem into my life."

She answers to this, "I cannot see how my love will hinder you."

He replies, "If you love *me*, who will love my art?"

So it goes--until the professors return with their freight of the world's Philistinism. And here came a scene, over which Thyrsis shook for many a day with merriment. The accounts of the concert are read; Moses awakens and comes in; and as the agony increases, the members of the family appear, one by one, clad in their dressing-gowns, and adding their lamentations to the chorus. Gone is all the prestige of the two professors, gone all the profits of Moses, gone all the visions of social triumphs in the city of the middle West!

To all of which uproar the two listen patiently; until at last the mother, in a transport of vexation, turns upon Helena, and accuses her of ensnaring the boy. And then--the climax of the scene--Lloyd springs up; all that Genius in him, which has so far gone into music, turns now into rage and scorn. He pictures these people--pawing over his inspiration with their unclean hands--peering at it, weighing it, chaffering over it--taking it into the market-place to be hawked about. He shows them what they are, and what that "world" is, to which they would offer his muse as a whore. And then at the climax of his speech, as he is waving his violin in the air, the Herr Prof. von Arne ventures to put in a word; and the boy whirls upon him, and brings down the three thousand-dollar treasure upon the eminent psychiatrist's head!

The third act, which was the hardest of all to write, was to take place in a garret. Lloyd has gone away alone, and three years have passed, and now he lies dying of a wasting disease. Helena has come to him again--and still they are fighting the duel. "A woman will do anything for a man but renounce him," says Lloyd; and she cannot understand this fierce instinct of his.

She has come and found him; and he lies gasping for breath, and speaking in broken sentences. Yet he will not have her bring grief into his chamber; he has fought his way through grief, and through hatred and contempt, and now he lies at peace upon the bosom of nature. No longer is he wrapped up in his own vision; he has learned from the million suns in the sky and the million trees of the forest. He tells her that the thing called "Genius" springs ceaselessly from the heart of life.

He has cast out fear; and with it he has cast out love. "What are you?" he asks. "What am I?" And he sets forth in blazing words his vision of the soul, which is as a flash of light in a raindrop, and yet one with the eternal process. As the fruit of his life he leaves one symphony in manuscript, and some pages of writing in which he has summed up his faith. That is enough, he says--that is victory; for that he fled away, and killed his love.

The two professors come, having learned that Lloyd is dying. But even they cannot divert him. He tells von Arne that his learning will submit itself, and that scientists will be as gardeners, tending the young flowers of faith. His mother and father come, and he whispers that even for them there is hope--that in the deepest mire of respectability the spark of the soul still glows. His mother bursts into weeping by his bed, and he tells her that even from the dungeon of pride there may be deliverance. So he sends them all away to pray.

Then Helena sits at the piano and plays a few bars of that sonata of Beethoven's which is an utterance of most poignant grief, and which some publisher has cruelly misnamed the "Moonlight". And after long silence, the dying man communes with his muse. A light suffuses the room, and he whispers, "Take thine own time; for the seeds of thy glories are planted in the hearts of men!"

Section 6. Over these things Thyrsis would work for six hours at a stretch, sitting without moving a muscle; for days and nights he would wander about at random in the woods. He ate irregularly, of such things as he could put his hands upon; and sleep fled from him like a mistress spurned. When, after a couple of months, he had finished the task, there was an incessant throbbing in his forehead, and--alas for the sudden tumble from the heights of Parnassus!--he had lost almost entirely the power of digesting food.

But the play was done. He sent it off to be copied, and wrote paeans of thanksgiving to Corydon. Once more he had a weapon, newly-forged and sharpened, wherewith to pierce that tough hide of the world!

There remained the practical question: What did one do when he had a play completed? What was the first step to be taken? Thyrsis pondered the problem for several days; and then, as chance would have it, his eye was caught by a newspaper paragraph to the effect that "Ethelynda Lewis, the popular *comedienne*, is to be starred in a serious drama next season, under the management of Robertson Jones. Miss Lewis's play has not yet been selected." Now, as it happened, "Ethelynda Lewis" had been on the play-bill of "The Princess of Prague", that tragic "musical comedy" to which Thyrsis had been taken; but he never noticed the names of actors and actresses, and had no suspicions. He sent his manuscript to this future star; and a week later came a note, written on scented monogram paper in a tall and distinguished chirography, acknowledging the receipt of his play and promising to read it.

Then Thyrsis turned to attack the manuscripts which had been accumulating while he was writing. They were coming more frequently now--apparently Mr. Ardsley liked his work. To Corydon, who had gone to the country with her parents, he wrote that he was getting some money ahead, and so she might join him before long.

This brought him a deluge of letters; and it forced him to another swift descent into the world of reality. "I have told you nothing of my sufferings," wrote Corydon. "At least a score of times I have written you long letters and then torn them up, saying that your work must not be disturbed. But oh, Thyrsis, I do not think I can stand it much longer! Can you imagine what it means to be shut up in a boarding-house, without one living soul to understand about me?"

She would go on to tell of her griefs and humiliations, her longings and rages and despairs. Then, too, Cedric was not growing as he should. "He is beautiful," she wrote, "and every one loves him. But he makes not the least attempt to sit up, and I am very much worried. I fear that I ought not to go on nursing him--I am too nervous to eat as I should. And then I think of the winter, and that we may still be separated, and I do not see how I am to stand it. It is as if I were in a prison. I think of you, and I cannot make you real to me."

To all of which Thyrsis could only reply with vague hopes--and then go away for a tramp in the forest, and call to his soul for new courage. He had still troubles enough of his own. For one thing, the fiend in his stomach was not to be exorcised by any spell he knew. It was all very picturesque to portray one's hero as dying of disease; but in reality it was not at all satisfactory. Thyrsis did not die, he merely ate a bowl of bread and milk, and then went about for several hours, feeling as if there were a football blown up inside of him.

He had a touching faith in the medical profession in those days, and whenever there was anything wrong with him, he would turn the problem over to a doctor and his soul would be at rest. In this case the doctor told him that he had dyspepsia--not a very difficult diagnosis--and gave him a bottle full of a red liquid to be taken after meals. To Thyrsis this seemed an example of the marvels of science, of the adjustment of means to ends; for behold, when he had taken the red liquid, the bread and milk disappeared as if by magic! And he might go on and eat anything else--if there was trouble, he had only to take more of the red liquid! So he plunged into work on a pot-boiler, and wrote Corydon to be of cheer, that the dawn was breaking.

Section 7. Corydon, in the meantime, had received a copy of his play; and he was surprised at the effect it had upon her. "It is marvellous," she wrote; "it is like a blaze of lightning from one end to the other. And yet, much as I rejoice in its power, the main feeling it brought me was of anguish; for it seemed to me as if in this play you had spoken out of your inmost soul. Can it be that you are really chafing against the bond of our love? That you feel that I have hold of you and cling to you; and that you resent it, and shrink from me? Oh Thyrsis, what can I do? Shall I bid you go, and blot the thought of you from my mind? Is that what you truly want? 'A woman will do anything for a man but renounce him!' Did you not shudder for me when you wrote those words?

"It is two o'clock in the morning, and so far I have not been able to sleep. I have lain awake with torturing thoughts; and then the baby wakened up, and I had to put him to sleep again--any indisposition of mine always affects him. I am sitting on the floor at the foot of the bed, writing with a candle; and hoping to get myself sufficiently exhausted, so that I shall no longer lie awake.

"Go and find your vision over my corpse, and may God bless you!...I wrote that hours ago, and I tried to mean it. I try to tell myself that I will take the child and go away, and crush my own hopes and yearnings, and give my life to him. But no--I cannot, I cannot! It is perfectly futile for me to think of that--I crave for life, and I cannot give up. There is that in me that will never yield, that will take no refusal. Sometimes I see myself as a woman of seventy, still seeking my life. Do you not realize that? I feel that I shall never grow old!

"How strange a thing it is, Thyrsis, that you and I, who might do so much with so little chance, should have no chance at all. I read of other poets and their wives--at least they managed to have a hut on some hillside, and they did not absolutely starve.

"I am tired now; perhaps I can sleep. But I will tell you something, Thyrsis--does it sound so very foolish? Not only will I never grow old, but I will never give up your love! Yes, some day you will find out how to seek your vision in spite of the fact that I am your wife!"

Section 8. Another day, there would be moods of peace, and even of merriment; it was always like putting one's hand into a grab-bag, to open a new letter from Corydon. In after years he would read them, and strange were the memories they brought!

"My Thyrsis," she wrote: "I have been reading a story of Heine in Zangwill's "Dreamers of the Ghetto". I did not know about Heine. He loved and married a sweet little woman of the people--Mathilde--who didn't appreciate his writings. I am not only going to love you, but I am going to appreciate your writings! Some day I am going to be educated--and won't it be fine when I am educated?

"I keep very busy, but I have not so much time as I had last summer. I live almost all my life in hope--the present is nothing. I think I get more strength by gazing at my baby than in any other way. I wonder if I can ever infuse into him my inspiration and my desire. It is wonderfully exciting to me to think of what a free soul could do, if it possessed my spirit and my dreams. Ah, even you don't know! I smile to myself when I think how surprised you might some day be! Oh, my baby, my baby, surely you will not fail me--little soul that is to be. This is what I say to him, and then I squeeze him in ecstasy, and he coughs up his milk. Dear funny little thing, that is so pleased with a red, white and blue rattle. At present he is grinning at it ecstatically--and he is truly most horribly cunning. His favorite expression is 'Ah-boo, ah-boo'; and is not that just *too* bright? Everybody tries to spoil him--even a twelve-year-old boy here wanted to kiss him. And wonder of wonders, he has two teeth appearing in his lower gums! Poor me--he bites hard enough as he is."

And then again:

"My Beloved: I am sitting with my candle once more. It is too hot for a lamp. I have been reading 'Paradise Lost', and truly I am astonished that it is so beautiful. Also I have been reading a book about Unitarianism, and I did not know that such things had been written. But I think it is hardly worth while to call one's self a Unitarian. I was thinking that I will go back and read the Bible through. I would not mind, if I knew I did not have to believe it.

"Also; this week, I read 'Paul and Virginia'. Oh, do not write anything to me about our meeting, until you are sure it can be! It breaks my heart.

"Did it ever occur to you that we might embark for the tropics? We'd have a hut, and I might learn to raise fruits and vegetables. I sigh for some verdant isle-- and I am not joking. We might find some place where steamers came now and then, and some one in New York could attend to your manuscripts.

"To-night I was trying to put my baby to sleep and he wouldn't go, but just lay in my lap and kicked and grinned. I tried to coax him to go to sleep, but if I was the least bit impatient he'd begin to cry. And then he'd grin at me so roguishly, as if to say, 'Let's play before I go to sleep!' Finally I looked right at him and said, 'Now, you have played long enough, and I wish you to be a good boy and go to sleep!' And then he laughed, and I put him on his side and he went to sleep! Wasn't that bright for a baby just seven months old?

"I think I write you much more interesting letters than you write me. To be sure I have no books into which to put my thoughts. Also, I have a great deal of time to compose letters to you; Cedric wakes me up so much in the night, and often I cannot go to sleep again. It plays havoc with me as a rule; and yet sometimes, when I'm not too exhausted, there is a certain joy in watching by the dim candle light the rosy upturned face and the little groping mouth. Oh Thyrsis, he is all mine and yours, and we must make him glad he was borned, mustn't we?"

Section 9. Such letters would come at a time when Thyrsis was almost prostrated with exhaustion; and great waves of loneliness and yearning would sweep over him. Ah God, what a fate it was--to labor as he labored, and then to have no means of recreation or respite, no hand to smooth his forehead, no voice to whisper solace! Who could know the tragedy of that aspect of his life?

There came one day an incident that almost broke his heart. Down the lake came a private yacht, beautiful and swift, clean as a new penny, its bronze and white paint glistening in the sunlight. It anchored not far out from the point where Thyrsis camped, and a boat put off, and from it three young girls stepped ashore. They were slender and graceful, clad all in white--as spotless as the vessel itself, and glowing with health and joyfulness. They cast shy glances at the tent, and asked Thyrsis to direct them to the nearest farm-house; he watched them disappear through the woods, and saw them return with a basket of fruit.

It was just at sunset, and there was a new moon in the sky, and the evening star trembled upon the bosom of the waters. There in the magic stillness lay the vessel--and suddenly came the sounds of a guitar, and of young voices singing. Wonderful to tell, they sang --not "ragtime" and "college songs," but the chorus of the "Rhein-toechter," and Schubert's "Auf dem Wasser zu singen", and other music, unknown to Thyrsis, exquisite almost beyond enduring. It pierced him to the heart; he sat with his hands clenched, and every nerve of him a-quiver, and the hot tears raining down his cheeks. It was loveliness not of this earth, it was an apparition; that presence which had been haunting him ever since he had come to this spot--

"So might I, standing on this pleasant lea,   Have glimpses that would make me less forlorn;   Have sight of Proteus rising from the sea,   And hear old Triton blow his wreathed horn."

The music died away, and rose again; and the deeps of his spirit were opened, and ecstasy and grief welled up together within him. Then he made out that the anchor was being lifted; and he was tempted to spring up and cry out to them to stay. But no--what did they know of him? What would they care about him? So he crouched by the bank, drinking greedily the precious notes; and as the yacht with its gleaming lights stole away into the twilight, all the poet's soul went yearning with it. Still he could hear the faint strains swelling--

"Blow, blow, breathe and blow,
Wind of the western sea!"

He sat with his face hidden in his hands, shuddering. Here he was, wrestling in the pit with sickness and despair--and there above him were the heights of art. If only he could live with such music, what prodigies could he not perform. And they who possessed it--did it mean to them what it meant to him? They who had everything that life could offer--music and art, freedom and beauty and health--all the treasures of life as their birthright--had they never a thought of those who had nothing, and were set to slave in the galleys of their pleasure-craft?

Thyrsis was always coming upon some aspect of this thing called Privilege. Corydon had suggested that there might be some work that she could do at home; and so one day he was looking over the advertisements in a newspaper, and came upon a composition by a man who was seeking a governess for his three children. It was written in a style all its own; it revealed a person accustomed to specify exactly what he wanted, and it occupied three or four inches, as if symbolic of the fact that he did not consider expense. He described the life of his children; they had servants and a tutor to attend to their physical and mental needs, and the father now sought a friend and, companion, to take charge of their spiritual and social development. The specifications evoked a picture of an establishment, in which all the community's resources, all the sciences and arts of civilization, were set at work to create joy and power for three young people. What a contrast it made with the care that little Cedric was getting, as revealed in his mother's letters!

Thyrsis could see in his mind's eye the master and provider of this establishment. How well he knew the type--how often had he sat in some quiet corner and listened while it revealed itself. A man alert and aggressive; immaculate in appearance as the latest fashion-plate, and overlaid with a veneer of culture--yet underneath it still the predatory talons, the soul of the hawk. He was a "practical" man; that is, he understood profit. He was trained to see where profit lay, and swift to seize upon it. As a business-man he ruled labor, and crushed his competitors, and directed legislatures and political machines; as a lawyer he protected his kind from attack, as a judge he bent the law to the ends of greed. So he lived in palaces, and travelled about in private-cars and yachts, and had servants and governesses for his children, and valets and secretaries to attend himself. And whenever by any chance he got a glimpse of Thyrsis' soul, how he hated it! On the other hand, to Thyrsis he was a portent of terror. He ruled in every field of human activity; and yet one saw that if his rule continued, it would mean the destruction of civilization! Whenever Thyrsis met one of these men, whether in imagination or reality, he found himself with hands clenched, and every nerve of him a-tingle with the lust of combat.

Section 10. A most trying thing it was to a man who carried the burden of the future in his soul--to have to wrestle with an obstinate stomach! But so it was again; the magic red liquid seemed to be losing its power. Then, the pot-boiler was not going well; and to cap the climax, the manuscripts stopped coming. Thyrsis, after waiting two or three weeks in suspense and dread, wrote to Mr. Ardsley, and received a reply to the effect that he would not be able to send any more. Mr. Ardsley had sent them because of his interest in the proposed "practical" novel; and now he had learned that the poet had been giving his time to the writing of an impossible play!

Thyrsis' predicament was a desperate one, and drove him to a desperate course. It was now midsummer; and run down from overwork as he was, could he face the thought of returning to the sweltering city, to go to work in some office? Or was he to hire out as a farm-laborer, under he knew not what conditions? He recoiled from either of these alternatives; and then suddenly, as he racked his brains, a wild idea flashed over him. For years he had talked and dreamed of escaping from civilization. He had pictured himself upon some tropic island, where bananas and cocoanuts grew; or again in some Northern wilderness, where he might hunt and fish, and live like the pioneers. And now--why not do it? He had an axe and a rifle and a fishing-rod; and only a few days previously he had heard a man telling of a lake in the Adirondacks, where not a dozen people went in the course of a year.

It was early one morning the idea came to him; and within an hour he had struck his tent and packed his trunk. He stowed his camp-stuff and bedding in a dry-goods box, and leaving his tent with the farmer, he purchased a ticket to a place on the edge of the wilderness. He put up at a village-hotel, and the next day drove fifteen miles by a stage, and five more by a wagon, and spent the night at a lumber-camp far in the wilderness. The next day, carrying as much of his belongings as he could, he walked three miles more, and came to the tiny lake that was his goal.

It was perhaps half a mile long; the virgin forest hung about it like a great green curtain, and the shadows of the blue mountains seemed as if painted upon its surface. Thyrsis gave a gasp of delight as he pushed through the bushes and saw it; he stripped and plunged into the crystal water--and hot and tired and soul-sick as he was, the coolness of it was like a clasp of protecting arms. There was a rock rising from the centre, and he swam out and stood upon it, and gazed about him at all the ravishing beauty, and laughed and whooped so that the mountains rang with the echoes.

He found an abandoned "open-camp", or shed, the roof of which he made water-proof with newspapers and balsam-boughs. He cut fresh boughs for his bed, and spread his blankets upon them, and went back to the lumber-shanties, and purchased a box of prunes and a bag of rice. There were huckleberries in profusion upon the hills, and in the lakes were fish, and in the forests squirrels and rabbits, partridges and deer. There were the game-laws, to be sure; but there was also a "higher law", as eminent authorities had declared. As one of the wits at the lumber-camp put it, "If any wild rabbit comes rushing out to bite you, don't you hesitate to defend yourself!"

So, with the sum of one dollar and twenty-three cents in his pocket-book, Thyrsis began the happiest experience of his life. He watched the sun rise and set behind the mountains; and sometimes he climbed to the summits to see it further upon its way. He watched the progress of the tempests across the lake, and swam in the water while the rain splashed his face and the lightning splintered the pines in the forest. He crouched in the bushes and saw the wild ducks feeding, and the deer that came at sunset to drink. He watched the loons diving, and spying him out with their wild eyes--sometimes, as they rose in flight, beating the surface of the water with a sound like thunder. At night he heard their loud laughter, and the creaking cries of the herons flying past. Sometimes far up in the hills a she-fox would bark, or some too-aged tree of the forest would come down with a booming crash. Thyrsis would lie in his open camp and watch the moonlight through the pines, and prayers of thankfulness would well up within him--

"Peace of the forest, rich, profound,
  Gather me closely, fold me round!"

There had been much carrying and hard work to do before he was settled, and there was more of it all through his stay. He had to cook all his meals and clean up afterwards; and because the nights were cold and his blankets few, there was much firewood to be cut. Also, there was no food unless he went out and found it, and so he spent hours each day tramping about in the forests. By the time he had got home and had cleaned the game and cooked it, he was ravenously hungry, and there was never any question as to what would digest. This was just what he had sought; and so now, deliberately, he banned all the muses from his presence, and poured the rest of the dyspepsia-medicine into the lake. His muscles became hard, and the flush of health returned to his cheeks, and as he went about his tasks he laughed and sang, and shouted his defiance to the world. And to Corydon he wrote his newest plan--to earn a little in the city that winter, and come back in the early spring and build a log-cabin for herself and the baby!

Section 11. Twice a week his mail came to the lumbercamp, in care of the friendly foreman. Each time that he went out to get it, he hoped for some new turn. There was a publisher interested in "The Hearer of Truth", and an editor was reading "The Higher Cannibalism"; also, and most important of all, Miss Ethelynda Lewis had now had "The Genius" for nearly two months, and had not yet reported. Thyrsis wrote to remind her, and after another two weeks, he wrote yet more urgently. At last came a note--"I have been away from the city, and have not had a chance to read the play. I will attend to it at once." And then, after three weeks more, Thyrsis wrote again--and at last came a letter that made his heart leap.

"I have read your play", wrote the popular *comedienne*: "I am very much interested in it indeed. I have asked my manager to read it, and will write you again shortly."

Thyrsis sent this to Corydon, and again there was rejoicing and expectation. "If only I can get the play on," he wrote, "our future is safe, for the profits from plays are enormous. It will be a great piece of luck if I have found the right person at the first attempt."

More weeks passed. Thyrsis watched the pageant of autumn upon the mountains--he saw the curtains of the lake-shore change to gold and scarlet, and from that to pale yellow and brown; and now, with every lightest breeze that stirred, there were showers of leaves came fluttering to the ground. The deer left the lake-shore and took to the "hard-wood", and the drumming of partridges thundered at sunset. The nights were bitterly cold, and he spent a good part of his day chopping logs and carrying them to camp, so that he might keep a blazing fire all night. There were hunting-parties in the woods, and he got a deer, and sold part of it, and had the rest hanging near his camp.

And then one night came the first snow-storm; in the morning it lay white and sparkling in the sunlight--and oh, the wonder of a hunting-trip, when the floor of the wilderness was like a page on which could be read the tale of all that happened in the night! One could hardly believe that so many creatures were in these woods--there were tracks everywhere one looked. Here a squirrel had run, and here a partridge; here had been a porcupine, with feet like a baby's, and here a fox, and here a bear with two cubs. And in yon hollow a deer had slept through the night, and here he had blown away the snow from the moss; here two bucks had fought; and here one of them had been started by a hunter, and had bounded away with leaps that it was a marvel to measure.

Thyrsis nearly lost his life at these fascinating adventures; for another storm came up, and covered his tracks, and when he tried to find his way back by the compass, he found that he had forgotten which end of the needle pointed to the North! So he wandered about for hours; and in the end had to decide by the toss of a penny whether he should get out to the main road, or wander off into twenty miles of trackless wilderness, without either food or matches. Fortunately the penny fell right; and he spent the night at a farmhouse, and the next day got back to the lumber-camp.

And there was a letter from Ethelynda Lewis! Thyrsis tore it open and read this incredible message:

"Your play has been carefully considered, and I am disposed to accept it. It is certainly very unusual and interesting, and I think it can be made a success. There are, however, certain changes which ought to be made. I am wondering if you will come to the city, so that we can talk it over. It would not be possible to settle a matter so important by mail; and there is no time to be lost, for I am ready to go ahead with the work at once, and so is my manager."

Section 12. Nothing that the mail had ever brought to Thyrsis had meant so much to him as this. He was transported with delight. Yes, for this he would go back to the city!--But then, he caught his breath, realizing his plight. How was he to get to the city, when he had only three dollars to his name?

He turned the problem over in his mind. Should he send a telegram to some relative and beg for help? No, he had vowed to die first. Should he write to the actress, and explain? No, for that would kill his chances. There was just one way to be thought of; venison in the woods was worth eleven cents a pound, and the smallest of deer would get him to the city!

And so began a great adventure. Thyrsis wrote Miss Ethelynda that he would come; and that night he loaded up some more buckshot "shells", and before dawn of the next day was out upon the hunt. The snow was gone now; and with soft shoes on his feet he wandered all day through the wilderness--and was rewarded by two chances to shoot at the white tails of flying deer.

And then came night, and he rigged up a "jack", a forbidden apparatus made of a soap-box and a lantern and a tin-plate for a reflector. He had an ingenious arrangement of straps and cords, whereby he could fasten this upon his head; and he had found an old lumber-trail where the deer came to feed upon the soft grass. Down this he crept like a thief in the night, with the light gleaming ahead, and the deer tramping in the thickets and whistling their alarms. Now and then one would stand and stare, his eye-balls gleaming like coals of fire; and at last came the roar of the gun, and the jacklight tumbled to the ground. When Thyrsis lighted up again and went to examine, there were spots of blood upon the leaves--but no deer.

So the next day he was up again at dawn, watching by one of the runways to the lake. And then came another tramp, through the thickets and over the mountains--and more shots at the "flags" of the elusive enemy. Thyrsis' back ached, and his feet were as if weighted with lead, but still he plodded on and on--it was his life against a deer's.

If only he had had a boat, so that he could have set up his "jack" in that! But he had no boat--and so he wrapped himself in blankets and sat to watch another runway at sunset; and when no deer came he decided to stay on until the moon rose. It was a bitterly cold night, and his hands almost froze to the gun-barrel when he touched it. And the moon rose, and forthwith went behind a cloud--and then came a deer!

There was hardly a trace of motion in the air, but somehow the creature half-scented Thyrsis; and so it stood and trumpeted to the night. Oh, the wildness of that sound--and the thumping of the heart of the hunter, and the breathless suspense, and the burning desire. The deer would take a step, and a twig would crack; and then it would stand still again, and Thyrsis would listen, crouching like a statue, clutching his weapon and striving to penetrate the darkness. And then the deer would take two or three more steps, and stand again; and then, in sudden alarm, bound away; and then come back again, step by step--fascinated by this mysterious thing there in the darkness. For three mortal hours that creature pranced and cavorted about Thyrsis, while he waited with chattering teeth; then in the end it took a sudden fright, and went bounding away through the thicket.

So came another day's hunting; and at sundown another watch by a runway; and another deer, that approached from the wrong direction, and came upon a man, worn out by three days and nights of effort, lying sound asleep at his post!

But there could be only one ending to this adventure. Thyrsis was out for a deer, and he would never quit until he got one. All his planning and wandering had availed him nothing; but now, the next morning, as he stepped out from his camp with a bucket in his hand--behold, at the edge of a thicket, a deer! Thyrsis stood rooted to the spot, staring blankly; and the deer stood staring at him.

It was a time of agony. Should he try to creep back to his gun, or should he make a sudden dash? He started to try the latter, and had a pang of despair as the deer whirled and bolted away. He leaped to the camp and grabbed his gun and sprang out into sight again--and there, off to the right, was another deer. It was a huge buck, with wide-spreading antlers, rising out of the bushes where it stood. It saw Thyrsis, and started away; and in a flash he raised his gun and fired. He saw the deer stumble, and he fired the other barrel; and then he started in wild pursuit.

He had been warned to beware of a wounded deer; but he forgot that--he forgot also that he had no more shells upon him. He ran madly through the forest, springing over fallen logs, plunging through thickets--he would have seized hold of the animal with his bare hands, if only he could have caught up with it.

The deer was badly hurt. It would leap ahead, and then stumble, half falling, and then leap again. Even in this way, the distance it covered was amazing; Thyrsis was appalled at the power of the creature, its tremendous bounds, the shock of its fall, and the crashing of the underbrush before it. It seemed like a huge boulder, leaping down a precipice; and Thyrsis stood at a safe distance and watched it. According to the poetry-books he should have been ashamed--perhaps moved to tears by the reproachful look in the great creature's eyes. But assuredly the makers of the poetry-books had never needed the price of a railroad-ticket as badly as Thyrsis did!

He only realized that night how desperate his need had been. He lay in his berth on board a train for the city--while back at his "open-camp" a wild blizzard was raging, and the thermometer stood at forty degrees below zero. But Thyrsis was warm and comfortable; and also he was brown and rugged, once more full of health and eagerness for life. All night he listened to the pounding of the flying train; and fast as the music of it went, it was not fast enough for his imagination. It seemed as if the rails were speaking--saying to him, over and over and over again, "Ethelynda Lewis! Ethelynda Lewis! Ethelynda Lewis!"

BOOK X
THE END OF THE TETHER

They sat still watching upon the hill-top, drinking in the scent of the clover.

"Ah, if only we might have come back here!" she sighed. "If only tee had never had to leave!"

"That way lies unhappiness" he said.

"Perhaps," she answered; and then quoted--

'Yet, Thyrsis, let me give my grief its hour
  In the old haunt, and find our tree-topp'd hill!
Who, if not I, for questing here hath power?"

"I wonder," said he, "if the poet put as much into these stanzas as we find in them!"

Section 1. Through the summer Corydon had been living week by week upon the hope that her husband would be able to send for her; all through the fall she had been dreaming of the arrangements they would make for the winter. But by now it had become clear that they would have to be separated for a part of the winter as well. She had sent him long letters, full of hopes and yearnings, anxieties and rebellions; but in the end she had brought herself to face the inevitable. And then it transpired that even a greater sacrifice was required of her--she was to be forbidden to see Thyrsis at all! If a man did not support his wife, said the world, it was common-sense that he should not have any wife; that was the quickest way to bring him to his senses. And so the two had threshed out that problem, and chosen their course; they would live in the same city, and yet confine themselves to writing letters!

A curious feeling it gave Thyrsis, to know that she was so near to him, and yet not to be going to meet her! He could not endure any part of the city where he had been with her, and got himself a hall bedroom on the edge of a tenement-district far up town. Then he had his shoes shined, and purchased a clean collar, and wrote Miss Ethelynda Lewis that he was ready to call. While he was waiting to hear from her, there came to him a strange adventure; assuredly one of the strangest that ever befell a struggling poet, in a world where many strange adventures have befallen struggling poets.

For six months Thyrsis had not seen his baby; and there had come in the meantime so many letters, telling so many miraculous things about that baby! So many dreams he had dreamed about it, so many hopes and so many prayers were centered in it! Twenty-two hours had he sat by the bedside when it was born; and through all the trials that had come afterwards, how he had suffered and wept for it! Now his heart was wrung with longing to see it, to touch it--his child. He wrote Corydon that he could not stand it; and Corydon wrote back that he was right--he should surely see the baby. And so it was arranged between them that Thyrsis was to be at a certain place in the park, and she would send the nurse-girl there with little Cedric.

He went and sat upon a bench; and the hour came, and at last down the path strolled a nurse-girl, wheeling a baby-carriage. He looked at the girl--yes, she was Irish, as Cordon had said, and answered all specifications; and then he looked at the baby, and his heart sank into his boots. Oh, such a baby! With red hair and a pug-nose, plebeian and dull-looking--such a baby! Thyrsis stared at the maid again--and she smiled at him. Then she passed on, and he sank down upon a bench. Great God, could it be that that was his child? That he would have to go through life with something so ugly, so alien to him? A terror seized him. It was like a nightmare. He was hardly able to move.

But then he told himself it could not be! Corydon had written him all about the baby; it was beautiful, with a noble head; everyone loved it. But then, were not mothers notoriously blind? Had there ever been a mother dissatisfied with her child? Or a father either, for that matter? Was it not a kind of treason for him to be so disgusted with this one--since it so clearly must be his?

There was none other in sight; and though he waited half an hour, none came.

At last he could stand it no more, but hurried away to the nearest telegraph-office. "Has baby red hair?" he wrote. "Did he come to the park?" And then he went to his room and waited, and soon after came the reply: "Baby has golden hair. Nurse was ill. Could not come."

Thyrsis read this, and then shut the door upon the messenger-boy, and burst into wild, hilarious laughter. He stood there with his arms stretched out, invoking all posterity to witness--"What do you think of *that?* What do you think of *that?*"

And a full hour later he was sitting by his bedside, his chin supported on his hands, and still invoking posterity. "Will you ever know what I went through?" he was saying. "Will you ever realize what my books have cost?" Then he smiled grimly, thinking of Voltaire's cruel epigram--that "letters addressed to posterity seldom reach their destination!"

Section 2. Thyrsis received a reply to his note, and went to call upon Miss Ethelynda Lewis. Miss Lewis dwelt in a luxurious apartment-house on Riverside Drive, where a colored maid showed him into a big parlor, full of spindle-legged gilt furniture upholstered in flowered silk. Also the room contained an ebony grand piano, and a bookcase, in which he had time to notice the works of Maupassant and Marie Corelli.

Then Miss Lewis entered, clad in a morning-gown of crimson "liberty". She was *petite* and exquisite, full of alluring dimples--and apparently just out of a perfumed bath. Thyrsis sat on the edge of his chair and gazed at her, feeling quite out of his element.

She placed herself on the flowered silk sofa and talked. "I am immensely interested in that play," she said. "It is *quite* unique. And you are so young, too--why, you seem just a boy. Really, you know I think you must be a genius yourself."

Thyrsis murmured something, feeling uncomfortable.

"The only thing is," Miss Lewis went on, "it will need a lot of revision to make it practical."

"In what part?" he asked.

"The love-story, principally," said the other. "You see, in that respect, you have simply thrown your chances away."

"I don't understand," said he.

"You have made your hero act so queerly. Everyone feels that he is in love with Helena--you meant him to be, didn't you? And yet he goes away from her and won't see her! Everyone will be disappointed at that--it's impossible, from every point of view. You'll have to have them married in the last act."

Thyrsis gasped for breath.

"You see," continued Miss Lewis, "I am to play the part of Helena, and I am to be the star. And obviously, it would never do for me to be rejected, and left all up in the air like that. I must have some sort of a love-scene."

"But"--protested the poet--"what you want me to change is what my play is *about!*"

"How do you mean?" asked the other.

"Why, it's a new kind of love," he stammered--"a different kind."

"But, people don't understand that kind of love."

"But, Miss Lewis, that's why I wrote my play! I want to *make* them understand."

"But you can't do anything like that on the stage," said Miss Lewis. "The public won't come to see your play." And then she went on to explain to him the conditions of success in the business of the theatre.

Thyrsis listened, with a clutch as of ice about his heart. "I am very sorry, Miss Lewis," he said, at last--"but I couldn't possibly do what you ask."

"Couldn't do it!" cried the other, amazed.

"It would not fit into my idea at all."

"But, don't you want to get your play produced?"

"That's just it, I want to get my play produced. If I did what you want me to, it wouldn't be my play. It would be somebody else's play."

And there he stood. The actress argued with him and protested. She showed him what a great chance he had here--one that came to a new and unknown writer but once in a lifetime. Here was a manager ready to give him a good contract, and to put his play on at once in a Broadway theatre; and here was a public favorite anxious to have the leading role. It would be everything he could ask--it would be fame and fortune at one stroke. But Thyrsis only shook his head--he could not do it. He was almost sick with disappointment; but it was a situation in which there was no use trying to compromise--he simply could not make a "love-story" out of "The Genius".

So at last there came a silence between them--there being nothing more for Miss Lewis to say.

"Then I suppose you won't want the play," said Thyrsis, faintly.

"I don't know," she answered, with vexation. "I'll have to think about it again, and talk to my manager. I had not counted on such a possibility as this."

And so they left it, and Thyrsis went away. The next morning he received a letter from "Robertson Jones, Inc.", asking him to call at once.

Section 3. Robertson Jones, the great "theatrical producer", was large and ponderous, florid of face and firm in manner--the steam-roller type of business-man. And it became evident at once that he had invited Thyrsis to come and be rolled.

"Miss Lewis tells me you can't agree about the play," said he.

"No," said Thyrsis, faintly.

And then Mr. Jones began. He told Thyrsis what he meant to do with this play. Miss Lewis was one of the country's future "stars", and he was willing to back her without stint. He had permitted her to make her own choice of a role, and she should have her way in everything. There were famous playwrights bidding for a chance to write for her; but she had seen fit to choose "The Genius".

"Personally," said Mr. Jones, "I don't believe in the play. I would never think of producing it--it's not the sort of thing anybody is interested in. But Miss Lewis likes it; she's been reading Ibsen, and she wants to do a 'drama of ideas', and all that sort of thing, you know. And that's all right--she's the sort to make a success of whatever she does. But you must do your share, and give her a part she can make something out of--some chance to show her charm. Otherwise, of course, the thing's impossible."

Mr. Jones paused. "I'm very sorry"--began Thyrsis, weakly.

"What's your idea in refusing?" interrupted the other.

Thyrsis tried to explain--that he had written the play to set forth a certain thesis, and that he was asked to make changes that directly contradicted this thesis.

"Have you ever had a play produced?" demanded the manager abruptly.

"No," said Thyrsis.

"Have you written any other plays?"

"No."

"Your first trial! Well, don't you think it a good deal to expect that your play should be perfect?"

"I don't think"--began Thyrsis.

"Can't you see," persisted the other, "that people who have been in this business all their lives, and have watched thousands of plays succeed and fail, might be able to give you some points on the matter?"--And then Mr. Jones went on to set forth to Thyrsis the laws of the theatrical game--a game in which there was the keenest competition, and in which the "ante" was enormously high. To produce "The Genius" would cost ten thousand dollars at the least; and were those who staked this to have no say whatever in the shaping of the play? Manifestly this was absurd; and as the manager pressed home the argument, Thyrsis felt as if he wanted to get up and run! When Mr. Jones talked to you, he looked you squarely in the eye, and you had a feeling of presumption, even of guilt, in standing out against him. Thyrsis shrunk in terror from that type of personality--he would let it have anything in the world it wanted, so only it would not clash with him. But never before had it demanded one of the children of his dreams!

Mr. Jones went on to tell how many things he would do for the play. It would go into rehearsal at once, and would be seen on Broadway by the first of February. They would pay him four, six and eight per cent., and his profits could not be less than three hundred dollars a week. With Ethelynda Lewis in the leading role the play might well run until June--and there would be the road profits the next season, in addition.

Thyrsis' brain reeled as he listened to this; it was in all respects identical with another famous temptation--"The devil taketh him upon a high mountain, and showeth him all the kingdoms of the earth!"

"And then there is England"--the man was saying.

"No, no!" cried Thyrsis, wildly. "No!"

"But *why* not?" demanded the other.

"It's impossible! I *couldn't* do it!"

"You mean you couldn't do the writing?"

"I wouldn't know how to!"

"Well then, that's easily arranged. Let me get some one to collaborate with you. There's Richard Haberton--you know who he is?"

"No," said Thyrsis, faintly.

"He's the author of 'The Rajah's Diamond'--it's playing with five companions now, and its third season. And he dramatized 'In Honor's Cause'--you've seen that, no doubt. We have paid him some sixty thousand dollars in royalties so far. And he'll take the play and fix it over--you wouldn't have to stir a finger."

Thyrsis sprang up in his agitation. "Please don't ask me, Mr. Jones," he cried. "I simply *could* not do it!"

It seemed strange to Thyrsis, when he thought it over afterwards, that the great Robertson Jones should have taken the trouble to argue so long with the unknown author of a play in which he did not believe. Was it that opposition incited him to persist? Or had he told Ethelynda Lewis he would get her what she wanted, and was now reluctant to confess defeat? At any rate, so it was--he went on to drive Thyrsis into a corner, to tear open his very soul. Also, he manifested anger; it was a deliberate affront that the boy should stand out like this. And Thyrsis, in great distress of soul, explained that he did not mean it that way--he apologized abjectly for his obstinacy. It was the *ideas* that he had tried to put into his play, and that he could not give up!

"But," persisted the manager--"write other plays, and put your ideas into them. If you've once had a Broadway success, then you can write anything you please, and you can make your own terms for production."

That thought had already occurred to Thyrsis; it was the one that nearly broke down his resistance. He would probably have surrendered, had the play not been so fresh from his mind, and so dear to him; if he had had time enough to become dissatisfied with it, as he had with his first novel--or discouraged about its prospects, as he had with "The Hearer of Truth"! But this child of his fancy was not yet weaned; and to tear it from his breast, and hand it to the butcher--no, it could not be thought of!

Section 4. So he parted from Mr. Jones, and went home, to pass two of the most miserable days of his life. He had pronounced his "*Apage, Satanas!*"--he had turned his back upon the kingdoms of the earth. And so presumably--virtue being its own reward--he should have been in a state of utter bliss. But Thyrsis had gone deeper into that problem, and asked himself a revolutionary question: Why should it always be that Satan had the kingdoms of the earth at his bestowal? Thyrsis did not want any kingdoms--he only wanted a chance to live in the country with his wife and child. And why, in order to get these things, must a poet submit himself to Satan?

Then came the third morning after his interview; and Thyrsis found in his mail another letter from Robertson Jones, Inc. It was a letter brief and to the point, and it struck him like a thunderbolt.

"Miss Ethelynda Lewis has decided that she wishes to accept your play as it stands. I enclose herewith a contract in duplicate, and if the terms are acceptable to you, will you kindly return one copy signed, and retain the other yourself."

Thyrsis read, not long after that, of a young playwright who died of heart-failure; and he was not surprised--if all playwrights had to go through experiences such as that. He could hardly believe his eyes, and he read the letter over two or three times; he read the contract, with Mr. Jones' impressive signature at the bottom. He did not know anything about theatrical contracts, but this one seemed fair to him. It provided for a royalty upon the gross receipts, to be paid after the play had earned the expenses of its production. Thyrsis had hoped that he might get some cash in advance, but that was not mentioned. In the flush of his delight he concluded that he would not take the risk of demanding anything additional, but signed the contract and mailed it, and sent a telegram to acquaint Corydon with the glorious tidings.

Section 5. One of the consequences of this triumph was that Thyrsis purchased a new necktie and half a dozen collars; and another was that an angry world was in some part appeased, and permitted the struggling poet to see his wife and child once more.

They met in the park; and strange it was to him to see Corydon after six months' absence. She was beautiful as ever, somewhat paler, though still with the halo of motherhood about her. He could scarcely realize that she was his; she seemed like a dream to him--like some phantom of music, thrilling and wonderful, yet frail and unsubstantial. She clung to his arm, trembling with delight, and pouring out her longing and her grief. There came to them one of those golden hours, when the deeps of their souls welled up, and they pledged themselves anew to their faith.

Even stranger it was to see the child; to be able to look at him all he pleased, and to speak to him, and to hold him in his arms! He was as beautiful as Thyrsis could have wished, and the father had no trouble at all in being interested in him;

his smiles were things to make the angels jealous. Thyrsis would push his carriage out into the park, and they would sit upon a bench and gaze at him--each making sure that the other had missed none of his fine points.

He was beginning to make sounds now, and had achieved the word "puss-ee". This originally had signified the woolly kitten he carried with him, but now by a metonymy it had come to include all kinds of living things; and great was the delight of the parents when a big red automobile flashed past, and the baby pointed his finger, exclaiming gleefully, "Puss-ee!" It is an astonishing thing, how little it takes to make parents happy; regarded, purely as an abstract proposition, it would be difficult to explain why two people who possessed between them a total of sixty-four teeth, more or less, should have been so much excited by the discovery that the baby had four.

But parenthood, as Thyrsis found, meant more than charming baby-prattle and the counting of teeth. Little Cedric's tiny fingers were twisted in his heart-strings--he loved him with a love the intensity of which frightened him when he realized it. And sometimes things went wrong, and then with a pang as from the stab of a knife would come the thought that he might some day lose this child. So much pain and toil a child cost, so much it took of one's strength and power; and then, such a fragile thing it was--exposed to so many perils and uncertainties, to the ravages of so many diseases, that struck like a cruel enemy in the dark! Corydon and Thyrsis were so ignorant--they were like children themselves; and where should they turn for knowledge? There were doctors, of course; but this took so much money--and even with all the doctors, see how many babies died!

Thyrsis was learning the bitter truth of Bacon's saying about "giving hostages to fortune." And dearly as he loved the child, the artist in him cried out against these ties. Where now was that care-free outlook, that recklessness, that joy in life as a spectacle, which made up so much of the artist's attitude? When one had a wife and child one no longer enjoyed tragedies--one lived, them; and one got from them, not *katharsis*, but exhaustion. One became timid and cautious and didactic, and other inartistic things. One learned that life was real, life was earnest, and the grave was not its goal!

Cedric had been weaned; but still he was not growing properly. Could it be that there was something wrong with what they fed him? Corydon would come upon advertisements telling of wonderful newly-discovered foods for infants, and giving pictures of the rosy and stalwart ones who were fed upon these foods. She would take to buying them--and they were not cheap foods either. Then, during the winter, the child caught cold; and they took that to mean that it had been in some way exposed--that was what everybody said, and what the name "cold" itself suggested. So Corydon would add more flannel dresses and blankets, until the unfortunate mite of life would be in a purple stew. And still, apparently, these mysterious "colds" were not to be thwarted. Thyrsis felt that in all this there must be something radically wrong, and yet he knew not what to do. Surely it should not have been such a task to keep life in one human infant.

Then, too, the training of the baby was going badly. He lived in close contact with nervous people who were disturbed if he cried; and so Corydon's energies were given to a terrified effort to keep him from crying. He must be dandled and rocked to sleep, he must be played with and amused, and have everything he cried for; and it was amazing how early in life this little creature learned the hold which he had upon his mother. His chief want had come to be to sleep all day and lie awake half the night; and during these hours of wakefulness he pursued the delightful pastime of holding some one's hand and playing with it. Corydon, nervous and sick and wrestling with melancholia, would have to lie awake for uncounted hours and submit to this torment. The infant had invented a name for the diversion; he called it "Hoodaloo mungie"--which being translated signified "Hold your finger". To the mother this was like the pass-word of some secret order of demons, who preyed upon and racked her in the night; so that never after in her life could she hear the phrase, even in jest, without experiencing a nervous shock.

Section 6. This was a period of great hopefulness for Thyrsis, but also of desperate struggle. For until the production of his play in January, he had somehow to keep alive, and that meant more hack-work. Also he had to lay something by, for after the rehearsals the play would go on the road for a couple of weeks, to be "tried on the dog"; and during that period he must have money enough to travel, and stay at hotels, and also to take Corydon with him, if possible.

The rehearsals began an interesting experience for him; he was introduced into a new and strange world. Thyrsis himself was shy, and disposed to run away and hide his emotions; but here were people--the actor-folk--whose business it was to live them in sight of the world. And these emotions were their life; they were very intense, yet quick both to come and to go. Such people were intensely personal; they were like great children, vain and sensitive, their moods and excitements not to be taken too seriously. But it was long before Thyrsis came to realize this, and meanwhile he had some uncomfortable times. To each of the players, apparently, the interest of a play centered in those places in which he was engaged in speaking his lines; and to each the author of the play was a more or less benevolent despot, who had the happiness of the rest of the world in his keeping. Once at a rehearsal, when Thyrsis was engaged in cutting out one of the speeches attributed to "Mrs. Hartman", he discovered that lady standing behind him in a flood of tears!

In the beginning Thyrsis paid many visits to the apartment on Riverside Drive; for Miss Lewis professed to be very anxious that he should consult with her and tell her his ideas of her part. But Thyrsis soon discovered that what she really wanted was to have him listen to *her* ideas. Miss Lewis was at war with Thyrsis' portrayal of Helena--it was incomprehensible to her that Lloyd should not be pursuing her, and she playing the coquette, according to all romantic models. Particularly she could not see how Lloyd was to resist the particularly charming Helena which she was going to make. She was always trying to make Thyrsis realize this incongruity, and to persuade him to put some "charming" lines into her part. "You boy!" she would exclaim. "I believe you are as obstinate as your hero!" Miss Lewis was only two years older than the "boy", but she saw fit to adopt this grandmotherly attitude toward him.

And then came Robertson Jones, suggesting a man who could play the part of Lloyd. But Miss Lewis declared indignantly that she would not have him, because he was not handsome enough. "If," she vowed, "I've got to make love to a man and be rejected by him, at least I'm not going to have it an ugly man!" When an actor was finally agreed upon and engaged, Thyrsis had a talk with him, and it seemed as if Miss Lewis, in her preoccupation with his looks, had overlooked the matter of his brains. But Thyrsis was so new at this game that he did not feel capable of judging. He shrunk from the thought of having any actor play his part--that was so precious and so full of meaning to him.

But when the rehearsals began, Thyrsis speedily forgot this feeling. The most sensitive poet to the contrary notwithstanding, the purpose of a play is to be acted;

and Thyrsis was like an inventor, who has dreamed a great machine, and now sees the parts of it appearing as solid steel and brass; sees them put together, and the great device getting actually under way.

The rehearsals were held in a little hall on the East Side, and thither came the company--six men and three women. There was no furniture or setting, they all wore their street clothing, and in the beginning they went through their parts with the manuscript in their hands. And yet--they had been selected because they resembled the characters in the play; and every time they went over the lines they gave them with more feeling and understanding. So--vaguely at first, and then more clearly--the poet began to see them as incarnations of his vision. These characters had been creatures of his fancy; they had lived in it, he had walked and talked and laughed and wept with them. Now to discover them outside him--to be able to hear them with his physical ears and see them with his physical eyes--was one of the strangest experiences of his life. It was so thrilling as to be almost uncanny. It was a new kind of inspiration, of that strange "subliminal uprush" which made the mystery of his life. And it was a kind that others could experience with him. Corydon would come every day to the rehearsals, and for four or five hours at a stretch they would sit and watch and listen in a state of perfect transport.

Section 7. Also, there were things not in the manuscript which were sources of interest and delight. There was Mr. Tapping, the stage director, for instance; Thyrsis could see himself writing another play, just to get Mr. Tapping in. He was a man well on in years, and wrecked by dissipation--almost bald and toothless, and with one foot crippled with gout. Yet he was a perfect geyser of activity-- bounding about the stage, talking swiftly, gesticulating--like some strange gnome or cobold out of the bowels of the earth. Thyrsis was the creator of the play, so far as concerned the words; but this man was to be the creator of it on the stage. And that, too, required a kind of genius, Thyrsis perceived.

Mr. Tapping had talked the problems out with him at the beginning--talking until two o'clock in the morning, in a super-heated office filled with the smoke of ten thousand dead cigars. He talked swiftly, eagerly, setting forth his ideas; to Thyrsis it was a most curious experience--to hear the vision of his inmost soul translated into the language of the Tenderloin! "Your fiddler's this kind of a guy," Mr. Tapping would say--"he knows he's got the goods, and he don't care whether those old fogies think he's dippy, or what the hell they think. Ain't that the dope, Mr. Author?" And Thyrsis would answer faintly that he thought that was "the dope."--This was a word that Mr. Tapping used every time he opened his mouth, apparently; it designated all things connected with the play--character, dialogue, action, scenery, music, costume. "That's the way to dope it out to them!" he would cry to the actors.

Miss Lewis, and Mr. Tilford, the leading man, moved through their parts with dignity; the stage director showed them the "business" he had laid out, but they did not trouble to act at rehearsals, and he did not criticize what they did. But all the other people had to be taught their roles and drilled in them; and that meant that Mr. Tapping had to have in him five actors and two actresses, and play all their seven parts as they came. Marvellous it was to see him do this; springing from place to place, and changing his whole aspect in a flash--now scolding shrewishly in the words of Violet Hartman, now discoursing, with the accent and manner of Prof, von Arne, upon the *psychopathia sexualis* of Genius.

He did not know all the parts, of course; but that was never allowed to trouble him. He would take a sentence out of the actor's lips, and then go on to elaborate it in his Tenderloin dialect; or, if the scene was highly emotional, and required swift speech, he would fall back upon the phrase "and so and so, and so and so." He could run the whole gamut of human emotions with those words, "and so and so."

"No, that's no good!" he would cry to "Mrs. Hartman." "What are those words?--'Wretched, ungrateful son--do you care nothing at all for your parents' feelings? Do you owe us nothing for what we have done? And so and so? And so and so? And so and so?'" Mr. Tapping's voice would rise to a wail; and then in a flash he would turn to Moses Rosen (he called all the actors by their character-names). "That's your cue, Rosen, you rush in left centre, and throw up your hands--right here--see? And what's your dope?--oh yes--'I have spent seven thousand dollars on this thing! You have ruined me! You have betrayed me! And so and so! And so and so! And so and so!'-- And then you run over here to the professor--'You have trapped me! And so and so!'"

Day by day as the work progressed, and the actors came to know their lines, Thyrsis' excitement grew. The great machine was running, he was getting some sense of the power of it! And new aspects of it were revealed to him; there came the composer who was to do the incidental music, and the orchestra-leader who was to conduct it; there came the costume-designer and the scene-painter, and even the press-agent who was to "boost" the play, and wanted picturesque details about the author's life. Corydon and Thyrsis were invited to go with Mr. Tilford to select a wig, and with Mr. Tapping to see the carpenters who were building the various "sets", in a big loft over near the North River. As the two walked home each day after these adventures, it was all they could do to keep from hugging each other on the street.

It was a thing of especial moment to Thyrsis, because it was the first time in his life that his art had received any assistance from the outside world--the first time this world had done anything but scold at him and mock him. Here at last was recognition--here was success! Here were material things submitting themselves to his vision, coming to him humbly to be taught, and to co-operate in the creation of beauty! So Thyrsis caught sudden glimpses of what his life might have been. He was like a man who had been chained in a black dungeon, and who now gets sight of the green earth and the blue sky, and smells the perfume of the flowers and hears the singing of the birds. With forces such as this at his command, the power of his vision would be multiplied tenfold; and he was transported with the delight of the discovery, he and Corydon found their souls once more in this new hope.

So out of these moods there began the burgeoning of new plans in his mind. Even amid the rush of rehearsals, he was dreaming of other things to write; some time before "The Genius" had reached the public, he had finished the writing of "The Utopians"--that fragment of a vision which was perhaps the greatest thing he ever did, and certainly the most characteristic.

Section 8. As usual, the immediate occasion of the writing was trivial enough. It was his "leading lady" who was responsible for it. Miss Lewis had taken a curious fancy to Thyrsis--he was a new type to her, and it pleased her to explore him. "How in the world did you ever get him to marry you?" she would exclaim to Corydon. "I could as soon imagine a marble statue making love to me!" And she told others about this strange poet, who was obviously almost starving, and yet had refused to let Richard Haberton revise his play for him, and had all but refused to let Robertson Jones Inc., produce it. Before long she came to Thyrsis to say that one of her friends desired to meet him, and would he come to a supper-party.

Thyrsis heard this with perplexity.

"A supper-party!" he exclaimed. "But I can't!"

"Why not?"

"Why--I have no clothes."

"Nobody expects a poet to have clothes," laughed Miss Lewis. "Come in the garments of your fancy. And besides, Barry's a true Bohemian."

Barry Creston, the giver of this party, was one of the sons of "Dan" Creston, the mine-owner and "railroad-king", who a short while before had been elected senator from a Western state under circumstances of great scandal. "The old man's a hard character, I guess," said Miss Lewis; "but you must not believe all you read in the papers about Barry."

"I never read anything about him," said the other; and so Miss Lewis went on to explain that Griswold, the Wall Street plunger, had got a divorce from his wife after throwing her into Barry's arms; and that Barry's sister had married an Austrian arch-duke who had maltreated her, and that Barry had kicked him out of a hotel-window in Paris.

This invitation was a cause of much discomfort to Thyrsis. He had not come to the point where he was even curious about the life of the Barry Crestons of the world; and yet he did not like to hurt Miss Lewis' feelings. She made it evident to him that she was determined to exhibit her "lion"; and so he said "all right."

The supper party was at the *Cafe de Boheme*, which was an Aladdin's palace buried underground beneath a building in the "Tenderloin". Fountains splashed in marble basins, and birds sang amid the branches of tropical flowering trees, while on a little stage a man in the costume and character of a Paris *apache* sang a song of ferocious cynicism. And after him came a Japanese juggler of prodigious swiftness, and then a fat German woman in peasant guise who sang folk-songs, and wound up with "O, du lieber Augustin!" After which the company joined in the chorus of "Funiculi, funicula" and "Gaudeamus igitur"--for the patrons of the "Boheme" were nothing if they were not cosmopolitan.

Cosmopolitan also was the company at Barry Creston's table. On one side of Thyrsis was Miss Lewis, and on the other was Mlle. Armand, the dancer who had set New York in a furore. Opposite to her was Scarpi, the famous baritone; and then there was Massey, a sculptor from Paris, and Miss Rita Seton, of the "Red Hussars" Company, and a Miss Raymond, a gorgeous creature with a red flamingo feather in her hat, who had been Massey's model for his sensational figure of "Aurora".

Finally there was Barry Creston himself: a new type, and a disconcerting one. He was not at all the "gilded youth" whom Thyrsis had expected to find; he was a man of about thirty, widely cultured, urbane and gracious in his manner, and quite evidently a man of force. He was altogether free from that crude egotism which Thyrsis had found to be the most prominent characteristic of the American man of wealth. He spoke in French with Armand and in Italian with Scarpi and in German with the head-waiter who worshipped before him; and yet one did not feel that there was any ostentation about it--all this was his *monde*. And although he exhaled an atmosphere of vast wealth, this, too, seemed a matter of course; he assumed that you also were provided with unlimited funds--that all the world, in fact, was in the same fortunate case. Evidently he was well-known at the "Boheme", for the waiters gathered like flies around the honey-pot, and the august head-waiter himself took the order, and beamed his approval at Barry's selections. So presently there flowed in a stream of costly viands, served in *outre* and fantastic fashion--many of them things not known even by name to Thyrsis. There were costly wines as well, and at the end an ice in the shape of a great basket of fruit, wonderfully carved and colored like life, resting upon a slab of ice, which in turn was set in a silver tray with handles.

Thyrsis was dazed at all this waste, and at the uproar in the place, where dozens of other parties were squandering money in the same blind fashion, and all laughing, chatting, joining in the choruses with the performers on the stage. Now and then he would catch a little of his host's conversation, which was of all the capitals of Europe, and of art-worlds, the very existence of which was unknown to him. And then, on his left hand, there was Mlle. Armand, deftly picking off the leaves of an artichoke and dipping them into *mayonnaise*, and saying in her little bird's voice, "They tell me, Monsieur, that you have *du genie*. Oh, you should go to Paree to live--it is not here that one appreciates *du genie*!" And, then while Thyrsis was working out an explanation of his failure to visit Paris, some one in the cafe caught sight of Scarpi, and there was a general call for him; and according to the genial custom of the "Boheme" he stood up, amid tumultuous applause, and sang one of his own rollicking songs.

So the revelry went forward, while Thyrsis marvelled, and tried to hide his pain. There could be no question of any enjoyment for him--when he knew that the cost of this affair would have paid all his expenses for a winter! Doubtless what Barry Creston spent for his cigars would have saved Thyrsis and his family from misery all their lives; and he wondered if the man would have cared had he known. Barry was one of the princes of the new dispensation; and sometimes princes were compassionate, Thyrsis reflected. Apparently this one was all urbanity and charm, having no thought in life save to play the perfect host to brilliant artists and ***demi-mondaimes***, and to skim the cream off the top of civilization.

But then suddenly the conversation took a new turn, and Thyrsis got another view of the young prince. There had been trouble out in the Western mines; and some one mentioned it--when in a flash Thyrsis saw the set jaw and the clenched fist and the steel grey eye of old "Dan" Creston. (Thyrsis had read somewhere a sketch of this senator, whose fortune was estimated at fifty millions, and who ran the governments of three states.) Barry, it seemed, had had charge of the mines for three years--that was how he had won his spurs. In those days, he said, there had been no unions--he told with a quiet smile how he had broken them. Now again "agitators" had crept in, so that in some of the camps the men were being moved out bodily, and replaced by foreigners, who knew a good job when they had it. To make this change had taken the militia; but it would be done thoroughly, and afterwards there would be no more trouble.

The supper-party broke up about two o'clock, and Miss Raymond, the lady of the flamingo hat, was the only one who showed any effects from all the wine that had been consumed. Thyrsis, to his great surprise discovered that his host had taken a fancy to him, and had asked Miss Lewis to bring him out to luncheon at the Creston place in the country. And so came the wonderful experience which brought to him the vision of "The Utopians."

Section 9. They went, one Saturday morning, in Miss Lewis' automobile--out to Riverside Drive, and up the valley of the Hudson. This was in itself a Utopian experience for Thyrsis, who had never before taken a trip in one of these magic chariots. It leaped over the frozen roads like a thing of life, and he lay back in the cushioned seats and closed his eyes and listened to the hum of the machinery, imagining what life might be for him, if he could rest like this when he was worn from overwork. It was like some great adventure in music, like a minstrel's chanting of heroic deeds; it was Nature with all her pageantry unrolled in a panorama before his eyes. And meantime Miss Lewis was chattering on about the play and its prospects; and about other plays and their prospects; and about the people at the supper-party and their various loves and hates.

So they came to the great stone castle of the Crestons, set upon a mountain-top overlooking the valley of this "American Rhine." Thyrsis gasped when he saw it, and he gasped many times again while Barry was showing them about. For this place was a triumph of a hundred arts and sciences; into its perfections had gone all the skill of the architects and designers, the weavers and carpenters, the painters and sculptors of a score of centuries and climes. The very dairies, the stables, the dog-kennels were things to be wondered at and studied; and in the vast halls were single pictures over which Thyrsis would fain have lingered for hours. Then, best of all, the great portico, with its stone pillars, and its view of the noble river, and of the snow-clad hills, dazzling in the sunlight!

They had luncheon; after which Barry played upon the organ, and Miss Lewis sat beside him and left Thyrsis to wander at will. He made his way out to the portico, and paced back and forth there; and while the organ rolled and thundered to him, the majesty of the scene swept over him, and in towering splendors his soul arose. He thought of the wretched room in which he was pent, he thought of his starved and struggling life; and all the rage of his defeated genius awoke in him. In the name of that genius he uttered his defiance, and by the title of it he took possession of this castle, and of all things it contained. Yes--for he was the true lord and master of it--he was the prince disinherited! And the meaning of it, its excuse for being, was this brief hour! For this its glories had been assembled; for this the architects and designers, the weavers and carpenters, the painters and sculptors had labored in a score of centuries and climes; for this the great organ had been built, and for this the great musician had composed--that he might behold, in one hour of transfiguration, what the life of man would be in that glad time when all the arts of civilization were turned to the fostering of the soul! When he who carried in the womb of his spirit the new life of the ages, would be loved instead of being hated, would be cherished instead of being neglected, would be reverenced instead of being mocked! When palaces would be built for him and beauty and joy would be gathered for him, and the paths would be made clear before his feet! So out of boundless love and rapture would he speak to men, and bring to them those gifts that were beyond price, the treasures of his unfolding inspiration.

So it was that the Utopians came to Thyrsis; those men of the future, worshippers of joy! They came to him, alive and in the flesh, beautiful and noble, gracious and free-hearted--as some day they will come, if so the earth endure; as they will stand upon that portico, and listen to that music, and gaze upon the valley of that American Rhine! And will they remember the long-dead dreamer, and how they walked with him there and spoke with him; how they put their arms about him, and gave him of their love and understanding? Will they remember what shuddering rapture their touch conveyed to him; how the tears ran down his cheeks, and he pledged his soul to yet more years of torment, so only their glory might come to be upon earth? Will they read the blazing words in which he pictured them, the trumpet-blast he sounded to the dead souls of his time?

Thyrsis knew that this was the greatest hour of his life, and he fought like mad to hold it. But that might not be--the music ceased, and he heard the voices of his host and Miss Lewis. They came to the door; and then Thyrsis' thoughts came back quickly to earth. For he saw that Barry Creston's arm was about the woman, and she was leaning upon him; nor did they separate when they saw him, but stood there, smiling; so that at last Thyrsis had solved for him the problem of their relationship. It was not so that the Utopians loved, he thought, as he watched them; and found himself wondering if young Creston was as imperious with his women as he was with the slaves in his Western mines.

The car came to the door, and they parted from their host and sped back to the city. "What do you think of him?" asked Miss Lewis--and went on in a burst of confidence to tell him that it was to this prince of the new dispensation that he owed the great chance of his life. For it was Barry Creston who had given the Broadway "show-girl" the start that had made her a popular *comedienne*; it was Barry Creston who had awakened in her an interest in the "drama of ideas", and had set her to fermenting with new ambitions; and finally it was Barry Creston who in a moment of indulgence had promised the money which had set the managers and actors and musicians, the stage-carpenters and scene-painters and press-agents to work at the task of embodying "The Genius"!

Section 10. It may have been a coincidence; but from that hour dated the process of Thyrsis' disillusionment concerning the production of his play. Could it be, he asked himself, that such wealth as Barry Creston's could buy true art? Could it be that forces set in motion by it could really express his vision? "Genius surrounded by Commercialism", had been the formula of his play; and did not the formula describe his own position as well as Lloyd's?

A strange thing was this theatrical business--the business of selling emotions! One had really to feel the emotions, in order to portray them with force; yet one had at the same time to appraise them with the eye of the business-man--one must not feel emotions that would not pay. Also, one boomed and boosted his own particular emotions, celebrating their merits in the language of the circus-poster. If you had taken up a certain play, you considered it the greatest play that had ever made its bow to Broadway; and you actually persuaded yourself to believe it--at least those who made the real successes were men who possessed that hypnotic power.

There was, for instance, Mr. Rosenberg, the press-agent and advertising-man. He was certain that "The Genius" was a play of genius, and its author a man of genius; and yet Thyrsis knew that if it had been Meyer and Levinson, across the street, who were producing it, Mr. Rosenberg would have called it "rot". Mr. Rosenberg was to Thyrsis a living embodiment of Moses Rosen in the play--so much so that he felt the resemblance in the names to be perilous, and winced every time he heard Rosenberg speak of Rosen. But fortunately neither Rosenberg nor Rosen possessed a sense of irony, and so there were no feelings hurt. Thyrsis had written the play without having met either a press-agent or the head of a music-bureau; he had drawn the character of Moses after the fashion of the German, evolving the idea of an elephant out of his inner consciousness. But now that it was done, he was amazed to see how well it was done; he was like an astronomer who works out the orbit of a new planet, and afterwards discovers it with his telescope.

As the preparations neared completeness, Thyrsis found himself more and more disturbed about the production. He was able to judge of the actors now, and they seemed to him to be cheap actors--to be relying for their effects upon exaggeration, to be making the play into a farce. But when he pointed this out to Mr. Tapping, Mr. Tapping was offended; and when he spoke to Mr. Jones, he was referred to Miss Lewis. All he could accomplish with Miss Lewis, however, was to bring up the eternal question of the lack of "charm" in her part. Poor Ethelynda was also getting into an unhappy frame of mind; she had begun to doubt whether the "drama of ideas" was her *forte* after all--and whether the ideas in this particular drama were real ideas or sham. She got the habit of inviting friends in to judge it, and she was always of the opinion of the last friend; so the production was like a ship whose pilot has lost his bearings.

The time drew near for the opening-performance, which was to be given in a manufacturing city in New England. The nerves of all the company were stretched to the breaking point; and overwrought as he was himself, Thyrsis could not but pity the unhappy "leading lady", who could hardly keep herself together, even with the drugs he saw her taking.

The "dress-rehearsal" began at six o'clock on Sunday evening; and from the very start everything went wrong. But Thyrsis did not know the peculiar fact about dress-rehearsals, that everything always goes wrong; and so he suffered untellable agonies at the sight of the blundering and stupidity. Mr. Tapping stormed and fumed and hopped about the stage, and swore, first at his gouty foot, and then at some member of the company; and he sent them back, over and over again through the scenes--it was midnight before they finished the first act, and it was six o'clock in the morning before they finished the second, and it was nearly noon of Monday before the wretched men and women went home to sleep.

Thyrsis had left before that, partly because he could not endure to see the mess that things were in, and partly because they told him he would have to make a speech that night, and he had to spend two of his hardearned dollars for the hire of a dress-suit. Here, as always, the scarcity of dollars was like a thorn in his flesh. He had been obliged to leave Corydon heart-broken at home, because he had not been able to lay by enough to bring her; he had to stay at a cheap hotel--cheaper even than any of the actors; and when Miss Lewis and Mr. Tapping went out to lunch, he would have to say that he was not hungry, and then go off and get something at a corner grocery.

The hour of the performance came; and Thyrsis, like a gambler who has staked all his possessions upon the turn of one card, sat in a box and watched the audience and the play. The house was crowded; and the play-wright saw with amazed relief that all his agonies of the night before had been needless--the performance went without a hitch from beginning to end. And also, to his unutterable delight, the play seemed to "score". He had gazed at the rows of respectable burghers of this prosperous manufacturing town, and wondered what understanding they could have of his tragedy of "genius". But they seemed to be understanding; at any rate they laughed and applauded; and when Lloyd smashed the violin over von Arne's head and the curtain went down, there was quite a little uproar.

Thyrsis came out and made his timid speech, which was also applauded; and then came the last act, and the women got out their handkerchiefs on schedule time, and Mr. Rosenberg stood behind Thyrsis in the box, rubbing his hands together gleefully. So the play-wright sent a telegram to his wife, saying that the play was a certain success; and then he went to bed, assuredly the happiest man who had ever slept in that fifty-cent hotel!

But alas--the next morning, there were the local papers; and with one accord they all "roasted" the play! Their accounts of it sounded for all the world like the play itself--those extracts which the two professors had read from the criticisms of Lloyd's concert! Thyrsis wondered if the critics must not have taken offence at the satire!

Then, going to the theatre, the first person he met was Rosenberg, who sent another chill to his heart. "First nights are always good," said Mr. Rosenberg. "It was all 'paper', you know. To-night is the real test."

And so the second performance came; and in the theatre were some two hundred people, and the occasion was the most awful "frost" that ever froze the heart of an unhappy partisan of the "drama of ideas". After which, according to schedule, the play moved to another manufacturing town; and in the theatre were some two hundred and fifty people--and a frost some ten degrees lower yet!

Section 11. So at twelve o'clock that night there was a consultation in a room at the hotel, attended by Thyrsis and Miss Lewis and Mr. Tapping and Mr. Jones.

"You see," said the last named; "the play is a failure."

"Absolutely!" said Mr. Tapping.

"I knew it would be!" cried Miss Lewis.

"And you?" asked Mr. Jones of Thyrsis.

"It has not succeeded in these towns," said Thyrsis. But then--how could it succeed, except where there are intellectual people? You promised to take it to New York."

"It's no use!" declared Jones. "New York would laugh it dead in one night."

"It would," said Mr. Tapping, decisively.

"I knew it all along," cried Miss Lewis.

So they went on for ten minutes; and then, "What are you going to do?" asked Thyrsis, in terror.

"The play must be altered," said Jones.

"How altered?"

"It must be altered as Miss Lewis asked you at first."

Thyrsis sprang up. "What!" he cried.

"It must be done!" said Mr. Jones.

"It must," said Mr. Tapping.

"I knew it all along!" cried Miss Lewis again.

"But I won't stand for it!" exclaimed Thyrsis, wildly.

"It must be done!" said Mr. Jones, in his heaviest steam-roller tone.

"But I won't have it!"

"What'll you do?"

"I'll go to law! I'll get an injunction."

"What is there in our contract to prevent our altering the play?" demanded the man.

"What!" gasped Thyrsis. "You know what our understanding was!"

"Humph!" said the other. "Can you prove it?"

"And do you mean that you would go back on that understanding?"

"And do you mean that you expect me to see this money wasted and the play sent to pot?"

Thyrsis, in his agony, turned to Miss Lewis. "Will you let him break our bargain?" he cried.

"But what else is there to be done?" she answered.

"Don't you see that the play is a failure? And don't you see the plight you've got me in?"

Thyrsis was dumb with dismay. He stared from one of these people to another, and his heart went down--down. He saw that his case was hopeless. He had no one to help him or to advise him, and he had less than eleven dollars in his pocket.

"What do you propose to do?" he asked, weakly.

"I have already telegraphed to Richard Haberton," said Jones. "He will meet us and see the next two performances; and then we'll lay the company off until we get some kind of a practical play."

And so the steam-roller rolled and the matter was settled; and Thyrsis, broken-hearted, bid the trio farewell, and took an early train back to New York.

He never saw any member of the company again--and he never saw the "practical play" which Mr. Richard Haberton made out of "The Genius". What was done he gathered from the press-clippings that came to him--the famous author of "The Rajah's Diamond" caused Helena to fall into Lloyd's arms at the end of the second act, and had them safely if not happily married at the beginning of the third. Also he wrote several "charming" scenes for Ethelynda Lewis, and two weeks later the play had a second opening in another manufacturing town of New England--where the critics, awed by the name of the distinguished dramatist upon the play-bills, were moved to faint praise. But perhaps it was that Mr. Richard Haberton required more than two weeks' time for the evolving of real "charm"; at any rate the audience came in no larger numbers to see this new version, and the misbegotten production lived for another six performances, and died a peaceful death at the very gates of the metropolis.

And such was the end of Thyrsis' career as a play-wright. In return for all his labors and his agonies he received some weeks later a note from Robertson Jones, Inc., to the effect that the books of "The Genius" showed a total deficit of six thousand seven hundred and forty-two dollars and seventeen cents; and accordingly, under the contract, there was nothing due to the author.

BOOK XI
THE TORTURE-HOUSE

They sat in the darkness, watching where the starlight gleamed upon the water.

"We had always hope," she was saying. "How endlessly we hoped!"

"Could we do it now?" he asked; and after a pause, he quoted from the poem--

"Unbreachable the fort
Of the long-batter'd world uplifts its wall;
    And strange and vain the earthly turmoil grows,
    And near and real the charm of thy repose,
And night as welcome as a friend would fall!"_

Section 1. Thyrsis came home beaten and crushed, worn out with overwork and worry, his heart black with rage and bitterness and despair. He met Corydon in the park, and she listened to his story, white and terrified. She had swallowed all her disappointment, had stayed at home with the baby while he went with the play; and now the outcome of it all was this!

"What are you going to do?" she whispered; and he answered, "I don't know. I don't know."

She saw the terrible state he was in, and she dared not utter a single word of her own grief. She bit her lip, and choked back her tears. "This is my life," she thought to herself; "I must endure, endure--that is all!"

He could not afford even to sit and talk with her very long; there was no time to indulge in the luxury of despair. His money was gone, and he was in debt for some that he had borrowed. Since irregular eating had been telling upon him again, he had been getting his meals with an acquaintance of the family, who kept a boarding-house uptown. On the strength of his prospects, she had trusted him for four dollars a week; and now the play had failed, and he had to go and tell her, and listen to new protests as to his folly in refusing to "get a position". But in the end she bade him stay on; and so he was divided between his shame, and the need of something to eat day by day.

Time dragged on, and still there was no gleam of light. There were shameful hours in these weeks--he touched the lowest point yet in his life. This was a typical cheap boarding-house, a place where the drudges of trade were herded; it was a home of sordidness and ugliness--to Thyrsis its people seemed like carefully selected types of all things that he hated in the world. There was a young broker's clerk, whose patter was of prices, and of fortunes made without service. There was a grey-haired bookkeeper for a giant "trust", a man who could not have had more pride in that great engine of exploitation, or more contempt for its victims, had he been the president and chief owner thereof. There was a young divinity-student, who made greedy reaches for the cake-plate, and who summed up for Thyrsis all the cant and commonness of the church. There was a dry-goods clerk, who wore flaring ties, and who played the role of a "masher" upon the avenue every evening. And finally there was a red-faced Irish-man who wore large shiny cuffs and a false diamond, and who held some political job, and was voluble in behalf of "the organization".

Among these people Thyrsis sat three times a day, silent and tortured, paying a high price for each morsel of food he ate. But also he was lonely, and craving any sort of respite; and in the course of time he became acquainted with several of the younger men. One of the diversions in their pitiful and narrow lives was to gather in some room and indulge in petty gambling; sitting for hours upon hours with their faculties alert upon the attempt to get from each other some small fraction of that weekly stipend which kept them alive. Sometimes they played "penny-ante", and sometimes *vingt et un*; once, as it chanced, they needed another player, and they urged Thyrsis to join them.

And so, for the first time in his life, Thyrsis learned what it meant to lay his soul upon the lap of the goddess of chance. From eight o'clock that evening until two the next morning, he sat in a suffocating room full of cigarette-smoke, trying in vain to win back the dollar or two he had lost at the outset; flushed and trembling with excitement, and hating himself with a bitter and tormenting hatred. And so he discovered his vice; he discovered that he had in him the soul of the gambler! And all the rest of the winter he had to wrestle with that shame. He would go to his dinner, tired and heartsick; and they would ask him to play again; and he--the man who carried a message for humanity in his heart--he would yield! Three times during that winter he fell into the mire; on Washington's birthday he began to play in the morning, and stopping only for meals, he played until long after midnight. Forever afterwards he was a humbler and a gentler man because of that experience; understanding how squalor abases one, and how swiftly and stealthily an evil passion closes its grasp about the soul.

Section 2. Of this shameful thing he said not a word to Corydon. But he avoided meeting her, because of the depths of his despair. And so at last there came a letter from her--a long and unusual one. Corydon, too, was having her troubles, it appeared.

"I am writing in haste," she said; "I shall mail the letter at once, before my resolution fails me. At least a dozen times I have made up my mind to tell you or to write you what is here, and each time I have turned back. But now I have got to a stage where I must have your help.

"I enclose a long letter which I wrote you years ago, before we were married. I was looking over some old papers the other day and came upon it. Generally when I wrote you letters that I did not send, I tore them up; but something led me to keep this one--I had a feeling that some day it would be interesting as a curiosity. You see, I am always persuading myself that I can get over this trouble, and learn to laugh at it; and I am always succeeding--but only to have it crop up in some different form. I have told you a little of it now and then--but stop and read the enclosed, and you will see."

So Thyrsis read the old letter--a missive of anguish and terror, and beginning with elaborate preludings and hesitations:

"I implore you to be patient with me this once; and when I have gotten through, I want you still to love me, if possible. I have been trying to get the courage to write you something that is so mean and low, childish and almost imbecile, that there have been moments in which my horror of it was absolutely unspeakable; when

I have imagined myself as a soul damned, when I thought that if you knew, you would think I had a diseased brain. I only ask you to read patiently what I am going to write; but know that every word is a horrible effort, that it is torture and humiliation to me to write it. I have a feeling now as though I were psychologically dissecting something.

"It must have been eight years ago, when I was sick in bed; in a fever or delirium I conceived the idea that there was a coffin under my bed. The thought took hold of me, somehow, like an octopus, and I used to writhe under it, and get into fearful perspirations. I never went near a bed that I didn't think of this thing with the same horror.

"And so I seemed to have created a nervousness, a sense of dread, before which I was absolutely helpless. I cannot tell you how hopelessly or fearfully I suffered, or what depths of despondency and despair and blackness I was cast into. I cannot understand how a creature could so manufacture torments for itself. But this is not all, just for once have mercy--and yet even now I am laughing at myself!

"The winter I was sixteen I was much disappointed that I could not go to college, and almost the whole winter, when I was not diverted, I would brood over this habit. As I grew older, it would come to me in spasms, and it seemed to my dawning sense so monstrously child- like, so insane, that I was aghast that it had power to affect me. I can find no words to tell you of the unspeakable horror with which I saw, in my older days, that a thought could so torment me; the mere fact of its being able to torment I could never forget. I know it was silly, unreasonable; and yet every time it came to me I would be plunged into a hopelessness and melancholy, than which I can honestly conceive nothing more fearful upon earth.

"Well, I continued to pursue myself with this morbidity (I would almost, rather kill myself than write this). As I got older my terror was less, but my melancholy greater, until I would be only half conscious of what I was allowing myself to do. I seemed to have engendered within myself a hob-goblin. Once--it was only last winter--I saw a nasty word written on a fence, and it sent a shudder through me, for I knew it would follow me and make me think of other things like it. I felt, since thoughts have such power to terrorize me, how can I ever get away from them?

"Oh, how I have struggled--tried to say it was not true--that I was just as sane as other people! And this made my thirst for beauty all the more maddening, and my melancholy all the more complete! So I have lived, at intervals, and words cannot describe the hell that I have endured, the more horrible because it seemed to me so unreasonable, so insane. It occurred to me more or less this summer, though in a milder form; but it often frightened me more than ever, as I felt how beautiful you were, and what you would think of me, if you knew I was capable of being the prey of such thoughts. So they were always more dreadful to me.

"Can you possibly understand how the thought of a word could make me shudder? The mere idea of my being capable of thinking of anything that was not beautiful! When I longed to be only the embodiment of beauty--and sometimes I *am* beautiful! I look into the glass, and I seem to have something in my face that is a promise of a glory to come--a light, a something,--I love to imagine it. And then, that a thought should knock me prone, and make me cringe--from the mere fact of its lowness and meanness!

"For the last two or three days I have again victimized myself; and when I was not studying I was asking myself in anguish what was the matter with me, and if there was no hope for me on earth. I dodged around and tried to laugh it off, then I went to the piano and lost myself in the dissatisfaction of my playing; but when I stopped, I was conscious of a great depression, as though I were chained in a dungeon. I jumped up, and said I could stand it no longer. I will tell Thyrsis, I said; but no, I will die first! I added. He could not tolerate me afterwards, he would think me only fit for the insane-asylum. Oh, why should I be so cursed? And then, somehow, I imagined that I told you, and that you laughed at me, that you pitied me--and that you held out your hand, and said, 'Come, you *shall* find beauty--poor, deluded, wretched, little creature!' I really imagined that this had happened, and I was relieved as with a draught of fresh air.

"Oh, God in Heaven, to think that I could ever have been so degraded! My head hurts, and I absolutely am dazed, to think that I have been able to write you of something for which (though it has not been my making) I am so ashamed and humiliated I can hardly hold my head up. I think in my short life I have atoned for the sins of many souls."

Section 3. Such was the old-time letter. "And now," wrote Corydon, "I don't want you to think that if I did not send you this, it was because I was afraid to do it, or unwilling to trust to your love. It was simply because I felt that I could conquer these things--that it would be weak and contemptible of me not to do so. Nor is the reason I write you now that I have not been able to conquer them, that I am still at the mercy of such habits. I am a grown woman, and I am not afraid of words; I tell myself this a hundred times; and it is true--and yet there is a way in which it is not true. The thing is so intricate--I never get to the end of it; I rid myself of the fear of a hateful idea, but there remains the fact that I should have been afraid; there is the fear of fear. And then comes a flood of shame--that I should have it in me to be afraid of fear!

"Thyrsis, as I write to you now I see clearly how perfectly preposterous and unreal all this is; and again there comes to me the impulse to tear up this letter, and banish the troop of hob-goblins from my mind. But no, this time I am determined to make a clean breast of the thing--for I see that secrecy and solitude are what it feeds on. If I were happy and busy with you such ideas would have no power over me. But think how it is, with my loneliness and despair! I don't want to say anything to make your task harder--but oh, Thyrsis, it is frightful to have nothing to do but wait, and wait, and wait! The baby wakes me up in the night and I lie for hours--it is at such times that these phantoms take hold of me. Do you realize that I literally never know what it is to have more than three or four consecutive hours of sleep?

"No, I am not insane, I tell myself; I am not insane! It is the circumstances of my life that cause this melancholia and misery. It has been my life, from the very beginning--for what a hopeful and joyous creature I would have been, had I only had a chance as a girl! I know that; and you must tell it to me, and help me to believe it."

Thyrsis read this with less surprise than Corydon had imagined; for she had been wont to drop hints about her trouble from time to time. He was shocked, however, to find what a hold it had taken upon her; the thing sent a chill of fear to his heart. Could it be after all that she had some taint? But he saw at once that he must not let her see any such feeling; the least hint of it would have driven her to distraction. On the contrary, he must minimize the trouble, must help her to laugh it away, as she asked.

He went to meet her in the park, and found her in an agony of distress; she had mailed the letter, and then she had wished to recall it, and had been struggling ever since with the idea that he would be disgusted with her. Now, when she found that such was not the case, that he still loved her and trusted her, she was transported with gratitude.

"But dearest," he said, "how absurd it is to be ashamed of an idea! If ugly things exist, don't we have to hear of them and know of them? And so why frighten ourselves because they are in our minds?"

"But Thyrsis," cried she, "they are so hateful!"

"Yes," he said. "But then the more you hate them, the more they haunt you!"

"That's just it!" she exclaimed.

"But what harm can they do? Can they have any effect upon your character? You must say to yourself that all this is a consequence of the structure of your brain-cells. What could be more futile than trying to forget? As if the very essence of the trying was not remembering!"

So Thyrsis went on to argue with her. He made her promise him that in future she would tell him of all her obsessions, permitting no fear or shame to deter her; and so thereafter he would have to listen periodically to long accounts of her psychological agonies, and help her to hunt out the "hob-goblins" from the tangled thickets of her mind. They were forever settling the matter, positively and finally--but alas, only to have something unsettle it again. So Thyrsis had to add to his other accomplishments the equipment of a psycho-pathologist; he brushed up his French, and read learned treatises upon the researches in the *Salpetriere*, and the theories of the "Nancy School".

Section 4. Another month passed by, and still there was no rift in the clouds. Once more Corydon was forbidden to see him, and so her pain grew day by day. At last there came another letter, voicing utter despertion. Something must be done, she declared, she was slowly going out of her mind. Thyrsis could have no idea of the shamefulness of her position, the humiliations she had to face. "I tell you the thing is putting a brand upon my soul," she wrote. "It is something I shall never get over all my life. It is withering me up--it is destroying my self-respect, my very decency; it is depriving me of my power to act, or even to think. People come in, relatives or friends--even strangers to me--and peer at me and pry into my affairs; I hear them whispering in the parlor--'Hasn't he got a position yet?' or 'How can she have anything to do with him?' The servants gossip about me--the woman I have for a nurse despises me and insults me, and I have not the courage to rebuke her. To-day I went almost wild with fury--I rushed into the bathroom and locked the door and flung myself upon the floor. I found myself gnawing at the rug in my rage--I mean that literally. That is what life has left for me!

"I tell you you must take me away, we must get out of this fiendish city. Let us go into the wilderness as you said, and live as we can--I would rather starve to death than face these things. Let us get into the country, Thyrsis. You can work as a farm-hand, and earn a few dollars a week--surely that could not be a greater strain upon us than the way things are now."

When Thyrsis received this, he racked his brains once more; and then he sat down and wrote a letter to Barry Creston. He told how he had worked over the play, and how it had gone to ruin; he told of his present plight. He knew, he said, that Mr. Creston had been interested in the play, and that he was a man understood the needs of the artist-life. Would he lend two hundred dollars, which would suffice until Thyrsis could get another work completed?

He waited a week for a reply to this; and when it arrived he opened it with trembling fingers. He half expected a check to fall fluttering to the floor; but alas, there was not a single flutter. "I have read your letter," wrote the young prince, "and I have considered the matter carefully. I would do what you ask, were it not for my conviction that it would not be a good thing for you. It seems to me the testimony of all experience, that artists do their great work under the spur of necessity. I do not believe that real art can ever be subsidized. It is for men that you are writing; and you must find out how to make men hear you. You may not thank me for this now, but some day you will, I believe."

After duly pondering which communication, Thyrsis racked his wits, and bethought him of yet another person to try. He sat himself down and addressed Mr. Robertson Jones. He explained that he was in this cruel plight, owing to his having devoted so many months to "The Genius." Even the actors had received something for the performances of the play they had given; but the author had received nothing at all. He asked Mr. Jones for a personal loan to help him in a great emergency; and he promised to repay it at the earliest possible moment. To which Mr. Jones made this reply--"Inasmuch as the failure of the play was due solely to your own obstinacy, it seems to me that your present experiences are affording exactly the discipline you need."

Section 5. However, there are many ups and downs in the trade of free-lance writer. The very day after he had received this letter, there came, in quick succession two bursts of sunlight through the clouds of Thyrsis' despair. The first was a letter, written in a quaint script, from a man who explained that he was interested in a "Free People's Theatre" in one of the cities of Germany. "You will please to accept my congratulations," he wrote; "I had never known such a play as yours in America to be written. I should greatly be pleased to translate the play, so that it might be known in Germany. Our compensation would have to be little, as you will understand; but of appreciation I think you may receive much in the Fatherland."

To which Thyrsis sent a cordial response, saying that he would be glad of any remuneration, and enclosing a copy of the manuscript of "The Genius". And then-- only two days later--came the other event, a still more notable one; a letter from the publisher who had been number thirty-seven on the list of "The Hearer of Truth". Thyrsis had got so discouraged about this work that he now sent it about as a matter of routine, and without thinking of it at all. Great, therefore, was his amazement when he opened the letter and read that this publisher was disposed to undertake it, and would be glad to see him and talk over terms.

Thyrsis went, speculating on the way as to what strange manner of being this publisher might be. The solution of the mystery he found was that the publisher was new at the business, and had entrusted his "literary department" to a very young man who had enthusiasms. The young man held his position for only a month or two; but in that month or two Thyrsis got in his "innings".

The publisher wished to bring the book out that spring. He offered a ten per cent royalty, and the trembling author summoned the courage to ask for one hundred dollars advance; when he got it, he was divided between his delight, and a sneaking regret that he had not tried for a hundred and fifty!

The very next day came the contracts and the money; Thyrsis marvelled at the fact that there were people who could sign checks for a hundred dollars, and apparently not mind it in the least. With the money he was able to pay all his debts, and also a bill which Corydon had received from a "specialist" who had been treating her. This was a new habit that Corydon was developing, as a result of headaches and backaches and other obscure miseries. These amiable "specialists" permitted one to run up a bill with them; and so, whenever Thyrsis made a new "strike", there were always debts to eat up the greater part of it.

They had now another hope to lure them; new proofs to read, and in due time, new reviews. But it would be fall before they could expect more money from the book, and meantime there was still the problem of the summer. So, as usual, Thyrsis was plotting and planning, groping about him and trying one desperate scheme after another; his head was like a busy workshop, from which came every hour new plans, new expedients, new experiments. And meanwhile, of course, deep down in his soul there was forming the new work, that some day would emerge and take possession of him, driving everything else from his consciousness.

People would repeat to him, over and over, their dreary formula--"Get a position! Get a position!" And patiently, unwearyingly, Thyrsis would set himself to explain to them what it was like to be inspired. It was not perversity upon his part, it was not conceit; it was no more these than it was laziness. It was something that was in him--something that he had not put there himself, something that he could not take out of himself; a thing that took possession of him, without any intention upon his part, without any permission; a thing that required him to do certain acts, and that tore him to pieces if he did not do them. And how should he be blamed because he could not do as other men--because he could not take care of himself, nor even of his wife and child? Because he could not have any rights, because he could not possess the luxuries of manhood and self-respect? Because, in short, he was cast out into the gutter for every dog to snarl at and for every loafer to spurn? Could it be that in this whole civilization, with its wealth and power, its culture and learning, its sciences and arts and religions--there was not to be found one single man or woman who could recognize such a state of affairs, and realize what it meant?

Section 6. About this time Thyrsis thought of another plan. Perhaps he might get some one to publish the play in book form--that would bring him a little money, and possibly also it might help him to interest some other manager or actor. So he took the manuscript to his friend Mr. Ardsley, who told him it would not sell, and then gave him another lecture upon his folly in not having written the "practical" novel; and then he took it to the publisher for whom Prof. Osborne acted as reader. So he had another conference with that representative of authority.

"I'll get him some day," Thyrsis had said to himself, after their last interview; and he found that he had almost "got" him now. There was no chance of the play's selling, said the professor, and therefore no recommending it for publication; but it was indeed a remarkable piece of work--one might possibly say that it was a **great** piece of work.

To which the author responded, "Why can't one say that surely?"

"I'm not quite sure," said the other, "whether your violinist is a genius, or only thinks he is."

Thyrsis pondered this. "That's rather an important question," he said.

"Yes," admitted the other.

"There ought to be some way of deciding such a question definitely."

"Yes, there ought to be."

"But there isn't?"

"No--I'm afraid there isn't. We know too little about genius as yet."

"But, professor," said Thyrsis, "you are a critic--you write books of criticism. And that's the one question a critic has to answer."

"Yes, I know," said Prof. Osborne.

"And yet, when you face the issue, you give up."

"It has generally taken a long time to decide such a matter," was the professor's reply.

"Yes, it has," said the other; "and meantime the man is starved out."

There was a pause. "You have never had any such experience yourself?" asked Thyrsis. "Of inspiration, I mean."

"No," was the answer. "I couldn't pretend to."

"So your judgments are never from first-hand knowledge?"

The professor hesitated. "I am dealing with you frankly---" he began.

"I know," said Thyrsis, "and I appreciate that. You understand that it's an important point for me to get clear. I've felt that all along about you--I've felt it about so many others who set themselves against me. And yet I have to bear the burden of their condemnation--"

"I never condemned you," interposed the other.

"Ah, but you did!" cried Thyrsis. "You told me that I knew less about writing than anyone in your class! And you spoke as one who had authority."

"But you had given no indications in the class-room--"

"I know! I know! I tried to get you to see the reason. I wanted to create literature; and you set me down with a lot of formulas--you told me to write about 'The Duty of the College Man to Support Athletics!'"

"It's difficult to see," began Prof. Osborne, "how we could teach college boys to create literature--"

"At least," said the other, "you need not follow a method which would make it impossible for one of them to create literature if he had it in him."

"Does it seem to you as bad as that?" asked the professor, a little disturbed.

"It truly does," said Thyrsis.

"But what would you say we could do?"

To which the boy replied, "You might try to get your pupils to feel one deep emotion about life, or to think one worth-while thought; then they might stand a chance of knowing how it feels to write."

Section 7. Thyrsis was still reading in the papers and magazines of philanthropists and public-spirited citizens; and he was still sitting down to write them and explain his plight. He would beg them to believe that he wanted nothing but a bare living; and he would send copies of his books or articles or manuscripts, and ask these people to read them. And about this time an unusual thing happened--one of these philanthropists answered his letter. He wrote that he did not agree with Thyrsis' ideas, by any means, but appreciated the power of his writing, and was certain that he had a career before him. Whereupon Thyrsis made haste to follow up his advantage, and wrote another letter--one of the most intense and impassioned that he ever composed in his life.

He told about the new book he was dreaming. For years he had read his country's history, and lived in it and thrilled with it. Especially had he read the Civil War; and now he was planning a book that should hold the War, and all the meanings of the War, as a wine-cup holds the rich flavors and aromas of the grape. A titan struggle it had been, the birth-agony of a nation; and it was a thing to be contemplated with amazement, that it should have produced so little in the way of art. Half a dozen poems there were; but of novels not one above the grade of juvenile fiction.

What Thyrsis was planning was a new form; a series of swift visions, of glimpses into the very heart of the nation's agony. He described some of the scenes that were haunting him and driving him. The winter's night in the ditches in front of

Marye's Heights, when the dead and dying lay piled in windrows, and the soul of a people sobbed in despair! The night on the field of Gettysburg, when the young soldier lay wounded, but rapt in his vision, seeing the hosts of the victorious future defiling upon that hallowed ground! The ghastly scenes in Andersonville, and the escape, and the long journey filled with perils; and the siege of Petersburg, and the surrender; and last of all the ecstasy of the dying man in the capital, when the grim, war-worn legions were tramping for two days through the city. Such, wrote Thyrsis, was the book that he wished to compose, and that was being stifled in him for the lack of two or three hundred dollars.

Upon the receipt of this letter the philanthropist wrote again, suggesting that the poet come to see him and talk things over. He sent the price of a railroad ticket to Boston; and so Thyrsis made the acquaintance of a new world--one might almost say of a whole new system of worlds.

For here was the Athens of America, the hub of the universe. In Boston they worshipped culture, they lived in literature and art and the transcendental excellences; and by the way of showing that there was no snobbery in them, they opened the gates of their most august mansions to this soul-sick poet, and invited him to tea.

Thyrsis got a strange impression among these people, who were living upon their knees before the shrine of their own literary history. One was treading here upon holy ground; in these very houses had dwelt immortal writers--their earthly forms had rested in these chairs, and their auras yet haunted the dim religious light of these drawing-rooms. There were old people who had known them in the flesh, and could tell anecdotes about them--to which one listened in reverent awe; at every gathering one met people who were writing biographies and memoirs of them, or editing their letters and journals, or writing essays and appreciations, criticisms and commentaries and catalogs and bibliographies. And to be worthy of the visitations of such hallowed influences, one must guard one's mind as a temple, a place of silences and serenities, to which no vulgar things could penetrate; one excluded all the uproar of these days of undisciplined egotism--above all things else one preserved an attitude of aloofness from that which presumed to call itself "literature" in such degenerate times.

To have become acquainted with these high standards was perhaps worth the rent of a room and the cost of some food and clean collars. So Thyrsis reflected when, after his week of waiting, he had his interview with the benevolent philanthropist, who explained to him, at great length, how charity had the effect of weakening the springs of character, and destroying those qualities of self-reliance and independence which were the most precious things in a man.

Section 8. It was a curious coincidence, one that seemed almost symbolic--that Thyrsis should have gone from the Brahmins of Boston to the Socialists of the East Side!

In one of the publishing-houses he visited, Thyrsis had met a young man who gave him a Socialist magazine to read; as the magazine was published in the next building, Thyrsis went in and met the editor. About this time they were crowning a new king in England, and Thyrsis, who had no use for kings, wrote a sarcastic poem which the Socialist editor published free of charge. And so the boy discovered a new way in which he could relieve his feelings.

"I see what you want," he admitted, in his arguments with this editor; "and it's the same thing as I want--every man with any sense must see that, in the ultimate outcome, all this capital will be owned by the public and not by private individuals. But what I object to is the way you go at it. The industrial process is a necessary thing; it is drilling and disciplining the workers. They are not yet fitted for the responsibility of managing the world."

"But," asked the editor, "what's to be the sign when they *are* fitted?"

"When they have been educated," Thyrsis answered.

To which the editor responded, "Who is to educate them, if we don't?"

That was an interesting point; and Thyrsis found little by little that a new light was dawning upon him. He had somehow conceived of industrial evolution as something vast and intangible and mechanical, something that went on independent of men, and that could not be hurried or delayed. What this editor pointed out was that the process was a definite one, that it went on in the minds of men, and involved human effort--of which the publishing of Socialist literature was a most essential part.

"You ought to hear Darrell," said the man; and a few days later he wrote Thyrsis a note, asking him to go to a hall over on the East Side that evening.

Thyrsis went, and found a working-men's meeting-room, ill-lighted and ill-ventilated, with perhaps two hundred people in it. The chairman introduced the speaker of the evening; and so Thyrsis got his first glimpse of Henry Darrell.

He was something over forty years of age, slight of build; his face was pale to the point of ghostliness, and this impression was heightened by a jet black mustache and beard. One's first thought was that this man was no stranger to suffering.

He was not a good speaker, in the conventional sense, he fumbled for words, and repeated himself--and yet from his first sentence Thyrsis found himself listening spellbound. The voice went through him like the toll of a bell; never in all his life had he heard a speaker who put such a burden of anguish into his words--who gave such a sense of gigantic issues, of age-long destinies hanging in the balance, of world-embracing hopes and powers struggling to be born. Here was a prophet who carried in his soul the future of the race; who in the sudden flashes of his vision, in the swift rushes of his passionate pleadings, evoked from the deeps of the consciousness forces that one contemplated with terror--confronted one with martyrdoms and agonies and despairs.

"Revolution" was his title; he pictured modern civilization as it presented itself to the proletarian man--a gigantic Moloch, to which human lives were fed, a monster from whose dominion there was no deliverance, even in the uttermost parts of the earth. He pictured accident, disease and death, unemployment and starvation, child-labor, prostitution, war; he was the voice of the dispossessed of the earth, the man beneath the machine, ground up body, mind and soul in this "world-wide mill of economic might". And he showed how this man dragged down with him all society; how the chain that bound the slave was fastened also to the master--so that from the poverty and oppression and degradation of this "downmost man" came all the ulcers that festered in the social body. He saw the great economic machine grinding on day and night, the mighty forces rushing to their culmination. He saw the toiling millions pressed deeper and deeper into the mire; he saw their blind, convulsive struggles for deliverance; he saw over them the gigantic slave-driver with his thousand-lashed whip--the capitalist state, class-owned class-administered--backed by the capitalist church and the capitalist press and capitalist "public sentiment". So the hopes of the people went down in blood and reaction sat enthroned. The nations, ridden by despotisms, and whirled into senseless wars, ran the old course of militarism, imperialism, barbarism; and so civilization slid back yet again into the melting-pot!

Thyrsis had never heard such a speech as this in his life. When it was over, he went up to the platform where Darrell sat, looking more exhausted and pain-driven than ever; and in a few hesitating words he told of his interest, and asked for the speaker's address, that he might write to him. And that night he posted a letter, introducing himself as a young writer, who felt impelled to learn more about Darrell's ideas.

In reply came a note from the other, asking him to dine with him; and Thyrsis answered accepting.

Then, as chance would have it, he mentioned the circumstance to his mother. "Darrell!" she cried. "You don't mean Henry Darrell!"

"Yes," said Thyrsis. "Why?"

"And you would meet that man?"

"Why not?" he asked, perplexed.

"Haven't you read anything about him in the papers? That monster!"

"What do you mean?"

"A man who deserted his wife and children, and left them to starve, and ran away with some rich woman!"

Thyrsis recollected vaguely some sensational headlines, about the clergyman and college professor who had done the shocking things his mother spoke of, and was now a social outcast, and a preacher of anarchy and revolution. He recalled also that there had been a woman, beautiful and richly-dressed, with Darrell at the meeting.

The boy was not disturbed by all this, for he had long ago made up his mind that every man had to work out his own sex-problems; in fact, his first impulse was to admire a man who had had the courage to face the world upon such an issue. But he was sorry he had mentioned it to his mother, for she wept bitterly when she found that he meant to accept the invitation. That was the culmination of her life's defeat--that her son, who had been designed for a bishop, should be going to sit at table with Henry Darrell and his paramour!

Section 9. Thyrsis went to the apartment-hotel where Darrell lived, and was introduced to the beautiful lady as Mrs. Darrell, and they went down to the dining-room--where he noticed that everyone turned to stare at them as they entered.

It made him feel that he must be doing something quite desperate; and yet it was not easy to imagine any wickedness of the man opposite to him--his voice was so kind, and his smile so gentle, and his whole aspect so appealing. He was dressed in black, and wore a soft black bow at his throat, which made still more conspicuous the pallor of his face; Thyrsis had never met a man he took to more quickly--there was something about him that was like a little child, calling for affection and sympathy.

Yet, also, there was the mind of a thinker. He was a man of culture, in the most vital sense of the word; he had swept the heavens of thought with a powerful telescope--had travelled, and knew many languages, and their literatures and arts. He had tested them all by a strong acid of his own; so that to talk with him was to discover the feet of clay of one's idols.

He spoke of Dante and Angelo, who were two of his heroes; he told of great experiences among the latter's titan frescos. He spoke of Mazzini, whose greatness as a writer the world had yet to appreciate; he spoke also of Wagner, whose music he valued less than his critical and polemical work. He told of modern artists both in Germany and Italy--revolutionary forces of whom Thyrsis had never heard at all. The day must come, said Darrell, when Americans would discover the great movements of contemporary thought, and realize their own provincialness. America thought of itself as "the land of the free", and that made it hard to teach. It was obvious enough that there had never been any real freedom in America--only government by propertied classes. The Revolution had been a rebellion of country gentlemen and city merchants; as one might know from the "constitution" they had adopted--one of the greatest barriers to human progress ever devised. And so with the Civil War, which to Darrell was one of the deeds of the newly-risen monster of Capitalism.

They went upstairs again, and Thyrsis found another man seated in the drawing-room. He was introduced by the name of Paret, and Thyrsis recognized him as the editor of "The Beacon", a magazine of which he had chanced upon a copy some time before. It was the first Socialist publication he had ever seen, and it had repelled him because its editor had printed his own picture in a conspicuous place, and also because in his leading editorial he had dealt flippantly with an eminent reformer and philanthropist for whom Thyrsis had a profound respect.

But here was the editor himself--not merely his photograph: a little man, clad in evening dress, very neat and dapper. He had a black beard, trimmed to a point, and also a sarcastic smile, and he impressed Thyrsis as a drawing-room edition of Mephistopheles. He lounged at ease in a big chair, not troubling to talk; save that every now and then he would punctuate the discussion with some droll reflection that stuck in one's mind like a burr.

Some one spoke of certain evangelists who were conducting a temperance campaign among the workers in the steel-mills. Said Paret: "If I had to live in hell, I'm sure I'd rather be drunk than sober!" And a little later Thyrsis spoke of a novel he had been reading, which set out to solve the problem of "capital and labor". Its solution seemed to be for the handsome young leader of the union to marry the daughter of the capitalist; and Paret remarked, with his dry smile, "No doubt if the capitalists and their daughters are willing, the union-leaders will come to the scratch." Again, Darrell was telling about the ten years' struggle he had waged to waken the Church to the great issue of the time; and how at last he had given up in despair. Paret remarked, "For my part, I never try to talk economics with preachers. When you talk to a business-man, he understands a business proposition, and you can get somewhere; but when you talk with a preacher, and you think he's been understanding you, you find that all the time he's been thinking what Moses would have said about it."

There came other guests: a German, hard-fisted, bullet-headed--editor of an East Side labor-paper. Some one spoke of working-men losing their votes through being unemployed and cast adrift; and Thyrsis remembered this man's grim comment, "They lose their votes, but they don't lose their voices!" There came a young man, fair as an Antinous, who with his verbal battering-ram shook the institutions of society so as to frighten even the author of "The Higher Cannibalism". There came also a poetess, whose work he had seen in the magazines, and with her a Russian youth who had come to study the thought of America, and was now going home, because America had no thought. Thyrsis had a good deal of patriotism left in him, and might have been angered by this stripling's contempt; but the stripling spoke with such quiet assurance, and his contempt was so boundless as to frighten one. "These people," he said--"they simply do not know what the intellectual life means!"

When Thyrsis went home that evening, he carried with him new ideas to ponder; also some of Darrell's pamphlets and speeches--the product of his ten years' struggle to make the teachings of Christ of some authority in the Christian Church. Thyrsis sat up late, and read one of these pamphlets, an indictment of Capitalism from the point of view of the artist and spiritual creator. It was a magnificent piece of writing; it came to Thyrsis like an echo out of his own life. So, before he slept that night he had written a letter to Darrell, telling of his struggles and his defeats. "I do not ask you to help *me*" he wrote. "I ask you to read my work, and decide if that be worth saving. For ashamed as I am to say it, I am at the end of my resources, and if some help does not come, I do not know what will become of me."

Thyrsis had now tried all varieties of the great and successful of the earth--the publishers and editors and authors, the college professors and clergymen, the statesmen and capitalists and philanthropists. And now, for the first time, he tried the Socialists. He trembled when he opened Darrell's reply. Could it be that this man would be like all the rest?

But no, he was different! "Dear Brother:" he wrote. "I understand what you have told me, and I appreciate your position. Send me your manuscripts at once; I leave to-morrow for a lecture-trip, and on my way I will read everything, and let you hear from me on my return. In the meantime, I should add that I am helping two Socialist publications, and a good many individuals too, and that my resources have been absurdly exaggerated in the public prints. I say this, that you may not overestimate what I might possibly be able to do."

Section 10. So Thyrsis sent a manuscript of his play, and a copy of his first novel, and a set of proofs of "The Hearer of Truth"; and then for a couple of weeks he waited in suspense and dread. He could not see how a man like Henry Darrell could fail to appreciate his work; but on the other hand, after so many disappointments and rebuffs, how could he bring himself to believe that any one would really give him aid?

At last came a second letter; a letter full of warm-hearted sympathy--pointing out the faults of immaturity in his work, but also recognizing its real merits. It closed with this all-important sentence: "I will do what I can to help you, so come and let us talk it over."

Thyrsis went; and as they sat in his study, Darrell put his arm about him, and told him a little of his own career. He had begun life as a street-waif, a newsboy and bootblack; and once when he was ill, he had gone to a drug-store for help, and the druggist had given him a poison by mistake, so that all his life thereafter he had more sick days than well. He told how, at an early age, he had gone to a country college to seek an education as a divinity-student; he had arrived, weary and foot-sore, and with his last cent had bought a post-card to let his mother know that he was safe He told how, as a clergyman and college professor the gospel of the time had come to him; how he had preached and labored, amid persecution and obloquy, until he had come to realize that the Church was a dead sepulchre; and how at last he had thrown everything to the winds, and given himself to the working-class political movement.

Then Thyrsis, scrupulous as ever, said, "I know nothing about Socialism. I mean to study it; but I might not come to believe in it--how can I tell? I would not want you to help me under any misapprehension."

At which the other smiled gently. "I am working for the truth," he said.

They talked about Thyrsis and his needs. Presumably, he said, he would have money from his new book in the fall, but meantime he wanted to take his family into the country. He could live on thirty dollars a month; it would be a matter of some two hundred and fifty dollars. Darrell said he would give him this; and Thyrsis sat there, powerless to thank him, his voice trembling, and a mist of tears in his eyes.

He went on to tell his friend of the work that he meant to do. Darrell had said that to him the Civil War was a crime; but Thyrsis did not know what he meant by that. "I believe in my country!" he said. "It has tried for high things--and it will come to them! I know that it can be thrilled and roused, and made to see the shame into which it is fallen."

Darrell pressed his arm, and answered, with a smile, "I won't argue with you about the War; you go ahead and write your book!"

So Thyrsis went home to Corydon, as one who brings a reprieve to a prisoner under sentence of death. Such a deliverance as it was to them! And such transports of relief and gratitude as they experienced! He sang the praises of Darrell, and of the new friends he had made at Darrell's; also he brought an invitation for Corydon to come with him to an evening reception the next week. They were anxious to meet her, he said; and Corydon was anxious to go.

But, alas, this did not work out according to expectations. Thyrsis discovered now what his wife had meant when she wrote that suffering and humiliation were breaking down her character. She could not bear to meet intellectual people, to take part in the competition of their life. For the most part these were men and women of intense personalities, absorbed in their own ideas, keenly critical, and not very merciful to any sort of weakness. And Corydon was morbidly aware of her own lack of accomplishments, and acutely sensitive as to what others thought about her. A strange figure she must have made in any one's drawing-room--with the old dress she had fixed up, and the lace-collar she had borrowed for the occasion, and the sad face with the large dark eyes. The talk of the company ran to politics; and Corydon had nothing to say about politics. She could only sit in a corner while Thyrsis talked, and suffer agonies of humiliation.

To make matters worse, there came a literary lion that evening; one of the few modern writers whose books Corydon knew and loved. But when they were introduced, he scarcely looked at her; he went on talking to an East Side poetess whose opinions were fluent and ready. So Corydon found herself shunted into a corner with an unknown old lady. It was one of Corydon's peculiarities that she abhorred old ladies; and this one questioned her about the feeding of infants and told her that she was ill-equipped for the responsibilities of motherhood!

On her way home she poured out her bitterness to Thyrsis. "I can see exactly how it is," she said. "They all think you've married a pretty face!"

"You haven't given them much chance to think otherwise," he pleaded.

"They don't want any chance," she exclaimed. "They've got it all settled! You are the rising light, which is to astonish the world--and I'm your youthful blunder. I stay at home and take care of the baby, and they all feel sorry for you."

"Do you want them to feel sorry for *you?*" he asked.

To which Corydon answered, "I don't want them to know about me at all. I want to get away, and stay by myself, and get back my self-respect." And so it was decided that in a couple of weeks more--the first of April--they would shake the dust of the city from their feet. They sent for their tent and other goods, and began inquiring about a place to camp.

Section 11. A few days more passed; and then, one Sunday morning, Thyrsis' mother came to him in tears, with a copy of a newspaper "magazine-supplement" in her hand.

"Look at this!" she cried; and Thyrsis stared.

There was a full-page article, with many illustrations, and a headline two inches deep--"Henry Darrell to found Free-Love Colony! Ex-college professor and clergyman buys farm to teach his doctrines." There was a picture of Darrell, standing upon a ladder and nailing up an announcement of his defiance to the institution of marriage; and there were pictures of his wife and child, and of the farm he had bought, and a long account of the colony which he was organizing, and in which he meant to preach and practice his ideas of "free love".

Thyrsis was half dazed. "I don't believe it!" he cried; whereat his mother wrung her hands.

"Not believe it!" she exclaimed. "Why, the paper even gives the price he paid for the place!"

So Thyrsis took the article and went to see Henry Darrell again; and there followed one of the most painful experiences of his life.

He found his friend like a man blasted by a stroke of lightning. His very physical appearance was altered; his voice shook and his eyes were wild, and he paced the room, his whole aspect one cry of agony.

He pointed Thyrsis to a lot of clippings that lay upon the table--the first editorial comments upon this new pronouncement. There was one from an evening paper, which had close upon a million circulation, and had devoted its whole editorial page to a scathing denunciation, in which it was declared that "Prof. Darrell's morality is that of the higher apes."

"Think of it!" the man cried. "And the thing will go from one end of the country to the other!"

"But"--gasped Thyrsis, bewildered--"then it is not true?"

"True?" cried Darrell. "True? How can you ask me?"

"But--the colony! What is it to be?"

"There is not going to be any colony. I never dreamed of such a thing!"

'And haven't you bought any farm?'

"My wife bought a farm, over a year ago--because we wanted to live in the country!"

"But then," gasped Thyrsis--"how dare they?"

"They dare anything with me!" cried the other. "***Anything!***"

"And have you no redress?"

"Redress? What redress?"

He went on to tell Thyrsis what had happened. He and Mrs. Darrell had gone down to the farm to see about getting it ready, and a woman had come, representing that she wished to write a magazine article about "the country-homes of literary Americans". Upon this pretext she had secured a photograph of the place, and of Darrell, and of his wife and child. She had even attempted to secure a photograph of his wife's aged mother, who lived with her, and who was involved in the affair because the money belonged to her. Then the woman had gone away--and a couple of weeks later had come this!

"And I thought they were through with us!" Darrell whispered, with a shudder. "I thought it was all over!"

He sat in a chair, with his face hid in his arms. Thyrsis put his hand upon his shoulder, and the man caught it. "Listen," he exclaimed. "You can see this thing from the outside, you know the literary world. Do you think that I can ever rise above this? Is there any use in trying?"

"How do you mean?" Thyrsis asked, perplexed.

"I mean--is it worth while for me to go on writing? Can I ever have any influence?"

Thyrsis was shocked at the question--as he had been at the way Darrell took the whole thing. He knew that his friend had money enough to live comfortably; and why should any sort of criticism matter to a man who was economically free?

"Brother," he said, "you have forgotten your Dante."

"How do you mean?" asked the other.

"***Segui il tuo corso e lascia dir le gente!***" quoted Thyrsis; and then he added, "You don't seem to realize that these are newspapers, and nobody really credits them."

"Ah, but they do!" cried Darrell. "You don't know what I have been through with! My oldest friends have cut me! Clergymen have refused to sit at table with me! The organization that I gave ten years of my life to founding has gone all to pieces. I have been utterly ruined--I have been wiped out, destroyed!"

"But, my dear man," Thyrsis argued, "you are setting out to teach a new doctrine, one that is abhorrent to people. And how can you expect to avoid being attacked? It seems to me that either you ought not to have done it, or else been prepared for some of this uproar."

"But because a man becomes a Socialist, are they to libel him in these foul ways?"

"I don't mean that. It's not only that you are a Socialist, but that you have defied their marriage-laws."

"But I haven't!" exclaimed Darrel.

"What do you mean?" asked Thyrsis, perplexed.

"I have defied no law--nor even any convention. I have done everything that the world requires."

Thyrsis stared at him, amazed. "Why, surely," he gasped, "you and--and Mrs. Darrell--you are not **married?**"

"Married!" exclaimed the other. "We were married here in New York, by a regularly-ordained clergyman!"

Thyrsis could not find words to express his dismay. "I--I had no idea of that!" he gasped. I thought--"

"You see the lies!" cried the other. "Even **you** had swallowed them!"

It took Thyrsis some time to adjust himself to this new point of view. He had thought of his friend as a man who had boldly defied the convention of marriage; and instead of that he was apparently a man cowering under the lash of the world's undeserved rage. But if so--what an amazing and incredible thing was the mesh of slander and falsehood in which he had been entangled!

Section 12. Little by little Thyrsis drew from Darrell the story of his marital experience. Before he had been of age, as a poor student, he had boarded with a woman many years his senior, who had set out to lure him into marrying her. "I don't believe that she ever loved me one hour," he said. "She had made up her mind that I was a man of brilliant parts, and that I would have worldly success. To me the thing was like an evil dream--I couldn't realize it. And I can't tell you about it now--it was too horrible. She was older than I, and so different--she was more like a man. And for twenty years she held me; I had to stay--I was utterly at her mercy!"

The man's voice fell to a whisper, and he pressed Thyrsis' hand convulsively;

there were tears upon his cheeks. "I could not tell it all to anyone," he said. "It makes me cry like a child to think of it. I'm only getting over it little by little--realizing how I was tortured. This woman had no interest in me, intellectual or spiritual; she brought up my children to despise me. I would stay upstairs in my study, writing sermons--that was all my life! For twenty years I waded through my own blood!"

Darrell paused to get control of himself, and then went on.

"One of my parishioners was my present wife's mother. She was one of the old-time abolitionists, and she was wealthy; and now, in her old age, she saw the new light, and became a Socialist. This, of course, was like gall to her family; they were powers in the state--the railroad people, who control the legislature and run the government. And so their newspapers denounced me, and denounced the university where I taught.

"Then came her daughter--a young girl out of college. I was at their home often, and we became friends. She saw how unhappy I was, and she tried to open my wife's eyes, and to win her over to me. But, of course, she failed in that; and then, little by little we found that we loved each other. You know me--you know that I am not a base man, nor a careless man; and you will believe me when I tell you that there was nothing between us that the world could have called wrong. We knew that we loved, and we knew that there was no hope. And that went on for eight years; for eight years I renounced--and strove with every power of my heart and soul to make something out of that renunciation, to transmute it into spiritual power. And I failed--I could not do it; and in the end I knew the reason. It was not beauty and nobility--it was madness and horror; it was not life--it was death! The time came when I knew that our renunciation was simply a crime against the soul. Can you see what I mean?"

"Yes," said Thyrsis, "I can see."

'And see what that meant to me--the situation I faced! I was a clergyman--and preaching a new crusade to the world. It was like being in a cage, with bars of red-hot metal. A hundred times I would go towards them--and a hundred times I would shrink back. But I had to grasp them in the end."

"I see!" whispered the other.

"The thing was becoming a scandal anyway; the world was bound to make a scandal of it, whether we would or no. It was a scandal that I visited in another woman's home, it was a scandal that I spent her money in my propaganda. The very children on the streets would taunt my children about it. And then, my health broke down from overwork; and the mother was going abroad, and she invited me to go with her and her daughter; and, of course, that made it worse. So at last the old lady came to me. 'You love my daughter,' she said, 'and the world has thrown her into your arms. You must let a divorce be arranged, and then marry my daughter.'"

"And you got the divorce yourself?" asked Thyrsis.

"No," said Darrell. "There were grounds enough; but it would have meant to attack my wife in the public prints, and I would not do it. I had to let her charge me with desertion, and say nothing."

"And, of course, they distorted that," said Thyrsis.

"They distorted everything!" cried the other. "My present wife gave my first wife all her patrimony; and I thought that was generous--I thought it was a proof of love. But the newspapers made it that she had bought me!"

"And they distorted your second marriage?" asked Thyrsis.

"They lied about it deliberately," was Darrell's reply--"Some of our friends gave little addresses of greeting; and so the newspapers called it a new kind of wedding--a 'Socialist wedding', which we had designed for our new kind of unions! And now, when we buy a farm, so that we can live quietly in the country, they turn that into a 'free love colony'!"

Section 13. Thyrsis went away from this interview with some new problems to ponder upon. He had seen a little of this power of the newspapers to defile and torment a man; but he had never dreamed of anything as bad as this. This was murderous, this was monstrous. He saw these papers now as gigantic engines of exploitation and oppression--irresponsible, unscrupulous, wanton--turned loose in society to crush and destroy whom they would.

They had taken this man Darrell and they had poured out their poisons upon him; they had tortured him hideously, they had burned him up as with vitriol. As a public force he was no longer a human being at all--he was a deformity, a spectre conjured up to bring fright to the beholder. And through it all he was utterly helpless--as much at their mercy as an infant in the hands of savages. And what had he done? Why had the torture been visited upon him?

Thyrsis pictured the men who had led in this soul-hunt. They were supposed to be enlightened Americans at the dawn of the twentieth century; and did they truly hold to the superstition of marriage as a religious sacrament, not to be dissolved by mortal power? Did they really believe that a man who had once been drawn into matrimony was obligated for life--no matter how unhappy he might be, no matter to what indignities he might be subjected? Or, if they did recognize the permissibility of divorce--then why this hue and cry after Darrell, who had borne his punishment for twenty years, and had waited for eight or ten years to test the depths of his new love?

The question answered itself; and the answer fanned Thyrsis' soul into a blaze of indignation. All this patter about the deserted wife, sitting at home with her children and weeping her eyes out--all that was so much hocus-pocus for the ears of the mob. The chiefs of this Inquisition and their torturers and slaves wrote it with their tongues in their cheeks. What they saw was that they had got securely strapped upon their rack the man who had threatened their power, who had laid bare its sources and exposed its iniquity. And they meant that if ever he came out of their torture-chamber, it should be so mangled and crippled that never again would he lift a finger against them!

The gist of the "Darrell case", when you got right down to it, was a quarrel over property; it was the snarling of wolves who had been disturbed at their feeding. Darrell had denounced wealth and the exploiters of wealth, and now he had married a woman of wealth; and was he to get away with his prize? That was the meaning of all the loud halloo--for that the hounds were unleashed and the hunting-horns sounded. Thyrsis pictured the men who "wrote up" the Darrell story. He had known them in the newspaper-world--the servants of the giant publicity-machine; living and working in the roar and rush of it, in a stifling atmosphere where the finer qualities of the soul were poisoned and withered over night. They lived their lives, almost without exception, by means of alcohol and coffee and tobacco; they were scornful, disillusioned, cynical beyond all telling and all belief. Their only god in heaven or earth or the waters under the earth was "copy". To such men there were two possible bonds of interest in a woman--the first being lust, and the second money. In the case of Henry Darrell they found both these motives; and so how clear the story was to them!

Thyrsis thought, also, of the men who owned and managed the papers; those who had turned loose the hunt and directed it. Rich men were they, who had built these publicity machines for their own purposes. And what were they in their private lives? Some of them were notoriously dissolute; and still others hid their ways under a veil of hypocrisy--just as in their editorials they hid their class-interests under pretenses of principle. And how easy it would have been for Darrell to get what he wanted without losing his reputation--if only he had been willing to follow the example of these eminent citizens! Thyrsis knew one man, the editor of an appallingly respectable journal, who had invited a young girl to his wife's home and there attempted to seduce her. He knew the proprietor of another, whose cheerful custom it was to go about among his newly-married women-friends and suggest that, inasmuch as he was a "superman," and their husbands were weaklings, they should let him become in secret the father of their children. This amateur eugenist was accustomed to maintain that the great men in history had for the most part been bastards; and Thyrsis, knowing this fact about him, would read editorials in his papers, in which Henry Darrell was denounced as an enemy of the home!

Meantime Thyrsis was reading Darrell's books and pamphlets, and coming to realize what a mind was here being destroyed. For this man, it seemed to him, was master of the noblest prose utterance that had been heard in America since Emerson died. He went again to hear him speak, in another ill-lighted and stuffy hall before less than a hundred people; and the pain of this was more than he could bear. He went home that night with his friend, and labored with him with all the force of his being. "You stay here," he declared, "and put yourself at the mercy of your enemies! You waste your faculties contending with them--even knowing about them is enough to destroy you. And all the while you might escape from them altogether--might do your real work, that the world knows nothing of. No one can hinder you. And when you have written the book of your soul, then your tormentors will be--they will be like the tormentors of Dante! Go away! Go away to Europe, where you can be free!"

And so before long, he stood upon a steamer-pier and waved Henry Darrell and his wife farewell. And every now and then would come letters, telling of long, long agonies; for Darrell had to fight for those few rare days when ill health would permit him to think. So year by year he labored at what Thyrsis knew, if it was ever finished, would be America's first world-poem; and in the meantime eminent statesmen and moralists who were alarmed at the progress of "Socialist agitation", would continue to conjure up before the public mind the night-mare spectre of the once-respected clergyman, who had deserted his weeping wife and children, and run away with a rich woman to found a "free-love colony"!

Section 14. A couple of days after the Darrells sailed, Thyrsis set out himself to find a home. On account of the new book, he would have to be near a library, and so he had selected a college-town not far from New York. He went there now, and put up for a week at a students' boarding-house, while prosecuting his search.

A strange experience it was to him, after the years of struggle and contact with the world, to come back to that academic atmosphere; to find men who were still peacefully counting up the "feminine endings" in Shakespeare's verse, and writing elaborate theses upon the sources of the Spenserian legends. Upon his excursions into the country some of these young men would tramp with him--threshing out, student-fashion, the problems of the universe; and how staggering it was to meet a man who was about to receive a master's degree in literature--and who regarded Arthur Hugh Clough as a "dangerous" poet, and Tennyson's "Two Voices" as containing vital thought, and T. H. Green as the world's leading philosopher! And this was the "education" that was dispensed at America's most aristocratic university--for this many millions of dollars had been contributed, and scores of magnificent buildings erected!

Thyrsis saw that a partial explanation lay in the fact that in connection with the university there existed a great theological seminary. Some of these future ministers came also to the boarding-house, and Thyrsis listened to their shop-talk--about the difference between "transubstantiation" and "consubstantiation", and the status of the controversy over the St. John Gospel. He heard one man cite arguments from Paley's "Moral Philosophy"; and another making bold to state that he was uncertain about the verbal inspiration of the Pentateuch!

To Thyrsis, as he listened to these discussions, it was as if he felt a black shadow stealing across his soul. He wondered why he should hate these men with a personal hatred; he tried to argue with himself that they must be well-meaning and earnest. The truth was that they seemed to him just like the law-students, men moved by sordid and low ideals; the only difference was that their minds were not so keen as the lawyers'. Thyrsis was coming little by little to understand the economic causes of things, and he perceived that this theological world represented a stagnant place in the stream of national culture; it being a subsidized world, maintained half by charity, vital men turned from it; it drew to itself the feebler minds, or such as wished to live at ease, and not inquire too closely into the difference between truth and falsehood.

Section 15. A few miles out from the town Thyrsis found a farm with an abundance of wild woodland, where the farmer gave him permission to camp. And so he went back and got some lumber, and loaded his tent and supplies on a wagon, and wrote Corydon that he would meet her the next afternoon. With the help of the farmer's boy he labored the rest of the day at building the platform, and putting up the tent, and getting their belongings in order. The next day he was up at dawn, constructing tables and stands; and later on he hired the farmer's "jagger-wagon", and drove in for Corydon and Cedric and the trunks.

It was a glorious spring day, of turquoise sky and glinting sunshine; and later, when the sun was low, the woods were flushed with a glow of scarlet and purple. It lent a glory to the scene, shedding a halo about the commonest tasks; the unpacking of blankets and dishes, the ranging of groceries upon shelves. They were free from all the world at last--they were setting out upon the journey of their lives together!

So it was with singing and laughter that they went at their work. The baby crawled about on the tent-floor and got into everybody's way, and crowed with delight at the novel surroundings; and later on his mother gave him his supper and put him to bed; and then she spread a feast of bread and butter, and fresh milk and eggs and a can of fruit, and they sat down to the first meal they had eaten together in many a long, long month.

They were tired and ravenously hungry; but their happiness of soul was keener even than any physical sensation, and they sat leaning upon their elbows and gazing across the table, reading the wonder in each other's eyes.

"It has been a year since we parted!" whispered Corydon.

"Just a year!" he said. "It seems like ten of them."

"And do you remember, Thyrsis, how we prayed! How we prayed for this very hour!"

He took her hands in his. Once more they renewed their pledges of devotion; once more the vision of their hopes unrolled before them. "From now on," he whispered, "our life is our own! We can make it whatever we will. Let us make it something beautiful."

And so there they made a compact. They would speak no more of the year that was past; it was a bad dream, and now it was gone. Let it be swept from their thoughts, and let them go on to make the future what they desired it to be.

BOOK XII
THE TREADMILL

They sat in the little cabin, where she had been reading some lines from the poem again--

"O easy access to the hearer's grace
    When Dorian shepherds sang to Proserpine!"

"Ah, yes!" he said. "But our lot was cast in a different time."

She put her hand upon his. "Even so," she said; and then turned the page, and read once more--

"What though the music of thy rustic flute
    Kept not for long its happy, country tone;
        Lost it too soon, and learnt a stormy note
Of men contention-tost, of men who groan,
        Which task'd thy pipe too sore, and tired thy
            throat--
            It failed, and thou wast mute!
    Yet hadst thou always visions of our light!_"

Section 1. The *mise-en-scene* of their new adventure in domesticity was a tent eighteen feet by twelve; but as the side-walls were low, they could walk only in the centre, and must range their belongings at the sides. To the left, as one entered the tent, there stood a soapbox with a tiny oil-stove upon it; and then a stand, made out of a packing-box, to hold their dishes, their cooking-utensils and their limited supply of provisions. Next down the line came a trunk, and in the corner the baby's crib--which had been outgrown by the farmer's children, and purchased by Thyrsis for a dollar. At the rear was a folding-table, and above it a board from which Corydon hung her clothing; along the other wall were her canvas cot, and a little stand with some books, and a wash-stand and another trunk.

Some distance off in the woods stood a second tent, seven feet square, in which Thyrsis had a cot for himself, and also a canvas-chair in which he sat to receive the visits of his muse. They got their drinking water from a spring near by; there was a tiny stream beside the tent which provided their washing-water. In this stream Thyrsis hollowed out a flat basin, in which they might set their butter-crock, and a pail of milk, and a larger pail that held their meat. Below that was a deeper pool from which they dipped water, and lower yet a third pool, with a board on which Corydon might sit and wash diapers, to her heart's content and her back's exhaustion.

The tent had been old when Thyrsis got it, and as this was the third season he had used it, it was dark and dun of hue. They had not noticed this at the outset as they had put it up on a bright, sunshiny day, and also before the trees had put out all their foliage. But now, when rain came, they found that they had to light a lamp in order to read in the tent; and, of course, it was on rainy days that they had to be inside. Thyrsis did not realize the influence which this tent had upon his wife's spirits; it was only after he saw her made physically ill by having to live in a room with yellow wall-paper, that he came to understand the power which her surroundings had over Corydon.

If they so much as touched a finger to the roof of the tent while it was raining, a steady dripping would come through at that point. Then, as the rains grew heavier, water took to running down the pole that stood in the centre of the tent, and formed a pool in the middle of the floor, so that Thyrsis had to get the axe and cut a hole there. And, of course, there was no way to dry anything; the woods, which were low, were turned into a swamp, and one's shoes became caked with mud, and there was no keeping the tent-floor clean.

In this place they had to keep an able-bodied, year-and-a-half-old baby! There was no other place to keep him. He could not be allowed on the damp floor, nor where he could touch the top of the tent; so Thyrsis set up sticks at all four corners of his crib, and tied strong twine about them, making a little pen; and therein they put the baby, and therein he had to stay. He had his rattle and his rubber-doll and his blocks and the rest of his gim-cracks; and after he had howled long enough to satisfy himself that there was no deliverance from his prison, he settled back and accepted his tragic fate. There came occasions when Corydon was sick, and unable to move; then Thyrsis would put up his umbrella and take Cedric to his own tent, where he would draw a chalk-line across the floor. One-half of the forty-nine square feet of space was his, and in it he would sit and read and study; in the other half the baby would play. After long experience he came to realize that at such times Papa would not pay any attention to him, and that crossing the chalk-line involved getting one's "mungies" spanked.

There were other troubles that fell upon them. At first, it being April, it was cold at night; and they had no stove, and no room for a stove. Later on the ceaseless rains brought a plague of mosquitoes; and so Thyrsis had to rig up a triangular door and cover the entrance to the tent with netting; and when the weather grew better, he had to get more netting and construct a little house, in which the baby could play outdoors. And then there had to be more spankings of "mungies", to teach the infant that this mysterious mosquito-bar must not be walked through, nor pulled at, nor poked with sticks, nor even eaten.

They prayed for fair days, and a little sunshine; and it seemed as if the weather-demons had discovered this, and were playing with them. There would come a bright morning, and they would spread a rug in the baby's cage, and hang out all their damp belongings to dry; and then would come a sudden shower, and baby and rug and belongings would all have to pile back into the tent. And then it would clear again, and everything would go out once more; and they would prepare dinner, and be comfortably settled to eat, when it would begin to sprinkle again. They would move in the clothing and the baby, and when it began to rain harder, they would move in the table and the food; and forthwith the rain would cease. Because it was poor fun eating in a dark tent by lamp-light, amid the odor of gas-stove and cooking, they might move out once more--but only to repeat the same experience over again.

For six weeks after their arrival there was not a day without rain, and it would rain sometimes for half a week without ceasing. So everything they owned became damp and mouldy--all their clothing, their food, the very beds upon which they slept. One of their miseries was the lack of place to keep things; all their odds and ends had to be stowed away under the cots--where one might find clothing, and books, and manuscripts, and a hammock, and an umbrella, and some shoes, and a box of prunes, and a sack of potatoes, and half a ham. When water got in at the sides of the tent and wet all these objects, and the bedclothing hung over the floor and got into them, it was trying to the temper to have to rummage there.

Section 2. Before she left the city Corydon had taken the baby to consult a famous "child-specialist"--at five dollars per consultation; she had received the dreadful tidings that Cedric was threatened with the "rickets". So she had come out to the country with one mighty purpose in her soul. "Under-nourishment", the doctor had said; and he had laid out a regular schedule. Six times daily the unhappy infant was to be fed; and each time some elaborate concoction had to be got ready--practically nothing could be eaten in a state of nature. The first meal would consist of, say a poached egg on a piece of toast, and the juice of an orange, with the seeds carefully excluded; the next of some chicken broth with a cracker or two, and the pulp of prunes with the skins removed; the next of some beef chopped up and pounded to a pulp and broiled, together with a bit of mashed potato or some other cooked vegetable; the next of some gruel, with cream and sugar, and some more prunes.

And these operations, of course, took the greater part of Corydon's day; she would struggle at them until she was ready to drop, and when she had to give up they would fall to Thyrsis. Some of them fell to him quite frequently--for instance, the pounding of the meat. It had to have all the fat and gristle carefully cut out; and there had to be a clean board, and a clean hammer, both of which must be scraped and washed afterwards; and whenever by any chance Corydon let the meat stay on the fire a second too long, so that it got hard, the whole elaborate operation had to be gone over again--was not the baby's life at stake?

It was quite vain for him to protest as to the pains that Corydon took to remove every tiniest fragment of the skin of a stewed prune. "Surely, dearest," he would argue, "the internal arrangements of a baby are not so delicate as to be torn by a tiny bit of prune-skin!"

But to Corydon the internal arrangements of babies were mysterious things--to be understood only by a child-specialist at five dollars per visit. "He told me what to do," she would say; "and I am going to do it."

So she would prepare the concoctions, and would sit and feed them to the baby, spoonful by spoonful; and long after the little one had been stuffed to the bursting-point, she would hold the spoon poised in front of its mouth, making tentative passes, and seeking by some device to cajole the mouth into opening and admitting one last morsel of the precious nutriment. The child had a word of its own invent-ing, wherewith it denoted things that were good to eat. "Hee, gubum, gubum!" he would exclaim; and Corydon would hold the spoon and repeat "Gubum, gubum,"--long after the baby had begun to sputter and gasp and make plain that it was no longer "gubum".

Also, under the instructions of the specialist, they made an attempt to break the child of the "hoodaloo mungie" habit. A baby should lie down and go to sleep without handling, the authority had declared; and now that there was all outdoors for him to cry in, they resolved that he should be taught. So they built up the fence about the crib, and laid the baby in for his afternoon nap, and started to go away. And the baby gave one look of perplexity and dismay, and then began to cry. By the time they had got out of the tent he was screaming like a creature possessed; and Corydon and Thyrsis sat outside and stared at each other in wonder and alarm. When she could stand it no more, they went away to a distance; but still the uproar went on. Now and then they would creep back and peep in at the purple and chok-ing infant; and then steal away again, and discuss the phenomenon, and wish that the "child-specialist" were there to advise them. Finally, when the crying had gone on for two hours without a moment's pause, they gave up, because they were afraid the baby might cry itself into convulsions. And so the "hoodaloo mungie" habit went on for some time yet.

Under the "stuffing regime" the infant at first thrived amazingly; he became fat and rosy, and Corydon's heart beat high with joy and pride. But then came midsum-mer, and the hot season; and first of all a rash broke out upon the precious body, and in spite of powders and ointments, refused to go away. Later on came the "hives", with which the baby was spotted like the top of a pepper-crust. And then, as fate willed it, the family of a woman who did some laundry for Corydon developed the measles; and Corydon found it out too late--and so they were in for the first of a long program of "children's diseases".

It was a siege that lasted for a month and more--a nightmare experience. The child had to be kept in a dark place, under pain of losing its eyesight; and when it was very hot in the tent, some one had to sit and fan it. It could not sleep, but writhed and moaned, now screaming in torment, now whimpering like a frightened cur--a sound that wrung Thyrsis' very heart. And oh, the sight of the little body--purple, a mass of eruptions, and with beads of perspiration upon it! Corydon's mother came to help her through this ordeal, and would sit for hours upon hours, rocking the wailing infant in her arms.

Section 3. But there were ups as well as downs in this tenting adventure. There came glorious days, when they took long tramps over the hills; or when Thyrsis would carry the child upon his shoulder, and they would wander about the meadows, picking daisies and clover, and making garlands for Corydon. Once Cedric sat down upon a bumble-bee, and that was hard upon him, and perhaps upon the bee. But for the most part the little one was enraptured during these excursions. He was fascinated with the flowers, and continually seeking for an opportunity to devour some of them; while he was doing it he would wear such a roguish smile--it was impossible not to believe that he understood the agitation which these abnormal appetites occasioned in his parents. Corydon would be seized with a sudden access of affection, and she would clutch him in her arms and squeeze him, and fairly smother him with kisses. Of course the youngster would protest wildly at this, and so not infrequently the demonstration would end tragically.

"I can't have any joy in my baby at all!" she would lament; and Thyrsis would have to soothe the child, and plead with her to find more practical ways of demonstrating her maternal devotion.

Cedric was beginning to make determined efforts to talk now, and he had the most original names for things. His parents would adopt these into their own speech, which thus departed rapidly from established usage. They had to bring themselves to realize that if they went on in that fashion, the child would never learn to speak so that any one else could understand him. The grandmothers were most strenuous upon this point, and would laboriously explain to the infant that chickens and pigeons and sparrows were not all known as "ducky-ducks"; they would plead with it to say "bottle of milk", while its reckless parents were delighting themselves with such perversions as "bobbu mookie-mook."

Two or three times each week the farmer would bring their mail; and once a week they would hire an old scare-crow of a horse, and a buggy which might have passed for the one-horse shay in its ninety-ninth year, and drive to a town for provisions. It was amazing what loads of provisions a family of three could consume in the course of a week--especially when one of them was following the "stuffing regime". There had to be a lot of figuring done to get it for the sum of thirty dollars a month; and this put another grievous burden upon Thyrsis. Corydon, alas, had no talents for figuring, and was cursed with a weakness for such superfluities as clean laundry and coffee with cream. This was one more aspect of the difference between the Hebrew and the Greek temperament; and sometimes the Hebrew temperament would lose its temper, and the Greek temperament would take to tears. The situation was all the more complicated because of their pitiful ignorance. They really did not know what was necessity and what was luxury. For instance, Thyrsis had read somewhere that people could live without meat; but Corydon had never heard of such an idea, and insisted with vehemence that it was an absurdity.

However, there was no evading the issue of poverty; for the thirty dollars was all they had. "The Hearer of Truth" had been out several months now, and had not sold a thousand copies; and so it was to be doubted if Thyrsis would ever get another dollar from that. Also, he had heard from the translator of "The Genius", and had agreed to accept twenty-five dollars as an "honorarium" for the production of his play in Germany--this princely sum to be paid when the play came out during the following winter.

Meantime, of course, he was driving away at his new work. Domestic duties took up most of his morning; but he would get away into the woods in the afternoons, and in the evenings, when the family was asleep, he would work until far after midnight. He was bringing out basketfuls of books from the library of the university; and he lived another life in these--sharing, in a hundred different forms, the agony of the War. He was not writing yet; he was filling up his soul with the thing, making it a reservoir of impressions. Some times it would seem that the reservoir was nearly full, and he would be seized with a hunger to be at work; he would go about possessed by it--absent-minded, restless, nervous when he was spoken to. It was hard for a man who listened all night to the death-groans of the thousands piled up before "Bloody Angle", to get up in the morning and be satisfactory in the role of "mother's assistant".

Here, again was the torment of this matrimonial bond to a man who wished to be an artist. He had to live two lives, when one was more than he could attend to; he had to be always aware of another soul yearning for him, reaching out to him and craving his attention. To be sure, Corydon was interested in what he was doing; she even made heroic efforts to read the books that he was reading. But she had so many duties, and so many headaches; and when night came she was so tired! She would ask him to tell her about his vision; and was not the thing untellable? Why else did he have to labor day and night, like a man possessed? He would explain this to her, and she would bid him go on and do his work and not mind her. But when he would take her at her word, and there would follow a week or two of indifference and preoccupation--then he would discover that she was again unhappy.

Section 4. This never ceased to be the case between them; but perhaps it was intensified at this time by the fact that their sex-life had to be suppressed. This was a problem which they had talked out between them before they came away. Thyrsis, who was groping for the truth about these matters, had come to the conclusion that the factor which gave dignity and meaning to intercourse between a man and woman was the desire, or at any rate the willingness, to create a child. Corydon was not sure that she agreed with him in this; but so far as their own case was concerned, it was quite clear that they could take no remotest chance of any accident--another child would mean certain destruction for all three of them. And so they had gone back to the "brother and sister" arrangement with which they had begun life. This was a simple matter for Thyrsis, who was utterly wrapped up in his book; it was not so simple for Corydon, though neither of them realized it, nor could have been brought to admit it. As usual, Corydon desired to be what he was, and to feel what he felt; and so Thyrsis did not realize how another side of her was being blighted. Hers was predominantly a love-nature; it was intolerable to her that any one she loved should not love her in return, and love her in the same way, and to the same extent; and now, when her entire being went out to him, she found herself obliged to suppress her emotions.

Sometimes the thing would break out in spite of her.

"Thyrsis," she would cry, "aren't you going to kiss me good-night?"

"Didn't I kiss you, dearest?" he would answer.

"Oh, but such a cold and perfunctory kiss!"

And so he would come and put his arms about her; but even while she held him thus, she would feel the life go out of his caresses, and see his eyes with a far-off expression. She would know that his thoughts were away upon some battle-field.

"Tell me, Thyrsis," she would exclaim. "Do you really love me?"

"Yes, dear," he would reply. "I love you."

"But how *much* do you love me?"

And then he would be dumb. What a question to ask him! As if he had the time and the energy to climb to those heights, to speak again that difficult language! Had he not told her a thousand times how much he loved her! and could she not believe it and understand it?

"But why should it be so hard to tell me?" she would protest.

And he would answer that to him it was a denial of love to explain or to make promises. He was as unchangeable as the laws of nature--he could no more be faithless to her soul than he could to his own.

"I want you to take that for granted," he would say; "to know it as you know that the sun will rise to-morrow morning."

"But, Thyrsis," she would answer, when he used this metaphor, "don't people sometimes like to go out and see the sun rise?"

Section 5. The summer passed; and Thyrsis found to his dismay that his relentless muse had not yet permitted him to write a word. He had not a sufficient grasp upon his mighty subject--nor for that matter had he freedom to get by himself and wrestle it out. He shrunk from that death-grapple, while they were in this unsettled state. They could not stay in tents through the winter-time; and where were they to go?

Thyrsis was consumed with the desire to build a tiny house in these woods. He had roamed the country over, without finding any place that was habitable; and besides, he did not want to pay rent--he wanted a home of his own, however humble. He had meant to build one with the money from "The Hearer of Truth"; but now there came a statement from the publisher, showing that there would be due him on the book a trifle over eleven dollars!

He tried a new plan. He wrote out a "scenario" of his projected novel, and sent this to his publisher, to see if he could get a contract in advance. He asked for five hundred dollars--with that he could build the house he wanted, and live for another six months, until the book was done. The publisher wrote him to come to the city, where, after some parleying, he submitted a proposition; he would advance the money and publish the book, paying ten per cent. royalty; but he must also have the option to publish the author's future writings for ten years upon the same basis.

This rather staggered Thyrsis. He was business-man enough by this time to realize that if he ever had a real success he could get fifteen or twenty per cent. upon his future work--there were even some authors who got twenty-five per cent. And moreover, he did not like to tie himself to this publisher, who was of the hard and grasping type. He went home to think it over, and in the end he wrote to Henry Darrell. He set forth the situation, and showed how much money it might mean to him--money which he would otherwise be able to devote to some useful purpose. It all depended upon what Darrell could do in the emergency.

He waited three weeks, and then came Darrell's reply, saying that he could not possibly do what Thyrsis wished. There were so many calls upon him--the Socialist paper was in trouble, and so on. Thereupon Thyrsis wrote to the publisher to say that he accepted the offer and would sign the contract; but in a couple of days he received a curt reply, to the effect that the publisher had changed his mind, and no longer cared to consider the arrangement. He had, as Thyrsis found afterwards, got rid of the enthusiastic young man who had inveigled him into "The Hearer of Truth"; and perhaps also he had been reading the ridicule which the critics were pouring out upon that unhappy book.

So once more Thyrsis wrote to Darrell--a letter of agonized entreaty. He was at the most critical moment of his life; and now, at the very culmination of his effort, to have to give up would be a calamity he could simply not contemplate. If only he could finish the task, he would be saved; for this was a book that would grip men and shake them--that it should fail was simply unthinkable. He could make out with two hundred dollars; and he besought his friend at any sacrifice to stand by him. He asked him to cable; and when, a couple of weeks later, the message came--"all right"--to Thyrsis it was like waking up and escaping from the grip of some terrible dream.

Section 6. And so began the house-building. It was high time, too--the latter part of September, and the nights were growing chill. He sought out a carpenter to help him, and had an interview with his friend the farmer, who agreed to rent a bit of land, in a corner of his orchard, by the edge of the wood. It was under the shade of a great elm-tree, and sufficiently remote from all the world to satisfy the taste of any literary hermit.

For months before this he and Corydon had discussed the plans of their future home; every square inch of it had been a subject of debate. In its architectural style it was a compromise between Corydon's aesthetic yearnings, and the rigid standards of economy which circumstance imposed. It was to be eighteen feet long and sixteen feet wide--six feet high at the sides and nine in the centre. It was to be "weather-boarded", and roofed with paper, instead of shingles--this being so much cheaper. Corydon heard with dismay that it would be necessary to paint this roofing-paper black; and Thyrsis, by way of compensation, agreed that the weather-boards should have some "natural finish", instead of common paint. There was to be a six-foot piazza in front, and a little platform in back, with steps descending to the spring.

There had been long discussions about the method of heating the mansion. Corydon had been observing the customs of her neighbors in this typical "small-farming" district, and declared that they had two leading characteristics: first, they were not happy until they had had all their own teeth extracted, and a complete set of "store-teeth" substituted; and second, as soon as they moved into a house, they boarded over the open fire-place and covered the boards with wall-paper. But Thyrsis, making investigations along practical lines, found that the open fire-place had a bad reputation as a consumer of fuel; and also, it would take a mason to build a chimney, and the wages of masons were high. So Corydon had to reconcile herself to a house with a stove, and a stove-pipe that went through a hole in the wall!

Nevertheless this house-building time was one of the happiest periods of their lives. For here was something constructive, in which they could both be occupied. Thyrsis would be up and at work early in the morning, before the carpenter came; and in between the baby's various meals, Corydon would come also, and take part in the operations. A miraculous thing it was to see the house of their dreams coming into being, with every feature just as they had planned it. And what a palatial structure it was--with so much space and air! One could actually move about in it without danger of striking one's head; coming into it from the tent, one felt as if he were entering a cathedral!

They were so consumed with a desire to see it finished, that Thyrsis would stay at the work until darkness came upon him, and sometimes even worked by moon-light, or with a lantern. And how proud they would be when the carpenter came next morning, and found the last roof-boards laid, or the flooring all completed! Thyrsis learned the mysteries of window-sills and door-frames, the excitements of "weather-boarding," and the perils of roof-painting. He realized with wonder how many achievements of civilization the privileged classes take as a matter of course. What a remarkable thing it was, when one came to think of it, that a door should swing true upon its hinges, and fit exactly into its frame, and latch with a precise and soul-satisfying snap! And that windows should slide up and down in their frames, and stop at certain places with a spring-catch!

Corydon too was interested in these discoveries, and became skilled at hold-ing weather-boards while her husband nailed them, and at helping to unroll and measure roofing-paper, and climbing up the ladder and holding it in place. Even the baby became fired with the spirit of achievement, and would get himself a ham-mer and a board, and plague his parents until they started a dozen or so of nails for him--after which he would sit and blissfully pound them into the board, and all but pound them through the board in his enthusiasm. Before long he even learned to start them himself; and a most diverting sight it was to see this twenty-two-months old youngster driving nails like an infant Hercules. For the fastening of the roofing-paper they used little circular plates of tin called "cotterels"; and these also Cedric must learn to use. So a new phrase was added to the vocabulary of "dam-fool talk". "Bongie cowtoos" was the name of the operation; for a couple Of years thereafter, whenever Corydon and Thyrsis wished to be let alone to discuss the problems of the universe, they would get the baby a hammer and some nails and a board, and repeat that magic formula, and the problem was solved.

Unfortunately, however, it was not all smooth sailing in the carpentry-business. There were mashed thumbs and sawed fingers; and then, in an evil hour, Thyrsis came upon an advertisement which told of a wonderful new kind of wall-paper which could be applied directly to laths--thus enabling one to dispense with plaster. He sent for ten or twelve dollars' worth of this material, and he and Corydon spent a whole morning making a mixture of glue and flour-paste and water, and boiling it in an iron preserving-kettle. But alas, the paper would not paste; and then they had a painful time. Corydon gave up in disgust, and went away; but Thyrsis, to whom economy was a kind of disease, would not give up, and was angry with the other for urging him to give up. He spent a whole day wrestling with the concoction, and gave himself a headache with the ghastly odor. But in the end he had to dump it out, and clean the kettle, and fasten the paper to the lathes with "bongie cowtoos". As the strips of paper did not correspond with the studding, he found himself driving nails into springy laths, an operation most trying to the temper of any man of letters. One of the trials of this house forever after was that upon the least jar a corner of the ceiling was liable to fall loose; and then one would have to get a ladder, and climb up into a hot region, and pound nails into a broken lath, with dust sifting down into one's eyes, and the hammer hitting one's sore thumb, and occasioning exclamations not at all suitable for the ears of a two-year-old intelligence.

Section 7. When the doors were fitted, and the windows set in, and the piazza laid, and the steps built, they got down to the furniture, which was also to be home-made. Thyrsis was gratified beyond telling by these tables and dressing-stands and shelves and book-cases, which he could build of hemlock boards in an hour or two, and which cost only thirty or forty cents apiece. He would labor with Corydon to induce her to share this joy; but alas, he would only succeed in losing his own joy, without increasing hers. On many occasions he attempted such things as this; it was only after long years that he came to realize that Corydon's temperament was the one fixed fact in the universe with which he had to deal.

Two hundred and twenty-five dollars was the total cost of this establishment when completed. And while the carpenter was putting the finishing touches, Thyrsis was using up thirty dollars more of lumber in constructing himself a "study" in the woods near by. Eight by ten this cabin was to be; it was to have a door and a window, and a little piazza in front, upon which the inhabitant might sit in fair weather. Also Thyrsis built for it a table and a bookcase; and as he had now eighty square feet instead of forty-nine, there was room for a cot and a chair, and a coal-stove fourteen inches in diameter. As fate would have it, there was some black paint left over; and to Corydon's horror it was announced that this would be used on the study. However, Thyrsis insisted that it was *his* study; and besides, there was some red paint left, with which he might decorate the window and the door-frame, and stripe the edges of the roof and the corners. Surely that would be festivity enough for the most exacting of Greek temperaments!

Then came the rapturous experience of moving into these new mansions. The joy of having shelves to put things on, and hooks to hang things from. Of being able to take books and manuscripts out of their trunks, and not pile them under their beds. Of carrying over their belongings, and having everything fit into the place that had been made for it!

Thyrsis purchased an old stove, and also a kitchen-range from a neighbor; he sank a barrel in the spring, and walled it round with cement; he built a stand in the kitchen, and set up a sink and a little pump.

This was the time of year when there were held at various places in the country what the neighbors called "vandews". He and Corydon found it diverting to get the scarecrow nag and the one-horse shay, and drive to some farm-house, where one might see the history of a family for the last fifty years spread out upon the lawn. They would stand round in the cold and snow while the auctioneer disposed of the horses and cows and hay and machinery, waiting until he came to the household objects upon which they had set their eye. So they would invest in some stove-pipe, and a couple of ghastly chromos (for the sake of the frames), and some odds and ends of crockery, and a spade, and some old rope to make a swing for the baby. They would get these things for five or ten cents each, and get in addition all the excitements of the bargain-hunt.

Once they had a real adventure--they came upon a wonderful old "grandfather's clock", about six feet high; and Corydon exclaimed in rapture, "Oh Thyrsis I'd be happy for the rest of my life if we could have that clock!" On such terms it appeared to Thyrsis that the clock might be worth making a sacrifice for, and he got up the courage to declare that he would offer as high as five dollars for it. And so they stood, trembling with excitement, and waiting.

"Don't lose it, even if it's as high as six dollars!" whispered Corydon; but alas, the first bid for the clock was twenty-five dollars. They stood staring with dismay, until the treasure was sold to a dealer from the city for the incredible sum of eighty-seven dollars; and then they drove home, quite awe-stricken by this sudden intrusion from the world of luxury outside their ken.

Section 8. However, this disappointment did not trouble them for long; there were too many luxuries in their own home. Not very long after it was finished, there fell a deluge of rain; and what a delight it was to listen to it, and know that they were safe from it! That not only did they have a dry roof over their head--but they were able to move about, and to reach up their hands without peril, and to sit down and read without a lamp! They would stand by the window with their arms about each other, watching the rain beating upon the fields, and dripping from the elm tree, and flowing in torrents past the house; they would listen to it pounding overhead and streaming off the roof before their faces. They were dry, quite dry! All their belongings were dry--their shoes were not mildewing, their books were not getting soft and shapeless, their bed-clothing would be all right when night came!

The down-pour lasted for three whole days, yet they enjoyed it all. It proved to be a memorable rain to Corydon, for it brought to her a great occasion--the beginning of her poetical career. It happened late one night, when, as usual, the cry of "hoodaloo mungie" awakened her from a sound slumber. The day had been a particularly hard one, and the heaviness of exhaustion was upon her. For a moment she stared up into the darkness, listening to the rain close above her, and trying to nerve herself to put out her arm in the cold. She shuddered at the thought; there came to her a perfectly definite impulse of hatred--hatred of the child, of its noise and its demands. She had felt it before--sometimes as a dull, cold dislike, sometimes as something passionate. Why should she have to sacrifice herself to this insatiable creature, whom she did not love? What did it matter to her if other women loved their children? She had wanted life--and was this life? At that moment the cry of "hoodaloo-mungie" symbolized for her all the sordid cares and nervous agony of her existence.

And suddenly, unexpectedly, a daring impulse seized her. "No!" she thought, and set her teeth--"I'll let him cry! I'll cure him of this--and I'll do it to-night!" So she turned and told Cedric to go to sleep; at which, of course, the child began to scream.

Corydon lay very still in the dark, her eyes wide and every nerve tense. She could not feel, she could not think; it seemed as though she were deprived of every sense except that of hearing; and in her, through her, and around her rang a senseless din, piercing, intense, increasing in volume every minute, and completely drowning out the beating of the rain.

"Can I stand it?" she thought. "Or will his lungs burst? And yet, I must, I must-- this can't go on forever! "And so she clenched her hands and waited. But the sounds did not diminish in the slightest; ten minutes twenty minutes must have passed, and the baby only seemed to gain increased power with each crescendo.

It seemed to Corydon at last as though she had always lain like this, and as though she must for endless time. She found herself getting used to it even; her muscles relaxed. There came to her a sense of the ludicrous side of it. "He means to conquer me!" she thought. "Can I hold out? If I only had something to think about, then I'd be a match for him." And suddenly the inspiration came to her. "I'll write a poem!"

What should it be about? The rain had been increasing in violence, and she became conscious of the steady downpour; it fascinated her, and she concentrated her attention upon it, and began---

"I am the rain, that comes in spring!"

So, after a while, she found herself in the throes of composition; she was eager, excited--and marvel of marvels, utterly forgetful of the baby! She had never tried to write verses before; but it did not seem at all difficult to her now.

The poem was simple and optimistic--it told of the beneficent qualities of rain, as it would appear to one whose roof did not leak. Somewhere in the course of it there was this stanza:

"I am the rain that comes at night,
 When all in slumber is folded light--
 Save one by weary vigils worn
 Who counteth the drops unto the morn."

This seemed to her an impressive bit, and she wondered what Thyrsis would think of it.

There were eight stanzas altogether, and when she finished the last of them the dawn was breaking, and it seemed hours since she had begun. As for the baby, he was still crying. She turned and peered at him; his eyelids drooped, and the crying came in spasms and gasps--it sounded very feeble, and a trifle perfunctory. Obviously he could not hold out much longer; Corydon would win, yes, she had won already. She lay still, and thrills of happiness went through her. Was it the poem, or the thought of her release, and the nights of quiet sleep in the future?

When Thyrsis came in, an hour or two later, he found her huddled up in blankets on the floor of the living-room, her cheeks bright, her hair dishevelled. How fascinating she looked in such a guise! She was eagerly pondering her poem; and the baby was sleeping quietly, save for a few convulsive gasps, the last stragglers of his routed forces.

"And oh, Thyrsis," she exclaimed, "to-morrow night he will only cry half as long, and still less the next night. And soon he will go to sleep quietly like any well brought-up, civilized baby. And, my dear, I believe I'm going to be a poetess--I think that to-night I was really inspired!"

So he made haste to build a fire, and then came and sat and listened to the poem. How eagerly she waited for his verdict! How she hung upon his words! And what should a man do in such a case--should he be a husband or a critic? Should he be an amateur or a professional?

But even as he hesitated, the damage was done. "Oh, you don't like it!" she cried. "You don't think it's good at all!"

"My dear," he argued, "poetry is such a difficult thing to write. And there are so many standards--a thing can be good, and yet not good! The heights are so far away--"

"But oh, how can I ever get there," wailed Corydon, "if nobody gives me any encouragement?"

Section 9. The time had now come for Thyrsis to put his job through. There was no longer any excuse for hesitation or delay. The book had come to ripeness in him; the birth-hour was at hand, and he must go and have it out with himself. He explained these things to Corydon, sitting beside her and holding her hands; they ascended once more to the heights of consecration; they renewed their vows of fortitude and faith, and then he went away.

For weeks thereafter he would be like the ghost of a man in the house, haggard and silent and preoccupied. All the work that he had ever done in his life seemed but child's play in comparison. Before this he had portrayed the struggles of men and women; but now he was to portray the agony of a whole nation--his heart must beat with the pulse of millions of suffering people. And the task was like a fiend that came upon him in the night-time and laid hold of him, dragging him away to sights of terror and madness. He was never safe from the thing for a moment--he could never tell when it might assail him. He might be washing the dishes, or wrestling with the refractory pump; but the vision would come to him, and he would wander off into the forest--perhaps to sit, crouching in the snow, trembling, and staring at the pageant in his soul.

He lived in the midst of battles; the smoke of powder always in his nostrils, the crash of musketry and the thunder of cannon in his ears. He saw the cavalry sweeping over the plains, the infantry crouching behind intrenchments; he heard the yells of the combatants, the shrieks of the wounded and dying; he saw the mangled bodies, and the ground slippery with blood. New aspects of the thing kept coming to him--new glimpses into meanings yet untold. They would come to him in great bursts of emotion, like tempests that swept him away; and these things he had to wrestle with and master. It meant toil, the like of which he had never faced before, a tension of all his faculties, that would last for hours and hours, and leave him bathed in perspiration, and utterly exhausted.

A scene would come to him, in some moment of insight; and he would drop everything else, and follow it. He would go over it, at the same time both creating and beholding it, at the same time both overwhelmed by it and controlling it--but above all things else, remembering it! He would be like Aladdin in the palace, stuffing his pockets with priceless jewels; coming away so loaded down that he could hardly stagger, and spilling them on every side. Then, scarcely pausing to rest, he would go back after what he had lost; he would grope about, gathering diamonds and rubies that he had all but forgotten--or perhaps coming upon new vaults and new treasure-chests.

So he would labor over a description, going over it and over it, not so much working it out, as letting it work itself out and stamp itself upon his memory. It made no difference how long the scene might be, he would not write a word of it; it might be some battle- picture, that would fill thirty or forty pages--he would know it all by heart, as Demosthenes or Webster might have known an oration. And only at the end would he write it down.

Over some of the scenes in this new book he labored thus for two or three weeks at a stretch; there would be literally not a moment of the day, nor perhaps of the night, when the thing was not working in some part of his mind. He would think about it for hours before he fell asleep; and when he opened his eyes it would be waiting at his bedside to pounce upon him. If he tried for even a few minutes to rest, or to divert his mind to some other work, he would find himself ill at ease and troubled, with a sense as of something pulling at him, calling to him. And if anything came to interrupt him, then he would be like a baker whose oven grows cold before the bread is half done--it would be a sad labor making anything out of that batch of bread.

Section 10. And this work he had to do as a married man, the father of a family and the head of a household; living with a child who was one incessant and irrepressible demand for attention, and a wife who was wrestling with weakness and sickness--eating out her heart in cruel loneliness, and cowering in the grip of fiends of melancholia and despair!

He had thought that when they moved into the new home, their domestic trials would be at an end. But now the cruel winter fell upon them. They had never known what a winter in the country was like; they came to see why the farmer had protested against their building in such a remote place. There were many days when they could not get to town, and some when they could not even get to the farm-house. Also there was the pump, which was continually freezing, and necessitating long and troublesome operations before they could get any water.

It was, as fate would have it, the worst winter in the oldest inhabitant's memory. The farmer's well froze over on three occasions, and it had never frozen before, so he declared. For such weather as this they were altogether unprepared; they had only a wood-stove, and could not keep a fire all night; and the cheap blankets they had bought were made all of cotton, and gave them almost no protection. They would not sleep with the windows down; and so, for weeks at a time, they would go to bed with their clothing, even their overcoats on; and would pile curtains and rugs upon these--and even so, they would waken at two or three o'clock in the morning, shivering and chilled to the bone.

And in this icy room they would have to get up and build a fire; and it might be half an hour before they could get the house warm. Also, they had no facilities for bathing; and so little by little they began to lose their habits of decency--there were days when Corydon left her face unwashed, and forgot to brush her hair. Everyday, it seemed, they slipped yet further down the grade. Thyrsis would work until he was faint and exhausted, and then he would come over, and find there was nothing ready to eat. By the time that he and Corydon had cooked a meal, they would both of them be ravenous, and they would sit and devour their food like a couple of savages. Then, because they had over-eaten, they would have to rest before they cleared things away; and like as not Thyrsis would get to thinking about his work, and go off and leave everything--and the dishes and the food might stay up on the table until the next meal. There was nearly always a piled-up mass of dishes and skillets and sauce-pans in the house--to Thyrsis these soiled dishes were the original source of the myth of Sisyphus and his labor.

And then there was the garbage-pail that he had forgotten to empty, and the lamps he had neglected to fill, and the slop-pails and the other utensils of domesticity. There were the diapers that somebody had to wash--and outside was always the bitter, merciless cold, that drove them in and shut them up with all this horror. The time came, as the winter dragged on, when the house which they had built with so many sacrifices, and into which they had moved with such eager anticipations, came to seem to them like a cave in which a couple of wild beasts cowered for shelter.

Section 11. There was another great change which this cold weather effected in their lives; it broke down the barriers they had been at such pains to build up between them. It was all very well for them to agree that they were "brother and sister," and that it was impossible for them ever to think of anything else. But now came a time when night after night the thermometer went to ten or fifteen degrees below zero; and first Thyrsis gave more bedding to Corydon--because she was able to suffer more than he; and he would go over to his cold hut alone, and crawl into a cold bed, and lie there the whole night through without a wink of sleep. But then, as the cold held on for a week or more, the resistance of both of them was broken down--they were like two animals which crawl into the same hole to keep each other from freezing. They piled all their bedding upon one narrow cot; and sleeping thus, they could be warm. Even then, they tried to keep to the resolution they had made; but this, it seemed, was not within the power of flesh and blood; and so, once more, the sex-factor was introduced into the complications of their lives.

To Thyrsis this thing was like some bird of prey that circled in the sky just above him--its shadow filling him with a continual fear, the swish of its wings making him cringe. He was never happy about it; there was no time in his life when he was not in a state of inward war. His intellect rebelled; and on the other hand, there was a part of his nature that craved this sex-experience and welcomed it--and this part, it seemed, was favored by all the circumstances of life. There was no chance to settle the matter in the light of reason, to test it by any moral or aesthetic law; blind fate decreed that one part of him should have the shaping of his character, the determining of his needs.

He tried to make clear to himself the basis of his distrust. Sexual intercourse as a habit--this was the formula by which he summed it up to himself. To be right, to win the sanction of the intellect and the conscience, the sex-act must be the result of a supreme creative impulse. Its purpose was the making of a new soul--and this could never be right until those who took that responsibility had used their reasons, and determined that circumstances were such that the new soul might be a sound and free and happy and beautiful soul. And how different was this from the customs which prevailed under the sanction of the "holy bonds of matrimony"! When sexual intercourse became a self-indulgence, like the eating of candy, or the drinking of liquor; a thing of the body, and the body alone; a thing determined by physical propinquity, by the sight and contact of the flesh, the dressing and undressing in the same room!

Then again, the means which they had to use to prevent conception--which destroyed all spontaneity in their relationship, and dragged the thing out into the cold light of day! And the continual fear that they might have made another blunder! Something of this sort was always happening, or seeming to have happened, or threatening to have happened, so that they waited each month in suspense and dread. It was this which made the terror of the whole matter to Thyrsis, and had so much to do with his repugnance. They were like people drawing lots for a death-sentence; like people who ate from dishes, one of which they knew to contain poison. What was the tragic destiny that hung over them--the Nemesis that gripped them, and forced them to take such a chance?

But the barriers were down, and there was no building them up again; Thyrsis never even tried, because of the revelation which came to him from Corydon's side. Corydon was craving, reaching out hungrily for something which she had not in herself, and which life did not give her in sufficiency. She called this thing "love"; and she had no hesitations and no limits to her demand for it. To Thyrsis this "love" was something quite else--it was sustenance and support. To demand it was an act of weakness, and to yield it was a kind of spiritual blood-transfusion. It was the first law of his life-code that every soul must stand upon its own feet and walk its own way; and to surrender that spiritual autonomy was the one blunder for which there could be no pardon.

But then--he would argue with himself--what folly it was to talk of such things in their position! They not souls at all--the life of the soul was not for them, the laws of the soul had nothing to do with them. They were two bodies--two miserable and cold and sick and tormented bodies; and with yet a third body, utterly helpless and dependent upon them--in defiance of all the most high-sounding pronouncements about "the soul"!

So Thyrsis would mock himself into subjection once more, and go on to play his part as husband and father and head of a household of bodies. He would play the game of "love" as Corydon wanted it played; he would yield to her demands, he would gratify her cravings, he would force himself to take her point of view. But then the other mood would come upon him--the mood that he knew to be the real expression of himself. He would begin the battle of his genius again; he would "hear the echoes afar off, the thunder of the captains and the shouting". If one gave one's self up to the body, and accepted the regimen and the laws of the body, how should the soul ever come to be free? To make such a concession was to pass upon it a sentence of life-imprisonment!

So would come to Thyrsis again that sense of the awful tragedy that was impending in their lives. Some day, he knew, he would break out of this prison. Some day, he knew, he would have to be himself, and live his own life!

And meanwhile, how pitiful were Corydon's attempts to shape him to her needs, and to persuade herself that she was succeeding in doing it! She would set forth to him elaborately how much he had improved; how much gentler and more human he was--in contrast with that blind and stupid and egotistical and impossible person she had first known. And with what bitterness Thyrsis would hear this--and how he had to struggle to suppress his feeling! For he knew that those qualities which were so hateful to her, were but the foam cast up to the surface of his soul by the seething of his genius within. When it had ceased altogether, how placid and still would be the pool-and what a beautiful mirror it would make for Corydon to behold her own features in!

Section 12. In later years they used to discuss this problem, and they could never be sure what would have happened in their lives--what would have been the reaction of their different temperaments--if they had been given any fair chance to live and grow as they wanted to. But here they were, mashed together in this stew-pot of domesticity, with all the most unlovely aspects of things forced continually upon their attention. Each was in some way a handicap and a torment to the other--a means which fate used to limit and crush and destroy the other; and as ever, they had in their hours of anguish no recourse save to sit down and reason it out together, and absolve each other from blame.

Thyrsis invented a phrase whereby he might make this point clear to Corydon, and keep it in her thoughts. The phrase was "the economic screw"; it pressed upon him, and through him it crushed her. All things that he sought to be and could not be, all things that he would not be and was; all that was hard and unloving in him--his irritability and impatience, his narrowness and bitterness--in all this he showed her that cruel force that was destroying them both.

It was a hard role for Thyrsis, to be the judge and the jury and the executioner of the stern will of this "economic screw". There was, for instance, the episode of the "turkey-red table-cover", which became a classic in their later lives. Corydon was always chafing at the bareness of their little home; and going into the shops in the town, and discovering things which might have made it lovely. One evil day she went alone; and when she came back, Thyrsis, as usual, pounced upon his mail, and came upon a letter from a magazine-editor whom he had been trying to please with an article, and who now scolded him mercilessly for his obstinacy and his egotism and his didacticism, and all his other unpublishable qualities. Then came the unwrapping of the bundles, and Corydon's guileless and joyful announcement that she had come upon a wonderful bargain in the dry-goods store, a beautiful piece of "turkey-red" cloth which would serve as the table-cover for which her soul had been pining--and which she had obtained for the incredibly small sum of thirty cents!

Whereupon, of course, Thyrsis began to exclaim in dismay. Thirty cents was a third of all they had to live upon for a day! And to pay it for a fool piece of rag for which they had no earthly need! So Corydon sank down in the middle of the floor and dissolved in floods of tears; and at the next trip into town the "turkey-red table-cover" was returned, and over the bare board table there were new expositions of the theory of the "economic screw"!

To these arguments Corydon would listen and assent. With her intellect she was at one with him, and she strove to make this intellect supreme. But always, deep underneath, was the other side of her being, that had nothing to do with intellect, but was pure primitive impulse--and that pushed and drove in her always, and carried her away the moment that intellect loosened its brake. Corydon was ashamed of this primitive self--she was always repudiating it, always shutting her eyes to it. There was no way to wound her so deeply as to posit its reality and identify it with her.

She was always fighting to make her temperament like Thyrsis'; she despised her own temperament utterly, and set up his qualities as her ideal. He was self-contained and masterful; he knew what he wanted and how to get it; he was not dependent upon anyone else, he needed no one's approval or admiration; he could control his emotions, and destroy those that inconvenienced him. So Corydon must be these things also; she *was* these things, and no one must gainsay it! And if ever she had felt or wished or said or done anything else--that was all misunderstanding or delusion or accident; she would repudiate it with grief and indignation, and proclaim herself the creature of pure reason that every person ought to be!

But then would come something that appealed to her emotions--to her love of beauty, her craving for joy; and there in a flash was the primitive self again. The task of compelling Corydon to economy reminded her husband of a toy which had been popular in his childhood days. The name of it was "Pigs in Clover"; there were five little balls which you had to coax into a narrow entrance, and while you were getting the last one in, the other four were almost certain to roll out. It was a labor of hours to get Corydon to recognize an unpleasant fact; and then--the next day she had forgotten it. There were some things about himself and his life that he could never get her to understand; for instance, his preoccupation with the newspaper--that symbol of all that was hateful in life. Just then was the beginning of the Russian revolution; and to Thyrsis the Russian revolution was like the coming of relief to a shipwrecked mariner. It was a personal thing to him--the overthrow of a horror that pressed upon the life of every human being upon earth. And so each day he hungered for the news, and when the paper came he would pounce upon it.

"Now dearest," he would say, "please don't disturb me. I want to read."

"All right," she would answer; and five minutes would pass.

Then--"Do you want potatoes for supper, Thyrsis?"

"Yes, dear. But I'm reading now."

"All right." And then another five minutes.

"Thyrsis, who was Boadicea?"

"I'm reading now, dearest."

"Oh yes." And then another five minutes.

"Thyrsis, do you spell choke with an a?"

At which Thyrsis would put down the paper. "Tell me, Corydon--isn't there something I can do so that you won't interrupt me?"

Instantly a look of pain would sweep across her face. "Do you have to speak to me like that, Thyrsis? If you'd only just tell me, kindly and pleasantly--"

"But I've told you three or four times!'

"Thyrsis! How can you say that?"

"But didn't I?"

"Why, of course not!"

And then they would have an argument. He would bring up each case and confront her with it; and how very unloving a procedure was that--and how exasperating was his manner as he did it!

Section 13. Then again, Corydon would be going into town to do some shopping; and he would ask her to bring out the afternoon paper. It would be the day of the October massacre, for instance; and he be on fire for the next batch of news. He would explain this to her; he would tell her again and again--whatever else she forgot, she must remember the afternoon paper. He would walk out to meet her, burning with impatience; and he would ask for the paper, and see a blank look come over her face.

Then, of course, he would scold. He had certain phrases--"How perfectly unspeakable! Perfectly paralyzing!" How she hated these phrases!

"I had so many things to get!" she would exclaim.

"But only one thing for me, Corydon!"

"Everything is for you--just as much as for myself! All these groceries--look at the bundles! I haven't had a single moment--"

"But how many moments does it take to buy a newspaper?"

"But Thyrsis--"

"And how many times would I have to tell you? Have I got to go into town myself, just for the sake of a newspaper?"

"I tell you I tried my very best to remember it--"

"But what's the matter with you? Is your mind getting weak?"

And then like as not Corydon would burst into tears. "Oh, I think you are a brute!" she would cry. "A perfect brute!"

Or else, perhaps, she would grow angry, and they would rail at each other, exchanging recriminations.

"I think I have burdens enough in my life," he would exclaim. "I've a right to some help from you."

"You have no sense of proportion!" she would answer. "You are impossible! You would drive any saint to distraction."

"Perhaps so. But I can't drive you anywhere, and I'm sick of trying."

"Oh, if you only weren't such a talker! You talk--talk--talk!"

And all the while they did this, what grief was in the depths of them! And afterwards, what ghastly wounds in Corydon's soul, that had to be bound up and tended and healed! The pity of it; the shame of it--that they should be able to descend to such sordidness! That their love, which they had planned as a noble temple, should turn out an ugly hovel!

"Oh Thyrsis!" the girl would cry. "The idea that you should think less of my soul than of an old newspaper!"

"But that is not so, dearest," he would answer. He would try to explain to her how much the newspaper had meant to him, and just why his annoyance had got the better of him. So they would rehearse the scene over again; and like as not their irritation would sweep over them, and before they realized it they would find themselves disputing once more.

Thyrsis would be making a desperate attempt to bring her to a realization of his difficulties; he would be in the midst of pouring out some eloquence, when she would interrupt him.

"But Thyrsis, wait a moment--you do not understand!"

"I am speaking!" he would say.

"But, Thyrsis--"

"I am speaking!" He would not be interrupted.

But then would come a time when they sat down together and talked all this out, perceiving it as one more aspect of the disharmony of their temperaments. It no fault of either of them, they would agree; it was just that they were different. Thyrsis had a simile that he used--"It's a marriage between a butterfly and a hippopotamus. You don't blame the butterfly because it can't get down into the water and snort; and on the other hand, when the hippopotamus tries to flap his wings and flit about among the flowers, he doesn't make a success of it."

There would be times when he took Corydon's point of view entirely. She was beautiful and good; her naivete and guilelessness were the essence of her charm and how preposterous it was to expect her to think about newspapers, or to be familiar with the price of beefsteaks! As for him--he was a blundering creature, dull and pragmatical; he was a great spiny monster that she had drawn up from the ocean-depths. She would cut off his spines, but at once they grew out again; she could do nothing with him at all!

But then she would protest--"It's not so bad as that, Thyrsis. You have your work."

"Yes, that's it," he would answer. "My work! I'm just a thinking-machine. I'm fit for nothing else. And here I am--married!"

He would say that, and he would mean it; he would try to act upon the conviction. Of course Corydon's nature was a thing more lovely than his; and, of course, it ought to have its way, to grow in freedom and joy. But alas--there was "the economic screw"! His qualities--hateful though they might be--were the product of stern conditions; they were the qualities which had to dominate in their lives, if they were to survive in the grim struggle for life.

Section 14. It was, as always, their tragedy that they had no means of communicating, except through suffering; they had no work, and they had no art, and they had no religion. To Thyrsis it seemed that this last was the supreme need of their lives; but it was quite in vain that he tried to supply it. He had no theologies to offer, but he had a rough working faith that served his needs. He had a way of prayer--informal prayers, to the undiscovered gods--"Oh infinite Holiness of life, I seek to be reminded of Thee!" He would contemplate their failures and agonies and despairs, and floods of pity would well up in him; and then he would come back to Corydon, seeking to make these things real to her. But this he could never do--he could never carry her with him, he could never find anything with her but failure and disappointment.

This was, in part, the outrage that the creed-mongers had done to her; with their dead formulas and their grotesque legends and their stupid bigotries they had sullied and defaced all the symbols of religion--they had made a noble temple into a sepulchre of dead bones. They had taken her by force, when she was a child, and dragged her into it, and filled her with terror and loathing. To abandon the language of metaphor, they had sent her to a Protestant-Episcopal Sunday-school, where a vinegary spinster had taught her the catechism and the ten commandments. And so forever after the whole content of Christianity was a thing alien and hateful to her.

But also, in their disharmony was something even more fundamental. Corydon's emotions did not come in the same way as her husband's. With her a joy had to be a spontaneous thing; there could be no reasoning about it, and it was not the product nor the occasion of any act of will. In fact, if anyone were to say to Corydon, "Come, let us experience a certain emotion"--then straightway it would become certain that she might experience any emotion in the world, save only that one.

Thyrsis told himself that he was to blame for this having destroyed her spontaneity in the very beginning But how was he to have known that, understanding as he did no temperament but his own, being powerless to handle any tools but his own? The process of his soul's life was to tell himself all his vices over; and so he would become filled with hatred of himself, and would forthwith evolve into something different. But with Corydon, this method produced, not rage and resolution, but only black despair. The process of Corydon's soul-life was that some one else should come to her, and tell her that she was radiant and exquisite; and straightway she would become these things, and yet more of them; and until such a person came to her, all her soul's life stood still.

This was illustrated whenever there was any misunderstanding between them, any crisis of unhappiness or fit of melancholia. It was quite in vain at such times that Thyrsis would ask her to sweep these things aside and forget them; it was disastrous to suggest that she put any blame upon herself, or scold herself into a different at-titude. He might take days to make up his mind to do what he had to do--yet that fit of misery would last until he had come and done it. He had to put his arms about her, and make her realize that she was precious to him, that she was necessary to him, that he loved her and appreciated her and believed in her; so, and so only, would the current of her life begin once more to flow.

And why could he not do this more quickly? Why did he have to wait until she had suffered agonies? Why did he have to be dragged to it by the hair of his head, as it were--as a means of keeping her from going insane from misery? Was it that he did not really love her? Mocking voices in his soul told him that was it--but he knew it was not so. He loved her; but he loved her in his way, and that was not her way. And how shall one explain that strange impulse in the heart of man, that makes it impossible for him to be content with anything that is upon the earth--that makes him restless in the presence of beauty and love and joy, and all those things with which he so obviously ought to be content?

It is so clearly irrational and unjustifiable; and yet that impulse continues to drive him forth, as it drove him to destroy the statues in the Athenian temples, and to burn the silken robes and the jewelled treasures in the public-squares of Venice. One contemplates the thing in its most unlovely aspects--in the form of Simeon Stylites upon his pillar, devoured by worms, or of Bernard Gui, with his racks and his thumb-screws and his "secular arm"--and it seems the very culmination of all human madness and horror. And yet, it does not cease to come; and he upon whom it seizes may not free himself by any power of his will, by any cunning of his wit; and no agony of yearning and grief may be sufficient to enable him to love a woman as a woman desires to be loved.

Section 15. Thyrsis would work over the book until he was utterly exhausted; and then, limp as a rag, he would come back to the world of reality and face these complications. He needed to rest, he needed to be soothed and comforted and sung to sleep; he needed to receive--and instead he had to give. Sometimes he wondered vaguely if this might not have been otherwise; he knew nothing about women--but surely there might have been, somewhere in the world, some woman who would have understood, and would have asked nothing from him. But he dwelt on that thought but seldom, for it seemed a kind of treason; he was not married to any such hypothetical woman--he was married to Corydon, and it was Corydon he had to save from the wolves.

So, time after time, he would come back to her, and take the cup of her pain in his trembling hands, and put it to his lips and drain it to the dregs. He would sit with her, and hear the tale of her struggles, he would fan the sparks of his exhausted emotions into flame, so that she might warm herself by the glow. And when the burden became too great for him, when the black floods of anguish and despair which she poured out upon him threatened to engulf him altogether--then he would tramp away into the forest, or out upon the snow-encrusted hills, and call up the demons of his soul once more, and proclaim himself unconquered and unconquerable. He would spread his wings to the glory of his vision; he would feel again the surge and sweep of it, he would sing aloud with the power of it, and pledge himself anew to live for it--if need be even to die for it.

The world was trying to crush it in him; the world hated it and feared it, and was bound that it should not live; and Thyrsis had sworn to save it--and so the issue was joined. He would hearten himself for the struggle--he would fling himself into the thick of it, again and again; he would summon up that thing which he called his Genius, that fountain of endless force that boiled up within him. Whatever strength they brought against him, he could match it; he might be knocked down, trampled upon, left for dead upon the field, but he could rise and renew the conflict! He would talk to himself, he would call aloud to himself, he would repeat to himself formulas of exhortation, cries of defiance, proclamations of resolve. He would summon his enemies before him, sometimes in hosts, sometimes as individuals--all those who ever in his life had mocked and taunted him, scolded him and threatened him. He would shake his clenched fists at them; they might as well understand it--they could never conquer him, not all the power they could bring would suffice! He would call upon posterity also; he would summon his friends and lovers of the future, to give him comfort in his sore distress. Was it not for them that he was laboring--that they might some day feed their souls upon his faith?

Thyrsis would think of the "Song of Roland", recalling that heroic figure and his three days' labor: when he had read that poem, his heart had seemed to throb with pain every time that Roland lifted his sword-arm. He would think of the old blind "Samson Agonistes"; he would think of the Greeks at Thermopylae, of the siege of Haarlem. History was full of such tales of the agonies that men had endured for the sake of their faith; and why should he expect exemption, why should he shrink from the fiery test?

Section 16. So he lived and fought two battles, one within and one without; and little by little these two became merged in his imagination. He had conceived a figure which should embody the War; and that figure had come to be himself.

The War of which he was writing had come upon a people unsuspecting and unprepared; they had not sought it nor desired it, they did not love it, they did not understand it. But the nation must be preserved; and so they set out to forge themselves into a sword. They had wealth, and they poured it out lavishly; and they had enthusiasm--whole armies of young men came forward. They were uniformed and armed and drilled and one after another they marched out, with banners waving, and drums rolling, and hearts beating high with hope; and one after another they met the enemy, and were swallowed up in carnage and destruction, and came reeling back in defeat and despair. It happened so often that the whole land moaned with the horror of it--there was Bull Run and then again Bull Run, and there was the long Peninsula Campaign--an entire year of futility and failure; and there was the ghastly slaughter of Fredericksburg, and the blind confusion of Chancellorsville, and the bitter, disappointment of Antietam.

Thyrsis wished to portray all this from the point of view of the humble private, who got none of the glory, and expected none, but only suffering and toil; whose lot it was to march and countermarch, to delve and sweat in the trenches, to be stifled by the heat and drenched by the rain and frozen by the cold; to wade through seas of blood and anguish, to be wounded and captured and imprisoned, to be lured by victory and blasted by defeat. And into it all he was pouring the distillation of his own experiences. For there was not much of it that he had not known in his own person. Surely he had known what it was to be cold and hungry; surely he had known what it was to be lured by victory and blasted by defeat. He had watched by the death-bed of his dearest dreams, he had listened to the moaning of multitudes of imprisoned hopes. He had known what it was to set before him a purpose, and to cling to it in spite of obloquy and hatred; he had known what it was to suffer until his forehead throbbed, and all things reeled and swam before his eyes. He had known also what it was to sacrifice for the sake of the future, and to see others, who thought of no one but themselves, preying upon him, and upon the community, and living in luxury and enjoying power.

Little by little, as he studied this War, Thyrsis had come upon a strange and sinister fact about it. Roughly speaking, the population of the country might have been divided into two classes. There were those to whom the Union was precious, and who gave their labor and their lives for it; they starved and fought and agonized for it, and came home, worn, often crippled, and always poor. On the other hand there were some who had cared nothing for the Union, but were finding their chance to grow rich and to establish themselves in the places of power. They were selling shoddy blankets and paper shoes to the government; they were speculating in cotton and gold and food. There were a few exceptions to this, of course; but for the most part, when one came to study the gigantic fortunes which were corrupting the nation, he discovered that it was just here they had begun.

So this was the curious and ironic fact; the nation had been saved--but only to be handed over to the money-changers! And these now possessed it and dominated it; and a new generation had come forward, which knew not how these things had come to be--which knew only the money-changers and their power. And who was there to tell them of the War, and all that the War had meant? Who was there to make that titan agony real to them, to point them to the high destinies of the Republic?

Along with his war-books, Thyrsis was reading his daily newspaper, which came to him freighted with the cynicism of the hour. It was when the revelations of corruption in business and political affairs were at their flood; high and low, in towns and cities, in states and in the nation itself, one saw that the government of the country had been bought. Everywhere throughout the land Mammon sat upon the throne, and men cringed before him--there was only persecution and mockery for those who believed in the things for which America stood to all the world.

And this new Lord, who had purchased the people, and held them in bond, was extracting a toll of suffering and privation, of accident and disease and death, that was worse than the agony of many wars. The whole land was groaning and sweating beneath the burden of it; and Thyrsis, who shared the pain, and knew the meaning of it, was sick with the responsibility it put upon him, yearning for a thousand voices with which he might cry the truth aloud.

Some one must bring America face to face with its soul again; and who was there to do it--who was there that was even trying? Thyrsis had seen the statues of St. Gaudens, and he knew there was one man who had dreamed the dream of his country. But who was there to put it into song, or into story, that the young might read? Like the newspapers and the churches, the authors had sold out; they were writing for matinee-girls, and for the Pullman-car book-trade; and meantime the civilization of America was sliding down into the pit!

So here again was War! Here again were pain and sickness, hunger and cold, solitude and despair, to be endured and defied; death itself to be faced--madness even, and soul-decay! Armies of men had gone out, had laid themselves down and filled up the ditches with their bodies, to make a bridge for Freedom to pass on. And the ditches were not yet full--another life was needed!

Nor must he think himself too good for the sacrifice; there had been greater men than he, no doubt, burned up in the Wilderness, and blown to pieces by the cannon at "Bloody Angle"; there had been dreamers of mighty dreams among them--and they were dead, and all their dreams were dead. And neither must he love his own too dearly; there had been women who had suffered and died in that War, and babes who had perished by tens of thousands; and they, too, had been born with agony, had been loved and yearned for, and wept and prayed for.

So, out of the dead past, were voices calling to Thyrsis; he heard them in the night--time as one mighty symphony of grief. They had died for nothing, unless the Republic should be saved, unless their dream of freedom and justice could be made real. And for what was the poet but that? So that the new generations might know what their fathers had done--that the youth of America might be roused and thrilled once more! Surely it could not be that the land was all sunk in selfishness and unfaith--that there were no longer any generous souls who could be stirred by a trumpet-call, and led forth to strike a new blow for the great hope of Humanity!

Section 17. The long winter dragged by, and the fury of it seemed to increase; they were as if besieged by demons of cold and storm. There came another blizzard, and the snows drifted down to their hollow by the edge of the woods, so that it was two days before they could get out, even to the farm-house. And there was no place for them to walk--a path from their house to Thyrsis' study was a labor of half a day to dig. Also Corydon caught a cold, which ran in due course through the little family, and added to their misery and discomfort.

The snow seemed to be symbolical, walling them in from all the world. "There is no help", it seemed to say to them; whatever strength they got they must wring out of their own hearts. Here in this place, it seemed to Thyrsis, he learned the real meaning of Winter; he saw it as primitive man had seen it, a cruel and merciless assailant, a fiend that came ravening, dealing destruction and death. He thought of the ode by Thomas Campbell--

> "Archangel! Power of desolation!
>   Fast descending as thou art,
>   Say, hath mortal invocation
>   Spells to touch thy stony heart?"

Surely no Runic Odin, who "howled his war-song to the gale", no Lapland savage who cowered in his hut, ever panted for the respite of the spring-time more than these two lovers in their tiny cottage.

It was evident that Corydon was going down-hill under the strain. She became more and more nervous and wretched, her headaches and her fits of exhaustion were more frequent. Then, too, her old mental trouble, the habit of "thinking things", was plaguing her again-- She would come to Thyrsis with long accounts of her psychological entanglements, and he would patiently unravel the skein. Or sometimes, if he was very tired, he might give some signs of a desire to escape the ordeal; and then he would see a look of terror stealing into Corydon's eyes. So these things were real after all--they were real even to Thyrsis!

One morning he opened his eyes, and looked from his study-window, to find that another heavy snow had fallen; and when he had dressed and gone over to the house, he found Corydon in bed. She complained of a headache, and had had chills during the night, and was now quite evidently feverish. He was alarmed, and after he had made her as comfortable as he could, he dressed the baby and took him upon his shoulder, and made his way with difficulty to the farm-house. He left the baby there, and with a horse and sleigh set out for town. The horse had to walk all the way, and several times the sleigh was upset in the drifts, so that it was two hours before he reached his destination. As the doctor was out upon his rounds, he had to wait a couple of hours more--and then only to learn that the man could not possibly attempt the trip. He had several patients who were dangerously ill, and he had to be on hand.

He sent Thyrsis to another doctor, but this one said exactly the same; and so the boy spent the day wandering about the town. The thought of Corydon's lying there alone, helpless and suffering, made him wild; but everywhere he met with the same response--the cold weather had apparently brought an epidemic of disease, and there was no doctor in the place who could spare three or four hours to make the long journey in the snow.

So there was nothing for him to do but go back. The farmer's wife offered to take care of the baby over night, and he went down to the cottage alone where he found Corydon much worse. He sat and held her hand, a terror clutching at his heart; and all night long he sat and tended her--he filled hot water bottles when she was chilled, and got ice when she was hot, and made cool lemonade, and prepared tidbits and tempted her to eat. He would whisper to her and soothe her; and later, when she fell into a doze, he sat nodding in his chair and shivering with cold, but afraid to touch the fire for fear of disturbing her.

Then, towards dawn, she wakened; and Thyrsis was almost beside himself with anguish and fear--for she was delirious, and did not know where she was, or what she was doing. She kept talking as if to the baby--in their baby-talk. Thyrsis would listen, until he would choke up with tears.

He left her, and went up to the farm, and got the horse and sleigh again, and drove to another town. It made no difference what doctor he got--to Thyrsis all doctors were alike, the keepers of the keys of health. After several hours' pursuit he found that this man also was busy. All he could say was that he would try to get out that night.

So Thyrsis went back again, to find his wife with flushed face, and beads of perspiration upon her forehead; now sitting up and babbling aimlessly, now sinking back exhausted. He sat once more through a night of torment, holding her hot hands in his, and praying in vain for the coming of the doctor.

It was afternoon of the next day before the man finally came, and brought some relief to Thyrsis' soul, and perhaps also to Corydon's body. He took her temperature and listened to her breathing, and pronounced it a severe attack of grippe, with a touch of bronchitis; and he laid out an assortment of capsules and liquids, and promised to come again if Thyrsis sent for him.

And so the boy set out in the double role of trained nurse and mother's assistant. He gave Corydon her medicines, and brought fresh water for her, and smoothed her pillows and talked to her, and prepared some delicacies for her when she wished to eat; also he dressed and bathed the baby, and cooked his complex meals and fed them to him; he put on his rubbers and his leggings and his mittens, and the overcoat and peaked hood (which Corydon had devised for him out of eighty cents' worth of woolly red cloth), and turned him out to "bongie cowtoos" in the snow. Likewise he got his own meals and washed the dishes, and tended the fires and emptied the ashes and filled the lamps and swept the floors; and in the interim between these various duties he fought new battles within himself, and got new side-lights upon Chickamauga and "Bloody Angle".

Section 18. It was two weeks before this siege was lifted, and Corydon was able to take up her burdens once more. It was then March, and the snow had given place to cold sleety rains, and the fields and the ground about their home were miniature swamps full of mud. Thyrsis would tramp through this to the hill-tops where the storm-winds howled, and there vow defiance to his foes, and come home to pour new hope and courage and resolution into a bottomless pit.

He was finishing his vision of the field of Gettysburg--the three-days' grapple between two titan armies, that meant to him three weeks of soul-terrifying toil. Men had said that Gettysburg meant the turning Of the tide, that victory was certain; and yet there had followed Sherman's long campaign, and all the horror of the Wilderness fighting, and Mine Run and Cold Harbor and the ghastly siege of Petersburg. And now Thyrsis had to fight his way through this. He saw the figure that he had dreamed, and that possessed him; a soldier who was the rage of the War incarnate, the awakened frenzy of the nation. He was a man lifted above pain and cold and hunger; he was gaunt and wild of aspect, restless and impatient, driving, driving to the end. He went about the duties of the camp like one in a dream; he marched like an automaton--for hours, or for days, as need might be--his thoughts flying on to those moments that alone were real to him, to the charge and the fury of the conflict, the blows that were the only things that counted. He lived amid sights and sounds of horror, with groans and weeping in his ears, with a mist of blood and cannon-smoke before his eyes; he drove on, grim and implacable, the very ground about him rocking and quivering in a delirium of torment. He was the War!

Meantime Corydon was growing paler, and more wretched than ever. For her, too, this winter was symbolized as a battle-ground. To him it was a field in which armies clashed, and the issue was uncertain; but to her it was a field of inevitable defeat, strewn with the corpses of her hopes. For hours she would lie upon her couch in the night-watches, silent, alone, staring out of the window at the wide waste of snow in the pitiless moonlight.

Thyrsis would have preferred to sleep in his own study, as he worked so late at night; but Corydon begged him not to do this, she would rather be wakened, she said.

So, on one occasion, he came over at about two o'clock in the morning, and found her sleeping, as he thought, and crawled into his own cot. He was just dozing off to sleep, when he heard what he thought was a stifled sob.

He listened; he thought that she was crying in her sleep. But then, as the sound grew clearer, he sat up. The moonlight was shining in upon her, and Thyrsis caught a bright glint of steel. Swift as a flash the meaning of that swept over him. He had provided her with a revolver, that she might feel safe when she was left alone; and now he bounded out of bed and sprang across the room, and found her with the weapon pointed at her head.

He struck it away; and Corydon, with a terrified cry, clutched at him and collapsed in his arms.

"Oh Thyrsis!" she wailed. "Save me! Save me!"

"What is it?" he gasped.

"I couldn't do it!" she cried, choking. "I couldn't! I tried--I tried so hard!"

"Sweetheart", he whispered, in terror.

"Don't let me do it!" she sobbed. "Oh, Thyrsis, you must save me!"

He pressed her to his bosom, shuddering with dread, and trying to soothe her hysterical outburst. So, little by little, he dragged the story from her. For three days she had been making up her mind to shoot herself, and she had chosen that night for the time.

"I've been sitting here for an hour," she whispered--"with the revolver in my hand. And I couldn't get up the courage to pull the trigger."

He clasped her, white with horror.

"I heard you coming," she went on. "I lay and pretended to sleep. Then I tried again--but I can't, I can't! I'm a coward!"

"Corydon!" he cried.

"There was only one thing that stopped me. You would have got on without me--"

"Don't say that, dearest!"

"You would--I know it! I'm only in your way. But oh, my baby! I loved him so, and I couldn't bear to leave him!"

She clung to him convulsively. "Oh, Thyrsis," she panted, "think what it meant to me to leave him. He'd have been without a mother all his life! And something might have happened to you, and he'd have had no one to love him at all!"

"Why did you want to do it?" he cried.

"Oh Thyrsis, I've suffered so! I'm weary--I'm worn out--I'm sick of the fight. I can't stand it any more--and what can I do?"

"My poor, poor girl," he whispered, and pressed her to his heart in a paroxysm of grief. "Oh, my Corydon! My Corydon!"

The horror of the thing overwhelmed him; he began to weep himself--his frame was shaken with tearless, agonizing sobs. What could he do for her, how could he help her?

But already he had helped her; it was not often that she saw him weeping, it was not often she found that she could do something for *him*. "Thyrsis, do you really *want* me?" she whispered. "Do you truly love me that much?"

"I love you, I love you!" he sobbed.

And she replied, "Then I'll stay. I'll bear anything, if you need me--if I can be of any use at all."

Section 19. So their tears were mingled; so once more, being sufficiently plowed up with agony, they might behold the deeps of each other's souls. Being at their last gasp, and driven to desperation, they would make the convulsive effort, and break the crust of dullness and commonplace, and reveal again the mighty forces hidden in their depths. At such hours he beheld Corydon as she was, the flaming spirit, the archangel prisoned in the flesh. If only he could have found the key to those deep chambers, so that he could have had access to them always!

But alas, they knew only one path that led to them, and that through the valley of despair. From despair it led to anguished struggle, and from struggle to defiance, to rage and denunciation--and thence to visions and invocations, raptures and enthralments. So this night, for instance, behold Corydon, first holding her husband's hands, and shuddering with awe, and pledging her faith all over again; and then, later on, when the dawn was breaking, sitting in the cold moonlight with a blanket flung about her, her wild hair tossing, and in her hand the revolver with which she had meant to destroy herself. Behold her, making sport of her own life-drama--turning into wildest phantasy her domestic ignominies, her inhibitions and her helpmate's blunderings; evoking the hosts of the future as to a festival, rehearsing the tragedy of her soul with all posterity as her audience. When once these mad steeds of her fancy were turned loose, one could never tell where their course would be; and strange indeed were the adventures that came to him who rode with her!

There seemed to be no limit to the powers of this subliminal woman within Corydon. Her cheeks would kindle, her eyes would blaze, and eloquence would pour from her--the language of great poetry, fervid and passionate, with swift flashes of insight and illumination, tumultuous invocations and bursts of prophecy. Thyrsis would listen and marvel. What a mind she had--sharp, like a rapier, swift as the lightning-flash! The powers of penetration and understanding, and above all the sheer splendors of language--the blazes of metaphor, the explosions of coruscating wit! What a tragic actress she might have made--how she would have shaken men's souls, and set them to shuddering with terror! What an opera-singer she could have been, with that rich vibrant voice, and the mien of a disinherited goddess!

It was out of such hours that the faith of their lives was made; and it was out of them also that Thyrsis formed his idea of woman. To him woman was an equal; and this he not only said with his lips, he lived it in his feelings. The time came when he went out into the world, and learned to understand the world's idea, that woman meant vanity and pettiness and frivolity; but Thyrsis let all this pass, knowing the woman-soul. Somewhere underneath, not yet understood and mastered, was pent this mighty force that in the end would revolutionize all human ideas and institutions. Here was faith, here was vision, here was the power of all powers; and how was it to be delivered and made conscious, and brought into the service of life?

Most women liked Thyrsis, because they divined in some vague way this attitude; and some men hated him for the same reason. These men, Thyrsis observed, were the slave-drivers; they held that woman was the weaker vessel, and for this they had their own motives. There were women, too, who liked to be ruled; but Thyrsis never argued with them--it was enough, he judged, to treat any slave as a free man, or any servant as a gentleman, and sooner or later they would divine what he meant, and the spirit of revolt would begin to flicker.

BOOK XIII
THE MASTERS OF THE SNARE

They stood upon the porch of the little cabin, listening to the silence of the night.

"How far away it all seems!" she said--

"How many a dingle on the loved hill-side
    Hath since our day put by
The coronals of that forgotten time!"

"It makes one feel old," he said--"like the coming of the night!"
"The night!" she repeated, and went on--

"I feel her finger light
Laid pausefully upon life's headlong train;--
    The foot less prompt to meet the morning dew,
    The heart less bounding at emotion new,
And hope once crush'd less quick to spring again!"_

Section 1. Throughout this long winter of discontent came to them one ray of hope from the outside world. "The Genius" was given in the little town in Germany, and Thyrsis' correspondent sent the twenty-five dollars, and wrote that it had made a great impression, and that more performances were to be expected. Then, after an interval, Thyrsis was surprised to receive from his clipping-bureau some items to the effect that his play was to be produced in one of the leading theatres in Berlin. He wrote to his correspondent for an explanation, and learned to his dismay that his play had been "pirated"; it was, of course, not copyright in Germany, and so he had no redress, and must content himself with what his friend referred to as "the renowns which will be brought to you by these performances".

The play came out, in the early spring, and apparently made a considerable sensation. Thyrsis read long reviews from the German papers, and there were accounts of it in several American papers. So people began to ask who this unknown poet might be. The publishers of "The Hearer of Truth" were moved to venture new advertisements of the book--whereby they sold perhaps a hundred copies more; and Thyrsis was moved to pay some badly--needed money to have more copies of the play made, so that he might try to interest some other manager. He carried on a long correspondence with a newly-organized "stage society", which thought a great deal about trying the play at a matinee, but did nothing.

Also, Thyrsis received a letter from one of the country's popular novelists, who had heard of the play abroad, and asked to read it. When he had read it and told what an interesting piece of work it was, Thyrsis sat down and wrote the great man about his plight, and asked for help; which led to correspondence, and to the passing round of the manuscript among a group of literary people. One of these was Haddon Channing, the critic and essayist, who was interested enough to write Thyrsis several long letters, and to read the rest of his productions, and later on to call to see him. Which, visit proved a curious experience for the family.

He arrived one day towards spring, when it chanced that Corydon was in town visiting the dentist. Thyrsis had just finished his dinner when he saw two people coming through the orchard, and he leaped up in haste to put the soiled dishes away, and make the place as presentable as possible. Mr. and Mrs. Channing had come in their car (they lived in Philadelphia), and were followed by an escort of the farmer's children--since an automobile was a rare phenomenon in that neighborhood. The entrance to the peach-orchard proved not wide enough for the machine, so they had to get out and walk; and this they found annoying, because the ground was wet and soft. All of which seemed to emphasize the incongruity of their presence.

Haddon Channing might have been described as a dilettante radical. He employed a highly-wrought and artificial style, which scintillated with brilliant epigram; one had a feeling that it rather atoned for the evils in human life, that they became the occasion of so much cleverness in Channing's books. Perhaps that was the reason why most people did not object to the vagueness of his ideas, when it came to any constructive suggestion. In fact he rather made a point of such vagueness--when you tried to do anything about a social evil, that was politics, and politics were vulgar. One could never pin Channing down, but his idea seemed to be that in the end all men would become free and independent spirits, able to make their own epigrams; after which there would be no more evil in the world.

And here he was in the flesh. It seemed to Thyrsis as if he must have made a study of his own books, and then proceeded to fit his person and his clothing, his accent and his manner, to make a proper setting thereto. He was tall and lean, immaculate and refined; he spoke with airy and fastidious grace, pouring out one continuous stream of cleverness--any hour of his conversation was equivalent to a volume of his works at a dollar and a quarter net.

Also, there was Mrs. Channing, gracious and exquisite, looking as if she had stepped out of one of Rossetti's poems. She was a poetess herself; writing about Acteon, and Antinous, and other remote subjects. Thyrsis assumed that there must be something in these poems, for they were given two or three pages in the thirty-five-cent magazines; but he himself had never discovered any reason why he should read one through.

Section 2. They seated themselves upon his six-foot piazza; and Thyrsis, who had very little sense of personality, and was altogether wrapped up in ideas, was soon in the midst of a free and easy discussion with them. It seemed ages since he had had an opportunity to exchange opinions with anyone except Corydon. With these people he roamed over the fields of literature; and as they found nothing to agree about anywhere, the conversation did not flag.

A strange experience it must have been to them, to come to a lonely shanty in the woods, and encounter a haggard boy, in a cotton-shirt and a pair of frayed trousers, who was all oblivious of their elegance, and unawed by their reputation, and who behaved like a bull in the china-shop of their orderly opinions. Mrs. Channing, it seemed, was completing her life-work, a volume which was to revolutionize current criticism, and lead the world back to artistic health; to her, modern civilization was a vast abortion, and in Greek culture was to be sought the fountain-head of health. She sang the praises of Athenian literature and art and life; there was sanity and clarity, there was balance and serenity! And to compare it with the jangled confusion and the frantic strife of modern times!

To which Thyrsis answered, "We'd best let modern times alone. For here you've all facts and no generalization; and in the case of the Greeks you've all generalization and no facts."

And so they went at it, hot and heavy. Mrs. Channing, her Greek serenity somewhat ruffled, insisted that she had studied the facts for herself. The other proceeded to probe into her equipment, and found that she knew Homer and Sophocles, but did not know Aristophanes so well, and did not know the Greek epigrams at all. Thyrsis maintained that the dominant note in the Greek heritage was one of bewilderment and despair; in support of which alarming opinion he carried the discussion from the dreams of Greek literature to the realities of Greek life. Did Mrs. Channing know how the Greeks had persecuted all their great thinkers?

Did she know anything about the cruelties of their slave-code?

"Have you ever studied Greek politics?" he asked. "Do you realize, for instance, that it was the custom of statesmen and generals who were defeated by their political rivals, to go over to the enemy and lead an expedition against their homes?"

"Isn't that putting it rather strongly?" asked Mrs. Channing.

"I don't think so," he answered. "Didn't the conquerors of both Salamis and Platasa afterwards sell out to the Persian king? And then you talk about the noble ideal of woman which the Greeks developed! Don't you know that it was nothing but a literary tradition?"

"I had never understood that," said Mrs. Channing.

To which the other answered: "It was handed down from imaginary Homeric days. The Greek lady of the Periclean age was a domestic prisoner and drudge."

Section 3. Then, late in the afternoon, came Corydon; and this part of the adventure must have seemed stranger yet to the Channings. Corydon wore a shirt-waist and a ten-cent straw hat, trimmed with some white mosquito-netting, and an old blue skirt which she had worn before her marriage, and had enlarged little by little during the period of her pregnancy, and had taken in again after the baby was born. Also she was pale and sad-looking, much startled by the sight of the automobile, and the sudden apparition of elegance. She got rid of her armfuls of groceries and bundles, and seated herself in an inconspicuous place, and sat listening while the argument went on. For a full hour she never uttered a word; only once during the controversy over the "Greek lady", Mrs. Channing turned to her and asked, "Don't you agree with me?" But Corydon could only answer, "I don't know, I have not read much history." And who was there to tell the visitor that this strange, wide-eyed girl knew more about the tragedies and terrors of the Greek temperament than she with all her culture and her college-degrees could have learned in many life-times?

The two stayed to supper, and Corydon and Thyrsis set out the meal upon the rustic outdoor table; they apologized for their domestic inadequacies, but Mrs. Channing declared that she "adored picknicking". The evening was spent in more discussion; and finally it was decided that the visitors should stay over night at the hotel in town, and come out again in the morning.

Thyrsis concluded, as he thought the matter over, that the two must have been fascinated by this domestic situation, and curious to look deeper into it. Perhaps they saw "material" in it; or perhaps it was that Haddon Channing was really impressed by Thyrsis' powers, and sought to understand his problems and help him. Whatever may have been the motive for it, when they came the next morning, the critic took Thyrsis for a walk in the woods and proceeded to discuss his affairs. And meanwhile his wife had set herself to the task of probing the innermost corners of Corydon's soul.

The burden of Channing's discourse was Thyrsis' impatience and lack of balance, his fanaticism and his too great opinion of his own work. "My dear fellow, he said, "you are the most friendless human being I have ever encountered upon earth. How can you expect to interest men if you don't get out into the world and learn what they are doing?"

"That means to get a position, I suppose?" said Thyrsis.

"No, not necessarily--" began the other.

"But I haven't money to live in the city otherwise."

That was too definite for Channing, and he went off on another tack. He had been reading "The Higher Cannibalism", and he could not forgive it. A boy of Thyrsis' age had no right to be seething with such bitterness; there must be some fundamental and terrible cause. He was destroying himself, he was eating out his heart in this isolation; he was so wrapped up in his own miseries, his own wrongs--in all the concerns of his own exaggerated ego!

They were seated beside a little streamlet in the woods. "What you need is something to get you out of yourself," the critic was saying--"something to restore your sanity and balance. It'll come to you some day. Perhaps it'll be a love-affair--you'll meet some woman who'll carry you away. I know the sort you need--they grow in the West--the great brooding type of woman-soul, that would fold you in her arms and give you a little peace."

Thyrsis was silent for a space. "You forget," he said, in a low voice, "that I am already married."

The other shrugged his shoulders. "Such things have happened, even so," he said.

Thyrsis had taken his part in the conversation before this, defending himself and setting forth his point of view. But now he fell silent. The words had cut him to the quick. It seemed to him an insult and a bitter humiliation; here, at his home, almost in the presence of his wife! What was the man's idea, anyway?

And suddenly he turned upon Channing with the question, "You think that I've married a doll?"

The other was staggered for a moment. "I don't know what you've married," he replied.

"No," said Thyrsis. "Then how can you advise me in such a matter?"

"I see that you're not happy--" the other began.

"Yes," said the boy. "But I don't want any more women."

There was a pause, while Thyrsis sat pondering, Should he try to explain to this man? But he shook his head. No, it would be useless to try. "She is not in your class," he said.

"How do you mean?" asked the other.

"She has none of your culture, none of your social graces. She can't write, and she can't sing--she can't do anything that your wife does."

"I'm afraid," said Channing, in a low voice, "you don't take my remarks in the right spirit."

"Even suppose that she were not what you call a 'great woman-soul'," persisted Thyrsis--"at least she has starved and suffered for me; and wouldn't common loyalty bind me to her?"

"I have tried to do something very difficult," said the other, after a silence. "I have tried to talk to you frankly. It is the most thankless task in the world to tell a man his own faults."

"I know," said Thyrsis. "And that's all right--I'm perfectly willing. I don't mind knowing my faults."

"It is evident that you have resented it," declared the other.

Thyrsis answered with a laugh, "Don't you admit of replies to your criticisms? Suppose I'm pointing out some of your faults--your faults as a critic?"

Channing said that he did not object to that.

"Very well, then," said Thyrsis. "I simply tell you that you have missed the point of my trouble. There's nothing the matter with me but poverty and lack of opportunity; and there's nothing else the matter with my wife. We're doing our best, and it's the simple fact that we've endured and dared more than anybody we've ever met. And that's all there is to it."

It was evident that Channing was deeply hurt. He turned the conversation to other matters, and pretty soon they got up and strolled on. When they came near to the house, he went off to see his chauffeur, and Thyrsis stood watching him, and pondering over the episode.

It was the same thing that had happened to him in the city; it was the thing that would be happening to him all the time. He saw that however wretched he might be with Corydon, he would always take her part against the world. Whatever her faults might be, they were not such as the world could judge. Rather would he make it the test of a person's character, that they should understand and appreciate her, in spite of her lack of that superficial thing called culture--the ability to rattle off opinions about any subject under the sun.

So it was that loyalty to Corydon held him fast. So her temperament was his law, and her needs were his standards; and day by day he must become more like her, and less like himself!

Section 4. He returned to the house, entering by the rear door. The baby was lying in the room asleep, and out upon the piazza, he could hear Corydon and Mrs. Channing. Corydon was speaking, in her intense voice.

"The trouble with me," she was saying, "is that I have no confidence! Other women are sure of themselves--they are self-contained, serene, satisfied."

"But why shouldn't you be that way?" Thus Mrs. Channing.

"I aim too high," said Corydon. "I want too much. I defeat myself."

"Yes," said the other, "but why--"

"It's been the circumstances of all my life! I've been defeated--thwarted--repressed! Everything drives me back into myself. There is nothing I can *do*--I can only endure and suffer and wait. So all the influences in my life are negative--

   'I was sick with the Nay of life--   With my lonely soul's refrain!'"

"What is that you are quoting?" asked Mrs. Channing.

"It's from a poem I wrote," said Corydon.

"Oh, you write poetry?"

"I couldn't say that," was the reply. "I have no technique--I never studied anything about it."

"But you try sometimes?"

"I find it helps me," said Corydon--"once in a great while I find lines in my mind; and I put them together, so that I can say them over, and remind myself of things."

"I see," said Mrs. Channing. "Tell me the poem you quoted."

"I--I don't believe you'd think much of it," said Corydon, hesitating. "I never expected anybody--

"I'd be interested to hear it," declared her visitor.

So Corydon recited in a low voice a couple of stanzas which had come to her in the lonely midnight hours. Thyrsis listened with interest--he had never heard them before:

> "What matters the tired heart,
>   What matters the weary brain?
> What matters the cruel smart
>   Of the burden borne again?
>
> I was sick with the Nay of life--
>   With my lonely soul's refrain;
> But the essence of love is strife,
>   And the meaning of life is pain."

There was a pause. "Do you--do you think that is worth while at all?" asked Corydon.

"It is evidently sincere," replied Mrs. Channing. "I think you ought to study and practice."

"I can't make much effort at it--"

But the other went on: "What concerns me is the attitude to life it shows. It is terrible that a young girl should feel that way. You must not let yourself get into such a state!"

"But how can I help it?"

"You must have something that occupies your mind! That is what you need, truly it is! You've got to stop thinking about yourself--you've got to get outside yourself, somehow!"

Thyrsis caught his breath. He could tell from the tone of the speaker's voice that she was laboring with Corydon, putting forth all her energies to impress her. He was tempted to step forward and cry out, "No, no! That's not the way! That won't work!"

But instead, he stood rooted to the spot, while Mrs. Channing went on--"This unhappiness comes from the fact that you are so self-centred. You must get some constructive work, my dear, if it's only training your baby. You must realize that you are not the only person who has troubles in the world. Why, I know a poor washerwoman, who was left a widow with four children to care for--"

And then suddenly Thyrsis heard a voice cry out in anguish, "Oh, oh! stop!" He heard his wife spring up from her chair.

"What's the matter?" asked Mrs. Channing.

"I can't listen to you any more!" cried Corydon. "You don't know what you're saying!--You don't understand me at all!"

There was a pause. "I'm sorry you feel that," said Mrs. Channing.

"I had no right to talk to you!" exclaimed the other. "There's no one can understand! I have to fight alone!"

At this point Thyrsis went into the kitchen, and made some noise that they would hear. Then he called, "Are you there, dearest?"

"Yes," said Corydon; and he went out upon the piazza. He saw her standing, white and tense.

"Are you still talking?" he said, with forced carelessness.

And as Mrs. Channing answered "Yes," Corydon said, quickly, "Excuse me a moment," and went into the house.

So the poet sat and talked with his guest about the state of the weather and the condition of the roads; until at last her husband arrived, saying that it was time they were starting. Corydon did not appear again, and so finally Thyrsis accompanied them out to their car, and saw them start off. They promised to come again, but he knew they would not keep that promise.

Section 5. He went back to the house, and after some search he found Corydon down in the woods, whither she had fled to have out her agony.

"Has that woman gone?" she panted, when he came near.

"Yes, dear," he said. "She's gone."

"Oh!" cried Corydon. "How dared she! How dared she!"

"Get up, sweetheart," said Thyrsis. "The ground is wet."

"She's gone off in her automobile!" exclaimed the girl, passionately. "She spent last night at a hotel that charged twelve dollars a day, and then she told me about her washerwoman! Now she's gone back to her beautiful home, with servants and a governess and a piano and everything else she wants! And she talked to me about 'occupation'! What *right* had she to come here and trample on my face?"

"But why did you let her, dearest?"

"How could I *help* myself? I had no idea--"

"But how did you get started?"

"I've nobody to confide in--nobody!" cried Corydon. "And she wanted to know about me--she led me on. I thought she sympathized with me--I thought she understood!"

"She's a woman of the world, my dear."

"She was just pulling me to pieces! She wanted to see how I worked! Don't you see what she was looking for, Thyrsis--she thought I was *material!*"

"She only writes about the Greeks," said Thyrsis, with a smile.

"I'm a horrible example! I'm neurasthenic and self-centred--I'm the modern woman! She read me a long lecture like that! I ought to get busy!"

"Dearest!" he pleaded, trying to soothe her.

"Busy"! repeated Corydon, laughing hysterically. "Busy! I wash and dress and amuse a baby! I get six meals a day for him, I get three meals for us, and clean up everything. And the rest of the day I'm so exhausted I can hardly stand up, and a good part of the time I'm sick besides. And then, if I think about my troubles, it's because I've nothing to do!"

"My dear," Thyrsis replied, "you should not have put yourself at her mercy."

"How I hate her!" cried Corydon. "How I *hate* her!"

"You must learn to protect yourself from such people, Corydon."

"I won't meet them at all! I'm not able to face them--I've none of their weapons, none of their training. I don't want to know about them, or their kind of life! They have no souls!"

"It isn't easy for them to understand," said Thyrsis. "They have never been poor--"

"That woman talks about the Greek love of beauty! What sacrifice has she ever made for beauty--what agony has she ever dared for it? And yet she can prattle about it--the phrases roll from her! She's been educated--polished--finished! She's been taught just what to say! And I haven't been taught, and so she despises me!"

"It's deeper than that, my dear," he said. "You have something in you that she would hate instinctively."

"What do you mean?"

"I've told you before, dearest. It's genius, I think.

"Genius! But what use is it to me, if it is? It only unfits me for life. It eats me up, it destroys me!"

"Some day," he said, "you will find a way to express it. It will come, never fear.--But now, dear, be sensible. The ground is wet, and if you sit there, you will surely be laid up with rheumatism."

He lifted her up; but she was not to be diverted. Suddenly she turned, and caught him by the arms. "Thyrsis!" she cried. "Tell me! Do you blame me as she does? Do you think I'm weak and incompetent?"

Whatever answer he might have been inclined to make, he saw in her wild eyes that only one answer was to be thought of. "Certainly not, my dear!" he said, quickly. "How could you ask me such a question?"

"Oh, tell me! tell me!" she exclaimed. And so he had to go on, and sing the song of their love to her, and pour out balm upon her wounded spirit.

But afterwards he went alone; and then it was not so simple. Little demons of doubt came and tormented him. Might it not be that there was something in the point of view of the Channings? He took Corydon at her own estimate--at the face value of her emotions; but might it not be that he was deluding himself, that he was a victim of his own infatuation?

He would ponder this; he tried to have it out with himself for once. What did he really think about it? What would he have told Corydon if he had told her the bald truth? But such doubts could not stay with him for long. They brought shame to him. He was like a man travelling across the plains, who comes upon the woman he loves, being tortured by a band of Apaches; and who is caught and bound fast, to watch the proceedings. Would such a man spend his time asking whether the woman was weak and incompetent? No--his energies would be given to getting his arms loose, and finding out where the guns were. He would set her free, and give her a chance; and then it would be time enough to measure her powers and pass judgment upon her.

Section 6. It was a long time before the family got over that visitation. Corydon burned all Channing's books and she wrote a long and indignant letter to Mrs. Channing, and then burned the letter. Thyrsis never told her about his conversation with the husband, for he knew she would never get over that insult. For himself, he concluded that the Channings were lucky in having got into a quarrel with them, as otherwise he would surely have compelled them to lend him some money.

In truth, the advent of some fairy-godmother or Lady Bountiful was badly needed just then. They had struggled desperately to keep within the thirty-dollar limit, but it could no longer be done. Illnesses were expensive luxuries; and there was the typwriting of the book--some twenty dollars so far; also, there were many things that happened when one was running a household--a tooth-ache, or a telegram, or a hot-water bottle that got a hole in it, or a horse that ran away and broke a shaft. Little by little the bills they had been obliged to run up at the grocer's and the butcher's and the doctor's had been getting beyond the limits of their monthly check; and to cap the climax, there came a letter from Henry Darrell, saying that the next two checks would be the last he could possibly send.

So Thyrsis set to work once more at the shell of that tough old oyster, the world. He made out a "scenario" of the rest of his new book, and sent it with the part he had already done to his friend Mr. Ardsley. Then for three weeks he waited in dread suspense; until at last came a letter asking him to call and talk over his proposition.

Mr. Ardsley had been reading all Thyrsis' manuscripts, nor had he failed to note the triumph of "The Genius" abroad. It became at once apparent to Thyrsis that the new book had scored with him; it was a book that could hardly fail, he said--if only it were finished as it had been begun. Thyrsis made it clear that he intended to finish it; no man could gaze into his wild eyes, and hear him talk of it in breathless excitement, without realizing that he would die, if need be, rather than fail.

So then the author went in to have a talk with the head of the firm. He spread out the treasures of his soul before this merchant, and the merchant sat and appraised them with a cold and critical eye. But Thyrsis, too, had learned something about trade by this time, and was watching the merchant; he made a desperate effort and summoned up the courage to state his demands--he wanted five hundred dollars advance, in installments, and he wanted fifteen per cent. royalty upon the book. To his wonder and amazement the merchant never turned a hair at this; and before they parted company, the incredible bargain had been made, and waited only the signing of the contracts!

Thyrsis went out from the building like a blind man who had suddenly received his sight. It seemed to him at that moment as if the last problem of his life had been solved. He sent off a telegram to Corydon to tell her of the victory, and a letter to Darrell, saying that he need send no more money--that the path was clear before his feet at last!

Section 7. This marked a new stage in the family's financial progress; and as usual it was signalized by a grand debauch in bill-paying. Also there was a real table-cover for Corydon, and a vase in which she might put spring-flowers; there were new dresses for the baby, and more important yet, a new addition to the house. This was to be a sort of lean-to at the rear, sixteen feet wide and eight feet deep, and divided into two apartments, one of which was to be the kitchen, and the other an extra bed-room. For they were going to keep a servant!

This was a new decision, to which they had come after much hesitation and discussion. It would be a frightful expense--including the cost of the extra food it would add over thirty dollars a month to their expenses; but it was the only way they could see the least hope of freedom, of any respite from household drudgery. It had been just a year now since they had set out upon their adventure in domesticity; and in that time Corydon figured that she had prepared two thousand meals for the baby. She had fed each one of them, spoonful by spoonful, into his mouth; and also she had washed two thousand spoons and dishes, and brushed off two thousand tables, and swept two thousand floors. And with every day of such drudgery the heights of music and literature seemed further away and more unattainable.

Thyrsis had seen something of servants in earlier days--he had memories of strange figures that during intervals of prosperity had flitted through his mother's home. There had been the frail, anaemic Swedish woman, who lived on tea and sugar, and afterwards had gone away and borne nine children, more frail and anaemic than herself; there had been the stout personage with the Irish brogue who had dropped the Christmas turkey out of the window and had not taken the trouble to go down after it; there had been the little old negress who had gone insane, and hurled the salt-box at his mother's head. But Thyrsis was hoping that they might avoid such troubles themselves; he had an idea that by watching at Castle Garden they might lay hold upon some young peasant-girl from Germany, who would be untouched by any of the corruptions of civilization. "A sort of Dorothea", he suggested to Corydon; and they agreed that they would search diligently and find such a "*treffliches Madchen*", who would be trusting and affectionate, and would talk in German with the baby.

So now he spent several days hunting in strange places; and at last, in a dingy East-side employment-office, he came upon his *Schatz*. She was buxom and hearty, and fairly oozed good-nature at every pore; she had only been a week in the country, and was evidently naive enough for any purpose whatever. She had no golden hair like Dorothea, but was swarthy--her German was complicated with a Hungarian accent, and with strange words that one had not come upon in Goethe and Freitag, and could not find in any dictionary.

Thyrsis helped to gather up her various bags and bundles, and transported her out to the country. On the train he set to work to gain her confidence, and was forthwith entertained with the tale of all her heart-troubles. Back in the Hungarian village she had fallen in love with the son of a rich farmer, quite in Hermann and Dorothea fashion; but alas, in this case there had been no "*gute verstandige Mut-*

ter" and no "*wurdiger Pfarrer*"--instead there had been a hateful step-mother, and so the "*treffliches Madchen*" had had to come away.

They reached the little cottage at last; and then what a house-cleaning there was, what scrubbing of floors; and brushing out the cobwebs, and scouring of lamp-chimneys and scraping of kettles and sauce-pans! And what a relief it was for Corydon and Thyrsis to be able to go off for a walk together, without first having to carry the baby up to the farm-house! And how very poetical it was to come back and discover Dorothea with the baby in her lap, feeding it a supper of *butter-brod* with a slice of raw bacon!

As time went on, alas, it came more and more to seem that the Dorothea idyl had not been meant to be taken as a work of realism. The "*treffliches Maedchen*" was perhaps *too* kind-hearted; her emotions were too voluminous for so small a house, her personality seemed to spread all over it. She would sing Hungarian love-ditties at her work; and somehow calling these "folksongs" did not help matters. Also, alas, she distributed about the house strange odors--of raw onions, boiled cabbage and perspiration. So, after three weeks, poor Dorothea had to be sent away--weeping copiously, and bewildered over this cruel misfortune. Corydon and Thyrsis went back again to washing their own dishes; being glad to pay the price for quietness and privacy, and vowing that they would never again try, to "keep a servant".

Section 8. The spring-time had come; not so much the spring-time of poets and song-birds, as the spring-time of cold rains and wind. But still, little by little, the sun was getting the better of his enemies; and so with infinite caution they reduced the quantity of the baby's apparel, and got him and his "bongie cowtoos" out upon the piazza.

Meantime Thyrsis was over at his own place, wrestling with the book again. He had told himself that it would be easy, now that he was free from the money-terror. But alas, it was not easy, and nothing could make it easy. If he had more energy, it only meant that his vision reached farther, and set him a harder task. Never in his life did he write a book, the last quarter of which was not to him a nightmare labor. He would be staggering, half blind with exhaustion--like a runner at the end of a long race, with a rival close at his heels.

Also, as usual, his stomach was beginning to weaken under the strain. He would come over sometimes, late in the afternoon, and lay his head in Corydon's lap, almost sobbing from weariness; and yet, after he had eaten a little and helped her with the hardest of her tasks, he would go away again, and work half through the night. There was nothing else he could do--there was no escaping from the thing; if he lay down to rest, or went for a walk, it would be only to think about it the whole time. He would feel that he was not getting enough exercise, and he would drive himself to some bodily tasks; but there was never anything that he could do, that he did not have the book eating away at his mind in the meantime. It was one of the calamities of his life that there was no way for him to play; all he could do was to take a stroll with Corydon, or to tramp over the country by himself.

He finished the book in May; and he knew that it was good. He sent it off to Mr. Ardsley, and Mr. Ardsley, too, declared himself satisfied, and sent the balance of the money. So Thyrsis sank back to get his breath, and to put back some flesh upon his skeleton. He was wont to say when he was writing, one could measure his progress upon a scales; every five thousand words he finished cost him a Shylock's price.

This summer was, upon the whole, the happiest time they had yet known. The book was scheduled to appear early in September; and they had money enough to last them meantime, with careful economy. Their little home was beautiful; they planted some sweet peas and roses, and Thyrsis even began to dig at a vegetable-garden. Also, it was strawberry-time, and cherry-time was near; nor did they over-look the fact that they lived in close proximity to a peach-orchard. These, perhaps, were prosaic considerations, and not of the sort which Thyrsis had been accus-tomed to associate with spring-time. But this he hardly realized--so rapidly was the discipline of domesticity bringing his haughty spirit to terms!

He built a rustic seat in the woods, where they might sit and read; he built a table beside the house, where the dishes might be washed under the blue sky; and he perfected an elaborate set of ditches and dykes, so that the rain-storms would not sweep away their milk and butter in the stream. He talked of building a pen for chickens--and might have done so, only he discovered that the perverse crea-tures would not lay except at the time when eggs were cheap and one did not care so much about them. He even figured on the cost of a cow, and the possibility of learning to milk it; and was so much enthralled by these bucolic occupations that he wrote a magazine-article to acquaint his struggling brother and sister poets with the fact that they, too, might escape to the country and live in a home-made house!

With the article there went a picture of the house, and also one of the baby, who had been waxing enormous, and now constituted a fine advertisement. The winter had seemed to agree with him, and the summer agreed with him even better. Thyrsis would smile now and then, thinking of his ideas of martyrdom; it was made evident that one member of the family was not minded for anything of the sort. The parents might become so much absorbed in their soul-problems that they forgot the dinner-hour; but one could have set his watch by the appetite of the baby. Nature had provided him, among other protections, with a truly phenomenal pair of lungs; and whenever life took a course that was not satisfactory to him, he would roar his face to a terrifying purple.

He was one overwhelming and incessant outcry for adventure. He would toddle all day about the place, getting his "mungies" into all sorts of messes. He was hard to fit into so small a place, and there were times when his parents were tempted to wish that some phenomenon a trifle less portentous had fallen to their lot. But for the most part he was a great hope--a sort of visible atonement for their sufferings. He at least was an achievement; he was something they had done. And he could not be undone, nor doubted--he put all skepticism to flight. In his vicinity there was no room for pessimistic philosophies, for **Weltschmerz** or **Karma**.

Thyrsis would sit now and then and watch him at play, and think thoughts that went deep into the meaning of things. Here was, in its very living presence, that blind will-to-be which had seized them and flung them together. And it seemed to Thyrsis that somehow Nature, with her strange secret chemistry, had reproduced all the elements they had brought to that union. This child was immense, volcanic, as their impulse had been; he was intense, highly-strung, and exacting--and these qualities too they had furnished. Curious also it was to observe how Nature, having accomplished her purpose, now flung aside her concealments and devices. From now on they existed to minister to this new life-phenomenon, to keep it happy and prosperous and she cared not how plain this might become to them --she feared not to taunt and humiliate them. And they accepted her sentence meekly, they no longer tried to oppose her. Her will was become an axiom which they never disputed, which they never even discussed. No matter what might happen to them in future, the Child must go on!

Section 9. Thyrsis utilized this summer of leisure to begin a course of reading in Socialism--a subject which had been stretching out its arms to him ever since he had made the acquaintance of Henry Darrell. He had held away from it on purpose, not wishing to complicate his mind with too many problems. But now he had finished with history, and was free to come back to the world of the present.

There were the pamphlets that Darrell had given him, and there was Paret's magazine. Strange to say, the latter's reckless jesting with the philanthropists and reformers no longer offended Thyrsis--he had been travelling fast along the road of disillusionment. Also, there was a Socialist paper in New York--"The Worker"; and more important still, there was the "Appeal to Reason". Thyrsis came upon a chance reference to this paper, which was published in a little town in Kansas, and he was astonished to learn that it claimed a circulation of two hundred thousand copies a week. He became a subscriber, and after that the process of his "conversion" was rapid.

The Appeal was an "agitation-paper". Its business was to show that side of the capitalist process which other publications tried to conceal, or at any rate to gild and dress up and make presentable. Each week came four closely-printed newspaper-pages, picturing horrors in mills and mines, telling of oppression and injustice, of unemployment and misery, accident, disease and death. There would be accounts of political corruption--of the buying of legislatures and courts, of the rule of "machines" of graft in city and state and nation. There would be tales of the manners and morals of the idle rich, set against others of the sufferings of the poor. And week by week, as he read and pondered, Thyrsis began to realize the absurd inadequacy of the placid statement which he had made to his first Socialist acquaintance--that the solution of such problems was to be left to "evolution". It became only too clear to him that here was another war--the class-war; and that it was being fought by the masters with every weapon that cunning and greed could lay hands upon or contrive. In that struggle Thyrsis saw clearly that his place was in the ranks of the disinherited and dispossessed.

This was not a difficult decision; for in the first place he was one of the disinherited and dispossessed himself; and in the next place, even before the "economic screw" had penetrated his consciousness, he had been a rebel in his sympathies and tastes. Jesus, Isaiah, Milton, Shelley--such men as these had been the friends of his soul; and he had sought in vain for their spirit in modern society--he had thought that it was dead, and that he, and a few other lonely dreamers in garrets, were the only ones who knew or cared about it. But now he came upon the amazing discovery that this spirit, driven from legislative-halls and courts of justice, from churches and schools and editorial sanctums, had flamed into life in the hearts of the working class, and was represented in a political party which numbered some thirty millions of adherents and cast some seven million votes!

Beginning nearly a century ago, these workmgmen had taken the spirit of Jesus and Isaiah and Milton and Shelley, and had worked out a scientific basis for it, and a method whereby it could be made to count in the world of affairs. They had analyzed all the evils of modern society--poverty and luxury, social and political corruption, prostitution, crime and war; they had not only discovered the causes of them, but had laid down with mathematical precision the remedies, and had gone on to carry the remedies into effect. In every civilized land upon the globe they were at work as a political party of protest; they were holding conventions and adopting programs; they had an enormous literature, they were publishing newspapers and magazines, many of them having circulations of hundreds of thousands of copies.

The strangest thing of all was this. Thyrsis was an educated man--or was supposed to be. He had spent five years in schools, and nine years in colleges and universities; he had given the scholars of the world full opportunity to guide him to whatever was of importance. Also, he had been an omnivorous reader upon his own impulse; and here he was, at the end of it all--practically ignorant that this enormous movement existed!

In economic classes in college there had, of course, been some mention of Socialism; but this had been of the utopian variety, the dreams of Plato and St. Simon and Fourier. There had been some account of the innumerable communities which had sprung up in America--with careful explanation, however, that they had all proven failures. Also one heard vaguely of Marx and Lassalle, two violent men, whose ideas were still popular among the ignorant masses of Europe, but could be of no concern to the fortunate inhabitants of a free Republic.

And then, after this, to come upon some piece of writing--such as, for instance, the "Communist Manifesto"! To read this mile-stone in the progress of civilization, this marvellous exposition of the development of human societies, and of the forces which drive and control them; and to realize that two lonely students, who had cast in their lot with the exploited toilers, had been able to predict the whole course of political and industrial evolution for sixty years, and to foresee and expound with precision the ultimate outcome of the whole process--matters of which the orthodox economists were still as ignorant as babes unborn!

Or to discover the writings of such a man as Karl Kautsky, the intellectual leader of the modern movement in Germany; such books as "The Social Revolution", and "The Road to Power"--in which one seemed to see a giant of the mind, standing in a death-duel with those forces of night and destruction that still made of the fair earth a hell! With what accuracy he was able to measure the strength of these powers of evil, to anticipate their every move, to plan the exact parry with which to meet them! To Thyrsis he seemed like some general commanding an army in battle, with the hopes of future ages hanging upon his skill. But this was a general who fought, not with sword and fire, but with ideas; a conqueror in the cause of "right reason and the will of God". He wrote simply, as a scientist; and yet one could feel the passion behind the quiet words--the hourly shock of the incessant conflict, the grim persistence which pressed on in the face of obloquy and persecution, the courage which had been tested through generations of anguish and toil.

Thyrsis' mind rushed through these things like prairie-fire; and all the time that he read, his wonder grew upon him. How *could* he have been kept ignorant of them? He was quick to pounce upon the essential fact, that this was no accident; it was something that must have been planned and brought about deliberately. He had thought that he was being educated, when in reality he was being held back and fenced off from truth. It was a world-wide conspiracy--it was that very class-war which the established order was waging upon these men and their ideas!

Section 10. It was not difficult for any one to understand the ideas, if he really wished to. They began with the fact of "surplus value". One man employed another man for the sake of the wealth he could be made to produce, over what he was paid as wages. That seemed obvious enough; and yet, what consequences came from following it up! Throughout human history men had been setting other men to work; whether they were called slaves, or serfs, or laborers, or servants, the motive-power which had set them to work had been the desire for "surplus value".

And as the process went on, those who appropriated the profits combined for mutual protection; and so out of the study of "surplus value" came the discovery of the "class-struggle". Human history was the tale of the arising of some dominating class, and of the struggle of some subject class for a larger share of what it produced. Human governments were devices by which the master-class preserved its power; and whatever may have been the original purposes of arts and religions, in the end they had always been seized by the master-class, and used as aids in the same struggle.

One came to the culmination of the process in modern capitalist society. Here was a class entrenched in power, owning the sources of wealth, the huge machines whereby it was produced, and the railroads whereby it was distributed, and above all, the financial resources upon which the other processes depended. One saw this class holding itself in power by means of the policeman's club and the militiaman's rifle, by machine-gun and battle-ship; one saw that, whether by bribery or by outright force, it had seized all the powers of government, of legislatures and executives and courts. One saw that in the same way it had seized upon the sources of ideas; it controlled the newspapers and the churches and the colleges, that it might shape the thoughts of men and keep them content. It set up in places of authority men whose views were agreeable to it--who believed in the beneficence of its rule and the permanence of its system; who would pour out ridicule and contempt upon those who suggested that any other system might be conceivable. And so the class-war was waged, not merely in the world of industry and politics, but also, in the intellectual world.

And step by step, as the processes of capitalism culminated, this war increased in bitterness and intensity. For, of course, as capital heaped up and its control became concentrated, the ratio of exploitation increased. The great mass of labor was unorganized and helpless; whereas the masters had combined and fixed their prices; and so day by day the cost of living increased, and misery and discontent increased with it. As capital expanded, and new machines of production were added, there were more and more goods to sell, and more and more difficulty in finding markets; and so came overproduction and unemployment, panics and crises; so came wars for foreign markets--with new opportunities of plunder for the exploiters and new hardships and new taxes for the producers. And so was fulfilled the prophecy of Marx and Engels; under the pressure of bitter necessity the proletariat was organizing and disciplining itself, training its own leaders and thinkers forming itself into a world-wide political party, whose destiny it was to conquer the powers of government in every land, and use them to turn out the exploiters, and to put an end to the rule of privilege.

This change was what the Socialists meant by the "revolution"--the transfer of the ownership of the means of production; and it was about that issue that the class-war was waged. Nothing else but that counted; without that all reform was futility, and all benevolence was mockery, and all knowledge was ignorance. So long as the means of producing necessities were owned by a few, and used for the advantage of a few, just so long must there be want in the midst of plenty, and darkness over all the earth. Whatever evil one went out into the world to combat, he came to realize that he could do nothing against it, because it was bound up with the capitalist system, was in fact itself that system. If little children were shut up in sweat-shops, if women were sold into brothels, it was not for any fault of theirs, it was not the work of any devil--it was simply because of the "surplus value". they represented. If weaker nations were conquered and "civilized", that, too, was for "surplus value". And these epidemics of "graft" that broke out upon the body politic--they were not accidental or sporadic things, and they were not to be remedied by putting any number of men in jail; they were to be understood as the system whereby an industrial oligarchy had rendered impotent a political democracy, and had fenced it out from the fields of privilege.

And so also was it with the dullness and sterility that prevailed in the intellectual world. The master-class did not want ideas--it only wanted to be let alone; and so it put in the seats of authority men who were blind to the blazing beacon-fires of the future. It would be no exaggeration to say that the intellectual and cultural system of the civilized world was conducted, whether deliberately or instinctively, for the purpose of keeping the truth about exploitation from becoming clear to the people.

The master-class owned the newspapers and ran them. It had built and endowed the churches, and taught the clergy to feed out of its hand. In the same way it had founded the colleges, and named the trustees, who in turn named the presidents and professors. The ordinary mortal took it for granted that because venerable bishops and dignified editors and learned college-professors were all in agreement as to a certain truth, there must be some inherent probability in that truth; and never once perceived how the cards were stacked and the dice loaded--how those clergymen and editors and professors had all been selected because they believed that truth to be true, and believed the contrary falsehood to be false!

And how smoothly and automatically the system worked! How these dignitaries stood together, and held up each other's hands, maintaining the august tradition, the atmosphere of authority and power! The bishops praising the editors, and the editors praising the professors, and the professors praising the bishops! And when the circle was completed, what *lese majeste* it seemed for an ordinary mortal to oppose their conclusions!

The bishops, one perceived, were "orthodox"--that is to say they were concerned with barren formulas; and they were "spiritual"--they were concerned with imaginary future states of bliss. The editors were "safe" and "conservative"--that is to say, their souls were dead and their eyes were sealed and their god was property. And when it came to the selecting of the college professors, of the men who were to guide and instruct the forthcoming generations--what precautions would be taken then! What consultations and investigations, what testimonials and interviews and examinations! For after all, in these new days, it could be no easy matter to find men whose minds were sterilized, who could face without blenching all the horrors of the capitalist regime! Who could see courts and congresses bought and sold; who could see children ground up in mills and factories, and women driven by the lash of want to sell their bodies; who could see the surplus of the world's wealth squandered in riot and debauchery, and the nations armed and drilled and sent out to slaughter each other in the quest for more. Who could know that all these things existed, and yet remain in their cloistered halls and pursue the placid ways of scholarship; who could teach history which regarded them as inevitable; who could care for literature that had been made for the amusement of slave-drivers, and art which existed for the sake of art, and not for the sake of humanity; who could know everything that was useless, and teach everything that was uninteresting, and could be dead at once to the warnings of the past, and to all that was vital and important in the present.

Section 11. Not since he had discovered the master-key of Evolution had Thyrsis come upon any set of ideas that meant so much to him. It was not that these were new to him--they were the stuff out of which his whole life had been made; but here they were ordered and systematized--he had a handle by which to take hold of them. The name of this handle was "the economic interpretation of history". And its import was that ideas did not come by hazard, or out of the air, but were products of social conditions; and that when one knew by what method the wealth of any community was produced, and by what class its "surplus value" was appropriated--then and then only could one understand the arts and customs, the sciences and religions, which that community would evolve.

In the light of this great principle Thyrsis had to revise all his previous knowledge; he had to cast out tons of rubbish from the chambers of his mind, and start his thinking life all over again. Just as, in early days, he had exchanged miracles and folk-tales for facts of natural science; so now he saw political institutions and social codes, literary and artistic canons, and ethical and philosophical systems, no longer as things valid and excellent, having relationship to truth--but simply as intrenchments and fortifications in the class-war, as devices which some men had used to deceive and plunder some other men. What a light it threw upon philosophy, for instance, to perceive it, not as a search for truth, but as a search for justification upon the part of ruling classes, and for a basis of attack upon the part of subject-classes!

So, for instance, on the one side one found Rousseau, and on the other Herbert Spencer. Thyrsis had read Spencer, and had cordially disliked him for his dogmatism and his callousness; but now he read Kropotkin's "Mutual Aid as a Factor in Evolution", and came to a realization of how the whole science of biology had been distorted to suit the convenience of the British ruling-classes. *Laissez-faire* and the Manchester school had taught him that "each for himself and the devil take the hindmost" was the universal law of life; and he had accepted it, because there seemed nothing else that he could do. But now, in a sudden flash, he came to see that the law of life was exactly the opposite; everywhere throughout nature that which survived was not ruthless egotism, but co-operative intelligence. The solitary and predatory animals were now almost entirely extinct; and even before the advent of man with his social brain, it had been the herbivorous and gregarious animals which had become most numerous. When it came to man, was it not perfectly obvious that the races which had made civilization were those which had developed the nobler virtues, such as honor and loyalty and patriotism? And now it was proposed to trample them into the mire of "business"; to abandon the race to a glorified debauch of greed! And this travesty of science was taught in ten thousand schools and colleges throughout America--and all because certain British gentlemen had wished to work their cotton-operatives fourteen hours a day, and certain others had wished to keep land which their ancestors had seized in the days of William the Conqueror! Shortly after this Thyrsis came upon Edmond Kelly's great work, "Government, or Human Evolution"; and so he realized that Herbert Spencer's social philosophy had at last been cleared out of the pathway of humanity. And this was a great relief to him--it was one more back-breaking task that he did not have to contemplate!

Section 12. Then one of his Socialist friends sent him Thorstein Veblen's "Theory of the Leisure Class"; a book which he read in a continuous ebullition of glee. Truly it was a delicious thing to find a man who could employ the lingo of the ultra-sophisticated sociologist, and use it in a demonstration of the most revolutionary propositions. The drollery of this was all the more enjoyable because Thyrsis could never be sure that the author himself intended it--whether his sesquipedalian irony might not be a pure product of nature, untouched by any human art.

Veblen's book might have been called a study of the ultimate destiny of "surplus value"; an economic interpretation of the social arts and graces, of "fashions" and "fads". Where men competed for the fruit of each other's labor, the possession of wealth was the sign of excellence. This excellence men wished to demonstrate to others; and step by step, as the methods of production and exploitation changed, one might trace the change in the methods of this demonstration. The savage chief began with nose-rings and anklets, and the trophies of his fights; then, as he grew richer, he would employ courtiers and concubines, and shine by vicarious splendor. He would give banquets and build palaces--the end being always "the conspicuous consumption of goods".

Later on came those stages when he no longer had to gain his wealth by physical prowess; when cunning took the place of force, and he ruled by laws and religions and moral codes, and handed down his power through long lines of descendants. Then ostentation became a highly specialized and conventionalized thing--its criterion changing gradually to "conspicuous waste of time". Those characteristics were cultivated which served to advertise to the world that their possessor had never had to earn wealth, nor to do anything for himself; the aristocrat became a special type of being, with small feet and hands and a feeble body, with special ways of walking and talking, of dressing and eating and playing. He developed a separate religion, a separate language, separate literatures and arts, separate vices and virtues. And fantastic and preposterous as some of these might seem, they were real things, they were the means whereby the leisure-class individual took part in the competition of his own world, and secured his own prestige and the survival of his line. Some philosopher had said that virtue is a product like vinegar; and it was a pleasant thing to discover that French heels and "picture-hats" and course-dinners were products also.

Thyrsis would read passages of this book aloud to Corydon, and they would chuckle over it together; but the reading of it did not bring Corydon the same unalloyed delight. In the leisure-class *regime*, the woman is a cherished possession--for it is through her that the ability to waste both time and goods can best be shown. So came Veblen's grim and ironic exposition of the leisure-class woman, an exposition which Corydon found almost too painful to be read. For Corydon's ancestors, as far back as documents could trace, had been members of that class. They had left her the frail and beautiful body, conspicuously useless and dependent; they had left her all the leisure-class impulses and cravings, all the leisure-class impotences and futilities to contend with. They had taught her nothing about cooking, nothing about sewing, nothing about babies, nothing about money; they had taught her only the leisure-class dream of "love in a cottage"--and she had run away with a poor poet to try it out!

The depth of these instincts in Corydon was amusingly illustrated by the fact that she always woke up dull and discouraged, and was seldom really herself until afternoon; and that along about ten o'clock at night, when for the sake of her health she should have been going to bed, she would be laughing, talking, singing, ablaze with interest and excitement. Thyrsis would point this out to her, and please himself by picturing the role which she should have been filling--wearing an empire gown and a rope or two of rubies, and presiding in an opera-box or a *salon*. Corydon would repudiate all this with indignation; but all the same she never escaped from the phrases of Veblen--she remained his "leisure-class wife" from that day forth. Not so very long afterwards they came upon Ibsen's "Hedda Gabler"; and

Thyrsis shuddered to observe that of all the heroines in the world's literature, that was the one which most appealed to her. Nor did he fail to observe the working of the thing in himself; the subtle and deeply-buried instinct which made him prefer to be wretched with a "leisure-class wife" rather than to be contented with a plebeian one!

BOOK XIV
THE PRICE OF RANSOM

The faint grey of dawn was stealing across the lake; and still the spell was upon them.

"There thou art gone, and me thou leavest here
  Sole in these fields! yet will I not despair."

So she whispered; and he answered her--

"He loved his mates; but yet he could not keep,
  Here with the shepherds and the silly sheep.
      Some life of men unblest
  He knew, which made him droop, and filled his head.
      He went; his piping took a troubled sound
      Of storms that rage outside our happy ground._"

Section 1. In the course of that summer there befell Corydon an adventure; Thyrsis had gone off one day for a walk, and when he came back she told him about it--how a young lady had stopped at the house to ask for a drink of water, and had sat upon the piazza to rest, and had talked with her. Now Corydon was in a state of excitement over a discovery.

Whenever Thyrsis met a stranger, it was necessary for him to go through elaborate intellectual processes, to find the person out by an exchange of ideas. And if by any chance the person was insincere, and used ideas as a blind and a cover, then Thyrsis might never find him out at all. In other words, he took people at the face-value of their cultural equipment; and only after long and tragic blunderings could he by any chance get deeper. But with his wife it happened quite otherwise; this case was the first which he witnessed, but the same thing happened many times afterwards. With her there would be a strange flash of recognition; it was a sort of intuition, perhaps a psychic thing--who could tell? By some unknown process in soul-chemistry, she would divine things about a person that he might have been a life-time in finding out.

It might be a burst of passionate interest, or on the other hand, of repugnance and fear. And long years of practice taught Thyrsis that this instinct of hers was never to be disregarded. Not once in all her life did he know her to give her affection to a base person; and if ever he disregarded her antipathies, he did it to his cost. Once they were sitting in a restaurant, and a man was brought up to be introduced by a friend; he was a person of not unpleasant aspect, courteous and apparently a gentleman, and yet Corydon flushed, and could scarcely keep her seat at the table, and would not give the man her hand. Years after Thyrsis came upon the discovery about this man, that he made a practice of unnatural vices.

He came home now to find Corydon flushed with excitement. "She has such a beautiful soul!" she exclaimed. "I never met anyone like her. And we just took to each other; she told me all about herself, and we are going to be friends."

"Who is she?" asked Thyrsis.

"She's visiting Mr. Harding, the clergyman at Bellevue," was the answer.

Bellevue was a town in the valley, on the other side from the university; it had a Presbyterian church, whose young pastor Thyrsis had met once or twice in his tramps about the country. This Miss Gordon, it seemed, was the niece of an elderly relative, his housekeeper; she was studying trained nursing, and afterwards intended to go out as a missionary to Africa.

"She's so anxious to meet you," Corydon went on. "She's coming up to see me to-morrow, and she's going to bring Mr. Harding. You won't mind, will you, Thyrsis?"

"I guess I can stand it if he can," said Thyrsis, grimly.

"You mustn't say anything to hurt their feelings," said Corydon, quickly. "She's terribly orthodox, you know; and she takes it so seriously. I was surprised--I had never thought that I could stand anybody like that."

Thyrsis merely grunted.

"I guess ideas don't matter so much after all," said Corydon. "It's a deep nature that I care about. But just fancy--she was pained because the baby hadn't been baptized!"

"You ought to have hid the dreadful truth," said he.

"I couldn't hide things from her," laughed Corydon, "But she says I can make a Socialist out of her, and she'll make a Christian out of me!"

His reply was, "Wait until she discovers the sensuous temperament!"

But Corydon answered that Delia Gordon had a sensuous temperament also. "She seemed to me like a Joan of Arc. Just think of her going away from all her family, to a station on the Congo River! She told me all about it--how wretched the people are, and what the women suffer. She woke up in the middle of the night, and a voice told her to go--told her the name of the place. And she'd never heard it before, and hadn't had the least idea of going away!"

Thyrsis was unmoved by this miracle. "I suppose," he said, "you'll be hearing voices yourself, and going with her. Tell me, is she pretty?"

"You wouldn't call her pretty," said Corydon, after a little thought. "She's just--just dear. Oh, Thyrsis, I simply fell in love with her!"

"You certainly chose an odd kind of an affinity," he said. "A Presbyterian missionary!"

"It's worse than that," confessed Corydon. "She's a Seventh-day Adventist."

"Good God! And what may that be?"

"Why, she keeps Saturday instead of Sunday. She calls it the Sabbath. And she thinks that 'evolution' is wicked, and she believes in some kind of a hell! She's not just sure what kind, apparently."

"You watch out," said he, "or the first thing you know she'll be baptizing the baby behind your back."

"Would that do any good?" asked Corydon, guilelessly.

He laughed as he answered, "It would, from her point of view."

To which she replied, "Well, if we didn't know it and the baby didn't, I guess it wouldn't do any harm."

"And it might save him from some kind of a hell!" added Thyrsis.

Section 2. Miss Gordon came the next morning, Mr. Harding with her; and the four sat out under the trees and talked. She was a girl some three years older than Corydon, but much more mature; she was short, but athletic in build, and with a bright personality. Thyrsis could see at once those fine qualities of idealism and fervor which had attracted Corydon; and to his surprise he found that, in addition to her religious virtues, the Lord had generously added a sense of humor. So Delia Gordon was really a person with whom one could have a good time.

The Lord had not been quite so generous with the Rev. Mr. Harding, apparently. Mr. Harding was about thirty years of age, tall and finely-built, with a slight, fair moustache, and a rather girlish complexion. He was evidently of a sentimental inclination, very sensitive, and a lovable person; but the sense of humor Thyrsis judged was underdeveloped. He was inclined towards social-reform, and had a club for working-boys in his town, of which he was very proud; he asked Thyrsis to come and give a literary talk to these boys, and Thyrsis replied that his views of things were hardly orthodox. When the clergyman asked for elucidation, Thyrsis added, with a smile, "I don't believe that Jonah ever swallowed the whale". Whereupon Mr. Harding proceeded with all gravity to correct his misapprehension of this legend.

The fires of friendship, thus suddenly lighted between the two girls, continued to burn. Delia Gordon came nearly every day to see Corydon, and once or twice Corydon went down to the town and had lunch with her. They told each other all the innermost secrets of their hearts, and in the evening Corydon would retail these to Thyrsis, who was thus put in the way to acquire that knowledge of human nature so essential to a novelist. Delia had never been in love, it seemed--her only passion was for savage tribes along the Congo; but Mr. Harding had been involved in a heart-tragedy some time ago, and was supposed to be still inconsolable. Incredible as it might seem, he was apparently not in love with Delia.

Also, needless to say, the pair did not fail to thresh out problems of theology. Delia made in due course the dreadful discovery of the sensuous temperament; and also she probed to the depths the frightful ocean of unorthodoxy that was hid beneath the placid surface of Corydon. But strange to say, this did not repel her, nor make any difference in their friendship. Thyrsis took that for the sign of a liberal attitude, but Corydon corrected him with a shrewd observation--"She's so sure of her own truth she can't believe in the reality of any other. She *knows* I'll come to

Jesus with her some day!"

It was a wonderful thing to Thyrsis to see his wife's happiness just then; she was like a flower which has been wilting, and suddenly receives a generous shower of rain. It was just what he had prayed for; having seen all along that her wretchedness was owing to her being shut up alone with him. So now he did his best to repress his own opinions, and to let the two friends work out their problem undisturbed.

"Oh, Thyrsis," Corydon exclaimed to him, one night, "if I could only have her with me, I'd be happy always!"

"Then why don't you get her to stay with you?" asked Thyrsis, quickly.

"Ah, but she wouldn't think of it," said Corydon. "She doesn't really care about anything in the world but her Congo savages!"

"We might try," said he. "When does she complete her course?"

"Not until the end of the year."

"Well, we can do a lot of arguing in that time. And when the book is out, we'll have money enough, so that we can offer to pay her. She might become a sort of 'mother's helper.'"

Section 3. So Thyrsis began a struggle with Jesus and the Congo savages, for the possession of Delia's soul. He set to work to interest her in his work; he gave her his first novel, which contained no theology at all; and also "The Hearer of Truth"--the social radicalism of which he was pleased to see did not alarm her. And then he gave her the war-novel, and saw with joy how she was thrilled over that. He laid himself out to make his purpose and his vision clear to her; and then, one afternoon, when Corydon had a headache and was taking a nap, he led her off to a quiet place in the woods, and set before her all the bitter tragedy of their lives.

He pictured the work he had to do, and the loneliness to which this consigned Corydon; he told her of the horrors they had so far endured, and what effect these had had upon his wife. He showed her what her power was--how she could make life possible for both of them. For she had that magic key which Thyrsis himself did not possess, she could unlock the treasure-chambers of Corydon's soul.

But alas, Thyrsis soon perceived that his efforts had been in vain. Delia was stirred by his eloquence, but the only effect was to move her to an equally eloquent account of the sufferings of the natives of the Congo basin. It was important that he should get his books written; but how much more important it was that some help should be carried to these unhappy wretches! They never saw any books, they were altogether beyond his reach; and who was to take the light to them? She told him harrowing tales of sick women, beaten and tortured and burned with fire to drive the devils out of them.

Thyrsis met this by attempting to broaden the girl's social consciousness. He showed her how the waves of intelligence, beginning at the top, spread to the lowest strata of society--changing the character of all human activities, and affecting the humblest life. He showed her the capitalist system, and explained how it worked; how it reached to the savage in the remotest corner of the earth, and seized him and made him over according to its will. It was true, for instance--and not in any poetic sense, but literally and demonstrably true--that the fate of the Congo native was determined in Wall Street, and in the financial centres of London and Paris and Brussels and Berlin. The essential thing about the natives was that they represented rubber and ivory. And Delia might go there, and try to teach them and help them, but she would find that there were forces engaged in beating them down and destroying them--forces in comparison with which she was as helpless as a child. It was true of the Congo blacks, as it was true of the people of the slums, of the proletariat of the whole earth, that there was no way to help them save to overthrow the system which made of them, not human beings, but commodities, to be purchased and passed through the profit-mill, and then flung into the scrap-heap.

But Thyrsis found to his pain that it was impossible to make these considerations of any real import to Delia. She understood them, she assented to them; but that did not make them count. Her impulses came from another part of her being. Her savages were naked and hungry and ignorant and miserable; and they needed to be fed and clothed, and more important yet, to be baptized and saved. She was all the more impelled to her task by the fact that all the forces of civilization were arrayed against her. The fires of martyrdom were blazing in her soul. She meant to throw herself over a precipice--and the higher the precipice, and the more jagged the rocks beneath, the greater was the thrill which the prospect brought her.

Section 4. They went back to the house; as Delia had arranged to spend the night with them, and as Corydon's headache was better, the controversy was continued far into the evening. Thyrsis took no part in it, he listened while Corydon pleaded for herself, and pictured her loneliness and despair.

Delia put her arms about her. "Don't you see, dear," she argued--"all that is because you are without a faith! You cast out Jesus, and deny him; and so how can *I* help you? If you believed what I do, you would not be lonely, even if you were in the heart of Africa."

"But how can I believe what isn't ***true?***" cried Corydon; and so the skeletons of theology came forth and rattled their bones once more.

A couple of hours must have passed, while Thyrsis said nothing, but listened to Delia and watched her, probing deeply into the agonies and futilities of life. He had given up all hope of persuading her to stay with them; he thought only of the tragedy, that this noble spirit should be tangled up and blundering about in the mazes of a grotesque dogma. And the time came when he could endure it no more; something rose up within him, something tremendous and terrible, and he laid hold of Delia Gordon's soul to wrestle with it, as never before had he wrestled with any human soul except Corydon's.

The truth of the matter was that Thyrsis loved the religious people; it was among them that he had been brought up, and their ways were his ways. This was a fact that came to him rarely now, for he was hard-driven and bitter; but it was true that when he sneered at the church and taunted it, he was like a parent who whips a child he loves. Perhaps Paret had spoken truly in one of his cruel jests--that when a man has been brought up religious, he can never really get over it, he can never really be free.

So now Thyrsis spoke to Delia as one who was himself of the faith of Jesus; he cried out to her that what she wanted was what he wanted, that all her attitudes and ways of working were his. And here were monstrous evils alive upon the earth--here were all the forces of hell unleashed, and ranging like savage beasts destroying the lives of men and women! And those who truly cared, those who had the conscience and the faith of the world in their keeping--they were wasting their time in disputations about barren formulas, questions which had no relationship to human life! Questions of the meaning of old Hebrew texts that had often no meaning at all, and of folk-tales and fairy-stories out of the nursery of the race--the problem of whether Jonah had swallowed the whale, or the whale had swallowed Jonah--the problem of whether it was on Friday or Saturday that the Lord had finished the earth. Because of such things as this, they drove all thinking men from their ranks, they degraded and made ridiculous the very name of faith! As he went on, the agony of this swept over Thyrsis--until it seemed to him as if he had the whole Christian Church before him, and was pleading with it in the voice of Jesus. Here was a new crucifixion--a crucifixion of civilization! Thyrsis cried out in the words, "Oh ye of little faith!" Truly, was it not the supreme act of infidelity, to make the spirit of religion, which was one with the impulse of all life--the force that made the flower bloom and oak-tree tower and the infant cry for its food--to make it dependent upon Hebrew texts and Assyrian folk-tales! Delia preached to him about "faith"; but what was her faith in comparison with his, which was a faith in all life--which trusted the soul of man, and reason as part of the soul of man, a thing which God had put in man to be used, and not to be feared and outraged.

Then came Delia. She would not admit that her faith depended upon texts and legends; it was a faith in the living God. She was not afraid of reason--she did not outrage it--

"But you do, you do!" cried Thyrsis. "Your whole attitude is an outrage to it! You never speak of 'science' except as an evil thing. You told Corydon that 'evolution' was wicked!"

"I don't see how evolution can help my faith"--began the other.

"That's just it!" cried Thyrsis again. "That is exactly what I mean! You do not pay homage to truth, you do not seek it for its own sake! You require that it should fit into certain formulas that you have set up--in other words that it should not interfere with your texts and your legends! And what is the result of that--you have paralyzed all your activities, you have condemned your intellectual life to sterility! For we live in an age of science, we cannot solve our problems except by means of it; the forces of evil are using it, and you are not using it, and so you are like a child in their hands! Not one of the social wrongs but could be put an end to--child-labor, poverty and disease, prostitution and drunkenness, crime and war! But you don't know how, and you can't find out how--simply because you have thrown away the sharp tools of the intellect, and filled your mind with formulas that mean nothing! How can you understand modern problems, when you know nothing about economics? You have rejected 'evolution'--so how can you comprehend the evolution of society? How can you know that civilization at this hour is going down into the abyss--dragging you and your churches and your Congo savages with it? I who do understand these things--I have to go out and fight alone, while you are shut up in your churches, mumbling your spells and incantations, and poring over your Hebrew texts! And think of what I must suffer, knowing as I do that the spirit that animates you--the fervor and devotion, the 'hunger and thirst after righteousness'--would banish horror from the earth forever, if only it could be guided by intelligence!"

Section 5. All this, of course, was effort utterly wasted. Thyrsis poured out his pleadings and exhortations, his longing and his pain; and when he had finished, the girl was exactly where she had been before--just as distrustful of "science", and just as blindly bent upon getting away to her savages and binding up their wounds and baptizing them. And so at last he gave up in despair, and left Delia to go to bed, and went out and sat alone in the moonlight.

Afterwards, though it was long after midnight, Corydon came out and joined him. He saw that she was flushed and trembling with excitement.

"Thyrsis!" she whispered. "That was a marvellous thing!"

He pressed her hand.

"And all thrown away!" she cried.

"You realized that, did you?" he asked.

"I realized many things. Why you set so much store by ideas, for instance! I see that you are right--one has to think straight!"

"It's like a steam-engine," said Thyrsis. "It doesn't matter how much power you get up, or how fast you make the wheels go--unless the switches are set right, you don't reach your destination."

"You only land in the ditch!" added Corydon. "And that's just the way I felt to-night--she'd take your argument every time, and dump it into a ditch. And she'd see it there, and not care."

"She doesn't care about facts at all, Corydon. And notice this also--she doesn't care about succeeding. That's the thing you must get straight--her religion is a religion of failure! It comes back to that criticism of Nietzsche's--it's a slave-morality. The world belongs to the devil; and the idea of taking it away from the devil seems to be presumptuous. Even if it could be done, the attempt would be "unspiritual'; for the 'world' is something corrupt--something that ought not to be saved. So you see, she's perfectly willing for the Belgians to have the rubber."

"'Render unto Caesar the things that are Caesar's'!" quoted Corydon.

"Yes, and let Caesar spend them on Cleo de Merode. What she wants is to save the *souls* of her savages--to baptize them, and to perish gloriously at the work, and then be transported to some future life that is worth while. So you see what the immortality-mongers do with our morality!"

"Ah!" cried Corydon, swiftly. "But that need not be so!"

"But it *is* so!" he answered.

"No, no!" she protested. "You must not say that! That is giving up--and I felt such a different mood in you to-night! I wanted to tell you--we must do something about it, Thyrsis! It made me ashamed of my own life. Here I am, failing miserably-- and all that work crying out to be done! I don't think I ever had such a sense of your power before--the things you might do, if only you could get free, if only I didn't stand in your way! Oh, can't we cast the old mistakes behind us, and go out into the world and preach that message?"

"But, my dear," said Thyrsis, "that wouldn't appeal to you always. Your temperament--"

"Never mind my temperament!" she cried. "I am sick of it, ashamed of it; I want the world to hear that trumpet-call! I want you to break your way into the churches--to make them listen to you, and realize their blasphemy of life!"

She caught hold of him and clung to him; he could feel, like an electric shock, the thrill of her excitement. He marvelled at the effect his words had produced upon her--realizing all the more keenly, in contrast with Delia, what a power of *mind* he had here to deal with. "Dearest," he said, "I must put these things into my books. You must stand by me and help me to put them into my books!"

Section 6. Delia Gordon went away to take up her work in the city; but for many months thereafter that missionary impulse stayed with them. They would find themselves seized with the longing to throw aside everything else, and to go out and preach Socialism with the living voice. They were still immersed in its literature; they read Bellamy's "Looking Backward", and Blatchford's "Merrie England", and Kropotkin's "Appeal to the Young". They read another book about England that moved them even more--a volume of sketches called "The People of the Abyss", by a young writer who was then just forging to the front--Jack London. He was the most vital among the younger writers of the time, and Thyrsis watched his career with eager interest. There was also not a little of wistful hunger in his attitude--he had visions of being the next to be caught up and transported to those far-off heights of popularity and power.

Also, they were kept in a state of excitement by the Socialist papers and magazines that came to them. There was a great strike that summer, and they followed the progress of it, reading accounts of the distress of the people. Every now and then the pain of these things would prove more than Thyrsis could bear, and he would blaze out in some fiery protest, which, of course, the Socialist papers published gladly. So little by little Thyrsis was coming to be known in "the movement". Some of his friends among the editors and publishers made strenuous protests against this course, but little dreaming how deeply the new faith had impressed him.

In truth it was all that Thyrsis could do to hold himself in; it seemed to him that he no longer cared about anything save this fight of the working-class for justice. He was frightened by the prospect, when he stopped to realize it; for he could not write anything but what he believed, and one could not live by writing about Socialism. He thought of his war-book, for instance. It was but two or three months since he had finished it, and it was his one hope for success and freedom; and yet already he had outgrown it utterly. He realized that if he had had to go back and do it over, he could not; he could never believe in any war again, never be interested in any war again. Wars were struggles among ruling-classes, and whoever won them, the people always lost. Thyrsis was now girding up his loins for a war upon war.

So there were times when it seemed that a literary career would no longer be possible to him; that he would have to cast his lot altogether with the people, and find his work as an agitator of the Revolution. One day a marvellous plan flashed over him, and he came to Corydon with it, and for nearly a week they threshed it over, tingling with excitement. They would sell their home, and raise what money they could, and get themselves a travelling van and a team of horses and go out upon the road on a Socialist campaign!

It was a perfectly feasible thing, Thyrsis declared: they would carry a supply of literature, and would get a commission upon subscriptions to Socialist papers. He pictured them drawing up on the main street of some country town, and ringing a dinner-bell to gather the people, and beginning a Socialist meeting. He would make a speech, and Corydon would sell pamphlets and books; they had animated discussions as to whether she might not learn to make a speech also. At least, he argued, she might sing Socialist songs!

Thyrsis was forever evolving plans of this sort; plans for doing something concrete, for coming into contact with the world of every day. The pursuit of literature was something so cold and aloof, so comfortable and conventional; one never pressed the hand of a person in distress, one never saw the light of hope and inspiration kindling in another's eyes. So he would dream of running a publishing-house or a magazine, of founding a library or staging a play, of starting a colony or a new religion. And then, after he had made himself drunk upon the imagining, he would take himself back to his real job. For that summer his only indiscretions were to buy several thousand copies of the "Appeal to Reason", and hire the old horse and buggy, and distribute them over some thirty square miles of country; also to help to organize a club for the study of Socialism at the university; and finally, when he was in the city, to make a fiery speech at a meeting of some "Christian Socialists." Because of this the newspaper reporters dug out the accounts of his earlier adventures, and "wrote him up" with malicious bantering. And this, alas--as the publisher pointed out--was a poor sort of preparation for the launching of the war-novel.

Needless to add, the two did not fail to wrestle with those individuals whom they met. Thyrsis got a collection of pamphlets, judiciously selected, and gave them to the butcher and the grocer, the store-clerks and the hack-drivers in the town. But a college-town was a poor place for Socialist propaganda, as he realized with sinking heart; its population was made up of masters and servants, and there was even more snobbery among the servants than among the masters. The main architectural features of the place were fraternity-houses and "eating-clubs", where the sons of the idle rich disported themselves; once or twice Thyrsis passed through the town after midnight, and saw these young fellows reeling home, singing and screaming in various stages of intoxication. Then he would think of little children shut up in cotton-mills and coal-mines, of women dying in pottery-works and lead-factories; and on his way home he would compose a screed for the "Appeal to Reason".

Section 7. Another victim of their fervor was the Rev. Mr. Harding, who stopped in to see them several times upon his tramps. Thyrsis would never have dreamed of troubling Mr. Harding, but Corydon found "something in him", and would go at him hammer and tongs whenever he appeared. It must have been a novel experience for the clergyman; it seemed to fascinate him, for he came again and again, and soon quite a friendship sprang up between the two. She would tell Thyrsis about it at great length, and so, of course, he had to change his ideas about Mr. Harding.

"Don't you see how fine and sensitive he is?" she would plead.

"No doubt, my dear," said Thyrsis. "But don't you think he's maybe just a bit timid?"

"Timid," she replied. "But then think of his training! And think what you are!"

"Yes, I suppose I'm pretty bad," he admitted.

This discussion took place after he and Mr. Harding had had an argument, in which Thyrsis had remarked casually that modern civilization was "crucifying Jesus all over again." And when Mr. Harding asked for enlightenment, Thyrsis answered, "My dear man, we crucify him according to the constitution. We teach the profession of crucifying him. We invest our capital in the business of crucifying him. We build churches and crucify him in his own name!"

After which explosion Corydon said, "You let me attend to Mr. Harding. I understand him, and how he feels about things."

"All right, my dear," assented Thyrsis. "When I see him coming, I'll disappear."

But that would not do either, it appeared, for Mr. Harding was a conventional person, and it was necessary that he should feel he was calling on the head of the family.

"Then," said Thyrsis, "I'm supposed to sit by and serve as a chaperon?"

"You're to answer questions when I ask you to," replied Corydon.

Through Mr. Harding they made other acquaintances in Bellevue. There was a Mrs. Jennings, the wife of the young principal of the High School; they were simple and kindly people, who became fond of Corydon, and would beg her to visit them. The girl was craving for companionship, and she would plead with Thyrsis to accompany her, and subject himself to the agonies of "ping-pong" and croquet; and once or twice he submitted--and so one might have beheld them, at a lawn-party, hotly pressed by half a dozen disputants, in a debate concerning the nature of American institutions, and the future of religion and the home!

Thyrsis seldom took human relationships seriously enough to get excited in such arguments; but Corydon, with her intense and personal temperament, made an eager and uncomfortable propagandist. How could anyone fail to see what was so plain to her? And so she would bring books and pamphlets, and lend them about. There was a young man named Harry Stuart, a fine, handsome fellow, who taught drawing at the High School. In him, also, Cordon discovered possibilities; and she repudiated indignantly the idea that his soulful eyes and waving brown hair had anything to do with it. Harry Stuart was a guileless and enthusiastic member of the State militia; but in spite of this sinister fact, Corydon went at him. She soon had her victim burning the midnight oil over Kautsky and Hyndman; and behold, before the autumn had passed, the ill-fated drawing-teacher had resigned from the State militia, and was doing cartoons for the "Appeal to Reason"!

Section 8. Corydon's excitement over these questions was all the greater because she was just then making the discovery of the relationship of Socialism to the problems of her own sex. Some one sent her a copy of Charlotte Gilman's "Women and Economics"; she read it at a sitting, and brought it to Thyrsis, who thus came to understand the scientific basis of yet another article of his faith. He went on to other books--to Lester Ward's "Sociology", and to Bebel's "Woman", and to the works of Havelock Ellis. So he realized that women had not always been clinging vines and frail flowers and other uncomfortable things; and the hope that they might some day be interested in other matters than fashion and sentiment and the pursuit of the male, was not a vain fantasy and a Utopian dream, but was rooted in the vital facts of life.

Throughout nature, it appeared, the female was often the equal of the male; and even in human history there had been periods when woman had held her own with man--when the bearing of children had not been a cause of degradation. Such had been the case with our racial ancestors, the Germans; as one found them in Tacitus, their women were strong and free, speaking with the men in the council-halls, and even going into battle if the need was great. It was only when they came under the Roman influence, and met slavery and its consequent luxury, that the Teutonic woman had started upon the downward path. Christianity also had had a great deal to do with it; or rather the dogmas which a Roman fanatic had imposed upon the message of Jesus.

It was interesting to note how one might trace the enslavement of woman, step by step with the enslavement of labor; the two things went hand in hand, and stood or fell together. So long as life was primitive, woman filled an economic function, and held her own with her mate. But with slavery and exploitation, the heaping up of wealth and the advent of the leisure-class *regime*, one saw the woman becoming definitely the appendage of the man, a household ornament and a piece of property; securing her survival, not by useful labor, but by sexual charm, and so becoming specialized as a sex-creature. For generations and ages the male had selected and bred in her those qualities which were most stimulating to his own desires, which increased in him the sense of his own dominance; and for generations and ages he taught the doctrine that the proper sphere of woman was the home. If he happened to be a German emperor, he summed it up in the sneer of "Kuche, Kinder, Kirche". So the woman became frail and impotent physically, and won her success by the only method that was open to her--by finding some male whom she could ensnare.

Such had been the conditions. But now, in the present century, had come machinery, and the development of woman's labor; and also had come intelligence, and woman's discovery of her chains. So there was the suffrage movement and the Socialist movement. After the overthrow of the competitive wage-system and of the leisure-class tradition, woman would no longer sell her sex-functions, whether in marriage or prostitution; and so the sex might cease to survive by its vices, and to infect the whole race with its intellectual and moral impotence. So would be set free the enormous force that was locked up in the soul of woman; and human life would be transformed by the impulse of emotions that were fundamental and primal. So Thyrsis perceived the two great causes in which the progress of humanity was bound up--the emancipation of labor and the emancipation of woman; to educate and agitate and organize for which became the one service that was worth while in life.

Section 9. The nights were beginning to grow chilly, and they realized that autumn was at hand, and faced the prospect of another winter in that lonely cabin. Paret, who had come down to visit them, had given it a name--"the soap-box in a marsh." Thyrsis saw clearly that he could not settle down to hard work while they were shut up there. Corydon's headaches and prostrations seemed to be growing worse, and she could simply not get through the winter without some help. As the book was ready, they had some money in prospect, and their idea was that they would buy a farm with a good house. So they might keep a horse and a cow and some chickens; and there might be some outdoor work for Thyrsis to do, instead of trudging aimlessly over the country.

They utilized their spare time by getting the old horse and buggy, and inspecting and discussing all the farms within five miles of them; an occupation which put a great strain upon their diverse temperaments. Thyrsis would be thinking of such matters as roads and fruit-trees and barns--and above all of prices; while Corydon would be concerned with--alas, Corydon never dared to formulate her vision, even to herself. She had vague memories of dilettante country-places with great open fire-places, and exposed beams, and a broad staircase, and a deep piazza, and above all, a view of the sunset. Whenever she came upon any vague suggestion of these luxuries, her heart would leap up--and would then be crushed by some reference to ten or fifteen thousand dollars.

Corydon was a poor sort of person to take an inspection-trip. She would gaze about and say, "There might be a piazza here"; and then she would look across the fields and add, "There'd be a good view if it weren't for those woods"--and wave the woods away with the gesture of a duchess. So, of course, the observant farmer would add a thousand dollars to the asking-price of his property.

On the other hand, when Thyrsis with his remorseless thoroughness would insist on getting out and inspecting some dilapidated and forlorn-looking place-- then what agonies would come! Corydon would pass through the rooms, suffering all the horrors which she might have suffered in years of occupancy of them. And there was no use pleading with her to be reserved in her attitude--she took houses in the same way that she took people, either loving them or hating them. So, from an afternoon's driving-trip, she would come home in a state of exhaustion and despair; and Thyrsis would have to pledge himself upon oath not to think of this or that horrible place for a single instant again.

There were times when Thyrsis, too, in spite of his lack of intuition, felt the atmosphere of evil which hung about some of these old farms. Having lived for a year and a half in the neighborhood, and been favored with the gossip of the washerwoman, and of the farmer's wife, and of the girl who came to clean house now and then, they had come to know the affairs of their neighbors--they had got a cross-section of an American small-farming community. It was in amusing accord with Thyrsis' social theories that the only two decent families in the neighborhood inhabited farms of over a hundred acres. There were several farms of fifty or sixty acres occupied by tenants, who were engaged, in plundering them as fast as they could; and then a host of little places, of from one to twenty acres, on which families were struggling pitifully to keep alive. And with scarcely a single exception, these homes of poverty were also homes of degradation. Across the way from Thyrsis was an idiot man; upon the next place lived an old man who was a hopeless drunkard, and had one son insane, and another tubercular; and then down in the meadows below the woods lived the Hodges--a name of direful portent. The father would work as a laborer in town for a day or two, and buy vinegar and make himself half insane, and then come home and beat his wife and children. There were eleven of these latter, and a new one came each year; the eldest were thieves, and the youngest might be seen in midwinter, playing half-naked before the house. The Hodges were known to all the neighbors for miles about, and the amount of energy which each farmer expended in fighting them would have maintained the whole family in comfort for their lives.

Thyrsis had travelled enough about the New England and Middle Atlantic states to know that these conditions were typical of the small-farming industry in all the remoter parts. The people with enterprise had moved West, and those who stayed behind divided and mortgaged their farms, and sunk lower and lower into misery and degradation. This was one more aspect of that noble system of *laissez faire*; this was the independent small-farmer, whose happiness was the theme of all orthodox economists! He was, according to the newspaper editorials, the backbone of American civilization; and once every two years, in November, he might be counted upon to hitch up his buggy and drive to town, and pocket his two-dollar bill, and roll up a glorious majority for the Grand Old Party of Protection and Prosperity.

Section 10. The date of publication of the book had come at last. It was being generously advertised, under the imprint of a leading house; and Thyrsis' heart warmed to see the advertisements. This at last, he felt, was success; and then the reviews began to come in, and his heart warmed still more. Here was a new note in current fiction, said the critics; here were power and passion, a broad sweep and a genuine poetic impulse. American history had never been treated like this before, American ideals had never been voiced like this before. And these, Thyrsis noted, were the opinions of the representative reviews--not those of obscure provincial newspapers. Victory, it seemed, had come to him at last!

He came up to the metropolis on the strength of these triumphs; for he had observed that when one had a new book coming out was the psychological moment to attack the magazine-editors. One was a personality then, and could command attention. It was the height of a presidential campaign, and the Socialists were making an impression which was astonishing every one. The idea had occurred to Thyrsis that some magazine might judge it worth while to tell its readers about this new and picturesque movement.

To his great delight the editor of "Macintyre's Monthly" looked with favor upon the suggestion, and asked to see an article at once. So Thyrsis shut himself up in a hotel-room and wrote it over night. It proved to be so full of "ginger" that the editorial staff of Macintyre's was delighted, and made suggestions as to another article; at which point Thyrsis made a desperate effort and summoned up his courage, and insinuated politely that his stuff was worth five cents a word. The editor-in-chief replied promptly that that seemed to him proper.

Two hundred dollars for an article! Here indeed was fame! The author went home, and thought out another one, and after a week came up to the city with it.

In this new article Thyrsis cited a presidential candidate before the bar of public opinion, and propounded troublesome questions to him. Here was the capital of the country, heaping itself up at compound interest, and demanding dividends; here were the people, scraping and struggling to furnish the necessary profits. Would they always be able to furnish enough; and what would happen when they could no longer furnish them? Here were franchises obtained by bribery, and capitalized for hundreds of millions of dollars; and these millions, too, were heaping up automatically. Were they to draw their interest and dividends forever? Here were the machines of production, increasing by leaps and bounds, and the product increasing still faster, and all counting upon foreign markets. What would happen when Japan had its own machines, and India had its own machines, and China had its own machines? Again, the processes of production were being perfected, and displacing men; here were panics and crises, displacing--yet more men. Already, in England, a good fourth of the population had been displaced; and what were these displaced populations to do? They had finished making over the earth for the capitalists; and now that the work was done, there seemed to be no longer any place on the earth for them!

Such were the problems of our time, according to Thyrsis; and why did the statesmen of the time have nothing to say about them? When this article had been read and discussed, young "Billy" Macintyre himself sent for Thyrsis. This was the "real thing", said he, with his genial ***bonhomie***; the five hundred thousand subscribers of Macintyre's must surely have these mirth-provoking meditations. Also, the editors themselves needed badly to be stirred up by such live ideas; therefore would Thyrsis come to dinner next Friday evening, and, as "Billy" phrased it, "throw a little Socialism at them"?

Section 11. So Thyrsis moved one step higher yet up the ladder of success. The younger Macintyre occupied half a block of mansion up on Riverside Drive-- just across the street from the town-house of Barry Creston's father. Thyrsis found himself in an entrance-hall where wonderful pictures loomed vaguely in a dim, religious light; and a silent footman took his cap, and then escorted him by a soft, plush-covered stairway to the apartments of "Billy", who was being helped into a dress-suit by his valet. Thyrsis, alas, had no dress-suit, and no valet to help him into it, but he sat on the edge of a big leather chair and proceeded to "throw a little Socialism" at his host. Then they went down stairs, and there were Morris and Hemingway, of the editorial staff, and "Buddie" Comings, most popular of novelists, and "Bob" Desmond, most famous of illustrators. And a little later on came Macintyre the elder, who had also been judged to stand in need of some Socialism.

Macintyre the elder was white-haired and rosy-cheeked. He had begun life as an emigrant-boy, running errands for a book-shop. In course of time he had become a partner, and then had started a cheap magazine for the printing of advertisements. From this had come the reprinting of cheap books for premiums; until now, after forty years, Macintyre's was one of the leading publishing-concerns of the country. Recently the important discovery had been made that the printing of half-inch advertisements headed "FITS" and "OBESITY" prevented the securing of full-page advertisements about automobiles. The former kind was therefore being diverted to the religious papers of the country, whose subscribers were now getting the "blood of the lamb" diluted with twenty-five per cent. alcohol and one and three-fourths per cent. opium. But such facts were not allowed to interfere with the optimistic philosophy of "Macintyre's Monthly".

The elder Macintyre seemed to Thyrsis the most naive and lovable old soul he had encountered in many a year. When he espied Thyrsis, he waited for no preliminaries, but went up to him as he stood by the fire-place, and put an arm about him, and led him off to a seat by the window. "I want to talk to you," said he.

"My boy," he went on, "I read that article of yours."

"Which one?" asked Thyrsis.

"The last one. And you know, Billy's got to stop putting things like that in the magazine!"

"What!" cried Thyrsis, alarmed.

"I won't have it! He must not print that article!"

"But he's accepted it!"

"I know. But he should have consulted me."

"But--but I wrote it at his order. And he promised to pay me--"

"Oh, that's all right," said the old gentleman, with a genial smile. "We'll pay for it, of course."

There was a moment's pause, while Thyrsis caught his breath.

"My boy," continued the other, "that's a terrible article!"

"Um," said the author--"possibly."

"Why do you write such things?"

"But isn't it true, sir?"

Mr. Macintyre pondered. "You know," he said, "I think you are a very clever fellow, and you know a lot; much more than I do, I've no doubt. But what I don't understand is, why don't you put it into a book?"

"Into a book?" echoed Thyrsis, perplexed.

"Yes," explained the other--"then it won't hurt anybody but yourself. Why should you try to get it into my magazine, and scare away my half-million subscribers?"

Section 12. They went in to dinner, which was served upon silver-plate, by the light of softly-shaded candles; and while the velvet-footed waiters caused their food to appear and disappear by magic, Thyrsis fulfilled his mission and "threw Socialism" at the company.

The company had its guns loaded, and they went at it hot and heavy. The editors wanted to know about "the home" under Socialism; to which Thyrsis made retort by picturing "the home" under capitalism. They wanted to know about liberty and individuality under Socialism; and so Thyrsis discussed the liberty and individuality of the hundred thousand wage-slaves of the Steel Trust. They sought to tangle him in discussions as to the desirability of competition, and the impossibility of escaping it; but Thyrsis would bring them back again and again to the central fact of exploitation, which was the one fact that counted. They insisted upon knowing how this, that, and the other thing would be done in the Cooperative Commonwealth; to which Thyrsis answered, "Do you ask for a map of heaven before you join the Church?"

It was "Billy" Macintyre who brought up a somewhat delicate question; how would such an institution as "Macintyre's Monthly" be run under Socialism? Thyrsis replied by quoting Kautsky's formula: "Communism in material production, Anarchism in intellectual". He showed how the state might print and bind and distribute, while men in "free associations" might edit and publish. But one could not get very far in this exposition, because of the excitement of the elder Macintyre. For the old gentleman was like a small boy who is being robbed of his marbles; if there had been a mob outside his publishing-house, he could not have been more agitated. He took occasion to state, with the utmost solemnity, that he disapproved of such discussions; and "Billy", who sat between him and Thyrsis, had to interfere now and then and soothe the "pater" down.

Mr. Macintyre's views on the subject of capitalism were simple and easy to understand. There could be nothing really wrong with a system which had brought so many great and good men into control of the country's affairs. Mr. Macintyre knew this, because he had played golf with them all and gone yachting with them all. And this was a perfectly genuine conviction; if there had been the slightest touch of sham in it, the old gentleman would have been more cautious in the examples he chose. He would name man after man who was among the most notorious of the country's "malefactors of great wealth"--men whose financial crimes had been proven beyond any possibility of doubting. He would name them in a voice overflowing with affection and admiration, as benefactors of humanity upon a cosmic scale; and of course that would end the argument in a gale of laughter. When the elder Macintyre entered the discussion, all the rest of the company moved forth-with to Thyrsis' side, and there were six Socialists confronting one business-man. And this was a very puzzling and alarming thing to the old gentleman--his son and his magazine were getting away from him, and he did not know what to make of the phenomenon!

Section 13. Thyrsis judged that the tidings must have got about that there was a new "lion" in town; for a couple of days after this he was called up by Comings, most popular of novelists, who asked him to have luncheon at the "Thistle" club. And when Thyrsis went, Comings explained that Mrs. Parmley Fatten had read his book, and was anxious to meet him, and requested that he be brought round to tea. The other was tactless enough to let it transpire that he knew nothing about Mrs. Patton; but Comings was too tactful to show his surprise. Mrs. Patton, he explained, was socially prominent--was looked upon as the leader of a set that went in for intellectual things. She was interested in social reform and woman's suffrage, and was worth helping along; and besides that, she was a charming woman--Thyrsis would surely find the adventure worth while. Then suddenly, while he was listen-ing, it flashed over Thyrsis that he *had* heard of Mrs. Patton before; the lady was in mourning for her brother, and Corydon had recently handed him a "society" item, which told of some unique and striking "mourning-hosiery" which she was introducing from Paris.

Thyrsis in former days might have been shy of this phenomenon; but at pres-ent he was a collecting economist on the look-out for specimens, and so he said he would go. He met Comings again at five o'clock, and they strolled out Fifth Avenue together to Mrs. Patton's brown-stone palace. Thyrsis observed that his friend had been considerate enough to omit his afternoon change of costume, and for this he was grateful.

Mrs. Patton was still in mourning, a filmy and diaphanous kind of mourning, beautiful enough to placate the angel Azrael himself. A filmy and diaphanous crea-ture was Mrs. Patton also--one could never have dreamed of so exquisite a black butterfly. She was very sweet and sympathetic, and told Thyrsis how much she had liked his book--so that Thyrsis concluded she was not half so bad as he had expect-ed. After all, she might not have been to blame for the hosiery story--it might even have been a lie. He reflected that the yellow journals no doubt lied as freely about young leaders of intellectual sets in "society" as they did about starving authors.

Mrs. Patton wanted to know about Socialism, and sighed because it seemed so far away. She made several remarks that showed real intelligence--and this was startling to Thyrsis, who would as soon have expected intelligence from a real butterfly. He got a strange impression of a personality struggling to get into contact with life from behind a wall some ten million dollars high. Mrs. Patton had three young children, and her husband was one of the "Standard Oil crowd"; she complained to Thyrsis that "Parmy"--so she referred to the gentleman--was always in terror over her vagaries.

It was a new discovery to the author that the very rich might live under the shadow of fear, quite as much as the very poor. Their wealth made them a target for newspaper satire, so that they dared not depart from convention in the slightest detail. Mrs. Patton told how once she had ventured to romp for a few minutes with some children on the grounds of the "Casino", and the next day all the world had read that she was introducing "tag" as a diversion for the Newport colony.

There came other callers, both women and men; Percy Ambler, man of fashion and dilettante poet; and with him little Murray Symington, who wrote the literary chat for "Knickerbocker's Weekly", and was therefore a power to be propitiated. There came Blanchard, the young and progressive publisher of the "Beau Monde", a weekly whose circulation rivalled that of "Macintyre's". There came also young Macklin, Mrs. Patton's nephew, with his monocle and his killing drawl. Macklin came by these honestly, having been brought up in England; but Thyrsis did not know that--he only heard the young gentleman's passing reference to his yacht, and to his passion for the poetry of Stephane Mallarme; and so he had it in for Macklin. Thyrsis had got involved in a serious discussion with Mrs. Patton and Symington, and was in the act of saying that the social problem could not be much longer left unsolved; and then he chanced to turn, and discovered young Macklin, surveying him with elaborate superciliousness, and asking with his British drawl, "Aw--I beg pawdon--but what do you mean by the social problem?" And Thyrsis, with a quick glance at him, answered, "I mean you." So Macklin subsided; and Thyrsis learned afterwards that his remark was going the rounds, being considered to be a ***mot***. It appeared the next week in the columns of a paper devoted to "society" gossip; and many a literary reputation had been made by a lesser triumph than that.

Thyrsis got new light upon the making of reputations, when he looked into the next issue of "Knickerbocker's Weekly". There he found that Murray Symington had devoted no less than three paragraphs to his personality and his book. It was all "sprightly"--that was Murray's tone--but also it was cordial; and it referred to Thyrsis' earlier novel, "The Hearer of Truth", as "that brilliant piece of work". Thyrsis read this with consternation--recalling that when the book had come out, not two years ago, "Knickerbocker's Weekly" had referred to it as a "preposterous concoction". Could it be true that an author's work was "preposterous" while he was starving in a garret, and became "brilliant" when he was found in the drawing-room of Mrs. "Parmy" Patton?

Section 14. Thyrsis went on to penetrate yet deeper into these mysteries; there came a call from Murray Symington, to say that Mrs. Jesse Dyckman wanted him to dinner. Jesse Dyckman he recognized as the name of one of the most popular contributors to the magazines --his short stories of Fifth Avenue life were the delight of the readers of the "Beau Monde".

"But I can't go to dinner-parties with women!" protested Thyrsis. "I don't dress!"

Murray took that message; but in a few minutes he called up again. "She says she doesn't care whether you dress or not."

"But then, I don't *eat!*" protested Thyrsis, who had recently discovered Horace Fletcher.

"I know *that* won't count," said the other, laughing. "She doesn't want you to eat--she wants you to talk."

Mrs. Jesse Dyckman inhabited an apartment in a "studio-building" not far from Central Park; and here was more luxury and charm--a dining-room done in dark red, with furniture of some black wood, and candles and silver and cut glass, quite after the fashion of the Macintyres. Thyrsis was admitted by a French maid-servant; and there was Mrs. Dyckman, resplendent in white shoulders and a necklace of pearls; and there was Dyckman himself, even more prosperous and contented-looking than his pictures, and even more brilliant and cynical than his tales. Also there was his sister, Mrs. Partridge, the writer of musical comedies; and a Miss Taylor, who filled the odd corners of the magazines with verses, which Corydon had once described as "cheap cheer-up stuff".

So here was the cream of the "literary world"; and Thyrsis, as he watched and listened to it, was working out the formula of magazine success. Mrs. Dyckman sat next to him, displaying her shoulders and her culture; it seemed to him that she must have spent all her spare time picking up phrases about the books and pictures and plays and music of the hour, so as to be ready for possible mention of them at her dinner-parties. She had opinions on tap about everything; opinions just enough "advanced" to be striking and original, and yet not too far "advanced" for good form. Jesse Dyckman's short stories were the sort in which you read how the hero handled his cigarette, and were told that the heroine was clad in "dimity *en princesse*". You learned the names of the latest fashionable drinks, and the technicalities of automobiles, and met with references to far-off and intricate standards of social excellence.

To Thyrsis it appeared that he could see before him the whole career of such a man. He had trained himself by years of apprenticeship in snobbery; he had studied the fashions not only in costume and manners, but also in books and opinions. He had been educated in a "fraternity", and had chosen a wife who had been educated in a "sorority"; they had set up in this apartment, with silver service and three French servants, and proceeded to give dinners, and cultivate people who "counted." And so had come the pleasant berth with the "Beau Monde"; one or two stories every month, and one thousand dollars for each story--as one might read in all newspaper accounts of the "earnings of authors".

The "Beau Monde" might have been described as a magazine for the standardizing of the newly-rich. A group of these existed in every town in the country, and had their "society" in every little city. They would come to New York and put up at expensive hotels, and get their education in theatres and opera-houses and "lobsterpalaces"; in addition they had this weekly messenger of good form. In its advertising-columns one read of the latest things in cigarettes and highballs and haberdashery and candies and autos; and in its reading-matter one found the leisure-class world, and the leisure-class idea of all other worlds. Young Blanchard himself was in the most "exclusive" society; and if one stayed close to him, one might worm his way past the warders. Among the regular contributors to the "Beau Monde" and to "Macintyre's", there were a dozen men who had risen by this method; and some of them had been real writers at the outset--had started with a fund of vigor, at least. But now they spent their evenings at dinner-parties, and their days lounging about in two or three expensive cafes, reading the afternoon papers, exchanging gossip, and acquiring the necessary stock of cynicism for their next picture of leisure-class life.

It was what might have been described as the "court method" of literary achievement. The centre of it was the young prince who held the purse-strings; and the court was a coterie of bookish men of fashion and rich women whose husbands were occupied in the stock-market. They set the tone and dispensed the favors; one who stood in their good graces would be practically immune to criticism, no matter how seedy his work might come to be. Nobody liked to "roast" a man with whom he had played golf at a week-end party; and who could be so impolite as to slight the work of a lady-poetess whom he had taken in to dinner?

Section 15. Thyrsis studied these people, and measured himself against them. He was not blinded by any vanity; he knew that it would not have taken him a week to turn out a short story which would have had the requisite qualities for Macin-tyre's--which would have been clever and entertaining, would have had genuine sentiment, and as large a proportion of sincerity as the magazine admitted. He could have suggested that he thought it was worth five hundred dollars, and "Billy" Ma-cintyre would have nodded and sent him a check. And then he could have moved up to town, and got a frock-coat, and paid another call upon Mrs. "Parmy" Patton. Then his friend Comings would have put him up for the "Thistle", he would have got to know the men who made literary opinion, and so his career would have been secure.

Nor need he have made any apparent break with his convictions. In "society" one met all sorts of eccentrics--"babus" and "yogis", Christian Scientists, spiritual-ists and theosophists, Fletcherites, vegetarians and "raw-fooders". And there would be ample room for his fad--it was quite "English" to be touched with Socialism. All that one had to do was to be entertaining in one's presentation of it, and to confine one's self to its literary aspects--not setting forth plans for the expropriation of the house of Macintyre!

Thyrsis had one grievous handicap, of course. He would have had to keep his wife and child in the background; for Corydon, alas, would not have scored as a giver of dinner-parties. From a woman like Mrs. Jesse Dyckman, skilled in intellectual fence, and merciless to her inferiors, Corydon would have turned tail and fled. Thyrsis was able to sit by and let Mrs. Dyckman wave the plumes of her wit and spread the tail-feathers of her culture before his astonished eyes, and at the same time occupy his mind with studying her, and working out her "economic interpretation". But Corydon took life too intensely, and people too personally for that.

But she would have let him go, if he had told her that it was best. So why should he not do it--why should he turn his back upon this opportunity, and return to the "soap-box in a marsh" to wrestle with loneliness and want? The fact of the matter was that the thing which seemed so easy to his intellect, was impossible to his character. Thyrsis could not have anything to do with these people without hypocrisy; merely to sit and talk pleasantly with them was to lie. They were to him the enemy, the thing he was in life to fight. And he hated all that they stood for in the world-- he hated their ideas and their institutions, their virtues as well as their vices.

He had been down into the bottom-most pit of hell, and the sights that he had seen there had withered him up. How could he derive enjoyment from silks and jewels, from rich foods and fine wines, when he heard in his ears the cries of agony of the millions he had left behind him in that seething abyss? And should he trample upon their faces, as so many others had trampled? Should he make a ladder of their murdered hopes, to climb out to fame and fortune? Not he!

It seemed to him sometimes, as he thought about it, that he alone, of all men living, had power to voice the despair of these tortured souls. Others had been down into that pit, and had come out alive; but who was there among them that was an ***artist;*** that could forge his hatred into a weapon, sharp enough and stout enough to be driven through the tough hide of the world of culture? To be an artist meant to have spent years and decades in toil and study, in disciplining and drilling one's powers; and who was there that had descended into the social inferno, and had come back with strength enough to accomplish that labor?

So it seemed to him that he was the bearer of a gospel, that he had to teach the world something it could otherwise not know. He had tried out upon his own person, and upon the persons of his loved ones, the effects of poverty and destitution, of cold and hunger, of solitude and sickness and despair. And so he knew, of his own knowledge, the meaning of the degradation that he saw in modern society--

of suicide and insanity, of drunkenness and vice and crime, of physical and mental and moral decay. He knew, and none could dispute him! Therefore he must nerve himself for the struggle; he must deliver that message, and pound home that truth. He must keep on and on--in defiance of authority, in the face of all the obloquy and ridicule that the prostitute powers of civilization could heap upon him. He must live for that work, and die for it--to make real to the thinking world the infamies and the horrors of the capitalist *regime*.

BOOK XV
THE CAPTIVE FAINTS

"Too quick despairer, wherefore wilt thou go?
    Soon will the high Midsummer pomps come on."

"Do you remember how you used to tell me that?" she whispered. "Hoping--always hoping!"

"And always young!" he added.

"How did I keep so?" she said, with wonder in her voice; and he read--

"Thou nearest the immortal chants--of old!-
    Putting his sickle to the perilous grain
      In the hot corn-field of the Phrygian king,
    For thee the Lityerses-song again
      Young Daphnis with his silver voice doth sing!"

Then a smile of mischief crossed her face, and she asked, "Which Daphnis?"

Section 1. Thyrsis came back to his home in the country, divided between satisfaction over the four hundred dollars worth of booty he had captured, and a great uneasiness concerning his novel. It had had with the critics all the success that he could have asked, but unfortunately it did not seem to be selling. Already it had been out three weeks, and the sales had been only a thousand copies. The publisher confessed himself disappointed, but said that it was too early to be certain; they must allow time for the book to make its way, for the opinions of the reviews to take effect.

And so, for week after week, Thyrsis watched and hoped against hope--the old, heart-sickening experience. In the end he came to realize that he had achieved that most cruel of all literary ironies, the ***succes d'estime***. The critics agreed that he had written a most unusual book; but then, the critics did not really count--they had no way of making their verdict effective. What determined success or failure was the department-store public. It would take a whim for a certain novel; and when a novel had once begun to sell, it would be advertised and pushed to the front, and everything else would give way before it, quite regardless of what the critic's had said. A book-review appeared only once, but an advertisement might appear a score of times, and be read all over the country. So the public would have pounded into its consciousness the statement that "Hearts Aflame", by Dorothy Dimple, was a masterpiece of character-drawing, full of thrilling incident and alive with pulsing passion. The department-store public, which was not intelligent enough to distinguish between a criticism and an advertisement, would accept all these opinions at their face-value. And that was success; even the critics bowed to it in the end--as you might note by the change in their tone when they came to review the next work by this "popular" novelist.

So Thyrsis faced the ghastly truth that another year and a half of toiling and waiting had gone for nothing--the heights of opportunity were almost as far away as ever. He had to summon up his courage and nerve himself for yet another climb; and Corydon would have to face the prospect of another winter in the "soap-box in a marsh".

It was now November, and Thyrsis had written nothing but Socialist manifestoes for six months. He was restless and chafing again; but living in distress as they were, he could not get his thoughts together at all. He must have been a trying person to live in the house with at such a time. "You ask me to take love for granted," said Corydon to him once; "but how can I, when your every expression is contradictory to love?"

How could he explain to her his trouble? Here again was the pressure of that dreadful "economic screw", that was crushing their love, and all beauty and joy and hope in their hearts. They might fight against it with all the power of their beings; they might fall down upon their knees together, and pledge themselves with anguish in their voices and tears in their eyes; but still the remorseless pressure would go on, day and night, week after week, without a moment's respite.

There was this little house, for instance. It was all that Thyrsis wanted, and all that he would ever have wanted; and yet he could not be happy in it, because Corydon was not happy in it. He must be plotting and planning and worrying, straining every nerve to get to another house; he might not even think of any other possibility--that would be treason to her. So always it seemed--he had to turn his face a way that he did not wish to travel, he had to go on against every instinct of his own nature. His love for Corydon was such that he would be ashamed whenever his own instincts showed themselves. But then he would go alone, and try to do his work, and then discover the havoc this had wrought in his own being.

Just now the tension had reached the breaking point; the craving for solitude and peace was eating him up.

"What is it that you want?" asked Corydon, one day.

"I want to be where I don't have to see anybody," he cried. "I want to rough it in a tent, as I did once before."

"But it's too late to go to the Adirondacks, Thyrsis!"

"I know that," he said. "But there are other places."

He had heard of one in Virginia--in that very Wilderness of which he had written so eloquently, but had never seen. "Isn't there some one who could come and stay with you?" he pleaded.

"I don't know," replied Corydon. But the next day, as fate would have it, there came a letter from Delia Gordon, saying that she had finished a certain stage of her study-course, and was tired out and in fear of break-down. So an invitation was sent and accepted, and Thyrsis secured the respite which he craved.

And so behold him as a hermit once more, settled in a deserted cabin not far from the battle-field of Spotsylvania. He had got rid of the vermin in the cabin by burning sulphur, and had stocked his establishment with a canvas-cot and a camp-stool and a lamp and an oil-can, and the usual supply of beans and bacon and rice and corn-meal and prunes. Also he had built himself a rustic table, and unpacked a trunkful of blankets and dishes and writing-pads and books. So once more his life was his own, and a thing of delight to him.

He had promised himself to live off the country, as he had before; but the principal game here was the wild turkey, and the wild turkey proved itself a shy and elusive bird. It was not occupied with meditations concerning literary masterpieces;

and so it had a great advantage over Thyrsis, who would forget that he had a gun with him after the first half-hour of a "hunt".

Section 2. It had now become clear to Thyrsis that he had nothing more to expect from his novel; it had sold less than two thousand copies, which meant that it had not earned the money which had already been advanced to him. But all that was now ancient history--the entrenchments and graveyards of the Wilderness battlefield were not more forgotten and overgrown with new life than was the war-book in Thyrsis' mind. He had had enough of being a national chronicler which the nation did not want; he had come down to the realities of the hour, to the blazing protest of the new Revolution.

For ten years now Thyrsis had been playing at the game of professional authorship; he had studied the literary world both high and low, and had seen enough to convince him that it was an impossible thing to produce art in such a society. The modern world did not know what art was, it was incapable of forming such a concept. That which it called "art" was fraud and parasitism--its very heart was diseased.

For the essence of art was unselfishness; it was an emotion which overflowed, and which sought to communicate itself to others from an impulse of pure joy. It was of necessity a social thing; the supreme art-products of the race had been, like the Greek tragedy and the Gothic cathedral, a result of the labor of a whole community. And what could the modern man, a solitary and predatory wolf in the wilderness of *laissez faire*--what could he conceive of such a state of soul? What would happen to a man who gave himself up to such a state of soul, in a community where the wolf-law and the wolf-customs prevailed?

A grim purpose had been forming itself in Thyrsis' mind. He would suppress the artist in himself for the present--he would do it, cost whatever agony it might. He would turn propagandist for a while; instead of scattering his precious seed in barren soil, he would set to work to make the soil ready. There was seething in his mind a work of revolutionary criticism, which would sweep into the rubbish-heap the idols of the leisure-class world.

It was his idea to go back to first principles; to study the bases of modern society, and show how its customs and institutions came to be, and interpret its art as a product of these. He would show what the modern artist was, and how he got his living, and how this moulded his work. He would take the previous art-periods of history and study them, showing by what stages the artist had evolved, and so gaining a stand-point from which to prophesy what he would come to be in the future. Only once had an attempt ever been made to apply to questions of art the methods of science--in Nordau's "Degeneration". But then Nordau's had been pseudo-science--three-quarters impertinence and conceit. The world still waited to understand its art-products in the light of scientific Socialism.

Such was the task which Thyrsis was planning. It would mean years of study, and how he was to get the means to do it, he could not guess. But he had his mind made up to do it, though it might be the last of his labors, though everything else in his life might end in shipwreck. He went about all day, possessed with the idea; it would be a colossal work, an epoch-making work--it would be the culmination of his efforts and the vindication of his claims. It would save the men who came after him; and to save the men who came after him had now become the formula of his life.

Section 3. Thyrsis would come back from a sojourn such as this with all his impulses of affection and sympathy renewed; he would have had time to miss Corydon, and to realize how closely he was bound to her. He would be eager to tell her all his adventures, and the wonderful plans which he had formed.

But this time it was Corydon who had adventures to narrate. He realized as soon as he saw her that she had something upon her mind; and at the first occasion she led him off to his own study, and shut the door. He got a fire going, and she sat opposite him and gazed at him.

"Thyrsis," she said, "I hardly know how to begin."

It was all very formal and mysterious. "What is it, dear?" he asked.

"It's something terrible," she whispered. "I'm afraid you're going to be angry."

"What is it?" he repeated, more anxiously.

"I was angry myself, at first," she said; "but I've got over it now. And I want you please to be reasonable."

"Go on, dear."

"Thyrsis," she whispered, after a pause, "it's Harry."

"Harry?"

"Harry Stuart, you know."

"Oh," said he. He had all but forgotten the young drawing-teacher, whom he had left doing Socialist cartoons.

"Well?" he inquired.

"You see, Thyrsis, I always liked him very much. And he's been coming up here--quite a good deal. I didn't see why he shouldn't come--Delia liked him too, and she was with us most of the time. Was it wrong of me to let him come?"

"I don't know," said he. "Tell me."

"Perhaps it's silly of me," Corydon continued, hesitatingly--"but I'm always imagining things about people. And he seemed to me to have such possibilities. He has--how shall I say it--"

"I recall your saying he had soulful eyes," put in Thyrsis.

"You'll make fun of it all, of course," said Corydon. "But it's really very tragic. You see, he's never met a woman like me before."

"I can believe that, my dear."

"I mean--a woman that has any real ideas. He would ask me questions by the hour; and we talked about everything. So, of course, we talked about love; and he--he asked if I was happy."

"I see," said Thyrsis, grimly. "Of course you said that you were miserable."

"I didn't say much. I told him that your work was hard, and that my courage wasn't always equal to my task. Anyone can see that I have suffered."

"Yes, dear," said Thyrsis, "of course. Go on."

"Well, one day--it was last Friday--he came up with a carriage to take us driving. And Delia had a headache, and wanted to rest, and so Harry and I went alone. I--I guess I shouldn't have gone, but I didn't realize it. It was a beautiful afternoon, and we both had a good time--in fact, I don't know when I have been so contentedly happy. We stopped to gather wild flowers, and once we sat by a little stream; and of course, we talked and talked, and before I realized it, twilight was falling, and we were a long way from home."

"Go on," said Thyrsis, as she hesitated.

"We started out. I recollected later, though I didn't seem to notice it at the time--that Harry's voice seemed to grow husky, and he spoke indistinctly. He had let the horse have the reins, and his arm was on the back of my seat. I hadn't noticed it; but then--then--fancy my horror--"

"Well?"

"It happened--all of a sudden." Corydon stammered, her cheeks turning scarlet. "I felt his arm clasp me; and I turned and stared, and his face was close to mine, and his eyes were fairly shining."

There was a pause. "What did you do?" asked the other.

"I just looked at him calmly, and said, 'Oh, how *could* you?' And at that he took his arm away quickly, and sat up stiff and straight, with a terribly hurt expression. 'Forgive me,' he said. 'I was mad.' And we neither of us spoke a word all the way home. And when we came to the house, I jumped out of the carriage without saying good-night."

Corydon sat staring at her husband, with her wide-open, anxious eyes. "And was that all?" he asked.

"To-day I had a letter from him. He said he was going away, over the Christmas holidays. He said that he was very much ashamed of himself, and he hoped that I would be able to forgive him. And that's all."

They sat for a while in silence. "You won't be too angry?" asked Corydon, anxiously.

"I'm not angry at all," he said. "But naturally it's disturbing. I don't like to have such things happen to you."

"It's strange, you know," said Corydon, "but I haven't seemed to stay very indignant. He was so hurt, you know--and I can realize how unhappy he's been. Curiously enough, I've even found myself thinking that I'd like to see him again. And that puzzled me. I felt that I ought to be quite outraged. That he should imagine he could hug me--like any shop-girl!"

They spent many hours discussing this adventure; in fact it was a week or two before they had disposed of it entirely. Thyrsis was hoping that the experience might be utilized to persuade Corydon to modify her utopian attitude towards young men with soulful eyes and waving brown hair. He was at some pains to set forth to her the psychology of the male creature--insisting that he knew more about this than she did, and that his remarks applied to drawing-teachers as well as to all other arts and professions.

The main question, of course, was as to their attitude towards Harry Stuart when he returned. Corydon, it became clear, had forgiven him; the phraseology of his letter was touching, and he was now invested in the glamor of penitence. She insisted that the episode might be overlooked, and that their friendship could go on as before. But Thyrsis argued vigorously that their relationship could never be the same again, and declared that they ought not to meet.

"But then," Corydon protested, "he'll be at the Jennings! And I can't snub him!"

"What does Delia think about it?" he asked.

"Dear me!" Corydon exclaimed. "I haven't told Delia a word of it!"

"Haven't told her! But why not?"

"Because she'd be horrified. She'd never speak to Harry Stuart again!"

"But then you want *me* to speak to him! And even to be cordial to him! You want to go ahead and carry on a sentimental flirtation with him--"

"Oh, Thyrsis!" she protested.

"But that's what it would come to. And how much peace of mind do you suppose I'd have, while I knew that was going on?"

At which Corydon sighed pathetically. "I'm a fine sort of emancipated woman!" she said. "Don't you see you're playing the role of the conventional jealous husband?"

But as she thought over the matter in the privacy of her own mind she was filled with perplexity, and wondered at herself. She found herself actually longing to see Harry Stuart. She asked herself, "Can it really be I, Corydon, who am capable of being interested in any other man besides my husband?" She could not bring herself to face the fact that it was true.

Section 4. Thyrsis went away, and took to wandering about the country, wrestling with his new book. After the fashion of every work that came to possess him, it seemed to possess him as no other work had ever done before. His mind was in a turmoil with it, his thoughts racing from one part to another; he would stop in the midst of pumping a bucket of water or bringing in a supply of wood, to jot down some notes that came to him. Each day he realized more fully the nature of the task. Seated alone at night in his tiny cabin, his spirit would cry out in terror at the burden that had been heaped upon it.

He had decided upon the title of the book--"Art and Money: an Essay in the Economic Interpretation of Literature". And then, late one night, as he was pondering it, there had flashed over him the form into which he should cast the work; he would make it, not only an exposition of his philosophy, but the story of his life, the cry of his soul. There had come to him an introductory statement; it was a smashing thing--a thing that would arrest and stun! Disraeli had said that a critic was a man who had failed as a creative writer; and Thyrsis would take that taunt and make it into his battle-cry. "I who write this," he would say--"I am a failure; I am a murdered artist! I sit by the corpse of my dead dreams, I dip my pen into the heart's blood of my strangled vision!" So he would indict the forces that had murdered him, and through the rest of the book he would pursue them--he would track them to their lair and corner them, and slay them with a sharp sword.

Meantime Delia Gordon had gone back to her studies, and Corydon had settled down to her lonely task. She washed and dressed and fed the baby, and satisfied what she could of his insatiable demands for play. Thyrsis would come and help to get the meals and wash the dishes; but even then he was poor company--he was either tired out, or lost in thought, and his nerves were in such a state that he could not bear to be criticized. It was getting to be harder for him to endure the strain of hearing complaints; and so Corydon shrunk more and more into herself, and took to pouring out her soul in long letters and journals.

"Is it possible," she wrote to Delia, "that to some people life is a continuous expiation--an expiation of submerged hereditary sins, as well as of conscious ones? A great deal of the time life seems to me a hopeless puzzle; I am so utterly unfitted for the roles I labor to play. Is it that I am too low for my environment? Or can it be that I am too high? Surely there must some day be other things that women can do in the world besides training children. I try to love my task, but I have no talent for it, and it is a frightful strain upon me. After one hour of blocks and choo-choo cars, I am perfectly prostrated. I have been cheated out of the joys of motherhood, that is the truth--the spring was poisoned for me at the very beginning.

"You must not mind my lamentations, dear Delia," she wrote in another letter. "You can't imagine how lonely my life is--no, for it is different when you are here. Oh, I am so weary! so weary! It didn't use to be like this. Every moment of leisure I had I would run and try to study; I would read something--I was always eager and hungry. But now I am dull--I do not follow my inspirations. If only Thyrsis and I might sometimes read together! I love to be read to, but he cannot bear it--he reads three times as fast to himself, he says. He will do it if I am sick; but even then it makes him nervous, and I cannot help but know that, however he tries to hide it. It is one of our troubles, but we know each other's states of mind intuitively.

"Oh, Delia, was there ever a tragedy in the world like that of our love? (Almost everything in our lives is pain, and so we are coming to stand for pain to each other!) I ask myself sometimes if any two people who love could stand what we have to stand. Sometimes I think they could, if their love was different; but then that thought breaks my heart! Why cannot our love be different, I ask!

"I had one of my frightful fits of unhappiness to-day. It was nothing--it was my fault, I guess. I am very sensitive. But I think it is a tendency of Thyrsis' temperament to try instinctively to overcome mine. Apparently the only thing that will conquer him is seeing me suffer; then he will give way--he will promise anything I want, blame himself for his rigidity, scourge himself for his blindness, do anything at all I ask. So I tell myself, everything will be different now; the last problem is solved! I see how good and kind he is, how noble his impulses are; he has never failed me in the big things of life.

"I suppose Mr. Harding writes you about us. He was up here this afternoon. He was very gentle and kind to me; he talked about his religion. Did you tell him much about me? It is a singular thing, how he seems to understand without being told. I realized to-day that whenever we talk about my life, we take everything for granted. Also, it seems strange that he does not blame me; generally people who are conventional think that I am selfish, that I ought to be loving my baby, instead of struggling with my pitiful soul.

"I wrote a little stanza the other night, dear Delia. Doesn't it seem strange, that when I am at the last gasp with agony, I should find myself thinking of lines of poetry? I called it 'Life'; you will say that it is too sombre--

"'A lonely journey in a night of storm, Lighted by flashes of inconstant faith, Goaded by multitudes of vague desires, And mocked by phantoms of remote delight!'"

Section 5. Just at this time Corydon found herself the victim of backaches and fits of exhaustion, for which there was no cause to be discovered. Each attack meant that Thyrsis would have to drop his work, and come and be housekeeper and nurse; he would have to repress every slightest sign of the impatience, which, was burning him up--knowing that if he gave vent to it, he would drive Corydon half-wild with suffering. After two or three such crises, he made up his mind that it was impossible for him to go on, until there was some one to help her in these emergencies.

As a result of their farm-hunting expeditions, they had in mind a place which was a compromise between their different requirements. It had a good barn and plenty of fruit, and at the same time a view, and a house with comfortable rooms, and wall-paper that was not altogether unendurable. It was offered for four thousand dollars, of which nearly three-quarters might remain upon mortgage; so they had agreed that their future happiness would depend upon the war-book's bringing them in a thousand dollars. Since this hope had failed, he had applied to Darrell, and to Paret, but neither of them had the money to spare. It now fell out, that just as he was at the point of desperation, he received a letter from the clergyman who had married them, Dr. Hamilton. This worthy man had been reading Thyrsis' manuscripts and following his career; and he now wrote to tell how greatly he had been impressed by the new novel. Whereupon the author was seized by a sudden resolve, and packed up a hand-satchel and set out for the city, with all the forces of his being nerved for an assault upon this ill-fated clergyman.

Dr. Hamilton sat in his little office, looking pale and worn, his face deeply seamed with lines of care. As the poet thought of it in later years, he realized that this man's function in life was to be a clearing-house for human misery--the wrecks of the competitive system in all classes and grades of society came to him to pour out their troubles and beg for help. It was not so very long afterwards that he went to pieces from overwork and nervous strain; and Thyrsis wondered with a guilty feeling how much his own assault had contributed to this result. Assuredly it could not happen often that a clergyman had to listen to a more harrowing tale than this "murdered artist" had to tell.

The doctor heard it out, and then began to argue: like the philanthropist in Boston, he was greatly troubled by the fear of "weakening the springs of character". Being an "advanced" clergyman, he was familiar with the pat phrases of evolutionary science--his mind was a queer jumble of the philosophy of Herbert Spencer and that of Thomas a Kempis. But Thyrsis just now was in a mood which might have moved even Spencer himself; he was almost frantic because of Corydon, whom he had left half-ill at home. He was not pleading for himself, he said--he could always get along; but oh, the horror of having to kill his wife for the sake of his books! To have to sit by day by day and watch her dying! He told about that night when Corydon had tried to kill herself; and now another winter was upon them, and he knew that unless something were done, the spring-time would not find her alive.

The suicide story turned the balance with the clergyman; Herbert Spencer was put back upon the shelf, and Thomas a Kempis ruled the day. Dr. Hamilton said that he would see one of his rich parishioners, and persuade him to take a second mortgage on the farm. And so Thyrsis went back, a messenger of wondrous tidings.

A few days later came the check. The deed had been got ready; and Thyrsis drove to the farm, and carried off the farmer and his wife to the nearest notary-public. The old man pleaded to stay in his home until the new year, but Thyrsis was obdurate, allowing him only a week in which to get himself and his belongings to another place. And meantime he and Corydon were packing up. They drove to another "vandew", and purchased more odds and ends of household stuff; and Thyrsis had his little study loaded upon a wagon, and taken to the new place.

A wonderful adventure was this moving! To enter a real house, with two stories, and two pairs of stairs, and eight rooms, and a cellar, and regular plastered walls, and no end of closets and shelves and such-like domestic luxuries! To be able to set apart a whole room in which the baby might spread himself with his toys and marbles and dolls and picture-books--and without any one's having to stumble over them, and break their owner's heart! To have a real parlor, with a stove to sit by, and a table for a lamp, and shelves for books; and yet another room to eat in, and another to cook in! To be able to have a woman come to wash the dishes without making a bosom friend of her, and having her hear all the conversation! To be able to walk through fields and orchards and woodland, and know that they belonged to one's self, and would some day shed their coat of snow and blossom into new life! Thyrsis wished that he could have the book out of his mind for a month, so that he might be properly thrilled by this experience.

It was at the Christmas season, and therefore an appropriate times for celebrating. He went down into the "wood-lot"--their own "wood-lot"--and cut a spruce tree, and set it up in the dining-room; they hung thereon all the contrivances which the associated grandparents had sent down to commemorate an occasion which was not only Christmas and house-warming, but the baby's third birthday as well. Because of the triple conjunction, they invested in a fat goose, to be roasted in the new kitchen-range; and besides this there were some spare-ribs and home-made sausages with which a neighbor had tempted them. It was a regular storybook Christmas, with a snow-storm raging outside, and the wind howling down the chimney, and an odor of molasses-taffy pervading the house.

Section 6. After which festivities Thyrsis bid farewell to his family once more, and went away to wrestle with his angel. Weeks of failure and struggle it cost him before he could get back what he had lost--before he could recall those phrases that had once blazed white-hot in his brain, and could see again the whole gigantic form and figure of his undertaking. Many an hour he spent pacing his little eight-foot piazza--four steps and a half each way, back and forth; many a night he would sit before his little fourteen-inch stove, so lost in his meditations that the stove would lose its red-hot glow, and the icy gale which raged outside and rattled the door would steal in through the cracks and set him to shivering.

Other times he would trudge through the snow and mud to the town, spending the day in the library, and then bringing out an armful of books to last him through the night. Thyrsis had read pretty thoroughly the literature of the six languages he knew; but now-- this was the appalling nature of his task--he had to go back and read it over again. He did not realize, until he got actually at the work, what an utter overturning there would be in all his ideas. How strange it was to return and read the "classics" of one's youth! What oceans of futility one discovered, what mountains of pretense--and with what forests of scholarship grown over them! It seemed to Thyrsis that everywhere he turned the search-light of his new truth, the structure of his opinions would topple like a house of cards. Truly, here was a *"Gotzendammerung"*, an *"Umwertung aller Werthe"*!

The worst of it was that he had to read, not only literature, but also history--often his own kind of history, that had not yet been written. If he wished to know the Shakespearean dramas as a product of the aristocratic and imperialist ideal in the glory and intoxication of its youth, he had to study, not only Shakespeare's poetry, but the cultural and social life of the Elizabethan people. And he could not take any man's word for the truth; he had to know for himself. The thing that would avail him in this battle was not eloquence and fervor, not the flashes of his irony and the white-hot shafts of his scorn. What he must have were facts, and more facts--and then again facts!

The facts were there, to be had for the gathering. Thyrsis again could only compare himself to Aladdin in his palace. Could it be believed that so many ideas had been left for one man to discover? It seemed to him, that the kingdoms of literature lay at his mercy; he was like a magician who has discovered a new spell, which places his rivals in his power. He knew that this book, if he could ever finish it, would alter the aspect of literary criticism, as a blow changes the pattern in a kaleidoscope.

Thyrsis had failed many times before, but this time he felt that success was in his hands; he knew the bookworld now, he was master of the game. This would set them to thinking, this would stir them up! He had got under the armor of his enemy at last, and he could feel him wince and writhe at each thrust that he drove home. So he wrought at his task, in a state of tense excitement, living always in imagination in the midst of the battle, following stroke with stroke and driving a rout before him.--So he would be for weeks; and then would come the reaction, when he fell back exhausted, and realized that his victory was mere phantasy, that nothing of it really counted until he had completed his labor. And that would take two years! Two years!

Section 7. From visions such as this Thyrsis came back to wrestle with all the problems of a household; with pumps that froze and drains that clogged, with stoves that went out and ashes that spilled, with milk-boys that were late and kitchen-maids that were snow-bound. He would leave his work at one or two o'clock in the morning, and make his way through the snow and the storm to the house, and crawl into bed, and then take his chances of being awakened by the baby, or by some spell of agony with Corydon.

He might not sleep alone; that supreme symbol of domesticity Corydon could not give up, and he soon ceased to ask for it. It seemed such a little thing to yield; and yet it meant so much to him! The room where he slept came to seem to him a chamber of terror, a place to which he went "like the galley-slave at night, scourged to his dungeon". It was a place where a crime was enacted; where the vital forces of his being were squandered, and the body and soul of him were wrung and squeezed dry like a sponge. This was marriage--it was the essence of marriage; it was the slavery into which he had delivered himself, the duty to which he was bound. And in how many millions of homes was this same thing going on--this licensed preying of one personality upon another? And the nightmare thing was upheld and buttressed by all the forces of society--priests were saying blessings over it and moralists were singing the praises of it--"the holy bonds of matrimony", it was called!

It was all the worse to Thyrsis because there was that in him which welcomed this animal intimacy. So he saw that day by day their lives were slipping to a lower plane; day by day they were discovering new weaknesses and developing new vices in themselves. Corydon was now a good part of the time in pain of some sort; and the doctors had accustomed her to stave off these crises with various kinds of drugs, so that she had a set of shelves crowded with pills and powders and bottles. She had learned to rely upon them in emergencies, to plead for them when she was helpless; and so Thyrsis saw her declining into an inferno. He would argue with her and plead with her and fight with her; he would spend days trying to open her eyes to the peril, to show her that it was better to suffer pain than to resort to these treacherous aids.

Section 8. They still had their hours of enthusiasm, of course, their illuminations and their resolutions. During the summer, while browsing among the English magazines in the library, Thyrsis had stumbled upon an astonishing article dealing with the subject of health. He read it in a state of great excitement, and then took it home and read it to Corydon. It told of the achievements of a gentleman by the name of Horace Fletcher, who had once possessed robust health, and lost it through careless living, and had then restored it by a new system of eating. To Thyrsis this came as one of the great discoveries of his life. For years every instinct of his nature had been whispering to him that his ways of eating were vicious; but he had been ignorant and helpless--and with all the world that he knew in opposition to him. As he read the article, he recalled a talk he had had with his "family doctor", way back before his marriage, when he had first begun to notice symptoms of stomach-trouble. He had suggested timidly that there might be something wrong with his diet, and that if the doctor would tell him exactly what he ought to eat, and how much and how often, he would be glad to adopt the regimen. But the doctor had only laughed and answered, "Nonsense, boy--don't you get to thinking about your food!" And so Thyrsis had gone away, to follow the old plan of eating what he liked. Health, it would seem, must be a spontaneous and accidental thing, it could not be a deliberate and reasoned thing.

But now he and Corydon became smitten with a passion of shame for all their stupidity and their gluttony; they invested in Fletcher's books, and set out upon this new adventure. They would help themselves to a very small saucerful of food; and they would take of this a very small spoonful--and chew--and chew--and chew. Mr. Fletcher said that half an hour a day was enough for the eating of the food one needed; but they, apparently, could have chewed for hours, and still been hungry. They labored religiously to stop as soon as they could pretend to be satisfied; the result of which was that Thyrsis lost fourteen pounds in as many days--and it was many a long year before he got those fourteen pounds back! He became still more "spiritual" in his aspect; until finally he and Corydon set out for a walk one day, and coming up a hill to their home they gave out altogether, and first Thyrsis had to crawl up the hill and get something to eat, and then take something down to Corydon!

However, in spite of all their blunders, this new idea was of genuine benefit to them; at least it put them upon the right track--it taught them the relationship between diet and disease. They saw the two as cause and consequence--they watched the food they ate affecting their bodies as one might watch a match affecting a thermometer. They were no longer victims of the idea that health must be a spontaneous and accidental thing--they were set definitely to thinking about it, as something that could be achieved by will and intelligence.

But the right knowledge lay far in the future; and meantime they were groping in ignorance, and disease was still a mysterious visitation that came upon them out of the night. "Thus saith the Lord, About midnight will I go out into the midst of Egypt; and all the firstborn in the land of Egypt shall die. And there shall be a great cry throughout all the land of Egypt, such as there hath been none like it, nor shall be like it any more."

Their own firstborn had low been on the *regime* of the "child specialist" for a year and a half. He was big and fat and rosy, and according to all the standards they knew, a picture of health. He was the pride of his parents' hearts--the one success they had achieved, and to which they could turn their eyes. He was a frightful burden to them--the most noisy and irrepressible of children. But they struggled and worried along with him, and were proud of him--and even, in a stormy sort of way, were happy with him. But now a calamity fell upon him, bringing them the most terrible distress they had yet had to face in their lives.

Section 9. It was all the worse because they laid the blame upon themselves. They were accustomed to attribute sickness to this or that trivial cause--if Corydon caught a cold, it was because she had sat in a draught, and if Thyrsis was laid up with tonsilitis, it was because he had gone out for kindling-wood without his hat. It had been their wont to bundle the child up and turn him out to play; and one very cold day he had stood a long time under the woodshed, and had got chilled. So that night his head was hot, and he was fretful; and in the morning he would not eat, and apparently had a fever. They sent off in haste for the doctor; and the doctor came and examined him, and shook his head and looked very grave. It was pneumonia, he said, and a serious case.

So Corydon and Thyrsis had to put all things else aside, and gird themselves for a siege. There were medicines to be administered every hour, and minute precautions to be taken to keep the patient from the slightest chill; he must be in a warm room, and yet with some ventilation. All these things they attended to, and then they would sit and gaze at the sufferer, dumb with grief and fear. Through the night Thyrsis sat by the bedside, while Cedric babbled and raved in delirium; and no suffering that he had ever experienced was equal to this.

How he loved this baby, how passionately, how cruelly! How he clung to him, blindly and desperately--the thought of losing him simply tore his heart to pieces! He would hold the hot hands, he would touch the little body; how he loved that body, that was so beautiful and soft and white! How many times he had bathed it and dressed it and hugged it to him! He would sit and listen to the fevered prattle, full of childish phrases which brought before him the childish soul--the wonderful, lovable thing, so merry and eager, so full of mischief and curiosity; with strange impulses of tenderness, and flashes of intelligence that thrilled one, and opened long vistas to the imagination. He was all they had, this baby--he was all they had saved out of the ruin of their lives, out of the shipwreck of their love. What sacrifices they had made for him--what agonies he represented! And now, the idea that they might never see him, nor touch him, nor hear his voice again!

Also would come agonies of remorse. Thyrsis would face the blunder they had made--it might have been avoided so easily, and now it was irrevocable! His whole body would shake with silent sobbing. Ah, this curse of their lives, this hideous shame--that they had not even been able to take proper care of their child! This wrong, too, the world meant to inflict upon them--this supreme vengeance, this cruel punishment!

Section 10. The doctor came next morning, and found the patient worse. This was the crisis, he said; if the little one lived through the night--And there he paused, seeing the agony in the eyes of the mother and father. They would do all they could, he said; they must hope for the best.

So the siege went on. Thyrsis sat through the night again--and Corydon, who could not rest either, would come into the room every little while, and listen and watch. They would hold each other's hand for hours, dumb with suffering; ghostly presences seemed to haunt the sick-chamber and set them to trembling. Thyrsis found himself thinking of that most terrible of all ballads, "The Erl-King". How he had shuddered once, hearing it sung!--

"Dem Vater grauset's, er reitet geschwind!"

All through the night he seemed to hear the hammer-strokes of the horse's hoofs echoing through his soul.

The child lived through the night, but the crisis was not yet over. The fever held on; the issue of life and death seemed to hang upon the flutter of an eyelid. There was one more night to be sat through and Thyrsis, whose restless intellect must needs be dealing with all issues, had by then fought his way through this ter-ror also. They must get control of themselves at all hazards, he said; they must face the facts. If so the child should die--

He tried to say something of the sort to Corydon, seeking to steady her. But Corydon became almost frantic at his words. "You must not say such a thing, you must not think such a thing!" she cried.

Corydon had been reading about "new thought", and she insisted that would be "holding the idea" of death over the child. "The thing for us to do," she said, "is to make up our minds--he must live, we must ***know*** that he will live!"--It was no time to argue about metaphysics, but Thyrsis found this proposition a source of great perplexity. How could a man make himself know what he did not know?

The crisis passed, and the child lived. But the illness continued for a couple of weeks--and how pitiful it was to see their baby, that had been so big and rosy, and was now pale and thin and weak! And when at last he got up and went outdoors again, he caught a cold, and there was a relapse, and another siege of the dread disease; the doctor had not warned them sufficiently, it seemed. So there was a week or two more of watching and worrying; and then they had to face the fact that little Cedric would be delicate for a long while--would need to be guarded with care all through the spring.

Thyrsis blamed himself for all that had happened; the weight of it rested upon him forever afterwards, as if it were some crime he had committed. Sometimes when he was overwrought and overdriven, he would lie awake in the small hours of the morning, and this spectre would come and sit by him. He had made a martyr of the child he loved, he had sacrificed it to what he called his art; and how had he dared to do it?

It was hard to think of a more cruel question to put to a man. Himself, no doubt, he might scourge and drive and wreck; but this child--what were the child's rights? Thyrsis would try to weigh them against the claims of posterity. What his own work might be, he knew; and to what extent should he sacrifice it to the unknown possibilities of his son? Some sacrifice there had to be--such was the stern decree of the "economic screw."

So Thyrsis once more was a field of warring motives; once more he faced the curse of his life--that he could not be as other men, he could not have other men's virtues. It was the latest aspect, and the most tragic, of that impulse in him which had made him fight so hard against marriage; which had made him quote to Corydon the lines of the outlaw's song--

"The fiend whose lantern lights the mead
Were better mate than I!"

BOOK XVI
THE BREAK FOR FREEDOM

The scarlet flush of morning was in the sky; and they stood upon the hill again, and watched the color spreading.

"We must go," she was saying. "But it was worthwhile to come."

"It was all worth-while," he said--"all!"

And she smiled, and quoted some lines from the poem--

"Thou too, O Thyrsis, on like quest wast bound;
　Thou wanderedst with me for a little hour!
　　Men gave thee nothing; but this happy quest,
　If men esteem'd thee feeble, gave thee power,
　　If men procured thee trouble, gave thee rest!"_

Section 1. This illness of the baby's had been a fearful drain upon their strength; and Thyrsis perceived that they had now got to a point where they could no longer stand alone. There must be a servant in the house, to help Corydon, and do for the baby what had to be done. It was a hard decision for him to face, for his money was almost gone, and the book loomed larger than ever. But there was no escaping the necessity.

They would get a married couple, they decided--the man could pay for himself by working the farm. So they put an advertisement in a city paper, and perused the scores of mis-spelled replies. After due correspondence, and much consultation, they decided upon Patrick and Mary Flanagan; and Thyrsis hired a two-seated carriage and drove in to meet them at the depot.

It was all very funny; years afterwards, when the clouds of tragedy were dispersed, they were able to laugh over the situation. Thyrsis had been used to servants in boyhood, but that was before he had acquired any ideas as to universal brotherhood and the rights of man. Now he hated all the symbols and symptoms of mastership; he shrunk from any sort of clash with unlovely personalities--he would be courteous and deprecating to the very tramp who came to his door to beg. And here were Patrick and Mary, very Irish, enormously stout, and devotedly Roman Catholic, having spent all their lives as caretakers of "gentlemen's country-places". They had most precise ideas as to what gentlemen's country-places should be, and how they should be equipped, and how the gentlemen of the country-places should treat their servants. And needless to say, they found nothing in this new situation which met with their approval. There were signs of humiliating poverty everywhere, and the farm-outfit was inadequate. As to the master and mistress, they must have been puzzling phenomena for Patrick and Mary to make up their minds about--possessing so many of the attributes of the lady and gentleman, and yet being lacking in so many others!

Patrick was a precise and particular person; he wanted his work laid out just so, and then he would do it without interference. As for Mary--he stood in awe of Mary himself, and so he accepted the idea that Corydon and Thyrsis should stand in awe of her too. Mary it was who announced that their dietary was inadequate; she took no stock at all in Fletcher and Chittenden--she knew that working-people must have meat at least four times a week. Also Mary maintained that their room was not large enough for so stout a couple. Also she arranged it that Corydon and Thyrsis should get the dinner on Sundays--the Roman Catholic church being five miles away, and the hour of mass being late, and the horse very old and slow.

For two months Corydon and Thyrsis struggled along under the dark and terrible shadow of the disapproval of the Flanagan family. Then one day there came a violent crisis between Corydon and Mary--occasioned by a discussion of the effect of an excess of grease upon the digestibility of potato-starch. Corydon fled in tears to her husband, who started for the kitchen forthwith, meaning to dispose of the Flanagans; when, to his vast astonishment, Corydon experienced one of her surges of energy, and thrust him to one side, and striding out upon the field of combat, proceeded to deliver herself of her pent-up sentiments. It was a discourse in the grandest style of tragedy, and Mary Flanagan was quite dumbfounded--apparently this was a "lady" after all! So the Flanagan family packed its belongings and departed in a chastened frame of mind; and Corydon turned to her spouse, her eyes still flashing, and remarked, "If only I had talked to her that way from the beginning!"

Section 2. Then once more there was answering of advertisements, and another couple was spewed forth from the maw of the metropolis--"Henery and Bessie Dobbs", as they subscribed themselves. "Henery" proved to be the adult stage of the East Side "gamin"; lean and cynical, full of slang and humor and the odor of cigarettes. He was fresh from a "ticket-chopper's" job in the subway, and he knew no more about farming than Thyrsis did; but he put up a clever "bluff", and was so prompt with his wits that it was hard to find fault with him successfully. As for his wife, she had come out of a paper-box factory, and was as skilled at housekeeping as her husband was at agriculture; she was frail and consumptive, and told Corydon the story of her pitiful life, with the result that she was able to impose upon her even more than her predecessor had done.

"Henery" was slow at pitching hay and loading stone, but when the season came, he developed a genius for peddling fruit; he was always hungry for any sort of chance to bargain, and was forever coming upon things which Thyrsis ought to buy. Very quickly the neighborhood discovered this propensity of his, and there was a constant stream of farmers who came to offer second-hand buggies, and wind-broken horses, and dried-up cows, and patent hay-rakes and churns and corn-shellers at reduced values; all of which rather tended to reveal to Thyrsis the unlovely aspects of his neighbors, and to weaken his faith in the perfectibility of the race.

Among Henery's discoveries was a pair of aged and emaciated mules. He became eloquent as to how he could fatten up these mules and what crops he could raise in the spring. So Thyrsis bought the mules, and also a supply of feed; but the fattening process failed to take effect-for the reason, as Thyrsis finally discovered, that the mules were in need of new teeth. When the plowing season began, Henery at first expended a vast amount of energy in beating the creatures with a stick, but finally he put his inventive genius to work, and devised a way to drive them without beating. It was some time before Thyrsis noted the change; when he made inquiries, he learned to his consternation that the ingenious Henery had fixed up the stick with a pin in the end!

At any time of the day one might stand upon the piazza of the house and gaze out across the corn-field, and see a long procession marching through the furrow. First there came the mules, and then came the plow, and then came Henery; and after Henery followed the dog, and after the dog followed the baby, and after the baby followed a train of chickens, foraging for worms. Little Cedric was apparently content to trot back and forth in the field for hours; which to his much-occupied parents seemed a delightful solution of a problem. But it happened one day when they had a visit from Mr. Harding, that Thyrsis and the clergyman came round the side of the house, and discovered the child engaged in trying to drag a heavy arm-chair through a door that was too small for it. He was wrestling like a young titan, purple in the face with rage; and shouting, in a perfect reproduction of Henery's voice and accent, "Come round here, God damn you, come round here!"

There were many such drawbacks to be balanced against the joys of "life on a farm". Thyrsis reflected with a bitter smile that his experiences and Corydon's had been calculated to destroy their illusions as to several kinds of romance. They had tried "Grub Street", and the poet's garret, and the cultivating of literature upon a little oatmeal; they had not found that a joyful adventure. They had tried the gypsy style of existence; they had gone back "to the bosom of nature"--and had found it a cold and stony bosom. They had tried out "love in a cottage", and the story-writer's dream of domestic raptures. And now they were chasing another will o' the wisp--that of "amateur farming"! When Thyrsis had purchased half the old junk in the township, and had seen the mules go lame, and the cows break into the pear-orchard and "founder" themselves; when he had expended two hundred dollars' worth of money and two thousand dollars' worth of energy to raise one hundred dollars' worth of vegetables and fruit, he framed for himself the conclusion that a farm is an excellent place for a literary man, provided that he can be kept from farming it.

Section 3. As the result of such extravagances, when they had got as far as the month of February, Thyrsis' bank-account had sunk to almost nothing. However, he had been getting ready for this emergency; he had prepared a *scenario* of his new book, setting forth the ideas it would contain and the form which it would take. This he sent to his publisher, with a letter saying that he wanted the same contract and the same advance as before.

And again he waited in breathless suspense. He knew that he had here a work of vital import, one that would be certain to make a sensation, even if it did not sell like a novel. It was, to be sure, a radical book--perhaps the most radical ever published in America; but on the other hand, it dealt with questions of literature and philosophy, where occasionally even respectable and conservative reviews permitted themselves to dally with ideas. Thyrsis was hoping that the publisher might see prestige and publicity in the adventure, and decide to take a chance; when this proved to be the case, he sank back with a vast sigh of relief. He had now money enough to last until midsummer, and by that time the book would be more than half done--and also the farm would be paying.

But alas, it seemed with them that strokes of calamity always followed upon strokes of good fortune. At this time Corydon's ailments became acute, and her nervous crises were no longer to be borne. There were anxious consultations on the subject, and finally it was decided that she should consult another "specialist". This was an uncle of Mr. Harding's, a man of most unusual character, the clergyman declared; the latter was going to the city, and would be glad to introduce Corydon.

So, a couple of days later came to Thyrsis a letter, conveying the tidings that she was discovered to be suffering from an abdominal tumor, and should undergo an immediate operation. It would cost a hundred dollars, and the hospital expenses would be at least as much; which meant that, with the bill-paying that had already taken place, their money would all be gone at the outset!

But Thyrsis did not waste any time in lamenting the inevitable. He was rather glad of the tidings, on the whole--at least there was a definite cause for Corydon's suffering, and a prospect of an end to it. Both of them had still their touching faith in doctors and surgeons, as speaking with final and godlike authority upon matters beyond the comprehension of the ordinary mind. The operation would not be dangerous, Corydon wrote, and it would make a new woman of her.

"If I could only have Delia Gordon with me," she added, "then my happiness would be complete. Only think of it, she left for Africa last week! I know she would have waited, if she'd known about this.

"However, I shall make out. Mr. Harding is going to be in town for more than a week--he is attending a conference of some sort, and he has promised to come and see me in the hospital. I think he likes to do such things--he has the queerest professional air about it, so that you feel you are being sympathized with for the glory of God. But really he is very beautiful and good, and I think you have never appreciated him. I am happy to-day, almost exhilarated; I feel as if I were about to escape from a dungeon."

Section 4. Such was the mood in which she went to her strange experience. She liked the hospital-room, tiny, but immaculately clean; she liked the nurses, who seemed to her to be altogether superior and exemplary beings--moving with such silence and assurance about their various tasks. She slept soundly, and in the morning they combed and plaited her hair and prepared her for the ceremony. There came a bunch of roses to her room, with a card from Mr. Harding; and these were exquisite, and made her happy, so that, when the doctor arrived, she went almost gaily to the operating-room.

Everything there aroused her curiosity; the pure white walls and ceiling, shining with matchless cleanness, the glittering instruments arranged carefully on glass tables, the attentive and pleasant-faced nurses, standing also in pure white, and the doctor in his vestments, smiling reassuringly. In the centre of the room was a large glass table, long enough for a reclining body, and through the sky-light the sun poured a pleasing radiance over all. "How beautiful!" exclaimed Corydon; and the nurses exchanged glances, and the old doctor failed to hide an expression of surprise.

"I wish all my patients felt like that," said he. "Now climb up on the table."

Corydon promptly did so, and another doctor who was to administer the anaesthetic came to her side. "Take a very deep breath, please," he said, as he placed over her mouth a white, cone-shaped thing that had a rather suffocating odor. Corydon was obedience itself, and breathed.

In a moment her body seemed to be falling from her. "Oh, I don't like it!" she gasped.

"Breathe deeply, and count as far as you can," came a voice from far above her.

"Stop!" whispered Corydon. "Oh, I don't want--I want to come back!"

Then she began to count--or rather some strange voice, not hers, seemed to count for her; as the first numbness passed, farther and farther away she seemed to dissolve, to become a disembodied consciousness poised in a misty ether. And at that moment--so she told Thyrsis afterwards--the face of Mr. Harding seemed to appear just above her, and to look at her with a pained and startled expression. It was a beautiful face, she thought; and she knew that everything she felt was being immediately registered in Mr. Harding's mind. They were two affinitized beings, suspended in the centre of a cosmos; "their soul intelligences were all that had been left of the sentient world after some cataclysm.

"I always knew that about us," thought Corydon, and she realized that the face before her understood, even though at the moment it, too, was dissolving. "I wonder why"--she mused--"why--" And then the little spark went out.

Two hours later the doctor was bending over her, anxiously scrutinizing her passive face. "Nurse, bring me some ice-water," he was saying. "She takes her time coming to." And sharply he struck her cheek and forehead with his finger-tips; but she showed no sign.

Deep down in some mysterious inner chamber, beneath the calm face, there was being enacted a grim spirit-drama. Corydon's soul was making a monstrous effort to return to its habitation; Corydon felt herself hanging, a tortured speck of being, in a dark and illimitable void. "This may be Hell," she thought. "I have neither hands nor feet, and I cannot fight; but I can *will* to get back!" This effort cost her inexpressible agony.

A strange incessant throbbing was going on in the black pit over which she seemed suspended. It had a kind of rhythm--metallic, and yet with a human resonance. It began way down somewhere, and proceeded with maddening accuracy to ascend through the semi-tones of a gigantic scale. Each beat was agony to her; it ascended to a certain pitch in merciless crescendo, then fell to the bottom again, and began anew its swift, maddeningly accurate ascent. Each time it ascended a little higher, and always straining her endurance to the uttermost, and bringing a more vivid realization of agony. "Will you stop here," it seemed to pulsate. "No, no, I will go on," willed Corydon. "You shall not keep me, I must escape, I must *get out*." But it kept up incessantly, ruthlessly, its strange, formless, soundless din, until the spirit writhed in its grasp.

Finally it seemed to Corydon that she was getting nearer--nearer to something, she knew not what. The blackness about her seemed to condense, and she found herself in what was apparently the middle of a lake, and some dark bodies with arms were trying to drag her down. "No, no," she willed to these forms, "you *shall* not. I do not belong here, I belong up--up!" And by a violent effort she escaped--into sensations yet more agonizing, more acute. The vibrations were getting faster and faster, whirling her along, stretching her consciousness to pieces. "Will it never end?" she thought. "Have mercy!" But after an eternity of such repetition, she found a bright light staring at her, and a frightful sense of heaviness, like mountains piled upon her. Also, eating her up from head to foot, was a strange, unusual pain; yes, it must be pain, though she had never felt anything like it before. She moaned; and there came a spasm of nausea, that seemed to tear her asunder.

The doctor was standing by her. "She gave me quite a fright," he was saying. "There, that's it, nurse. She'll be sleeping sweetly in a minute." The nurse hurried forward, and Corydon felt a stinging sensation in her side, and then a delightful numbness crept over her. "Oh, thank you, doctor," she whispered.

Section 5. The next week held for Corydon continuous suffering, which she bore with a rebellious defiance--feeling that she had been betrayed in some way. "If you had only told me," she wailed, to the doctor. "I would rather have stayed as I was before!" For answer he would pat her cheek and tell her to go to sleep.

The days dragged on. Every afternoon her mother came and read to her for several hours; and in the afternoons Mr. Harding would come, and sit by her bedside in his kind way and talk to her. Sometimes he only stayed a few minutes, but often he would spend an hour or so, trying to dispel the clouds of gloom and despondency that were hanging over her. Corydon told him of her vision in the operating-room, and strange to say he declared that he had known it all; also he said that he had helped her to fight her way back to life.

He seemed to understand her every need, and from his sympathy gave her all the comfort he could. But he little realized all that it meant to her--how deeply it stirred her gratitude and her liking for him. During the day she would find herself counting the hours until the time he had named; and when the expected knock would come, and his tall figure appear at the door, her heart would give a sudden jump and send the blood rushing to her head. Her lips would tremble slightly as she held out her hand to him; and as he sat and looked at her, she would become uncomfortably conscious of the beating of her heart; in fact at times it would almost suffocate her, and her cheeks would become as fire.

She wondered if he noticed it. But he seemed concerned only for her welfare, and anxiously inquired how she felt. She was not doing well, it seemed, and the doctor was greatly troubled; her temperature had not become normal since the operation, and they could not account for it, as she was suffering no more than the usual amount of pain. To Corydon this was a matter of no importance; she was willing to lie there all day, if only the hour of Mr. Harding's visit would come more quickly. She was beginning to be alarmed because she had such difficulty in controlling her excitement.

The magic hour would strike, and the door of hope open, and there upon the threshold he would appear, in all his superb manhood. Corydon thought she had never before met a man who gave her such an impression of vitality. He was splendid; he was like a young Viking, who brought into the room with him the pure air of the Northern mountains. When he looked at her, his eyes assumed a wonderful expression, a "golden" expression, as Corydon described it to herself. And day after day she clothed this Viking in more lustrous garments, woven from the threads of her imagination, her innermost desires and her dreams. And always at sight of him, her heart beat faster, her head became hotter; until the bed she lay upon became a bed of burning coals. She realized at last what had happened to her, that she loved-- yes, that she loved! But she must not let her Viking see it; that would be unpardonable, it would damn her forever in his sight. And so she struggled with her secret. At night she slept in fitful starts, and in the morning she lay pale and sombre. But when he came she was all brilliancy and animation.

Section 6. Each night the doctor would look anxiously at his thermometer; it was a source of great worry to him and to Corydon's parents that the fever did not abate. Also, needless to say, the news worried Thyrsis; all the more, because it meant a long stay in the hospital, and more of their money gone. At last he came up to town to see about it; and Corydon thought to herself, "This is very wrong of me. It is Thyrsis I ought to be interested in, it is his sympathy I ought to be craving."

She brought the image of Thyrsis before her; it seemed vague and unreal. She found that she remembered mostly the unattractive aspects of him. And this brought a pang to her. "He is good and noble," she told herself; she forced herself to think of generous things that he had done.

He came; and then she felt still more ashamed. He had been working very hard, and was pale and haggard; it was becoming to him to be that way. Recollections came back to her in floods; yes, he was truly good and noble!

He sat by her bedside, and she told him about the operation, and poured out the hunger of her soul to him. He stayed all the morning with her, and he came again and spent the afternoon with her. He read to her and kissed her and soothed her--his influence was very calming, she found. After he had gone for the night, Corydon lay thinking, "I still love him!"

How strange it was that she could love two men at once! It was surely very wrong! She would never have dreamed that she, Corydon, could do such a thing. She thought of Harry Stuart, and of the unacknowledged thrill of excitement which his presence had brought to her. "And now here it is again," she mused--"only this time it is worse! What *can*--be the matter with me?"

Then she wondered, "Do I really love Mr. Harding? Haven't I got over it now?" But the least thinking of him sufficed to set her heart to thumping again; and so she shrunk from that train of thought. She wanted to love her husband.

He came again the next morning, and Corydon found that she was very happy in his presence. Her fever was slightly lower, and she thought, "I will get well quickly now."

But alas, she had reckoned in this without Thyrsis! To sit in the hospital all day was a cruel strain upon him; the more so as he had been entirely unprepared for it. Corydon had assured him that the operation would be nothing, and that she would not need him; and so he had just finished a harrowing piece of labor on the book. Now to stay all day and witness her struggle, to satisfy her craving for sympathy and to meet and wrestle with her despair--it was like having the last drops of his soul-energy squeezed out of him. He did not know what was troubling Corydon, but the *rapport* between them was so close, that he knew she was in some distress of mind.

He stood the ordeal as long as he could, and then he had to beg for respite. Cedric was down on the farm, with no one but the servants to care for him; so he would go back, and see that everything was all right, and after he had rested up for two or three days, he would come again. Corydon smiled faintly and assented--for that morning she had received a note from Mr. Harding, saying that he would be in town the next day, and would call.

So Thyrsis went away, and Corydon lay and thought the problem over again.

"Yes, I love my husband; but it's such an effort for him to love me! And why should that be? I don't believe it would be such an effort for Mr. Harding to love me!"

So again she was seized by the thought of the young clergyman. And she was astonished at the difference in her feelings--the flood of emotion that swept over her. Her heart began to beat fast and her cheeks once more to burn. He was coming up to the city on purpose, this time; it must be that he wanted to see her very much!

That night was an especially hard one for her; she felt as though the frail shell that held her were breaking, as though her endurance were failing altogether. The fever had risen, and her bed had seemed like the burning arms of Moloch. Once she imagined that the room was stifling her, and in a sudden frenzy of impatience she struggled upon one elbow and flung her pillow across the room. In that instant she had noticed a new and sharp pain in her side; it did not leave her, though at the time she thought little about it.

She was all absorbed in the coming of Mr. Harding; by the time morning had come she had made up her mind that her one hope of deliverance was in confession. She must tell him, she must make known to him her love; and he would forgive her, and then her heart would not beat so violently at sight of him, her fever would abate and she might rest.

But when he sat there, talking to her, and looking so beautiful and so strange, she trembled, and made half a dozen vain efforts to begin. Finally she asked, "Have you ever read that poem of Heine's-- 'Ein Jungling liebt ein Madchen, Die hat einen Andern erwahlt?'"

"Oh, yes," he answered; then they were silent again. Finally Corydon nerved herself to yet another effort. "Mr. Harding," she said, "will you come a little nearer, please. I have something very important to say to you." And then, waveringly and brokenly, now in agonized abashment, now rushing ahead as she felt his encouragement and sympathy, she gave him the whole story of her suffering and its cause. When she came to the words "because I love you", she closed her eyes and her spirit sank back with a great gasp of relief.

When she opened them again, his head was bowed in his hands and he did not move. "Mr. Harding," she whispered, "Mr. Harding, you forgive me, do you not? You do not hate me?"

He roused himself with an effort. "Dear child," said he, and as he looked at her she thought she had never seen a face so sad, so exquisite--"it is I who ask forgiveness."

He rose and came to her bedside, and took her hand in both of his. "It would not be right for me to say to you what you have said to me. We must not speak of this any more. You will promise me this, and then you will rest, and to-morrow you will be better. Soon you will be well; and how glad your husband will be--and all of us."

With that he pressed her hand firmly, and left the room; and Corydon turned her face to the wall, and whispered happily to herself, "Yes, he loves me, he loves me! And now I shall rest!"

Section 7. For a while she slept the sleep of exhaustion, nor did there fall across her dreams the shadow of the angel of fate who was even then placing his mark upon her forehead. Toward morning she was awakened suddenly with the sharp pain in her side; but it abated presently, and Corydon thought blissfully of the afternoon before. He would come again to her, she would see him that very day; and so what did pain matter? She was really happy at last. But as the day advanced, she became uneasy; her fever had not diminished, and the pain was becoming more persistent.

The nurse was anxious, too. Her mother came and regarded her in alarm. But she was thinking of Mr. Harding. He was coming; he might arrive at any moment.

There was a knock upon the door. Corydon's pulse fluttered, and she whispered, "Here he is!" She could scarcely speak the words, "Come in". But when the door opened, she saw that it was the doctor. Her heart sank, and she closed her eyes with a moan of pain. Could it be that he was not coming? Could it be that she had been mistaken--that he did not love her after all? She must see him--she must! She could not endure this suspense; she could not endure these interruptions by other people.

The doctor came and sat by her. "I must see what is the matter here," he said. "Why do you not get well, Corydon?"

He questioned her carefully and looked grave. "I must have a consultation at once," he said.

Corydon's hand caught at his sleeve. "No, no!" she whispered.

"Don't be afraid," said the doctor. "It won't hurt."

"It isn't that," said Corydon. She all but added, "I must see Mr. Harding!"

She was wheeled into the operating-room, but this time there was no interest in her eyes as she regarded the smooth table and the shining instruments. As they lifted her upon it, she shuddered. "Oh I cannot, I cannot!" she wailed.

"There, there," said the doctor. "Be brave. We wish simply to see what the matter is. It won't take long."

And they put the cone to her mouth. Corydon struggled and gasped, but it was no use, she was in the clutches of the fiend again; only this time there was no ecstasy, and no vision of Mr. Harding. Instead there was instant and sickening suffocation. Again she descended into the uttermost depths of the inferno; and it seemed as though this time the brave will was not equal to the battle before it.

The surgeons made their examination, and they discovered more diseased tissue, and a slowly spreading infection. So there was nothing for it but to operate again--they held a quick consultation, and then went ahead. And afterwards they labored and sweated, and by dint of persistent effort, and every device at their command, they fanned into life once more the faint spark in the ashen-grey form that lay before them. But it was a feeble flame they got; as Corydon's eyelids fluttered, the only sign of recognition that came from her lips was a moan, and from her eyes a look of dazed stupidity. But there was hope for her life, the doctors said; and they sent a telegram which Thyrsis got three days later, when he had fought his way to the town through five miles of heavy snow-drifts.

Meantime the grim fight for life was going on. In the morning Corydon opened her eyes to a burning torture, the racked and twisted nerves quivering in rebellion. It did not come in twinges of pain, it was a slow, deadening, persistent agony, that pervaded every inch of her body. She wondered how she could bear it, how she could live. And yet, strangely, inexplicably, she wanted to live. She did not know why--she had been outraged, she had been deserted by all, she was but a feeble atom of determination in the centre of a hostile universe. And yet she would pit her will against them all, God, man, and devil; they should not conquer her, she would win out.

So she would clench her teeth together and fight. For hours she would stare at the wall, the blank, unresponsive, formless wall before her; and then, when the shadows of the evening fell, and they saw she was fainting from exhaustion, they would come with the needle of oblivion, and the dauntless soul would die for the night, and return in the morning to its pitiless task.

Section 8. Thyrsis received a couple of letters at the same time as the telegram, and he took the next train for the city. It is said that a drowning man sees before him in a few moments the panorama of his whole life; but to Thyrsis were given three hours in which to recall the events of his love for Corydon. He had every reason to believe that he would find her dying; and such pangs of suffering as came to him he had never known before. He was in a crowded car, and he would not shed a tear; but he sat, crouched in a heap and staring before him, fairly quivering with pent-up and concentrated grief. God, how he loved her! What a spirit of pure flame she was--what a creature from another sky! What martyrdom she had dared for him, and how cruelly she had been punished for her daring! And now, this was the end; she was dying--perhaps dead! How was he to live without her--in the bare and barren future that he saw stretching out before him?

Flashes of memory would come to him, waves of torment roll over him. He would recall her gestures, the curves of her face, the tones of her voice, the songs that she had sung; and then would come a choking in his throat, and he would clench his hands, as a runner in the last moments of a desperate race. He thought of her as he had seen her last. He had gone away, careless and unthinking--how blind he had been! The things that he had not said to her, and that he might have said so easily! The love he had not uttered, the pardons he had not procured! The yearnings and consecrations that had remained unspoken all through their lives--ah God, what a tragedy of impotence and failure their lives had been!

Then before his soul came troops of memories, each one a fiend with a whip of fire; the words of anger that he had spoken, the acts of cruelty that he had done! The times when he had made her weep, and had not comforted her! Oh, what a fool he had been--what a blind and wanton fool! And now--if he were to find her dead, and never be able to tell her of his shame and sorrow--he knew that he would carry the memories with him all his days, they would be like blazing scars upon his soul.

She was still alive, however; and so he took a deep breath, and went at his task. There was no question now of what he could bear to do, but of what he must do; she must be saved, and who could do it but himself? Who else could take her hands and whisper to her, and fill her with new courage and hope; who else could bid her to live--to live; could rouse the fainting spirit, and bid it rise up and set forth upon the agonizing journey?

So out of the very abyss they came together. But when at last the fight was won, when the doctors an-nounced that she was out of danger, Thyrsis was fairly reeling with exhaustion. When he left her in the afternoon, he would go to his hotel-room and lie down, utterly prostrated; he would lie awake the whole night through, wrestling with the demons of horror that he had brought with him from her bedside.

So he realized that he was on the verge of collapse, and that cost what it would, he must get away. Corydon's mother was with her, and when she was strong enough to be moved, she would be taken back to the farm. He mentioned this to Corydon, and she replied that she would be satisfied. There would be Mr. Harding also, she said; Mr. Harding wrote that he would come up to the city, and do what he could to help her in her dire distress.

Section 9. There came from the higher regions a pass upon a steamer to Florida; and so Thyrsis sailed away. With a determined effort he took all his cares, and locked them back in a far chamber of his mind. He would not think about Corydon, nor about what he would do for money when he came home; more important yet, he would clear the book out of his thoughts--he would not permit it to gnaw at him all day and all night.

And by these resolves he stood grimly. He walked the deck for hours every day; he watched the foaming green waters, and the gulls wheeling in the sky, and the sun setting over the sea, and the new moon showering its fire upon the waves. Gradually the air grew warm, and ice and snow became as an evil dream. A land of magic it seemed to which Thyrsis came--the beauty of it enfolded him like a clasp of love. He saw pine-forests, and swamps with alligators in them, and live oaks draped with trailing grey moss. The clumps of palmettos fascinated him--he had seen pictures of such trees in the tropics, and would hardly have been astonished to see a herd of elephants in their shadows.

He found a beach, snow-white and hard, upon which he walked for uncounted miles. He gathered strange shells and crabs, and watched the turkey-buzzards on the shore, and the slow procession of the pelicans, sailing past above the tops of the breakers. He saw the black fins of the grampuses cutting the water, and thought that they were sharks. He stood for hours at a time up to his waist in the surf, casting for sea-bass; he got few fish, but joy and excitement he got in abundance.

Then, back upon the hammocks--to walk upon the hard shell roads, and see orange and lemon-groves, and gardens filled with roses and magnolias, and orchards of mulberry and fig-trees. Truly this must have been the land which the poet had described--

"Where every prospect pleases,
And only man is vile."

Thyrsis stayed in a humble boarding-house, but nearby was one of the famous winter-resorts of the Florida East Coast, and he was free to go there, and wander about the lobbies and piazzas of the palatial hotels, and watch the idle rich at their diversions. A strange society they were--it seemed as if the scum of the civilization of forty-five states had been blown into this bit of back-water. Here were society women, jaded with dissipation; stock-brokers and financiers, fleeing from the strain of the "Street"; here were parasites of every species, who, having nothing to do at home--or perhaps not even having any home--had come to this land of warmth to prolong their orgies. They raced over the roads and beaches in autos, and over the water in swift motor-boats; they dressed themselves half a dozen times a day, they fed themselves upon rich and costly foods, they gambled and gossiped and drank and wantoned their time away. As he watched them it was all that Thyrsis could do to keep himself from beginning another manifesto for the "Appeal to Reason". Oh, if only the toilers of the nation could be brought here, and shown what became of the wealth they produced!

As if to complete his study of winter-resort manners and morals, Thyrsis encountered a college acquaintance whose father had become enormously rich through a mining speculation, and was here with a party of friends in a private-train. So he was whirled off in one of half a dozen automobiles, and rode for a hundred miles or so to an inland lake, and sat down to an *al fresco* luncheon of such delicacies as *pate de fois gras* and jellied grouse and champagne. Afterwards the young people wandered about and amused themselves, and the elders played "bridge", in the face of all the raptures of this wonderland of nature.

A strange and sombre figure Thyrsis must have seemed to these people, with his brooding air and his worn clothing; he rode home in an auto with half a dozen youths and maidens, and while they flashed by lakes and rivers that gleamed in the golden moon-light, and by orchards and gardens from which the mingled scents of millions of blossoms were wafted to them, these voung people jested together and laughed and sang.

And Thyrsis lay back and watched them and studied them. Their music was what is called "rag-time"--they had apparently found nothing better to do with their lives than to learn hundreds of verses and melodies, of which the subject-matter was the whims and moods of the half-tamed African race--their vanities and their barbarous impulses, and above all their hot and lustful passions. Song after song they poured forth, the substance of which was summed up in one line that Thyrsis happened to carry away with him--

"Ah lubs you, mah honey, yes, Ah do!"

It seemed to him such a curious and striking commentary upon the stage which leisure-class culture had reached, in the course of its reversion to savagery.

Section 10. Thyesis came home after three weeks, browned and refreshed, and ready to take up the struggle again. He came with the cup of his love and sympathy overflowing; eager to see Corydon, and to tell her his adventures, and to share with her his store of new hope.

He found her reclining on the piazza of the farm-house. The April buds were bursting upon the trees, and the odor of spring was in the air; also, the flush of health was stealing back into Corydon's cheeks. How beautiful she looked, and how soft and gentle was her caress, and what wistfulness and tenderness were in the smile with which she greeted him!

There was the baby also, tumultuous and excited. Thyrsis took him upon his knee, and while he fondled him and played with him, he told Corydon about his trip. But in a short while it became evident to him that she had something on her mind; and finally she sent the baby away to play, and began, "There is something I have to tell you."

"Yes, dear?" he said.

"It is something very, very important."

"Yes?" he repeated.

"I--I don't know just how to begin," said Corydon. "I hope you are not going to be angry."

"I can't imagine myself being angry just now," he replied; and then, struck by a sense of familiarity in this introduction, he asked, with a smile, "You haven't been seeing Harry Stuart, have you?"

Corydon frowned at the words. "Don't speak of that!" she said, quickly. "I am not joking."

He saw that she was agitated, and so he fell silent.

"I hesitated a long time about telling you," she went on. "But you must know. I am sure it's right to tell you."

"By all means, dearest," he answered.

"It's a long story," she said. "I must go back to my first operation." And then she began, and told him how she had found herself thinking of Mr. Harding, and of the strange vision she had had; she told of all her fevered excitements, and of her confession to him. When she finished she was trembling all over, and her face and throat were flushed.

Thyrsis sat for a while in silence, looking very grave. "I see," he said.

"You--you are not angry with me?" she asked.

"No, I'm not angry," he replied. "But tell me, what has been going on since?"

"Well," said Corydon, "Mr. Harding has been coming here to see me. He saw I needed help, and he couldn't refuse it. It was--it was his duty to come."

"Yes," said the other. "Go on."

"Well, I think he had an idea that the whole thing was a product of my sickness; and when I was well again, it would all be over."

"And is it, Corydon?"

She sat staring in front of her; her voice sank to a whisper. "No," she said. "It--it isn't."

"And does he know that?" asked Thyrsis.

"He knows everything," she replied. "I don't need to tell him things."

"But have you talked about it with him?"

"A little," she said. "That is, you see, I had to explain to him--to apologize for what I had done in the hospital. I wanted him to know that I wouldn't have said anything to him, if I hadn't been so very ill."

"I see," said Thyrsis.

"And I want you to understand," added Corydon, quickly-"you must not blame him. For he's the soul of honor, Thyrsis; and he can't help how he feels about me-any more than I can help it. You must know that, dear!"

"Yes, I know that."

"He's been so good and so noble about it. He thinks so much of you, Thyrsis--he wouldn't do you wrong, not by a single word. He said that to me---over and over again. He's frightened, you know, that either of us might do wrong. He's so sensitive-I think he takes things more seriously than anybody we've ever known."

"I understand," said Thyrsis; and then, after a pause, he inquired, "But what's to come of it?"

"How do you mean?" she asked.

"What are you going to do?"

"Why, I don't know that there's anything to do, Thyrsis. What would there be?"

"But are you going on being in love with him forever?"

"I--I don't see how I can tell, Thyrsis. Would it do any harm?"

"It might grow on you," he said, with a slight smile. "It sometimes does."

"Mr. Harding said we ought never to speak of it again," said she. "And I guess he's right about that. He said that our lives would always be richer, because we had discovered each other's souls; that it would help us to grow into a nobler life."

"I see," said Thyrsis. "But it's a trifle disconcerting at first. I'll need a little time to get used to it."

"Mr. Harding is very anxious to know you better," remarked Corydon. "But you see, he's afraid of you, Thyrsis. You are so direct--you get to the point too quickly for him."

"Um--yes," said he. "I can imagine that."

"And he thinks you distrust him," she went on--"just because he's orthodox. But he's really not half as backward as you think. His faith means a great deal to him. I only wish I had such a faith in my own life."

To which Thyrsis responded, "God knows, my dear, I wish you had."

Section 11. The young clergyman came to call the next afternoon, and the three sat upon the lawn and talked. They talked about Florida, and then about Socialism--as was inevitable, after Thyrsis had described the population of the East Coast hotels. But he felt constrained and troubled--he did not know just how a man should conduct himself with his wife's lover; and so in the end he excused himself and strolled off.

He came back as Mr. Harding was leaving; and it seemed to him that the other's face wore a look of pain and distress. Also, at supper he noted that Corydon was ill at ease.

"Something has gone wrong with your program?" he inquired.

To which Corydon answered, "Mr. Harding thinks he ought not to come any more."

"Not come any more?"

"He says I don't need him now. And he thinks--he thinks it isn't right. He's afraid to come."

And so a week passed, and the young clergyman was not seen again. Thyrsis noticed that his wife was silent a great deal; and that when she did talk, she talked about Mr. Harding. His heart ached to see her as she was, so pitifully weak and appealing. She was scarcely able to walk alone yet; and she complained also that her mind had been weakened by the frightful ordeal she had undergone. It exhausted her to do any thinking at all; and she seemed to have forgotten nearly all she knew--there were whole subjects upon which her mind appeared to be a blank.

So he gave up trying to think about his book, and went about all day pondering this new problem. It was one of the laws of the marriage state that he must suffer whenever she suffered. It was never permitted to him to question the reality of any of her emotions; if they were real to her, they were real in the only sense that counted; and he must take them with the entire tragic seriousness that she took them, he must regard them as inevitable and fatal. For himself, he could change or suppress emotions--that ability was the most characteristic fact about him; but Corydon could not do it, and so he was not permitted to do it. That would be to manifest the "cold" and "stern" self, which was to Corydon an object of abhorrence and fear.

So now he went about all day, brooding over this trouble. He would come to Corydon and see her gazing across the valley with a melancholy look upon her features; he would see her, with her sweet face as if suffused with unshed tears. And what was he to do about it? Was he to rebuke her--however gently--and urge her to suppress this yearning? To do that would be to plunge her into abysses of grief. Or was he to come to her, and utter his own love to her, and draw her to him again? He knew that he could do that--he was conceited enough to believe that with his eloquence and his power of soul, he could have wiped Mr. Harding clean out of her thoughts in a few days. But then, when he had done it, he would have to go back to the task of revolutionizing the world's critical standards; and what would become of Corydon after that? What she needed, he told himself, was a love that was not a will o' the wisp and a fraud, but a love that was real and unceasing; she needed the love of a man, and not of an artist!

Here were two young people who were in love with each other; and according to the specifications of the moral code, they had their minds made up to sublime renunciation. But then, Thyrsis had a moral code of his own, and in it renunciation was not the only law of life.

It was only when he thought of losing Corydon, that he realized to the full how much he loved her. Then all their consecrations and their pledges would come back to him; he would hold her as the greatest human soul that he had ever met. But it was a strange paradox, that precisely the depth of his love for her made him willing to think of losing her. He loved her for herself, and not for anything she gave him; he wanted her to be happy, he wanted her to grow and achieve, and in order to see her do this he would make any sacrifice in the world. In how many hours of insight had it become clear to him that he himself could never make her happy--that he was not the man to be her husband! Now it seemed as if the time had come for him to prove that he meant what he had said--that he was willing to stand by his vision and to act upon it.

So after one day of especial unhappiness, he made up his mind to a desperate resolve; and at night, when all the household was asleep, he went over to his lonely study and sat down with a pen in his hand, and summoned the spirit of Mr. Harding before him.

"I have concluded to write you a letter," he began. "You will find it a startling and unusual one. I can only beg you to believe that I have written it after much hesitation, and that it represents most earnest and prayerful thought upon my part.

"Since my return, I have become aware of the situation which has developed between yourself and my wife. Her welfare is dearer to me than anything else in the world; and after thinking it over, I concluded that her welfare required that I should explain to you the relationship which exists between us. It seems unlikely that you could know about it otherwise, for it is a very unusual relationship.

"I suppose there is no need for me to tell you that Corydon is not happy. She never has been happy as my wife, and I fear that she never will be. She is by nature warm-hearted, craving affection and companionship. I, on the other hand, am by nature impersonal and self-absorbed--I am compelled by the exigencies of my work to be abstracted and indifferent to things about me. I perceived this before our marriage, but not clearly enough to save her; it has been her misfortune that I have loved her so dearly that I have been driven to attempt the impossible. I am continuually deceiving myself into the belief that I am succeeding--and I am continually deceiving Corydon in the same way. It has been our habit to talk things out between us frankly; but this is a truth from which we have shrunk instinctively. I have always seen it as the seed of what must grow to be a bitter tragedy.

"The possibility that Corydon might come to love some other man was one that I had not thought of--it was very stupid of me, no doubt. But now it has happened; and I have worked over the problem with all the faculties I possess. A man who was worthy of Corydon's love would be very apt, under the circumstances, to feel that he must crush his impulses towards her. But when we were married, it was with the agreement that our marriage should be binding upon us only so long as it was for the highest spiritual welfare of both; and by that agreement it is necessary that we should stand at all times. My purpose in writing to you is to let you know that I have no claim upon Corydon which prohibits her from continuing her acquaintance with you; and that if in the course of time it should become clear that Corydon would be happier as your wife than as mine, I should regard it as my duty to step aside. Having said this, I feel that I have done my part. I leave the matter in your hands, with the fullest confidence in your sincerity and good faith."

Thyrsis wrote this letter, and read it a couple of times. Then he decided to sleep over it; and the next morning he wakened, and read it again--with a shock of surprise. He found it a startling letter. It opened up vistas to his spirit; vistas of loneliness and grief-- and then again, vistas of freedom and triumph. If he were to mail it, it would be irrevocable; and it would probably mean that he would lose Corydon. And *could* he make up his mind to lose her? His swift thoughts flew to their parting; there were tears in his eyes-- his love came back to him, as it had when he thought she was dying. But then again, there came a thrill of exultation; the captive lion within him smelt the air of the jungle, and rattled his chains and roared.

Throughout breakfast he was absent-minded and ill at ease; he bid Corydon a farewell which puzzled her by its tenderness, and then started to walk to Bellevue with the letter. Half way in, he stopped. No, he could not do it--it was a piece of madness; but then he started again--he *must* do it. He found himself pacing up and down before the post office, where for nearly an hour he struggled to screw his courage to the sticking-point. Once he started away, having made up his mind that he would take another day to think the matter over; but after he had walked half a mile or so, he changed his mind and strode back, and dropped the letter in the box.

And then a pang smote him. It was done! All the way as he walked home he had to fight with an impulse to go back, and persuade the postmaster to return the letter to him!

Section 12. Thyrsis figured that the fatal document would reach Mr. Harding that afternoon; and the next morning in his anxiety he walked a mile or two to meet the mail-carrier on his way. Sure enough, there was a reply from the clergyman. He tore it open and read it swiftly:

"I received your letter, and I hasten to answer. I cannot tell you the distress of mind which it has caused me. There has been a most dreadful misundertanding, and I can only hope that it has not gone too far to be corrected. I beg you to believe me that there has been nothing between your wife and myself that could justify the inference you have drawn. Your wife was in terrible distress of spirit, and I visited her and tried to comfort her--such is my duty as a clergyman, as I conceive it. I did nothing but what a clergyman should properly do, and you have totally misunderstood me, and also your wife, who is the most innocent and gentle and trusting of souls. She is utterly devoted to you, and the idea that the help I have tried to give her should be the occasion of any misunderstanding between you is dreadful for me to contemplate.

"I must implore you to believe this, and dismiss these cruel suspicions from your mind. If I were to be the cause of breaking up your home, and wrecking Corydon's life, it would be more than I could bear. I have a most profound belief in the sanctity of the institution of marriage, and not for anything in the world would I have been led to do, or even to contemplate in my own thoughts, anything which would trespass upon its obligations. I repeat to you with all the earnestness of which I am capable that your idea is without basis, and I beg you to banish it from your mind. You may rely upon it that I will not see your wife again, under any circumstances imaginable."

Thyrsis read this, and then stared before him with knitted brows. "Why, what's the matter with the man?" he said to himself. And then he read the letter over again, weighing its every phrase. "Did he think my letter was sarcasm?" he wondered. "Did he think I was angry?"

He went to his study and got the rough draft of his own letter, and reread and pondered it. No, he concluded, it was not possible that Mr. Harding had thought he was angry. "He's trying to dodge!" he exclaimed. "He can't bring himself to face the thing!"

But then again, he wondered. Could it be that the man was right; could it be that Corydon had misunderstood him and his attitude? Or had he perhaps experienced a reaction, and was now trying to deny his feelings?

For several hours Thyrsis pondered the problem; and then he went and sat by her, as she was reading on the piazza. "You haven't heard anything more from Mr. Harding, have you?" he asked.

"Nothing," said Corydon.

"What do you suppose he intends to do?"

"I--I don't know," she said. "I don't think he means to come back."

"But why not, dear?"

"He's afraid to trust himself, Thyrsis."

"You think he really cares for you, then?"

"Yes, dear."

"But, how can you be sure?" he asked.

At which Corydon smiled. "A woman has ways of knowing about such things," she said.

"I wish you'd tell me about it," said he.

But after a little thought, she shook her head. "Maybe some day, but not now. It wouldn't be fair to him. It isn't going any further, and that's enough for you to know."

"He must be unhappy, isn't he?" said Thyrsis, artfully.

"Yes," she answered, "he's unhappy, I'm sure. He takes things very seriously."

Thyrsis paused a moment. "Did he tell you that he loved you?" he asked.

"No," said Corydon. "He--he wouldn't have permitted himself to do that. That would have been wrong."

"But then--what did he do?"

"He looked at me," she said.

"When he went off the other day--did he know how you still felt?"

"Yes, Thyrsis; why do you ask?"

"I thought you might have been deceiving yourself.'"

At which she smiled and replied, "I wouldn't have bothered to tell you in that case."

Section 13. So Thyrsis strolled away, and after duly considering the matter, he sat himself down to compose another letter to the young clergyman.

"My dear Mr. Harding:

"I read your note with a great deal of perplexity. It is evident to me that I have not made the situation clear to you; you probably do not find it easy to realize the frankness which Corydon and I maintain in our relationship. I must tell you at the outset that she has narrated to me what has passed between you, and so I am not dealing with 'cruel suspicions', but with facts. Can I not persuade you to do the same?

"It is difficult for me to be sure just what is in your mind. But for one thing, let me make certain that you are not trying to read anything between the lines of what I write you. Please understand I am not angry, or jealous, or suspicious; also, I am not unhappy--at least not so unhappy but that I can stand it. I have stood a good deal of unhappiness in my life, and Corydon has also.

"You tell me about your attitude towards my wife. Of course it may be that as you come to look back upon what has passed between you, it seems to you that your feeling for her was not deep and permanent, and that you would prefer not to continue your acquaintance with her. That would be your right--you have not pledged yourself in any way. All that I desire is, that in considering the state of your feelings, you should deal with them, and not with any duty which you may imagine you owe to *me*. I have no claim in the matter, and any that I might have, I forego.

"The crux of the whole difficulty I imagine must lie in what you say about your 'profound belief in the sanctity of the institution of marriage'. That is, of course, a large question to attempt to discuss in a letter. I can only say that I once had such a belief, and that as a result of my studies I have it no longer. I see the institution of marriage as a product of a certain phase of the economic development of the race, which phase is rapidly passing, if it be not already past. And the institution to me seems to share in the evils of the economic phase; indeed I am accustomed, when invited to discuss the institution of marriage, to insist upon discussing what actually exists--which is the institution of marriage-plus-prostitution.

"Our economic system affords to certain small classes of men--to capitalists, to merchants, to lawyers, to clergymen--opportunities of comfort and dignity and knowledge and health and virtue. But to certain other classes, and far larger classes-to miners, to steel- workers, to garment-makers--it deals out misery and squalor and ignorance and disease and vice. And in the case of women it does exactly the same; to some it gives a sheltered home, with comfort and beauty and peace; while to others it gives a life of loneliness and sterility, and to others a life of domestic slavery, and to yet others only the horrors of the brothel. And when you come to investigate, you find that the difference is everywhere one of economic advantage. The merchant, the lawyer, the clergyman, has education and privilege, he can wait and make his terms; but the miner, the steel-worker, the sweat-shop-toiler, has to sell his labor for what will keep him alive that day. And in the same way with women--some can acquire accomplishments, virtues, charms; and when it comes to giving their love, they can secure the life-contract which we call marriage. But the daughter of the slums has no opportunity to acquire such accomplishments and virtues and charms, and often she cannot hold out for such a bargain--she sells her love for the food and shelter that she needs to keep her alive.

"This will seem radical doctrine to you, I suppose; I have noticed that you take our institutions at their face-value, and do not ask how much in them may be sham. But it seems to me there is no need to go into that matter here, for no trespass upon the marriage obligation is proposed. The conventions undoubtedly give me the right to be outraged because my wife is in love with another man; I can denounce him, and humiliate her. But if I am willing to forego this right, if I do not care to play Othello to her Desdemona, what then? Who can claim to be injured by my renunciation?

"Of course I know it is said that marriages are made in Heaven, and that what God hath joined together, no man may put asunder. But it is difficult for me to imagine that an intelligent man would take this attitude at the present day. If I were dead, you would surely recognize that Corydon might remarry; you would recognize it, I presume, if I were hopelessly insane, or degenerate. What if I were in the habit of getting drunk and maltreating her--would you claim that she was condemned to suffer this for life? Or suppose that I were found to be physically impotent? And can you not recognize the fact that there might be impotence of an intellectual and spiritual sort, which could leave a woman quite as unhappy, and make her life quite as barren and futile?

"Let us suppose, for the sake of the argument, that I have stated correctly the facts between Corydon and myself; that there exists between us a fundamental difference in temperament, which makes it certain that, however much we might respect and admire, and even love each other, we could never either of us be happy as man and wife; and suppose that Corydon were to meet some other man, with whom she could live harmoniously; and that she loved him sincerely, and he loved her; and that I were to recognize this, and be willing that she should leave me--do you mean that you would maintain that such a course was wrong? And if it were, with whom would the blame be? With her, because she did not condemn herself to a lifetime of failure? Or with me, because I did not desire her to do this--because I did not wish to waste my life-force in trying to content a discontented woman?

"I might add that I have said nothing to Corydon about having written to you; she has no idea that I have thought of such a thing, and she would be horrified at the suggestion. I have taken the responsibility of doing it, realizing that there was no other way in which you could be made acquainted with the true situation. There is much more that I could say about all this, but it seems a waste of time to write it. Can we not meet sometime, and get at each other's point of view? I am going to be in town the day after to-morrow, and unless I hear from you to the contrary, I will drop in to see you some time in the morning."

Section 14. Thyrsis read this letter over two or three times; and then, resisting the impulse to elaborate his exposition of the economic bases of the marriage institution, he took it in to town and mailed it. He waited eagerly for a reply the next day; but no reply came.

The morning after that, he walked down to town as he had agreed to, and called at Mr. Harding's home. The door was opened by his housekeeper, Delia Gordon's aunt. "Is Mr. Harding in?" asked Thyrsis.

"He's gone up to the city," was the reply.

"To the city," said Thyrsis. "When did he go?"

"He left this morning."

"And when will he be back?"

"I don't know. He left rather suddenly, and he didn't say."

"I see," said Thyrsis. "Tell him I called, please."

And so he went home and mailed another note to Mr. Harding, asking him to make an appointment for a meeting; after which he waited for three or four days--but still there came no reply.

"Have you heard anything more from Mr. Harding?" he asked of Corydon, finally.

"No, dear," she answered. "I don't expect to hear." But he saw that she was nervous and *distrait*; and he knew by her unwonted interest in the mail that she was all the time hoping to get some word from him.

When it came to handling any affair with Corydon, Thyrsis was a poor diplomatist. He would tell himself that this or that should be kept from her for the present; but the secrecy always irked him--his impulse was to talk things out with her, to go hand in hand with her to face the facts of their life. So now, in this case; one afternoon he settled her comfortably in a hammock, and sat beside her and took her hand.

"Corydon," he said, "I've something I want to tell you. I've been having a correspondence with Mr. Harding."

She started, and stared at him wildly. "What do you mean?" she gasped.

"I wrote him two letters," said he.

"What about?"

"I wanted to explain about us," he said; and then he told her what he had put in the first letter, and read Mr. Harding's reply, which he had in his pocket.

"What do you make of it?" he asked.

"Tell me what your answer was!" cried Corydon, quickly; and so he began to outline his second letter.

But she did not let him get very far. "You wrote him that way about marriage!" she exclaimed.

"Yes, dear," said he.

"But, Thyrsis! He'll be perfectly horrified!"

"You think so?"

"Why, Thyrsis! Don't you understand? He's a clergyman!"

"I know; but it's the truth---"

"You don't know anything about people at all!" she cried. "Can't you realize? He doesn't reason about things like you; you can't appeal to him in that way!"

"Well, what was I to do---"

"We'll never see him again!" exclaimed Corydon, in despair.

"That won't be any worse than it was before, will it?"

"Tell me," she rushed on, in her agitation. "Did you tell him that I had no idea what you were doing?"

"Of course I told him that."

"But did you make it perfectly clear to him?"

"I tried to, dear."

"Tell me what you said! Tell me the rest of the letter."

And so he recited it, as well as he could, while she listened, breathless with dismay. "How could you!" she cried.

Then she read over Mr. Harding's letter once more. "You see," she said; "he was simply dazed. He didn't know what to say, he didn't know what to think."

"He'll get over it in time. He had to know, somehow."

"But *why* did he have to know? Why couldn't things have stayed as they were?"

"But my dear, you are in love with the man, aren't you?"

"But I don't want to marry him, Thyrsis! I don't--I don't love him enough."

"You might have come to it in the course of time," he replied.

"Don't you see that he'd have to give up being a clergyman?" she exclaimed.

"That's been done before," he said.

"But--see it from his point of view! Think of the scandal!"

"I don't think much about scandals," Thyrsis answered. "That part could be arranged."

"But do the laws give people divorces in that way?"

"Our divorce laws are relics of feudalism," he answered. "One does not take them seriously."

"But how can you get around them, Thyrsis?"

"You simply have to admit whatever offense they require."

"But Thyrsis! Think how that would seem to Mr. Harding!"

"My dear," he answered, "if I knew that a divorce was necessary to your happiness, I would take upon myself whatever disgrace was necessary."

Corydon sat gazing at him. "Is it so easy to give me up?" she asked.

"It wasn't easy at all, my dear," he answered. "It was a fight that I fought out."

"But you decided that you could do it!" she exclaimed; and that, he found, was the aspect of the matter that stayed with her in the end. It seemed a poor sort of compliment he had paid her; and how could he make real to her the pangs the decision had cost him? He expected her to take that for granted--in all these years, had he not been able to convince her of his love?

It was the old story between them, he reflected; he was always being called upon to express his feelings, and always reluctant to attempt it. Just now she wanted him to enter upon an eloquent exposition of how he had suffered and hesitated before he mailed the letter; and she would hang upon his words, and drink them in greedily--and of course, the more convincing he made them, the more she would love *him*.

She could never leave him, she insisted--the idea of giving him up was madness. She had not meant any such thing by falling in love with Mr. Harding. Why must he be so elemental, so brutally direct? He was like some clumsy animal, blundering about in the garden where she kept her sentimental plants. He frightened her, as he had frightened Mr. Harding. She stood appalled at this thing which he had done; the truth being that his action had sprung from a certain deep conviction in him, which he never found courage to utter to her.

Section 15. Thyrsis pledged his word that he would write no more to Mr. Harding; and so they settled down to wait for a reply. But a couple more days passed, and still there came nothing.

Corydon was restless and impatient. "What **can** he be doing?" she exclaimed. Finally it chanced that Thyrsis had to go to Bellevue upon some errand; and so the two drove into town together, and came upon the solution of the mystery.

On the street they met Mr. Jennings, the high-school principal.

"Good-morning," said he. "A fine day." And then, "Have you heard the news about Harding?"

"What news?" asked Thyrsis.

"He's gone away."

"Gone away!"

"He's resigned his pastorate."

Thyrsis stared at the man, dazed; he felt Corydon beside him give a start. "Resigned his pastorate!" she echoed.

"Yes," said the other, "just so."

"But why?"

"We none of us know. We're at our wits' end."

"But--how did you hear it?"

"I'm one of the trustees of the church, and his letter was read last night."

Thyrsis could not find a word to utter. He sat staring at the man in bewilderment. "What did he say?" cried Corydon, at last.

"He said that for some time he had been dissatisfied with his work, and felt the need of more study and reflection. It quite took our breath away, for nobody'd had the least idea that anything was wrong."

"But what's he going to do?"

"Apparently he's going abroad," was the answer--"at least he ordered his mail to be forwarded to an address in Switzerland. And that's all we know."

Then, after a few remarks about the spiritual ferment in the churches, the worthy high-school principal went on his way, and left Corydon and Thyrsis in the middle of the street. For a minute or two they sat staring before them as if in a trance; and then suddenly from Thyrsis' lips there burst a peal of wild laughter. "By the Lord God, he ran away from it!" he cried; and he seized Corydon by the arm and cried again, "He ran away from it!"

"Thyrsis!" exclaimed the other. "Don't laugh about it!"

"Don't laugh!" he gasped; and again the convulsion of hilarity swept over him.

But Corydon turned upon him swiftly. "No!" she cried. "Stop! It's no joke!"

She was staring at him, her eyes wide with consternation and dismay. "Think!" she exclaimed. "He's given up his career!"

"Yes," he said, "so it seems."

"It's awful!" she cried. "Oh, how *could* he!"

He saw the way the news affected her, and he made an effort to control himself. "The man simply couldn't face it," he said. "He didn't dare to trust himself. He ran."

"But Thyrsis!" she exclaimed. "I can't believe it! He's given up his whole life-work!"

"He's fled like Joseph," said Thyrsis--"leaving his cloak in the hands of the temptress!"

And then, the strain proving too much for him, he began to laugh again. Becoming aware of the stares of some people on the street, he started up the horse, and drove on into the country, where he could be alone, and could give unrestrained expression to the emotions that possessed him.

He imagined the dismay and perplexity of the unhappy clergyman, with his belief in the sacred institution of marriage--and with the vision of Corydon pursuing him all day, and haunting his dreams at night. He imagined him trying to face the interview with the husband--with the terrible, conventionless husband, whose arguments could not be answered. "He simply couldn't face me! He went the very morning I was coming!"

So he would laugh again; he would laugh until he was so weak that he had to lie back in his seat. "I can't believe that it's true!" he exclaimed. "My dear, I think it's the funniest thing that ever happened since the world began!"

"But Thyrsis!" she protested. "Think what we've done to him! The man's life is wrecked!"

"Nonsense!" said he. "It's the best thing that could have happened to him. He might have gone on preaching sermons all his life--but now he's got some ideas to work out. He'll have time to read books, and to think."

"But he must be suffering so!" exclaimed Corydon, who could not forget her love, even in the presence of his ribaldry.

"He needs to suffer," Thyrsis replied. "He may meet some of the radicals over there, and come back with a new point of view."

But Corydon shook her head. "You don't know him," she said. "He couldn't possibly change. I don't think I'll ever hear from him again."

Thyrsis looked at her and saw that there were tears in her eyes. He put his hand upon hers. "We'll have to worry through for a while longer, dear," he said. "Never mind--we'll manage to make out somehow!"

Section 16. They drove home; and all through supper they talked about this breathless event. Afterwards they sat in the twilight, upon the porch, and threshed it out in its every aspect.

"Corydon," said he, "I don't believe you really loved him as much as you thought. Did you?"

She stared before her without answering.

"Would you have loved him for long?" he persisted.

She pondered over this. "I don't think one could love a man always," she answered, "unless he had a mind."

At which he pondered in turn. "Then it was too bad to drive him away!"

"That's just it," said she. "That's what I couldn't make clear to you."

"But still, we had to find out."

" *You* may have," she said. "I didn't."

Thyrsis looked, and saw that she was smiling through her tears. He took her hand in his. "We'll see each other through, dear," he said. "We'll have to wait until the world grows up."

He felt an answering pressure of her hand. "Thyrsis," she said, "you must promise me that you will never do anything dreadful like that again. You must understand me; I might think that I was in love, but it would never be real--truly it wouldn't. No man could ever mean to me what you mean--I know that! And I couldn't give you up--you must never let yourself think of such a thing! I couldn't give you up!"

So there came to Thyrsis one of those bursts of tenderness that she knew so well. He put his arms about her and kissed her with fervor; but even while he spoke with her, and gave her the love she desired, there was something in him that sank back and moaned with despair. So the captive sinks and moans when he finds that his break for freedom has led only to the tightening of his chains.

They stood for the last time before the cabin, bidding farewell to the little glen and all its memories.

"There are lines in the poem for everything," she said. "Even for that!" And she quoted--

"He hearkens not! light comer, he is flown!"

He laughed. "I can do better yet," he said--

"Alack, for Corydon no rival now!"

There was a pause. "That was five years," she mused. "And there were five more!"

"It will mean another book," he said. "To tell about the new work; and how Thyrsis became a social lion; and how, like Icarus, he flew too high and melted his wings. And then, 'The Exploiters,' the book of his vengeance! And then Corydon---"

"Yes, do not forget Corydon," she said.

"How he watched her dying before his eyes, and how he prayed for months for courage to kill her, and could not, but ran away. And then---"

"It will make a long story."

"Yes--a long story. 'Love's Deliverance,' let us call it."

"They will smile at that. It sounds like Reno, Nevada."

"'Love's Deliverance,' even so," he said. "To tell how Thyrsis went out into the wilderness and found himself; and of the new love that came to Corydon."

"It will be a Bible for lovers," said she.

"Yes," he replied, and smiled-"with a book of Chronicles, and a book of Proverbs, and a book of Psalms, and a book of Revelations--"

"And several books of Epistles," she interposed.

"The tablets in the temple are cracked," he said, "and the fortresses of privilege are crumbling. When the Revolution is here--when there are no longer priests nor judges nor class-taboos--then out of the hunger of our own hearts we shall have to shape our sex-ideals, and organize our new aristocracies."

"They will call it a book of 'free love'," said she.

To which he answered, gravely: ***"Let us redeem our great words from base uses. Let that no longer call itself Love, which knows that it is not free!"***

The Codes Of Hammurabi And Moses
W. W. Davies

QTY

The discovery of the Hammurabi Code is one of the greatest achievements of archaeology, and is of paramount interest, not only to the student of the Bible, but also to all those interested in ancient history...

Religion   **ISBN:** *1-59462-338-4*   **Pages:132**
MSRP $12.95

The Theory of Moral Sentiments
Adam Smith

QTY

This work from 1749. contains original theories of conscience amd moral judgment and it is the foundation for systemof morals.

Philosophy **ISBN:** *1-59462-777-0*   **Pages:536**
MSRP $19.95

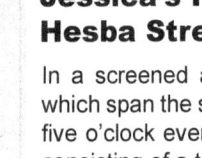

Jessica's First Prayer
Hesba Stretton

QTY

In a screened and secluded corner of one of the many railway-bridges which span the streets of London there could be seen a few years ago, from five o'clock every morning until half past eight, a tidily set-out coffee-stall, consisting of a trestle and board, upon which stood two large tin cans, with a small fire of charcoal burning under each so as to keep the coffee boiling during the early hours of the morning when the work-people were thronging into the city on their way to their daily toil...

Pages:84

Childrens   **ISBN:** *1-59462-373-2*   *MSRP $9.95*

My Life and Work
Henry Ford

QTY

Henry Ford revolutionized the world with his implementation of mass production for the Model T automobile. Gain valuable business insight into his life and work with his own auto-biography... "We have only started on our development of our country we have not as yet, with all our talk of wonderful progress, done more than scratch the surface. The progress has been wonderful enough but..."

Pages:300

Biographies/   **ISBN:** *1-59462-198-5*   *MSRP $21.95*

QTY

The Art of Cross-Examination
Francis Wellman

I presume it is the experience of every author, after his first book is published upon an important subject, to be almost overwhelmed with a wealth of ideas and illustrations which could readily have been included in his book, and which to his own mind, at least, seem to make a second edition inevitable. Such certainly was the case with me; and when the first edition had reached its sixth impression in five months, I rejoiced to learn that it seemed to my publishers that the book had met with a sufficiently favorable reception to justify a second and considerably enlarged edition. ..

Pages:412

Reference   **ISBN:** *1-59462-647-2*   *MSRP $19.95*

QTY

On the Duty of Civil Disobedience
Henry David Thoreau

Thoreau wrote his famous essay, On the Duty of Civil Disobedience, as a protest against an unjust but popular war and the immoral but popular institution of slave-owning. He did more than write—he declined to pay his taxes, and was hauled off to gaol in consequence. Who can say how much this refusal of his hastened the end of the war and of slavery ?

Law   **ISBN:** *1-59462-747-9*   **Pages:48**

MSRP $7.45

Dream Psychology Psychoanalysis for Beginners
Sigmund Freud

QTY

Sigmund Freud, born Sigismund Schlomo Freud (May 6, 1856 - September 23, 1939), was a Jewish-Austrian neurologist and psychiatrist who co-founded the psychoanalytic school of psychology. Freud is best known for his theories of the unconscious mind, especially involving the mechanism of repression; his redefinition of sexual desire as mobile and directed towards a wide variety of objects; and his therapeutic techniques, especially his understanding of transference in the therapeutic relationship and the presumed value of dreams as sources of insight into unconscious desires.

Pages:196

Psychology   **ISBN:** *1-59462-905-6*   *MSRP $15.45*

The Miracle of Right Thought
Orison Swett Marden

QTY

Believe with all of your heart that you will do what you were made to do. When the mind has once formed the habit of holding cheerful, happy, prosperous pictures, it will not be easy to form the opposite habit. It does not matter how improbable or how far away this realization may see, or how dark the prospects may be, if we visualize them as best we can, as vividly as possible, hold tenaciously to them and vigorously struggle to attain them, they will gradually become actualized, realized in the life. But a desire, a longing without endeavor, a yearning abandoned or held indifferently will vanish without realization.

Pages:360

Self Help   **ISBN:** *1-59462-644-8*   *MSRP $25.45*

QTY

The Rosicrucian Cosmo-Conception Mystic Christianity *by Max Heindel*   ISBN: *1-59462-188-8*   **$38.95**
The Rosicrucian Cosmo-conception is not dogmatic, neither does it appeal to any other authority than the reason of the student. It is: not controversial, but is: sent forth in the, hope that it may help to clear...   New Age/Religion Pages 646

Abandonment To Divine Providence *by Jean-Pierre de Caussade*   ISBN: *1-59462-228-0*   **$25.95**
"The Rev. Jean Pierre de Caussade was one of the most remarkable spiritual writers of the Society of Jesus in France in the 18th Century. His death took place at Toulouse in 1751. His works have gone through many editions and have been republished...   Inspirational/Religion Pages 400

Mental Chemistry *by Charles Haanel*   ISBN: *1-59462-192-6*   **$23.95**
Mental Chemistry allows the change of material conditions by combining and appropriately utilizing the power of the mind. Much like applied chemistry creates something new and unique out of careful combinations of chemicals the mastery of mental chemistry...   New Age Pages 354

The Letters of Robert Browning and Elizabeth Barret Barrett 1845-1846 vol II   ISBN: *1-59462-193-4*   **$35.95**
by Robert Browning and Elizabeth Barrett   Biographies Pages 596

Gleanings In Genesis (volume I) *by Arthur W. Pink*   ISBN: *1-59462-130-6*   **$27.45**
Appropriately has Genesis been termed "the seed plot of the Bible" for in it we have, in germ form, almost all of the great doctrines which are afterwards fully developed in the books of Scripture which follow...   Religion/Inspirational Pages 420

The Master Key *by L. W. de Laurence*   ISBN: *1-59462-001-6*   **$30.95**
In no branch of human knowledge has there been a more lively increase of the spirit of research during the past few years than in the study of Psychology, Concentration and Mental Discipline. The requests for authentic lessons in Thought Control, Mental Discipline and...   New Age/Business Pages 422

The Lesser Key Of Solomon Goetia *by L. W. de Laurence*   ISBN: *1-59462-092-X*   **$9.95**
This translation of the first book of the "Lemegton" which is now for the first time made accessible to students of Talismanic Magic was done, after careful collation and edition, from numerous Ancient Manuscripts in Hebrew, Latin, and French...   New Age/Occult Pages 92

Rubaiyat Of Omar Khayyam *by Edward Fitzgerald*   ISBN:*1-59462-332-5*   **$13.95**
Edward Fitzgerald, whom the world has already learned, in spite of his own efforts to remain within the shadow of anonymity, to look upon as one of the rarest poets of the century, was born at Bredfield, in Suffolk, on the 31st of March, 1809. He was the third son of John Purcell...   Music Pages 172

Ancient Law *by Henry Maine*   ISBN: *1-59462-128-4*   **$29.95**
The chief object of the following pages is to indicate some of the earliest ideas of mankind, as they are reflected in Ancient Law, and to point out the relation of those ideas to modern thought.   Religion/History Pages 452

Far-Away Stories *by William J. Locke*   ISBN: *1-59462-129-2*   **$19.45**
"Good wine needs no bush, but a collection of mixed vintages does. And this book is just such a collection. Some of the stories I do not want to remain buried for ever in the museum files of dead magazine-numbers an author's not unpardonable vanity..."   Fiction Pages 272

Life of David Crockett *by David Crockett*   ISBN: *1-59462-250-7*   **$27.45**
"Colonel David Crockett was one of the most remarkable men of the times in which he lived. Born in humble life, but gifted with a strong will, an indomitable courage, and unremitting perseverance...   Biographies/New Age Pages 424

Lip-Reading *by Edward Nitchie*   ISBN: *1-59462-206-X*   **$25.95**
Edward B. Nitchie, founder of the New York School for the Hard of Hearing, now the Nitchie School of Lip-Reading, Inc, wrote "LIP-READING Principles and Practice". The development and perfecting of this meritorious work on lip-reading was an undertaking...   How-to Pages 400

A Handbook of Suggestive Therapeutics, Applied Hypnotism, Psychic Science   ISBN: *1-59462-214-0*   **$24.95**
by Henry Munro   Health/New Age/Health/Self-help Pages 376

A Doll's House: and Two Other Plays *by Henrik Ibsen*   ISBN: *1-59462-112-8*   **$19.95**
Henrik Ibsen created this classic when in revolutionary 1848 Rome. Introducing some striking concepts in playwriting for the realist genre, this play has been studied the world over.   Fiction/Classics/Plays 308

The Light of Asia *by sir Edwin Arnold*   ISBN: *1-59462-204-3*   **$13.95**
In this poetic masterpiece, Edwin Arnold describes the life and teachings of Buddha. The man who was to become known as Buddha to the world was born as Prince Gautama of India but he rejected the worldly riches and abandoned the reigns of power when...   Religion/History/Biographies Pages 170

The Complete Works of Guy de Maupassant *by Guy de Maupassant*   ISBN: *1-59462-157-8*   **$16.95**
"For days and days, nights and nights, I had dreamed of that first kiss which was to consecrate our engagement, and I knew not on what spot I should put my lips..."   Fiction/Classics Pages 240

The Art of Cross-Examination *by Francis L. Wellman*   ISBN: *1-59462-309-0*   **$26.95**
Written by a renowned trial lawyer, Wellman imparts his experience and uses case studies to explain how to use psychology to extract desired information through questioning.   How-to/Science/Reference Pages 408

Answered or Unanswered? *by Louisa Vaughan*   ISBN: *1-59462-248-5*   **$10.95**
Miracles of Faith in China   Religion Pages 112

The Edinburgh Lectures on Mental Science (1909) *by Thomas*   ISBN: *1-59462-008-3*   **$11.95**
This book contains the substance of a course of lectures recently given by the writer in the Queen Street Hall, Edinburgh. Its purpose is to indicate the Natural Principles governing the relation between Mental Action and Material Conditions...   New Age/Psychology Pages 148

Ayesha *by H. Rider Haggard*   ISBN: *1-59462-301-5*   **$24.95**
Verily and indeed it is the unexpected that happens! Probably if there was one person upon the earth from whom the Editor of this, and of a certain previous history, did not expect to hear again...   Classics Pages 380

Ayala's Angel *by Anthony Trollope*   ISBN: *1-59462-352-X*   **$29.95**
The two girls were both pretty, but Lucy who was twenty-one who supposed to be simple and comparatively unattractive, whereas Ayala was credited, as her Bombwhat romantic name might show, with poetic charm and a taste for romance. Ayala when her father died was nineteen...   Fiction Pages 484

The American Commonwealth *by James Bryce*   ISBN: *1-59462-286-8*   **$34.45**
An interpretation of American democratic political theory. It examines political mechanics and society from the perspective of Scotsman James Bryce   Politics Pages 572

Stories of the Pilgrims *by Margaret P. Pumphrey*   ISBN: *1-59462-116-0*   **$17.95**
This book explores pilgrims religious oppression in England as well as their escape to Holland and eventual crossing to America on the Mayflower, and their early days in New England...   History Pages 268

QTY

The Fasting Cure *by Sinclair Upton*   **ISBN:** *1-59462-222-1*   **$13.95**
In the Cosmopolitan Magazine for May, 1910, and in the Contemporary Review (London) for April, 1910, I published an article dealing with my experiences in fasting. I have written a great many magazine articles, but never one which attracted so much attention... New Age/Self Help/Health Pages 164

Hebrew Astrology *by Sepharial*   **ISBN:** *1-59462-308-2*   **$13.45**
In these days of advanced thinking it is a matter of common observation that we have left many of the old landmarks behind and that we are now pressing forward to greater heights and to a wider horizon than that which represented the mind-content of our progenitors... Astrology Pages 144

Thought Vibration or The Law of Attraction in the Thought World   **ISBN:** *1-59462-127-6*   **$12.95**
by William Walker Atkinson   Psychology/Religion Pages 144

Optimism *by Helen Keller*   **ISBN:** *1-59462-108-X*   **$15.95**
Helen Keller was blind, deaf, and mute since 19 months old, yet famously learned how to overcome these handicaps, communicate with the world, and spread her lectures promoting optimism. An inspiring read for everyone... Biographies/Inspirational Pages 84

Sara Crewe *by Frances Burnett*   **ISBN:** *1-59462-360-0*   **$9.45**
In the first place, Miss Minchin lived in London. Her home was a large, dull, tall one, in a large, dull square, where all the houses were alike, and all the sparrows were alike, and where all the door-knockers made the same heavy sound... Childrens/Classic Pages 88

The Autobiography of Benjamin Franklin *by Benjamin Franklin*   **ISBN:** *1-59462-135-7*   **$24.95**
The Autobiography of Benjamin Franklin has probably been more extensively read than any other American historical work, and no other book of its kind has had such ups and downs of fortune. Franklin lived for many years in England, where he was agent... Biographies/History Pages 332

Name	
Email	
Telephone	
Address	
City, State ZIP	

☐ **Credit Card**   ☐ **Check / Money Order**

Credit Card Number	
Expiration Date	
Signature	

Please Mail to: Book Jungle
                     PO Box 2226
                     Champaign, IL 61825
or Fax to: 630-214-0564

ORDERING INFORMATION

web: *www.bookjungle.com*
email: *sales@bookjungle.com*
fax: *630-214-0564*
mail: *Book Jungle PO Box 2226 Champaign, IL 61825*
or PayPal *to sales@bookjungle.com*

Please contact us for bulk discounts

DIRECT-ORDER TERMS

**20% Discount if You Order
Two or More Books**
Free Domestic Shipping!
Accepted: Master Card, Visa,
Discover, American Express